Mrs. Hudson

and

The Malabar Rose

MARTIN DAVIES

BERKLEY PRIME CRIME, NEW YORK

THE BERKLEY PUBLISHING GROUP
Published by the Penguin Group
Penguin Group (USA) Inc.
375 Hudson Street, New York, New York 10014, USA
Penguin Group (Canada), 90 Eglinton Avenue East, Suite 700, Toronto, Ontario M4P 2Y3, Canada
(a division of Pearson Penguin Canada Inc.)
Penguin Books Ltd., 80 Strand, London WC2R 0RL, England
Penguin Group Ireland, 25 St. Stephen's Green, Dublin 2, Ireland (a division of Penguin Books Ltd.)
Penguin Group (Australia), 250 Camberwell Road, Camberwell, Victoria 3124, Australia
(a division of Pearson Australia Group Pty. Ltd.)
Penguin Books India Pvt. Ltd., 11 Community Centre, Panchsheel Park, New Delhi—110 017, India
Penguin Group (NZ), Cnr. Airborne and Rosedale Roads, Albany, Auckland 1310, New Zealand
(a division of Pearson New Zealand Ltd.)
Penguin Books (South Africa) (Pty.) Ltd., 24 Sturdee Avenue, Rosebank, Johannesburg 2196, South Africa

Penguin Books Ltd., Registered Offices: 80 Strand, London WC2R 0RL, England

This is a work of fiction. Names, characters, places, and incidents either are the product of the author's imagination or are used fictitiously, and any resemblance to actual persons, living or dead, business establishments, events, or locales is entirely coincidental. The publisher does not have any control over and does not assume any responsibility for author or third-party websites or their content.

MRS. HUDSON AND THE MALABAR ROSE

A Berkley Prime Crime Book / published by arrangement with the author

PRINTING HISTORY
Berkley Prime Crime trade edition / August 2005
Berkley Prime Crime mass-market edition / October 2006

Copyright © 2005 by Martin Davies.
Cover illustration by Stephen Gardner.
Cover design by Monica Benalcazar.

ISBN: 0-425-20651-3

BERKLEY® PRIME CRIME
Berkley Prime Crime Books are published by The Berkley Publishing Group,
a division of Penguin Group (USA) Inc.,
375 Hudson Street, New York, New York 10014.
The name BERKLEY PRIME CRIME and the BERKLEY PRIME CRIME design are trademarks belonging to Penguin Group (USA) Inc.

PRINTED IN THE UNITED STATES OF AMERICA

10 9 8 7 6 5 4 3 2 1

To MM and ALLeQ
with thanks

CHAPTER ONE

Snow Falls on Baker Street

"News!" the newsboy cried. "All the news! Famous gem arrives in London. Guard of honour for priceless stone!"

When I heard his shout that night, the snow was already falling and the carriages had turned the cobbled streets to slush. It was hardly the night for a young girl to dream of adventure. At first I scarcely heard the cry over the clattering hooves and grumbling wheels, and if I had any thoughts at all as I battled homewards that night, they were of dry clothes and dry feet and a warm fire. But then the boy's shout reached me again, this time a little louder and a little clearer.

"Indian jewel is gift to nation! Priceless stone in safe hands!"

I knew nothing then of priceless stones, still less of the fierce and fiery passions they can inspire. But even on that ill-tempered December evening the words kindled a little spark inside me, and I paused in my progress to look around.

Through the flurries of flailing snow, between the jousting hansoms and the lumbering victorias, I could distinguish dimly the figure of the newsboy, pale in the gaslight on the far side of the street. He was a thin boy, hunched with cold, and his boots when he tried to stamp them were so heavy with snow that he struggled to lift them clear of the pavement. Between us the cobbled street was thick with mud, and I hesitated for a moment on the edge of the kerb, reaching into my coat pocket for the penny to buy a paper.

It was then that I felt the hand. It brushed mine so softly and so unexpectedly that for a moment I thought it was no more than the fabric of my coat against my fingers. But that first touch was followed by a firm and jarring tug at my purse and in an instant the purse was gone, my fingertips left grasping at air. I let out a cry and grabbed wildly for the invading hand, knowing that in a fraction of a second it would be gone. But my reactions were fast that night, and so swift was my movement that I felt my fingers close on my assailant. At the same time my eyes met those of a tiny street urchin, frozen for an instant in utter surprise. I could see him clearly by the light of the lamps and saw at once that he was no more than ten or eleven years old, and skinny as a Thames eel.

My lucky grab had caught hold of his wrist, and so small was it that my fingers closed right round it. But it was something else that struck me about him: his eyes. They were unlike any I had seen before, a very pale blue, almost cornflower blue, and his cap was pulled down low over his brow as if to hide them from public scrutiny. Something about that peculiar colour caught me off guard, for in the next moment, with his free hand, he seized the stolen purse and with all his strength thrust it back inside my coat.

So surprised was I by this manoeuvre and by the force with which he pushed me that I stepped back and loosened my grip on his arm; and in that moment he broke free, darting into the road between the wheels of the hansoms and the coat-tails of pedestrians, until the crowds and the darkness closed around him and he was gone.

He did not look back as he made his escape. I stood and watched him go, clutching my rescued purse against my chest and panting slightly from the shock.

"News!" the paper boy continued to cry. "News! World's rarest ruby arrives in London! Read all the news!"

IN the end I didn't read the news until later, when I was warm and dry again. I arrived home flushed and still foolishly shaken by the attempt on my purse, and strangely unsettled by the youth and boldness of my assailant. And yet I was no stranger to the darker side of London's streets, nor to the dangers that lurked there. It was little more than three years since those cold and unforgiving streets had been my only home, until hunger and despair had led me to attempt a theft of my own. But the strictness of the orphanage had left me an inexpert thief, and my capture by Scraggs, the grocer's boy, had been the moment that changed my life. Marched by him into the stern and substantial presence of Mrs. Hudson, a housekeeper respected by all who knew her for her common sense and her most uncommon perspicacity, I found myself adopted as her scullery maid. And three years on, that same imposing figure welcomed me now, her sleeves pushed up and her formidable forearms white with flour as she kneaded a mess of fruit-dough with the most punishing severity.

"Why, Flotsam!" she began when she looked up from her work and noticed the wateriness of my smile. But Mrs. Hudson was not a woman to employ words when actions were required, and saying nothing more she advanced and removed my coat with her strong, floury hands, then seated me close to the fire and chaffed some warmth into my fingers while I explained what had befallen me.

"And it was the strangest thing, ma'am," I told her, "but when he shoved me backwards to get free, my purse fell straight into the pocket inside my coat. It was as though I'd placed it there myself."

Mrs. Hudson nodded appreciatively and rose to her feet.

"Then he was a boy who knew his trade, Flotsam. For if you'd managed to hold him fast and wrestle him into the arms of a policeman, you'd have found there was no crime to report. Just an innocent child in front of you and a purse in your pocket, exactly as it should be."

I sat back and watched her as she returned to her baking. She had just begun to plait the dough into a delicate braid. I had watched her do the same thing many times before, but I never failed to be fascinated by the speed and the dexterity of her fingers. It was a dexterity I had never been able to emulate, though the art of baking was one of the many I had learned in my years as Mrs. Hudson's helper. For Mrs. Hudson believed in education, and the things I had been required to learn from her were both varied and surprising. I had learned how to skin a hare and to scrub floors; how to polish silver and how to take tea in polite society. I had read every book in Baker Street, from Horace to *On Housekeeping*, and from *Blood Stains* to *Belinda;* and I could with equal confidence pluck a chicken or dress a lobster or announce correctly a visiting peer of the realm. By the age of fifteen it was impossible to recognise in me the ragged orphan of before, a change surely accelerated by our arrival in the service of Mr. Sherlock Holmes and Dr. Watson, and by the excitements I had encountered there.

"Well, Flotsam," Mrs. Hudson continued, still shaping the dough, "since our gentlemen are to be away for a few days, this would be a good opportunity to sort out their study. So if you've told me everything, it wouldn't do any harm to run round there with a duster." She paused for a moment. "Is there something else, Flotsam?"

"Ma'am?"

"About the little incident this evening. It's not like you to be so very thrown by such a thing."

I hesitated, not sure at first if it really was something. But she was right. Something else that evening *had* unsettled me. I had been given a glimpse of another place, a winter's day in another lifetime. But I wasn't sure it was a place I wanted to revisit.

"It's nothing really, ma'am. It's just that there was a boy once. A long time ago, back in the orphanage. I suppose I must have been about six or seven. He was little more than a baby, really. They brought him in one night. His parents had just died, both of them together. There'd been some scandal, I think, and there was no one to look after him."

Mrs. Hudson nodded and said nothing. I told the tale hesitantly, struggling to remember. So much had happened since then, so many things both good and bad, that it was hard to take myself back to that other time, a time when everything hurt. All of us at the orphanage were used to that—used to the cold and the hunger, the knocks and the curses. But this boy was different. He'd known nothing but kindness until that day. He must have been about two years old—too young to understand his loss, but old enough to feel the terrible change that had come upon him.

For no reason I ever understood, the boy adopted me. Perhaps because I had once lost a brother, he sensed in me some sympathy that was absent from our companions. He would come to me at the end of the day, when we met for prayers, and would press close to me, silently, afraid to speak for fear of being punished. He was only tiny; he barely came up to my waist. I remember that he had one possession that he had been able to keep, a portrait of his mother in a locket around his neck. She had seemed to me little more than a girl herself, and so pretty that, although I have no memory of my own mother's eyes, for some reason I can still remember hers, smiling out from that little golden frame as if happiness was all that could ever happen.

Mrs. Hudson had been listening to my tale, her fruit-dough temporarily laid to one side.

"But, Flotsam, why did you remember him tonight?"

"It was those blue eyes, ma'am. That boy in the orphanage had blue eyes, too. It just made me wonder what happened to him . . ."

I shrugged, not sure why the question filled me with such sadness. But Mrs. Hudson seemed to understand, and for a moment or two she said nothing. However, when she spoke again it was in a brisk, businesslike tone.

"Now, young lady . . ." She startled me out of my reverie by clapping her hands together so firmly that a light mist of flour rose into the air above her. "I'm not saying that this evening hasn't given you a bit of a shock, young Flottie, but there's still work to be done, and if the gentlemen's study hasn't been dusted by the time supper's ready, I daresay you'll be getting another one. So if you would seize that duster and some old newspapers for the grate . . ."

I rose obediently and was about to go about my tasks when the sight of the newspapers reminded me of the paper I had gone to such pains to bring home.

"Oh, ma'am, there was something else. I was that shaken by everything I almost forgot it. It's tonight's evening paper. I just thought it sounded exciting, ma'am."

I passed Mrs. Hudson the newspaper, and she moved towards the fire to study the front page. For a moment she stood still, her eyes intent on it, and then, to my surprise, I noticed a tiny smile on the corner of her lips.

"Well, well, well!" she chuckled. "A fine kettle of fish and no mistake. Have you read this yet, Flotsam?"

"No, ma'am, I only heard what the newsboy was shouting."

"Then get back over here by the fire, girl, and take a look. I'll spread it out so we can both see."

So I dropped another coal on the fire while Mrs. Hudson rose to adjust the lamp and to pour herself a small glass of our finest pale sherry. Then we settled down with the newspaper in front of us to examine together the leading item.

I can't deny that the words we read were plain enough, but as I read them I felt again something of the quickening excitement that had come to me in the street when I heard the newsboy's cry. It was as if, behind the lines of plain newsprint, there lurked a story deeper and richer and more complex.

PRICELESS JEWEL ARRIVES IN LONDON
Malabar Rose is to be Gift to Crown

A guard of honour led by Major General Sir John Plaskett was on duty at the Pool of London today to greet the return of HMS *Imperious* and to receive its unique cargo, the famous ruby known as the Malabar Rose. The great stone, among the largest of its kind ever found, is believed to have been mined on the Malabar Coast of India in the course of the last century and has long been the property of the maharajahs of Majoudh. Now the current maharajah has made it known that he wishes to present the stone to the Crown in recognition of the great services rendered to his people by Her Majesty over many years.

The Malabar Rose is famed not only for its unprecedented size, but also for the spectacular flame that appears to burn at its heart, a fire so exquisite that jewellers have declared the stone beyond value.

At the maharajah's request, the stone is to be displayed to a select audience later this month before being presented to the Crown as part of the New Year celebrations. The audience for the private viewing will include the Dowager Duchess of Marne, Princess Alicia Karageorgevich, and many other notable dignitaries and will take place in the Satin Rooms of the Blenheim Hotel on Thursday 26th December.

When Mrs. Hudson had finished reading, she raised an eyebrow in my direction. "So, Flotsam, just what do you make of that?"

I looked down at the paper again, uncertain of what I did make of it.

"Well, ma'am, it seems very generous of the maharajah."

"Oh, I'm sure the maharajah has his reasons, Flottie," she assured me, waving away a whole world of diplomatic machinations with a sweep of her hand. Her face in the firelight was set in firm lines as if she were thinking something through very carefully. I waited quietly until she spoke again.

"Did you notice what that ruby was said to be worth, Flotsam?"

"It's supposed to be priceless, ma'am."

At this Mrs. Hudson sat back with a sigh and held her sherry at eye level, then rolled the glass gently between her fingers so that the golden liquid caught the firelight. Its motion sent little fragments of light spinning around the darkened room.

"Priceless things are all very well, Flottie, but one thing you can be sure of: there's never any shortage of people willing to put a price on them." She stood up purposefully and placed her glass on the stool in front of her. "Now, Flotsam, I believe you have some dusting to do. And, if we want any supper, I have some vegetables to chop. You've got twenty minutes until I'm finished, so jump to it. . . ."

I went about the work happily. Mr. Holmes and Dr. Watson were away in the West Country investigating a matter that, judging from their telegrams, was as baffling as it was remote. In their absence, Mrs. Hudson and I had brought some order to their rooms, returning stray items of clutter to their allocated places in the filing system. Thus a collection of exotic dried beetles that had been scattered over the hearth were returned to a drawer labelled "Infestations—Unexplained" and the mess of cigar ash that had been smeared carelessly across a side table was most carefully scraped into an envelope that Mrs. Hudson marked "Counterfeit Trinchinopoly—Christmas gift of Lord Fieldborough—possibly toxic." It was always a pleasure for me to dust Mr. Holmes' various cabinets and to wonder at their contents, and for a while I quite forgot about pickpockets, rubies, and even the smell of supper wafting invitingly up the stairs.

When the last speck of dust had been banished and I felt myself safe to return downstairs, I was surprised to hear voices coming from the kitchen. As well as Mrs. Hudson's low rumble there was male laughter, too, and when I opened the door it was to see a boy of sixteen with riotous hair and an unruly smile munching happily on a carrot pinched from Mrs. Hudson's chopping board.

"Hello, Flot," he chirruped happily. "You're just in time to see Mrs. H set about me with that ladle of hers."

"I shall be doing no such thing, Scraggs," Mrs. Hudson growled. "That carrot will be coming off your bill at the end of the month, young man. Now if you want to eat with us, I'll see some proper manners and some soap on your hands before we go any further."

Scraggs, the grocer's boy, had been supplying Mrs. Hudson

with news, information, and general comestibles since he'd been old enough to stack blocks of soap, and I knew that underneath her gruff manner she trusted him more than any newspaper to tell her what was passing in the streets outside.

"So, Scraggs," she asked when the three of us were sitting down to supper, "what's new today?"

"Well, there's been a bit of a rumpus down at Fortescue's. Turns out the caviar they've been buying from Russia isn't the real thing. Lots of talk about cheap fish and black ink. There's been quite a row."

Mrs. Hudson nodded as if the news came as no surprise. "Old Mr. Fortescue used to know his caviar, but those sons of his are sadly lacking. Anything else?"

Scraggs turned to me and winked. "This is one you'll like, Flot. There's been a big stir at the Regal Theatre. Seems they've booked some foreign conjurer for just after Christmas. They say he's the toast of society over on the Continent—Paris, Berlin, Budapest, all the posh places. Packed houses everywhere he goes, and he never does more than one night. Keeps himself mysterious. And he does tricks no one's ever even seen before. And it gets even better. You've heard of Lola Del Fuego?"

I nodded breathlessly. "The dancer? Yes, of course. They say she's the most beautiful woman in Europe. And half of the gentlemen on the Continent seem to be in love with her. They say she's turned down offers of marriage from royalty in three different countries. You can't mean that *she's* coming to London, Scraggs?"

He chewed slowly on a mouthful of hot dumpling, enjoying my pent-up excitement. "She most certainly is," he confirmed at last. "On the same bill as the magician. Just for the one night. They say it will be the biggest event for years. The tickets are starting at a guinea a go, and they reckon they'll all be gone by the end of tomorrow."

The fact that a guinea was a quite impossible price did nothing to dampen my enthusiasm. Just the thought that the most famous dancer in the world was going to be in London, walking the same pavements as I walked, was more than enough for me.

"Do you think we shall see her?" I asked, looking across at Mrs. Hudson. "In the street, I mean, on the way to the theatre perhaps?"

Mrs. Hudson rose and began to pile up our empty plates. "I daresay we might, Flotsam. Though I can't say that particular line of dancing is one I greatly approve of. I should imagine that Miss Del Fuego's admirers are not always intent on her dance steps. Tell me, Scraggs, you say that there is really only one performance?"

"That's right, Mrs. H. Apparently, it's going to contain some stupendous piece of magic never seen before. Everyone at the theatre's talking about it. Simkins, the boy who does the chestnuts outside, says they're expecting the toffs to be fighting for tickets."

"I imagine he's right. The ladies will want to see the magic, and the gentlemen won't be averse to the dancing. As Hudson always used to say . . ."

But at that moment there came a crisp, decisive knock at the front door. Mrs. Hudson paused in her handling of the dirty dishes.

"Hmmm," she murmured thoughtfully. "It's rather late for callers. Flotsam, would you be so kind?"

So pausing only to smooth down my apron and to push out of sight the strands of hair that habitually escaped down my forehead, I slipped out of the kitchen and up the dark passageway that led me to the front door. The bolts were not yet drawn for the evening and the door, though heavy, swung open easily.

The first thing that struck me was the snow. It had come

on much stronger since we'd closed the curtains for the night, and now it was piling high on the rooftops and coating everything below with a crisp layer of greying white. In front of me, exposed to the full hostility of the elements, stood a short, bespectacled man with the most marked air of self-regard. He had removed his hat on my opening the door and as a result the snow was beginning to land unimpeded on the bald dome of his head, but his chest was pushed out very determinedly, and his manner when he spoke was one of the most scrupulous formality.

"I believe this is the residence of Mr. Sherlock Holmes?"

"Yes, sir."

"Very good. And is Mr. Holmes at home?"

"No, sir. I'm afraid Mr. Holmes is out of London."

This information appeared to disconcert the caller, and he wiped a gloved hand over his forehead where the flakes of snow were beginning to melt.

"I have a letter here of the utmost importance. Please see to it that it is brought to his attention at the very earliest opportunity."

He reached inside his coat and produced a heavily embossed envelope that he pressed into my hands, then turned on his heel and trotted to a dark carriage that was waiting on the other side of the street. Even through the falling snow I could see that its doors were adorned with a bright gold crest, but before I could make out the details the carriage had pulled away, and a thicker than usual flurry of snow reminded me of the need to close the door against the swirling night.

Returning to the kitchen with snowflakes still unmelted on my shoulders, I found Mrs. Hudson washing plates and instructing Scraggs in the art of polishing glasses. "Not your hand," she was rumbling, "always move the glass instead. That's more like it . . ." She looked up at me as I entered.

"A message, Flotsam?"

"A letter for Mr. Holmes, ma'am. The gentleman said it was very urgent."

"Did he now?" She performed three emphatic wipes of her cloth on a large meat platter, then placed it on the draining board and joined me by the fire. "Just what did this gentleman look like?" she asked, taking the envelope and turning it thoughtfully between her fingers.

"A small man, ma'am. Bald with little round glasses. And all puffed up like a bantam."

"Was he on foot?"

"No, ma'am, he came in a carriage, a big, black one with a gold crest on the door."

"I see. And was the crest like this one?"

She showed me a golden emblem pressed into the surface of the envelope.

"Yes, I think so. It was a little hard to see because of all the snow."

While Scraggs strained to peer over her shoulder, she ran her finger over the envelope once more. "This paper is handmade, Flottie, and of the very highest quality. And this is the Home Office crest. But the Home Office doesn't use paper like this every day. And the Brunswick carriage doesn't come out in the snow for any old errand. I have a suspicion that this letter comes from the minister himself."

"Surely not the little man at the door, ma'am?"

"Certainly not, Flotsam. The Home Secretary does not deliver his own mail."

"Blimey, just think of that!" Scraggs sounded impressed. "Lord Shastonbury himself writing to old Sherlock."

"So what do we do with the letter now, ma'am? Do we send it on?"

She looked at me then and I could see she had come to a decision.

"Matters of state must not be trifled with," she said

firmly. "Not a moment must be wasted." She began to examine the envelope's big wax seal.

"But Mrs. Hudson, ma'am, you surely don't mean . . ."

"This is a time for common sense, Flotsam. There'll be plenty of time later to stand on ceremony. Now pass me the paper knife—it's in the dresser, next to the nutmeg grinder—and let's see what His Grace has to say."

While I fetched the knife from the big dresser at the back of the kitchen, Mrs. Hudson settled down in her familiar chair by the fire, and Scraggs pulled up a seat alongside her. She took the paper knife from me with barely concealed relish and sliced open the envelope with a flourish of the wrist.

Inside there was a single sheet of paper, headed with the same gold crest. The few words on it were written in a strong, flowing hand, and the wording was that of a man accustomed to command.

Sir,

It is in your power to assist in a matter of vital importance. The honour of the nation is at stake. You are requested to attend at the address below at the earliest opportunity. Please consider it your duty to do so.

Yours, etc, etc,
SHASTONBURY

Printed neatly below was an address in Whitehall. The envelope contained no further instructions.

For a moment none of us spoke, and I could hear the fresh coals spitting on the fire.

"What a very interesting letter," Mrs. Hudson said at last. "I hadn't thought things would progress so quickly. What do you think, Flotsam?"

"We must telegraph Mr. Holmes at once, ma'am! He must start for Whitehall immediately."

I think I must have sounded rather breathless in my excitement, but Mrs. Hudson greeted this call to action with only a very slow nod of her head.

"Yes, Flottie, I suppose Mr. Holmes must be alerted. Come, you two, we have telegrams to write."

She moved across the room to the kitchen table and, from its drawer, produced paper and a bit of pencil. She had seated herself comfortably at the table and seemed about to write when she noticed that Scraggs and I were still hovering uncertainly by the fire.

"Come on, Flotsam. Over here. You must tell me if you think my wording is appropriate. And Scraggs, you'll be taking these to the office so start getting your things on. There's no time to lose."

Mrs. Hudson wrote two telegrams that evening, and both were remarkable. The first was addressed to the Earl of Shastonbury:

REGRET CANNOT REACH LONDON UNTIL WEDNESDAY EARLIEST STOP INDISPOSITION RENDERS ME UNABLE TO ATTEND WHITEHALL STOP BEG YOU TO CALL AT BAKER ST WED FROM NOON STOP HOLMES

"But Mrs. Hudson, ma'am," I spluttered, "Mr. Holmes is in perfect health. How can he refuse to attend Whitehall? And won't he be furious if you answer for him like that?"

"On the contrary, Flottie. You know Mr. Holmes. He likes to hear these things in the comfort of his own study. I think this arrangement will be altogether more to his liking, don't you?"

While I contemplated the audacity of this argument,

Mrs. Hudson was composing a telegram to Mr. Holmes in the West Country. If I had found the contents of the first telegram startling, the second left me blinking with bewilderment.

PRESENCE REQUIRED BAKER STREET STOP MOST URGENT STOP HOME SECRETARY WISHES TO CONSULT YOU RE SAFETY OF THE MALABAR ROSE

CHAPTER TWO

A Notable Cane

The next day passed in a haze of excitement. A telegram from Mr. Holmes confirmed that he and Watson would catch the night train and would be in Baker Street the following morning. Mrs. Hudson had been planning accordingly and even before that message reached us, preparations for the gentlemen's return had begun. Beds needed to be aired, provisions bought, and a veritable banquet of baking, roasting, stuffing, and chopping was required before Mrs. Hudson was satisfied that the pantry was in a sufficient state of readiness. My day was spent running errands and carrying messages to tradesmen through the slushy streets of a leaden day. In between, I was searching the markets for winter vegetables or collecting supplies of pipe tobacco from Mr. Hicks, the tobacconist on York Street. There was no time to be cold or to worry about the mud, and when I spotted Scraggs pushing a heavy barrow through Smithfields I barely had time to wave my hand before I was off in the other direction, in search of sausages and silver polish.

Only when the dusk began to close in from the docks and my list of tasks was finally complete did I find an opportunity to ask Mrs. Hudson the question that she had somehow evaded the night before. I returned weighed down with packages and weary from head to toe, and found Mrs. Hudson lighting the lamps. Outside, the cold of the previous evening had returned, and with the fading light there had appeared a strange yellowness in the clouds that threatened snow; but inside, in Mrs. Hudson's kitchen, the fire was burning with a hearty roar, and the air was heavy with the scent of cinnamon and cloves. The effect was to send a little shiver of pleasure through me, and Mrs. Hudson, noticing it, feared it might be a sign of too much time out of doors.

"Now, Flotsam," she ordered, "sit yourself down in front of the fire. We've done fine work today, and I've just taken two fine game pies out of the oven. The gentlemen won't miss a slice or two of one of them. So get yourself out of that coat, and we'll have a little something by the fire."

Mrs. Hudson's idea of a little something turned out to be a cup of hot shrub and lemon for me, and for herself a glass of the old Madeira. I waited until she had taken a first, contented sip before I dared to begin my questions.

"Mrs. Hudson, ma'am?"

"Yes, Flotsam?"

"There's something I don't quite understand. Last night, that letter . . ."

"Yes, Flotsam?"

Twenty hours' worth of curiosity came bubbling out. "Well, how can you *know* it's about the Malabar Rose, ma'am? There was nothing in it about rubies. It could be about anything. And what if Mr. Holmes rushes all the way back here, and it turns out to be about something else altogether?"

She permitted herself the faintest twitch of a smile and sighed happily.

"Ah, yes. The Malabar Rose. Very interesting. Wait a moment while I fetch that newspaper . . ." She bustled to the back of the kitchen and returned with the item we had read together the previous day. "Now, Flottie, there are one or two very noticeable things in this report. For instance, yesterday's guard of honour was led by Major General Sir John Plaskett. Does that name mean anything to you?"

"Isn't he the Hero of Ishtabad, ma'am?"

"And the safest pair of hands in a British uniform, Flottie. Now he's hardly the sort of man to be chosen for minor ceremonial duties at a time when there are so many rumblings abroad. He'd expect to be out on the Irrawaddy, or wintering in Kabul, not leading guards of honour around the streets of London. And then there's HMS *Imperious,* the newest ship in the Navy. She was supposed to be in the Indian Ocean, Flotsam, but instead we find her over here, playing the role of glorified cargo ship."

"I suppose they want to keep the Malabar Rose very safe, ma'am."

She nodded thoughtfully. "That's right, Flotsam. Somebody is worried. Very worried. A gift like the Malabar Rose sounds like good news, but until they get it safely into the vaults, it's a terrible headache for the government. And they can't just lock it away at once, which is probably what they'd like to do, because the maharajah, God bless him, insists that his stone is shown off beforehand."

I paused to consider this while Mrs. Hudson took another sip of Madeira. "But, ma'am," I continued after a moment, "you still can't be sure that last night's letter was about the Malabar Rose. It could be about *anything.*"

Mrs. Hudson gave a little chuckle. "The Home Secretary

is hardly likely to require Mr. Holmes' views on the suffrage or on the income tax, now is he, Flotsam? But who better to turn to when it is feared that plans may be afoot to steal a national treasure?"

Mrs. Hudson took another sip of Madeira while I considered the simple logic of her reasoning and found myself looking forward with quickening interest to our impending visit by the Home Office.

"Mrs. Hudson, ma'am?" I asked timidly. "You know that you sent me for some silver polish today?"

"Yes, Flotsam?" Her tone could not have been more innocent.

"I was thinking that we'll need to get to work on the silver tomorrow, won't we?"

"We certainly will, Flotsam."

"And we usually work on the silver in the little storeroom by the study, don't we, ma'am?"

"That's what we usually do, yes, Flottie."

I was about to say more but just then our eyes met and Mrs. Hudson nodded gently. So I said nothing, but sipped my drink and wiggled my toes and waited for the morrow.

THE return of Mr. Holmes and Dr. Watson created a great deal of hustle and bustle. They were much later than we had expected them, and no sooner was the door open than they stamped up to the study, blowing on their fingers and leaving little frozen lumps of slush in their wake.

"Really, Mrs. Hudson, it was the smallest dusting of snow imaginable!" Dr. Watson's outrage was almost incandescent.

"Indeed it was," agreed Mr. Holmes more calmly. "It is difficult to see how such a thin covering of snow would be enough to halt a locomotive of approximately fifty tons. However, as it is the same story every winter, I suppose we should have anticipated some such delay."

The two men had taken up positions in front of the fire in their study, the main room of the house, where as well as reading and discussing their cases, the two men would smoke, take their meals, interview visitors, and enjoy the comfort of Mrs. Hudson's excellent housekeeping. Now, as they allowed the warmth of the room to sweep over them, the flushed, puffing indignation of Dr. Watson contrasted quite noticeably with the angular intelligence and rather hawkish features of his friend.

"Dashed incompetence is what I call it!" Dr. Watson insisted. "You'd think our train companies might anticipate a degree of bad weather in December, eh?"

"Well, my friend, we're here now with a good fire and a new case in front of us." Mr. Holmes looked about him, his features softened by the pleasure of once more being amid familiar surroundings. The study was a large, bright room with two good windows, a table in front of them, and comfortable armchairs arranged around a generous fireplace. Around the walls stood the various cabinets that held his collections. He gave a contented sigh.

"I see that you have once again created order out of chaos, Mrs. Hudson. Your talent for the domestic arts never ceases to impress."

"Thank you, sir. We've done a little tidying, and I believe Flotsam here has done some dusting. Now, gentlemen, if you'll allow us to take those coats? . . . "

But Mr. Holmes wasn't listening. He had advanced to the fireplace and while I helped Dr. Watson out of his overcoat, Mr. Holmes knelt down and seized upon an object that had fallen to the ground close to one of the armchairs. As he straightened I could see that he was holding in his hand a gentleman's cane.

"So!" he exclaimed. "I perceive we have had visitors already this morning, Mrs. Hudson."

"Yes, sir," Mrs. Hudson responded, evidently unimpressed by this particular deduction. "A gentleman called at noon and waited for a few minutes. He promised to return within the hour."

"I see . . ." Mr. Holmes was studying the cane with the most minute attention and only when he had run his gaze four or five times up its full length did he pass it over to his companion. "Well, Watson, what does this stick tell us of our visitor?"

"Eh, Holmes? What's that?" Dr. Watson, having escaped from his rather damp coat, had made haste to the tray of whisky and soda water that Mrs. Hudson had positioned on the sideboard.

"Come, Watson, demonstrate for us your powers of deduction!"

"Very well, Holmes." He took up the cane and proceeded to observe it rather glumly. "Well, this is a very fine stick. Irish blackthorn, I should say. Had one myself once. Lasted for years until I left it on a train just outside West Wittering. Never saw it again after that."

"Indeed?" Holmes smiled fondly. "Now if you could confine your musings to that particular stick . . ."

"Oh, yes. Of course . . . Well, it goes without saying that the tip and handle are both silver. A bit worn, so I should say it's been well-used. Now this inscription here . . ." He peered at the top of the cane and rubbed at something with his thumb. "It seems to be someone's initials. They're quite worn. Is that a *G* and a *D*?"

Mr. Holmes took the cane from him with a smile. "What if I told you, Watson, that the owner of this stick is a grey-haired man of above-average height who walks with a slight limp in his right leg, and who travelled here from Whitehall this morning by carriage?"

Dr. Watson snorted. "Why, then I should call you a fraud, Holmes. How could you possibly deduce all that from a man's cane?"

Mr. Holmes leaned the stick against the mantelpiece and began to divest himself of his coat.

"You know, Watson, sometimes I despair of you. Everything I have just told you is written there as plain as day. All you need to read it is some basic observation. That is the key, Watson! It is only by being alert to every detail that you can be sure of arriving at the truth. And in this case I am confident that nothing has escaped me."

"Really, Holmes," grunted Watson, sinking into his seat, then brightening somewhat as Mrs. Hudson replenished his glass. "It's only a stick after all."

"Well, let's see . . ." Mr. Holmes took up the cane again and sat down opposite his friend. "As you yourself point out, this object is made to last a lifetime and has clearly seen service over a very substantial number of years. So, it is a reasonable guess that the gentleman may himself be a man of advancing years. In which case it is very likely indeed that his hair will be grey. And the length of the stick is notable, a good three or four inches greater than average, so it is likely that he is a taller man than most."

Mr. Holmes paused for a moment while he focussed his attention on the tip of the cane.

"This is where there is most to observe, Watson. Note that the silver point is warn very decidedly on one side. That would suggest that the owner is in the habit of using it at a slight angle, as if he requires it to take a portion of his weight. Hence the limp, which of course must be in the right leg if the wear on the tip and the wear on the handle are to make any sense."

"That certainly sounds simple enough, Holmes," Dr. Watson nodded, apparently greatly restored by a long sip from his glass. "But what of the carriage from Whitehall? You can't tell me that is somehow written on the man's stick!"

Holmes leaned back and surveyed his audience with an air of profound satisfaction.

"Ah, that is precisely what I can tell you, Watson. It is at this point that my powers of observation are most clearly demonstrated. Here, take a careful look at the tip of this cane and you will see that it bears traces of tar upon it. In that tar there are embedded very small chips of fine white marble. See, the tar is still soft. It has not yet had time to harden. Now the only part of London where fine marble is currently being worked on the public streets is where the marble columns are being repaired in Whitehall. So it is reasonable to suppose that it was in Whitehall that our visitor picked up both the tar and the chippings. And yet, apart from the marble, there is no other debris trapped in that tar, as there must have been if the cane's owner had travelled on foot through the dirty winter streets. So it is evident that our visitor must have travelled by carriage and been dropped at our very door."

"I say, Holmes, you make it sound the easiest thing in the world!"

"A simple thing, Watson, though it would perhaps be ingenuous to call it an easy one. Observation is the key. Observation!" Mr. Holmes had turned his attention to the inscription at the top of the cane. "These initials, Watson. You are correct that the first two are *G* and *D*, but I believe there is a third. I suspect that our visitor's surname begins with the letter *P.*" He passed the stick casually to Mrs. Hudson who took it and, after glancing at it in the most cursory way, gave a little cough.

"If you please, sir, I think you'll find his name begins with a *B*."

"You think so, Mrs. Hudson? I fear that the script is too faded for any certainty in the matter."

"That's probably true, sir. But you will observe that the silver tray by your right hand contains the gentleman's card. Mr. Godwin Branchester, sir."

I am ashamed to confess that the name of Godwin Branchester meant nothing to me. It was only later that the eminence and influence of the man was explained and I came to understand why, at the mention of his name, a startled silence fell. For although the name of Branchester was never widely known amongst the public at large, amongst the circles of government it was—and still is to this day—whispered in awe.

Godwin Branchester was at that time a man of seventy-eight years, but still a powerful figure in every sense of the word. His family was not remarkable, but his magnificent legal brain, his razor-sharp wits and, most of all, his tremendous personal authority had made him the pre-eminent adviser to the government of the day, regardless of its political hue. For nearly forty years he had maintained that position. He had advised prime ministers, admirals, archbishops, Lord Chancellors, and, it was whispered, was the most trusted adviser to the Queen herself. He had long since retired from any official position, but it was said that no foreign policy was formed that he had not first commented on, no new measures introduced that had not first been placed before him.

"Godwin Branchester? Here?" Dr. Watson sounded slightly hoarse, as if the very thought made him nervous.

"Yes, sir." Only Mrs. Hudson seemed unmoved. "I explained that your train was probably delayed by the snow, and he agreed that was almost certainly the case, there having been so little of it."

"Well done, Mrs. Hudson." Mr. Holmes reached into his pocket for his pipe. "Watson, we must be on our mettle for such a distinguished visitor. I suggest we spend the time between now and his return in a period of quiet contemplation so that our faculties are rested and our minds prepared."

Whether a period of calm would have achieved this outcome was never to be tested because as Mr. Holmes finished speaking, there was a sharp knock at the front door. Dr. Watson, who had just returned to the drinks tray, jumped visibly. Mr. Holmes raised his eyebrows. And I, crouched in one corner and mopping at a pool of water left by the gentlemen's boots, decided to crouch a little lower in the hope that my presence would not be noticed.

In the silence that followed the knock, Mr. Holmes allowed himself a low laugh that spoke more of anticipation than of amusement.

"Well, Watson, it seems we are to wrestle with the problem without the benefit of rest. But the great affairs of state will not wait on our convenience. Mrs. Hudson, would you be so good as to show our caller straight up? There is no need to announce him. This is one visitor who needs no introduction."

In the minute or so that followed Mrs. Hudson's departure, a tense and rather awkward silence fell on the study. Mr. Holmes remained seated with his eyes closed. Dr. Watson, having poured another drink, seemed suddenly unsure what to do with it and finally solved the problem by drinking it off in one gulp. Unnoticed by either, I made haste to make the room ready for our visitor, sweeping the coal dust from the hearth and wiping away further marks of melted snow that the two gentlemen had left on the carpet. Intent on finishing my task, I didn't look up when I heard footsteps outside the door, nor when Mrs. Hudson's polite cough heralded the new arrival. It seems that neither of the two gentlemen had looked up either because the next words Mrs. Hudson spoke took us all by surprise.

"Mrs. Smithers, sir," she announced calmly. "Mrs. Smithers wishes to consult you, sir. It appears her son-in-law has vanished into thin air."

CHAPTER THREE

A Disappearance in Ealing

Mrs. Hudson's announcement was met with some considerable consternation. Where we had anticipated a figure of magisterial gravity, there stood before us a rather corpulent woman of about fifty-five, dressed in an old-fashioned coat and a hat that, although maintaining the awkward air of Sunday best, had clearly in its time witnessed a great many Sundays. And if her appearance caused a surprise in the study at Baker Street, that surprise seemed nothing to the astonishment felt by our visitor at finding herself the focus of such direct and bemused scrutiny. She stood before us wringing her hands nervously and looking from Sherlock Holmes to Dr. Watson and back again, until Dr. Watson, remembering his manners, leapt to his feet.

"Mrs. Smithers, you say?" he began, clearly still in some confusion. "Surely not from the Home Office, madam?"

The stout woman's nervousness began to intensify into outright panic.

"The Home Office, sir? No, sir, from Sefton Avenue. That's in Ealing, sir."

"Mrs. Smithers has come to consult you and Mr. Holmes on a personal matter, sir." Mrs. Hudson ushered the visitor smoothly to the centre of the room. "Her difficulty sounds most intriguing, sir, and your instructions were to bring the caller straight up . . . I am sure the matter she wishes to discuss will be of some interest to you gentlemen."

Mr. Holmes had raised himself to the edge of his chair upon Mrs. Smithers' arrival, and he now rose to his feet and paced towards the window.

"Quite right, Mrs. Hudson. And under normal circumstances I'm sure we would be delighted to assist. But at this particular moment . . ." He began to feel in his pockets for his pipe, as if his attention was already returning to matters of greater import.

"You must excuse us, madam," Dr. Watson continued. "Mr. Holmes and I are expecting a most distinguished visitor. If you were to return at another time, perhaps in the new year . . ."

Mrs. Smithers nodded frantically and began to back away.

"Yes, of course," she murmured. "No wish to be a trouble. Another time . . ." But I could see that Mrs. Hudson was having none of that. The housekeeper reached out a reassuring arm that had the effect of holding our visitor firmly on the edge of the rug. When she spoke, there was iron in her voice.

"I fear, sir, that Mrs. Smithers' business is more pressing than that. And it is her belief that, in the whole of London, only Mr. Holmes can assist her."

"Oh, yes, sir," burst out Mrs. Smithers eagerly. "I've heard so much about you, sir, and when I found that the police were right flummoxed by the whole thing, I said to my Lavinia, 'This is a case for Mr. Sherlock Holmes, this is. Mark my words, he's the man to sort this out,' I told her."

Dr. Watson appeared at a loss how to respond to this statement, but Mr. Holmes, who had now succeeded in lighting his pipe, appeared strangely moved by her words.

"Now, Watson," he reproved, "let us not be too hasty in this. There is no doubt a lot of truth in what our visitor says." Here he favoured Mrs. Smithers with a polite nod and motioned her vaguely towards a chair. "While we have a few moments, I can see no harm in hearing her story. That the police are bewildered means nothing, of course. It may be something that we can clear up here and now, without the need for further investigation."

He turned again to Mrs. Smithers, who had remained standing, her hand now clamped tightly to Mrs. Hudson's arm. "Now, madam, if you would tell your tale clearly, confining yourself strictly to the facts, Dr. Watson and I will endeavour to assist in any way we can. Mrs. Hudson, since Mrs. Smithers appears to find your presence reassuring, perhaps you would be so good as to remain with us?"

And with that, he returned to his seat, drew deeply on his pipe, and closed his eyes again. Watson perched himself on the arm of his chair and smiled encouragingly.

"Go ahead, Mrs. Smithers. Whenever you're ready . . ."

By now I had retreated to a corner of the room that was partially hidden by Dr. Watson's collection of primitive medical instruments. Realising that neither the gentlemen nor Mrs. Smithers were aware of my presence, I decided that I would be least in the way by sitting still and saying nothing.

Even when settled in a low chair, Mrs. Smithers seemed uncertain where to begin, but eventually she took a deep breath and plunged in.

"Well, sir," she began, "it all happened last Sunday. Sunday is the day when my daughter—my Lavinia, that is—likes to take tea in town. It's a little thing of hers. I daresay you will think it a little piece of nonsense, and it's certainly an extravagance, but in truth my Vinnie was spoiled something terrible by her father, and when he died she was that upset, I've never liked to rein her in. She's certainly grown up more ladylike than the daughter of a haberdasher has any right to be."

Now that she'd begun, Mrs. Smithers began to gather speed.

"That's why I was quite surprised when she married Phillimore, sir. He being only a clerk, and a quiet chap at that. Reserved, you'd call him. But she saw something in him and, to be fair to her, he's always kept her as she likes to be kept, and he's never said anything against indulging her little habits. Take Sunday afternoons, for instance. She likes to dress up so you wouldn't know her from a duchess, and he takes her into town to have afternoon tea in a proper 'otel. Always somewhere fancy, it is."

Throughout this speech, Mr. Holmes' eyes had remained tightly shut, but now he opened one of them and fixed her with a baleful glare.

"Very nice, I'm sure, Mrs. Smithers," he opined. "However, perhaps if we were to get back to this particular Sunday . . ."

"Yes, sir. Well, this Sunday they were going off as normal. The three of us live together in Ealing, sir. Sefton Avenue—I don't know if you know it. It's just the three of us there. Vinnie and her husband haven't had no children yet, sir, but of course there's plenty of time for that. To be honest with you, sir, I'm not sure Lavinia is that bothered by it, though of course I'd like grandchildren for myself, sir."

Sherlock Holmes stirred dangerously in his seat.

"This *particular* Sunday, Mrs. Smithers?"

"Yes, sir. Well, sir, this Sunday they were going out at

about half past two. I happened to be going out at the same time because I wanted to call on a cousin of mine who lives in Perivale. So the three of us left the house together, sir, which is a bit unusual. Anyway, we'd only gone about twenty steps when Phillimore began to fret about the weather. He said he thought there'd be showers."

"Eh?" Dr. Watson scratched his head. "But Sunday was a fine day, Mrs. Smithers. Remember it well because we haven't had many this winter. I almost went for a walk myself, if I remember rightly."

"That's right, sir. That's what I told Phillimore, but he seemed uneasy. Said he'd just step inside for an umbrella."

"Very well, Mrs. Smithers. So what happened then?"

"That's just it, sir. Nothing happened. We waited, but he didn't come out again. And when we went in to look for him, well, you could have knocked me down with a feather! You see, he just wasn't there! He couldn't have left the house, sir, not without us noticing. Be he weren't inside, neither. And we've never seen him since, sir. It's as Mrs. Hudson here said: he's gone and vanished into thin air."

Mrs. Smithers' story made Sherlock Holmes sit up sharply and open his eyes. Although he remained silent, and made a show of attending to his pipe, I could tell by the gleam in his eye that her narrative had engaged his interest. Even so, it was Dr. Watson who spoke first, blinking slightly as if a crucial element of the tale had passed him by.

"I'm sorry, Mrs. Smithers, I don't quite see . . . Could your son-in-law not have left the house unnoticed by some back route?"

"Oh, no, sir. I can be sure he did not."

"But you have a back door and rear windows, Mrs.

Smithers?" Mr. Holmes was still apparently absorbed in his pipe. "It must have been impossible for you to observe them from the street."

"Yes, sir." Mrs. Smithers turned to him eagerly, her honest face full of confidence. "But the back door was locked from the inside and all the windows were latched. You see, when we couldn't find Phillimore anywhere in the house, I thought he must be playing some joke on us. I thought, 'He's gone out the back.' But he couldn't have done. I took care to check all the windows, sir. Everything was locked from the inside."

"Remarkable!" Dr. Watson reached for his glass. "What do you make of it, Holmes?"

"That remains to be seen, Watson." Mr. Holmes removed his pipe and looked directly at our visitor. "You say, Mrs. Smithers, that your daughter is a woman of expensive tastes?"

"Well, sir, let's just say that my Vinnie has always liked nice things."

"And her husband, this Mr. Phillimore, is a clerk, you say?"

"Yes, sir."

"So I imagine that your daughter's little indulgences must account for a considerable portion of his salary?"

"Well, I couldn't say that for sure, sir. I suppose they must. He's always been very generous." She paused and frowned rather thoughtfully. "But then again, Phillimore is a very ordinary sort of man. Never seems to have any interests of his own. And Vinnie never could abide the idea of money sitting idle, sir."

"I see." Outside, the day had turned rather dark, and I could hear rain driving against the windows. While Mr. Holmes pondered, Mrs. Hudson moved silently to one of the side tables and lit a lamp. Its light fell obliquely on Mr. Holmes' face, and I saw that the glimpse of excitement there had turned to one of amusement.

"Would you say Mr. Phillimore was a man content with his lot, Mrs. Smithers?"

This question seemed to surprise her, and she pursed her lips as she puzzled it.

"I don't rightly know, sir. I've never really thought about it. But he had a roof over his head and a wife who is so elegant that any man would be glad to marry her."

"Indeed." Mr. Holmes turned to his colleague. "It is one of the great mysteries, Watson, how the two sexes can see the same objects so very differently. Tell me, Mrs. Smithers, in the days before he disappeared had Mr. Phillimore's behaviour been in any way unusual? Think very carefully before you answer."

"Unusual, sir? I wouldn't say so. He isn't the sort to do anything out of the ordinary." She pondered her son-in-law's extreme predictability for a moment, and then her face changed suddenly. "There was one thing, though. Something I found in a drawer along with his new pair of gloves." She began to fumble with her handbag, her cheeks flushing even redder than before. "I brought it with me, sir, because I didn't want Vinnie to see it. It would bring on the vapours, it would. To think of her husband bringing such a thing into the house!"

After a moment of determined rooting in the depths of her bag, she produced a folded square of paper and passed it to Dr. Watson with such alacrity that it might have been burning her fingers. I watched Mrs. Hudson lean forward slightly as the doctor opened it up and glanced at its contents.

"Why, it's a playbill, Holmes! For some dancer who's set to perform in Piccadilly. A Spanish lady by the sound of it."

Mrs. Smithers snorted. "She's no lady, sir, at least not in *my* book. I know about those sort of dancers. Why, it's downright indecent! To think of a quiet man like Phillimore entertaining such thoughts! If Vinnie knew, she'd be broken-hearted."

Dr. Watson held the bill out to his friend, but Mr. Holmes waved it away and rose to his feet, taking up a position by the mantelpiece from where he faced his audience.

"I think, Watson, it requires no act of genius to solve this particular problem." A flicker of amusement played around the corners of his mouth. "Mrs. Smithers, the answer to the next question is vital. It will give me the final piece to the puzzle. Now tell me . . ." He paused one moment more and drew happily on his pipe. "When you and your daughter were waiting in the street for your son-in-law to appear, *was it dresses that you were discussing, or was it the latest fashion in hats?*"

It would be hard to say whether Dr. Watson or Mrs. Smithers was the most taken aback at this question. Both seemed to blink a little in surprise, and Mrs. Smithers needed a second or two before she could respond.

"Why, that's amazing, that is! It just as you say, sir, though it beats me how you could know it. It was hats we was talking about, sir. Vinnie thinks a lot about hats. That day she was wearing a new style, and she wanted to know how she looked. And then there was a woman walking past who had a hat very like her own, so of course we had to talk about *that,* too . . ." She trailed off as though a thought had struck her. "But, sir, how does that explain what's happened to Phillimore?"

Mr. Holmes surveyed his audience and smiled. "If I were to tell you it were possible, under certain conditions, for a man to become invisible, you would no doubt mock me. And yet, I assure you that is the case."

"Nonsense, Holmes!" Dr. Watson exclaimed. "Under what conditions could that possibly be?"

"Why, Watson, my observations of the opposite sex have shown me that during any prolonged discussion of feminine attire, it is possible for any number of men to disappear entirely. As far as the female protagonists are concerned, they simply cease to exist. In this case, seeing his wife engrossed in what is, no doubt, her favourite subject, Mr. Phillimore quite accurately concluded that he might slip past both women in a cloak of total invisibility."

"But, sir!" Mrs. Smithers' ruddy face was becoming mottled with confusion.

"No, madam! No discussion! I am quite convinced. Let me tell you this: that if you wait two weeks, it is very likely that your son-in-law will come to his senses and return home begging to be forgiven. If the situation is worse, if he has discovered a taste for freedom, then I would suggest a small notice, perhaps in the theatrical papers, urging him to return home to discover something to his advantage. That should do the trick. After all, a man who abandons his wife, whatever the provocation, is a poor fellow and highly likely to succumb to other forms of temptation. Would you not agree, Mrs. Hudson?"

During Mr. Holmes' explanation the housekeeper had been listening to his comments with a furrowed brow, absently wiping at tiny marks on the sideboard with the hem of her apron. Now she paused and seemed to consider her response.

"His behaviour certainly leaves something to be desired, sir."

"But I'm quite sure he didn't pass us . . ." Mrs. Smithers rose, shaking her head as if a butterfly of doubt was fluttering around it. "But if you really think so, sir . . . I suppose he might . . ." She bobbed a little curtsey as if making up her mind. "I must thank you for your time, sir."

Mrs. Hudson paused to direct a rather frosty look at Mr.

Holmes, then guided our visitor gently to the door. "I'm sure the gentlemen will think further on your problem," she reassured her. "And if anything else occurs to them, they will no doubt wish to be in touch. I'll take a note of your address as I show you out . . ."

When the door closed behind them, I gave a little bow and began to follow them out, stopping on the way, for the sake of tidiness, to pick up the playbill that Dr. Watson had left lying on the floor. When I reached the sanctuary of the kitchen, I stopped to study it. At its head, a very familiar name was trumpeted in large letters.

LOLA DEL FUEGO!
The World Famous!
The Spectacular!
The Uniquely Talented!
The Most Beautiful Woman in Europe!!
The Greatest Dancer in the World!!
THE LADY OF THE FIRES
comes to London!!
For one night only!
At the Regal Theatre, Piccadilly
December 26th
Tickets by application to the Box Office
Advance sales only

Not sure what to do with it, I smoothed it flat and placed it neatly in the middle of the kitchen table where Mrs. Hudson would be sure to notice it on her return.

WITH the departure of Mrs. Smithers, the house became strangely subdued. Dr. Watson, seizing his chance, retired to his room for a restorative nap. Mr. Holmes, in retaliation, took up his violin, and soon the house hummed with a low, wistful melody. Outside, the rain that lashed the windows was slowly turning into sleet and although it was not yet one o'clock, the streets seemed grainy, as if dissolving into a preternatural dusk.

In the kitchen Mrs. Hudson and I prepared lunch in silence. The housekeeper had escorted Mrs. Smithers to the door and had returned with a little crooked furrow in her brow. For a while after that she said nothing, but from time to time she would take up the playbill and look at it as if it contained the answer to a question she had not yet fully formulated. When I tried to ask her about it, she shook her head.

"Not now, Flotsam. There's only one thing I can tell you just at the moment."

"Yes, ma'am?"

"That in any decent world, an honest woman's peace of mind is worth quite as much as rubies."

And that was all she would say on the matter until the cold roast beef was carved and the horseradish grated. Then, as we prepared to carry the trays to the study, she paused and looked at the rain running down the window.

"If it's fine tomorrow, Flottie, I think we might make a little expedition. It is some time since I was last in Ealing, but I believe it has some very fine public buildings. And, do you know, on top of that, I find myself inclined to pay a short visit to Sefton Avenue . . ."

I knew her too well to ask more and soon the subject was pushed from my mind, for as the afternoon advanced and no further caller made themselves known, an air of expectancy began to stifle all that we did.

"Dash it, Holmes! It's too bad of Branchester to leave us waiting like this!" grumbled Dr. Watson when his lunch had been cleared away and the morning paper had been looked through twice.

"Yet his cane tells us that he will return, my friend," Mr. Holmes replied gently, and the two lapsed into silence. Then, while Holmes smoked pipe after pipe and studied with extraordinary care a small portion of the ceiling, Dr. Watson took up a pack of cards and began to play patience, a pastime he conducted with a singular lack of the quality which gave it its name. At about three o'clock, when the kitchen was smart as an Irish hussar and fresh as a Whitstable oyster, Mrs. Hudson finally gestured towards the pot of silver polish.

"I think we might go up now, Flotsam," she said softly, and after we had gathered up our things, she led the way upstairs with a candlestick in each hand and two more under her arm.

The small linen room upstairs had never been intended for the polishing of silver but, although it lacked in space, it had certain other unique advantages. For one thing, its position just opposite the gentlemen's study meant that silver items in everyday use could be stored there, without the need for always carrying them up and down the stairs; for another, its proximity to the warm pipes meant that even in the coldest weather you could work with warm fingers and bare arms. Furthermore, although the fact was never commented upon between us, it was undeniable that when the door of the linen room was a little open and the door of the study not quite closed, then a clear line of vision ran between the two rooms, and any conversation in one might easily be heard in the other. Aware of this, and obviously not wishing to disturb the gentlemen, Mrs. Hudson and I tended to work there in complete silence.

We had not been working there for very many minutes before we heard the knock on the door that we had been so keenly expecting, three strong, imperious blows that told of a forceful hand and an equally forceful disposition.

"If you'd be so kind, Flotsam . . ." Mrs. Hudson carried on rubbing at the large candelabra as though she had no other interest on earth, so it was me, heart beating a little faster and errant curls peeping from beneath my cap, who had the honour of attending to the arrival in Baker Street of Mr. Godwin Branchester, confidant of princes, adviser to governments, and the man charged with the safety of the Malabar Rose.

CHAPTER FOUR

An Affair of State

That afternoon the rain became sleet, and the sleet became snow, and the wind turned so that it blew from the east. It was a day when the early darkness and the relentless, blustering flurries of snow combined to make the city strange and different. Familiar buildings blurred at the edges, and the friendly faces of neighbours disappeared beneath scarves and mufflers. The cold played its games with minds as well as bodies, so while on market stalls the wares were being fumbled and dropped by icy hands, so straightforward thoughts became difficult and strangely clouded by snow. Housewives battling back from market took wrong turns on routes they'd known forever. Policemen on their regular patrols found themselves inexplicably down alleyways they didn't recognise on beats that were not their own. The constable on duty in Baker Street thought more than once that he had spotted a small urchin lingering near our door, but each time, when he managed to battle across the road to grab him by the ear, the boy, if he had ever existed, had disappeared.

Down on the docks, Scraggs, who had taken the afternoon off, was watching a ship being unloaded. Great packing cases of unusual shapes and strange dimensions were being piled on the harbour side by men cursing as they slipped and strained in the snow. Each box was stamped with the same device: a crescent moon and three small stars. And overseeing the handling of each one was a short, dark-skinned man wrapped in an enormous cloak and with an astrakhan hat pulled low over his face. Describing him later, Scraggs could remember nothing but a neatly clipped moustache and an urgent pair of brown eyes that followed every inch of every movement of every case.

Elsewhere that afternoon, there were others braving the snow. In Randolph Place, a slim, angular man was hunched against the railings, watching the carriages pass by. He had turned up the collar of his coat against the snow, and under one arm he carried a small, brown-paper parcel. Eventually, when the moment was right, he crossed the road and knocked on one of the smart red front doors. This door was opened by a butler of very advanced years who ran a careful eye over his visitor's clothes while he listened to his request. Apparently satisfied by what he saw and heard, he beckoned the man inside and indicated that he should wait in the hallway. It was not a particularly inviting room, with cold marble floors and very little furniture to make it welcoming, only a stand for coats, a small table in the classical style, and a low chest, no more than three feet long and a couple of feet high, that may once have contained the personal effects of a military man on foreign service. As the stranger looked around him, a small pool of water began to gather at his feet.

The butler was away for no more than a minute before he returned with an answer to the man's enquiry. But to his surprise he found the front door open and the hall empty but for the marks of the stranger's feet retreating to the door. Before calling for a maid and a mop, the butler looked both up and down the street, but the snow confused the view and it was hard to tell amongst the hurrying crowds which direction the stranger had taken.

In Mr. Holmes' study, the haphazard snow and the growling wind were kept very firmly in their places. Mr. Godwin Branchester stood with his back to a roaring fire and eyed his audience carefully. The curtains had been closed to shut out the weather and the warm glow of the lamps softened the austerity of the great man's features. He was, as Mr. Holmes had predicted, a tall man and broad with it, so that his presence dominated the room. He stood straight despite his limp, and his mane of white hair made his figure even more imposing. When he spoke, his voice was gruff and businesslike.

"You will understand, gentlemen," he began, "that it is highly unusual for Her Majesty's Government to seek assistance in this way."

"Of course, sir." At Mr. Branchester's insistence, Mr. Holmes and Dr. Watson had remained seated. Mr. Holmes was studying his guest carefully. "But equally it is highly unusual for Her Majesty's Government to find itself in possession of a ruby such as the Malabar Rose."

Mr. Branchester, his air of authority a little dented, allowed himself to smile. "My word, sir, you are every bit as sharp as I have been led to believe. So you have divined that it is of the Malabar Rose that I wish to speak?"

Mr. Holmes waved the compliment away but allowed himself to look ever so slightly pleased. "It is not a difficult deduction to make, sir. A jewel beyond price is as much a burden as a blessing."

"Well, you are right enough, Mr. Holmes. The maharajah's gift comes with certain conditions. One is that it should be put on display before the end of this year so that London society might admire it. I don't mind admitting that this is causing unease at the very highest levels. The *very* highest levels, you understand." He paused for a moment to allow the significance of this remark to sink in. Although Sherlock Holmes appeared unimpressed and continued to examine the bowl of his pipe, Dr. Watson sat a little straighter in his chair.

"Very honoured, I'm sure, sir," he muttered. "At Her Majesty's service. Try to do our best, and all that."

Mr. Holmes waited for his friend to subside before speaking.

"Tell me, sir, with all the resources available to you, I am surprised that you require any special help from us. This is a police matter, surely?"

The gentleman nodded his great maned head in agreement.

"I must admit, sir, if I had my way, that would be the case. I'd have the stone in the vaults of the Bank of England quicker than the eye can see, and that would be an end of it. But the maharajah has stipulated a viewing and, worse, he demands it should be in the suite of rooms he keeps at the Blenheim Hotel. The maharajah himself, of course, has remained in Madras, but we have no choice but to comply with his instructions. Her Majesty insists upon it."

Mr. Holmes scratched his chin with the stem of his pipe. "I agree that arrangement creates certain difficulties, but nothing that a cordon of moderately alert policemen can't solve. Where is the stone now? Is it safe?"

"I have made certain of that, Mr. Holmes. I have placed Sir John Plaskett in charge of it, and I have asked him to call here within the hour to brief you on the steps he has taken."

"The Hero of Ishtabad?" Mr. Holmes allowed a smile to appear at the corners of his mouth. "It is to be hoped that a military brain is appropriate for this problem. Let us hope it remains a simple one."

"I fear it is very far from that, Mr. Holmes. There is one other aspect to the situation that I wish to share with you, the aspect that has panicked the Home Secretary and unnerved our police force. Have you ever heard, sir, of an illusionist who calls himself the Great Salmanazar?"

"An illusionist? I think not. Hardly my line, I fear. What about you, Watson?"

"Eh? Oh, no, Holmes. Not really my sort of thing, either. Though I did know a chap in the army who could make a rupee disappear into his elbow. Never was sure how he did it, you know."

Mr. Holmes turned to his guest and smiled apologetically. "I'm afraid, sir, that prestidigitation is not an art much studied in this house."

"Well, Mr. Holmes, they say the Great Salmanazar is a master of his craft. He first showed up half a dozen years ago, in Budapest. It isn't clear where he came from before that. He might be Persian by the look of him, but I've heard him called an Arab, a Farsi, a Berber . . . We've made inquiries, of course, but we know no more of him now than when he first appeared."

From where I stood in the linen room, I could see Mr. Branchester rub his jaw ruefully, as if amazed by this failure of British intelligence.

"Anyway, from his first show in Hungary, he has moved on to conquer Europe. Vienna, St. Petersburg, Paris, Madrid, Berlin . . . He has appeared across the continent, always for one night only, always playing to audiences containing the cream of society and never failing to enchant and baffle them. Now, in a week's time, he is booked to perform at the Regal Theatre in Piccadilly."

Mr. Holmes nodded in immediate understanding. "And the Regal Theatre is, of course, only a dozen yards from the Blenheim Hotel."

Godwin Branchester nodded meaningfully. "The two events are scheduled for the very same night. You have heard of the Godolphin Blue, Mr. Holmes?"

"Of course. The sapphire stolen in Milan last September."

"And the Von Metzen diamonds?"

"Disappeared in Berlin two years ago."

"And the Lafayette necklace?"

"Vanished from the vaults of a Paris bank some time in May of last year."

"Correct on all counts, Mr. Holmes. Each of those thefts has something in common, and it is that which is playing on the nerves of Lord Shastonbury and is fraying the tempers of our senior policemen. You see, *each of those thefts coincided exactly in time and place with performances by the Great Salmanazar.*"

In the silence that followed these words, Mr. Holmes put down his pipe and looked slowly across at Dr. Watson, who in turn tugged at his moustache and looked perturbed. In the darkness of the linen room, I looked across at Mrs. Hudson, who for the first time that evening had stopped polishing the silver. In response to my gaze she raised one eyebrow fleetingly and then returned to her work.

Back in the warmly lit study, Godwin Branchester was continuing.

"There can be no doubting the connection, Mr. Holmes, and I assure you it doesn't stop there. Everywhere this Salmanazar has gone, it has been the same. Jewels stolen, bullion disappeared. In Prague, it was the Templar Crucifix; in Lisbon, the Isabella figurine. And now he's in London, Mr. Holmes, and so is the Malabar Rose. We are relying on you to make sure that the paths of the two do not cross."

It was clear from the great many questions that followed that both Mr. Holmes and Dr. Watson were aware of the responsibility being placed on their shoulders. They asked everything you could imagine about the history and habits

of the Great Salmanazar, but Mr. Branchester could add little to what he had already told them. It appeared the man
really was a mystery. Eventually their discussion was interrupted by a further knock at the door, and I found myself
once again announcing one of the nation's great men.

"Major General Sir John Plaskett, sir. And Inspector
Lestrade of Scotland Yard."

The new arrivals could not have been more different in
appearance. Sir John was short and solid, filling out the red
and gold of his dress uniform like a particularly proud fighting cock. He had a bald pate, swirling grey whiskers, and a
moustache that ended at both ends with a magnificent flourish. Lestrade on the other hand was a tall, slightly lugubri-
ous man, with small features and a smooth chin, slight in
both stature and in impact. When I retreated from the room
the necessary introductions were being made, and by the
time I was safely ensconced in the linen room, Sir John was
addressing his audience in robust, booming tones.

"This has not been a conventional operation, gentlemen.
If there is one lesson I have learned in the field, it is that a
moving target is harder to hit. Makes sense, eh? As for the
enemy, well, we've had intelligence for weeks now that a
number of criminal gangs are interested in the Malabar
Rose, and to make matters worse there is the threat of this
man, Salmanazar, a threat that is currently hard to quantify."

With the arrival of Sir John, Godwin Branchester had finally accepted a seat, and now it was the major general's turn
to stand before his listeners. As he spoke, he took short steps
to and fro in front of the fire and emphasised his points with
jabs of the finger as if he were addressing a group of trusted
officers on the brink of battle.

"The kernel of my plan can be expressed in seven words,
gentlemen. *They can't steal what they can't find.* In the last
twenty-four hours, with the help of Lestrade here, we have

been putting that plan into action. That box, if you please, Inspector."

From behind his chair, the policeman produced a small velvet box of about a foot square. Sir John took the object and held it in front of him.

"When the ruby is displayed in the Blenheim Hotel, it will be in such a box as this. If I remove the lid, you will see that it is designed to act as both a case for the jewel and as a stand on which to display it." He levered the velvet lid of the box away and discarded it. Inside I could see that the velvet case had been shaped upwards to form a low pyramid, truncated at the top by a little hollow where the stone would sit. At a nod from Sir John, Lestrade produced a black pouch from his jacket and handed it across. Sir John emptied it into his hand and revealed to the audience a rose-red jewel, the size of a duck egg, nestling in his palm.

Dr. Watson gasped at the sight of it, and even Mr. Holmes sat forward, but Sir John merely smiled and placed the object gently onto the velvet stand.

"No, gentlemen. That is not the Malabar Rose. I took the precaution of having a dozen identical boxes made and eleven imitation rubies. This one is nothing more sophisticated than cleverly cut glass. By daylight you would not be fooled. But they will play their part well enough, for all that."

"I see." Mr. Holmes pursed his lips thoughtfully. "Eleven decoys."

"That's right, Mr. Holmes. Ten of which are currently being held under guard in different locations, each of them in a place where we might legitimately be expected to guard such a treasure. As of tonight, clumsy attempts have been made on three of these decoys. Each attempt has failed, and the gangs responsible are in custody. The one I show you here is the eleventh. We have no plans to deploy it, so you may keep both jewel case and jewel for your researches."

"And the twelfth, Sir John?"

At that question, the soldier stiffened. "The twelfth is the real gem, Mr. Holmes. I fear I can tell you only that it is kept separate from its box and held somewhere where I can guarantee it will be safe. The box that goes with it I have retained in my own home, and the two shall be brought together at the Blenheim Hotel on the night of the twenty-sixth, when the ruby goes on display. It is in the management of that occasion, and in determining the threat from this Salmanazar fellow, that we require your help."

All eyes seemed to be on Mr. Holmes, who was looking far from happy.

"You will understand Sir John's caution, Mr. Holmes," Mr. Branchester put in. "I myself am as much in the dark as you are."

Dr. Watson leaned forward and placed his hand on his friend's arm. "Come, Holmes. Think of England."

The great detective looked at the hand on his sleeve as if he scarcely recognised it, and only after a full three seconds of consideration did he raise his head.

"Very well, Sir John. I cannot be expected to work to my best if I am not in possession of every fact, but I shall assume that the ruby will be safe under your supervision until the night when it is put on display. In the meantime, Dr. Watson and I will work with Lestrade here to make sure that every precaution is taken to keep it safe for the entire time it is in the Blenheim Hotel. Now, Sir John, how shall we contact you?"

"During the day, you should try the regimental headquarters." Sir John reached into his pocket for a card. "Failing that, Mr. Holmes, a message will always reach me if addressed to my home in Randolph Place."

.   .   .

THAT night, I found it difficult to sleep. There were too many things lingering in my mind that were still not fully understood. Who was the Great Salmanazar, and how could he be stopped? What would happen if the Malabar Rose were stolen? And how would I be able to catch a glimpse of the famous Lola Del Fuego? Tucked up in my little cupboard bed beside the kitchen, these thoughts chased each other through my mind. I heard the clock outside strike midnight, then the quarter, then the half, and through the crack of my door I could see how the gaslight from the street filtered onto the kitchen floor. The fall of snow had changed its usual patterns, making the light somehow softer, so that the kitchen seemed full of new shadows, perplexing and eerie in their strangeness.

I don't know how long I had lain there looking at them when I suddenly became aware of a shadow that was shorter and clearer than the others. Something, perhaps a faint movement, must have drawn my attention to it and my attention, once caught, was unable to leave it alone. Now it seemed still, then it seemed to waver. Now it seemed no more than the branch of a tree caught at an awkward angle, next it seemed to have the form and substance of a human figure.

Puzzled now, and a little unnerved, I swung myself out of bed and crossed the kitchen to the window. Outside the street seemed still, motionless but for the gently falling snowflakes. But I had the impression that at the moment of my looking, something had just ceased to move. I scanned the view again, pausing on every pool of shadow, but nothing stirred, nothing disturbed the emptiness of the night. And then, just as I was turning away, too cold to sustain my lookout any longer, something definitely moved—a glimpse of a dark cap, the blur of a black coat. A shadow rearranged itself, then fell still again, as innocent as night.

Tiptoeing warily, almost afraid to breathe, I moved across

the kitchen and began to dress. When I had squeezed on every layer I could, I moved again, still keeping to the shadow, this time towards the kitchen door where my big winter coat was hanging. The movement I had seen was in the patch of darkness near the area steps, so instead of going out that way I made my way up through the house to the main front door. I drew the bolts as quietly as possible, and the door opened soundlessly. If the figure in the darkness was the person I thought, he would little expect an approach from this direction.

In the event, I had crept to within five or six yards of him before he heard me and, with a gasp of surprise and an oath, burst from cover. I was after him in a moment and almost grasped him there and then, before he escaped into the open street. He was small, and swift as an elver, and in moments he was beyond my reach and running as if for his life. I gave chase, but my chances of catching him seemed remote. The extra layers I had pulled on made me ungainly, and my skirts were soon damp and in my way. Had he held a straight line he might have escaped, but just as my breath was shortening a policeman's whistle sounded from the street ahead of us and stopped the fugitive in his tracks.

Hearing me close behind him, he made a quick decision and sidestepped into a tiny alley that opened to the street just at the place where he had paused. I saw him disappear into its darkness and felt a little glow of triumph. The alley-way may have served to hide him from the policeman, but it was a path I knew, and I knew it led only to a small court-yard. Without hesitating, I followed the figure into the dark-ness, slowing as I did so to catch my breath. When I reached the courtyard a minute or so later, I found him crouched in the farthest corner, staring back at me. The only light was from the sky, but it was enough to be sure of my quarry. It was the boy with the blue eyes.

"Where's the peeler?" he asked, peering behind me, expecting to see a dark uniform emerging from the darkness.

"Back in the street. He didn't see where we went." I stopped at the mouth of the alley, careful not to get close too quickly.

"Done nothin' wrong, anyways. Why're yer chasin' me? Didn't do nothin' tonight. An' I never took yer purse. Yer purse was in yer pocket all the time."

"I didn't chase you about the purse," I told him.

"What, then? Wasn't doin' no harm. Just standin'. It's a public highway, ain't it?"

"What did you come for? Did you want to break in? I haven't got that purse on me now, you know."

"I can see that," he spat back contemptuously, though *how* he could see, given the thickness of my coat and the many layers beneath it, wasn't very clear to me. "I didn't come for no purse. Told yer that."

"So why did you come?" While I stayed by the mouth of the alley his chances of escape were slight, and I could see the prospect of the policeman beyond was still bothering him.

"No reason. Now lemme go."

I shook my head and waited. I could hear his breathing, as heavy as my own. Suddenly he shivered. His coat was a thin one, and ragged, too.

"What's your name?" I asked him.

"What's it to you?" I could see he was angry with himself for getting caught.

"What's your name?" I said again, louder this time.

"They call me Blue."

I thought about that for a moment. "Have they ever called you John?" I asked.

His eyes narrowed suspiciously. "What d'yer mean?"

"I knew someone once who looked like you."

We carried on looking at each other. I tried again. "Did you recognise me? Is that why you followed me?"

"Don't know why I followed you. It's cos . . . Cos when I saw you, I thought yer looked nice. Not like them ladies as shriek an' shout as though they've been murdered, even though they's got nothing in their purses that they couldn't lose ten times over. But you didn't shout, did yer?" He looked as though that question had been worrying him. "Why didn't you shout?"

"I don't know. I think because you reminded me of someone. This boy, he had eyes like yours. He was only very small then. In the orphanage. His parents had just died."

"Never had no parents," he retorted angrily.

"Have you ever been in an orphanage?"

"Mighter done. Don't remember no girls there."

"When the boys reach three, they get moved. This was before that. This boy, I think his name was John."

"Pah!" He spat into the gutter. "No one's ever called me John. I've always been Blue."

I took a step forward.

"John had a picture."

"Picture? What d'yer mean?" He seemed tenser than ever, and his eyes were darting around the courtyard, alighting on everything but my own.

"A tiny one. A picture of his mother."

He breathed out a sigh. "Never had no mother. You goin' to lemme go?"

I stood aside so that I was no longer blocking his escape. "All right, Blue. The policeman will have gone by now." He straightened up and began to sidle around the wall of the courtyard towards the gap that had opened for him. "There's one thing, though, before you go."

"What?" His voice was suspicious again.

"What are you going to do now?"

"I'm goin' home."

"And where's home?"

"What's that to you?"

"When you get there, are you just going to keep stealing until one day that policeman out there does catch you? Is that your plan?"

"Plan? Pah!" He spat again.

"You could find work . . ."

"Work? Here? For the likes of me? Pah! Yer jokin'!"

I looked at the blue eyes and saw the anger and the mistrust in them, and somehow I felt defeated by them. There was nothing I could do for this boy, whoever he was.

"I'll leave you then," I told him, and turned to walk away down the alley. But something inside me softened, and I turned back. "You know where I live, Blue. If you ever really need help, ask for me. My name's Flotsam."

It was after I had left the alley and turned into Baker Street that I heard his footsteps behind me.

"Oi, Flotsam!" He seemed to linger on the name. "Flotsam," he said again.

I turned and saw him standing in the snow at the mouth of the alley. "There was a bloke asking around. Offerin' work. Just the other day."

I waited. He seemed to be looking at me very closely, trying to remember something.

"Well?"

He shrugged. "Well, I reckon I could go and look him up."

I HAD made my way to my own front door before I turned again and looked back up the street. It was hard to see amid the snow and the shadows, but I think when I closed the door behind me, he was still there, watching.

CHAPTER FIVE

An Ordinary Pair of Gloves

When I woke the next day, the whole world seemed to be talking of rubies. Long before the newspapers appeared, the Covent Garden costers and the Billingsgate fishmongers had heard of the three attempts on the Malabar Rose, and by dawn the news was all over London. Even before the dawn, while the lamps were still lit, the name of Sir John Plaskett was on the lips of every barrow boy and street hawker. Sir John was the man for the job; he had saved the ruby by his great astuteness; he had thwarted a plot by Fenians, by Polish revolutionaries, by criminal masterminds of every description; Scotland Yard had the measure of the plotters; the ruby was saved for the nation! By the time Scraggs arrived on our doorstep with a present for Mrs. Hudson of eggs fresh from the hen, it was already common knowledge that Mr. Holmes was also on the case; that he and Dr. Watson were to visit the Blenheim Hotel that very afternoon; that pitted against them were the world's most devious criminal minds; that only their most inspired efforts would be enough to guarantee the safety of the most remarkable gem in the world.

"And I'll tell you another thing, Flot," Scraggs declared, when Mrs. Hudson stepped upstairs to answer Dr. Watson's call for breakfast. "There's whispers on the streets about this magician chap, this Salmanazar. They say he collects precious stones, uses his magic to spirit them away into his own pocket."

"But that might be true, Scraggs!" There was something in my voice very like excitement, as though part of me hoped that the mysterious Salmanazar really *did* have such amazing powers. "The police are really worried about him. I heard them saying so last night."

Scraggs let out a low whistle. "Are they now? Then there's going to be some fireworks that night, an' no mistake, what with the magician on stage and the ruby next door and that Lola Del Fuego doing her fire dance on the same bill. Not surprising that the tickets are moving quicker than frogs in an eel pond. I'm just hoping that Jennings the chestnut seller can sneak me into the roof space to watch the fun."

"Oh, Scraggs, I wish I could go! I'd love to see that dance, and all the magic, too."

Scraggs was already pulling on his coat and preparing to leave. In the time since I'd first met him, Scraggs had grown taller, and sometimes, especially in this sort of half-light, his face seemed stronger and firmer than I remembered it.

"Well, Flot," he replied, placing his hand on my shoulder, "you never know. Perhaps there'll be some tickets to spare in the end after all. I'll be off now, so you can tell old Mrs. H good-bye from me."

"*Old* Mrs. H, Scraggs?" Mrs. Hudson boomed, bustling back into the kitchen bearing an empty tray and two pairs of Dr. Watson's socks for darning. "You can tell her that yourself and get a clip round the ear for your pains. But first, I've got something for you." She reached into her apron and produced a folded piece of paper which she then slipped deftly into Scraggs' pocket. "You can make yourself useful for once and deliver that to Mr. Rumbelow for me."

Scraggs looked pleased. "Yes, ma'am," he replied, almost respectfully. "I'm always pleased to go and see Mr. Rumbelow. Is it a legal matter, ma'am?"

"Never you mind, Scraggs. Now you should be on your way, and no more chatter. As for you, Flotsam my girl, have you forgotten that you've got a chemistry lesson this morning?"

I *had* forgotten. The excitement of the previous day had completely put it from my mind, with the result that I had no more than ten minutes to scramble myself out of my work things and into the neat, smart clothes required for such a visit.

The chemistry lessons had been Mrs. Hudson's idea. She had noticed in me an instinctive fascination for the phials of liquid and the brightly coloured test tubes that from time to time made their appearance in Mr. Holmes' study; and since she needed little in the way of encouragement when it came to furthering my education, she had pressed into service as my tutor no less a person than the Right Honourable Rupert Spencer, nephew to the Earl of Brabham. Mr. Spencer was a rising young man and already a chemist of some note, and known to Mrs. Hudson since his childhood when she once worked in the big house at Brabham-on-Stream. I suspect that he was as surprised to discover himself my teacher as I was to find myself his pupil, but Mrs. Hudson had a way of stating that things would happen which meant that they *did* happen, and it never occurred to either Mr. Spencer or myself to do anything but comply.

These lessons had become special to me for many reasons. For one, when I arrived at the townhouse in Bloomsbury

Square, I was under strict instructions to present myself at the front door, like a real caller. "You are a student like his other students, Flotsam, and when it comes to study it is achievement that counts."

"But, Mrs. Hudson, I haven't *achieved* anything yet," I would whimper feebly.

"No, Flotsam, not yet. Not yet." And she would chuckle to herself and continue her chores with a satisfied smile.

And once I had grown used to knocking at such a grand front door, and to the ritual of tea served in a drawing room bigger than all the rooms in Baker Street knocked together, then I found myself free to concentrate my thoughts on the lessons themselves, and the amazing hidden world they revealed to me. Mr. Spencer talked of the sciences with a rare enthusiasm, and I would treasure every word, drawing it all in with rapt attention. It was unprecedented for me to forget a lesson.

That morning, as I scurried through the slushy streets towards Bloomsbury Square, I noticed that the poster bills were everywhere. "The Great Salmanazar!" they proclaimed, and promised "the Greatest Feat of Magic ever Witnessed on these Shores." Next to each of them was a bill about Lola Del Fuego, like the one I had seen the night before. From the attention of the crowds gathering around them, I could see that "Lola Del Fuego, the Lady of the Flames!" was anticipated with quite as much eagerness as the illusionist she accompanied. And I was clearly not the only person with a passionate desire to watch Miss Del Fuego dance, for as I was being welcomed into the hall of the great house in Bloomsbury, a voice somewhere in one of the downstairs rooms could be heard squealing with excitement.

"But, Rupert, darling, you must, you must, you must, you must, *you must!* You simply *must!* She is so unutterably *gorgeous.* Everyone says so. I simply must see if she is as amazing as everyone says."

Reynolds, the butler, raised an eloquent eyebrow as he took my coat from me. "Miss Peters, miss. As you will gather, she has formed an urgent desire to witness the forthcoming theatricals at the Regal Theatre. I fear Mr. Spencer will have little choice but to purchase tickets."

I smiled back at him warmly. Reynolds was an old acquaintance of mine from my visits with Mrs. Hudson to the servants' door, and ever since my lessons began he had always done everything possible to put me at my ease.

"I think he may have to hurry," I told him. "Scraggs says the tickets will probably sell out very soon."

"Indeed, miss. I believe the last ticket sold at twenty minutes past nine this morning. But that is hardly an end to the matter. I understand that tickets already purchased are now changing hands through unofficial channels for up to five guineas apiece. If asked, I would strongly advise Mr. Spencer to act promptly in the matter, as I believe that price is unlikely to hold for very many hours."

At that moment we were interrupted by another shriek from the drawing room and with the shadow of a wink, Reynolds ushered me in.

Prepared though I was for a scene of some excitement, I was greeted by the most unlikely sight. For I had expected to find Miss Peters pouring tea at the little Louis XIV table in the centre of the room, and was alarmed to find that she was in fact standing on top of it. And not just standing, either. She was, from time to time, giving little jumps into the air, all the time waving around her head a bamboo cane with a small muslin net attached to it. Although this looked vigorous work, it was not enough to impede even slightly the flow of her argument.

"Surely you *want* to see the most beautiful woman in Europe, Rupert?" She paused to make another little jump. "I mean, despite all your dull old experiments, no one can really be *that* dry and dusty. They simply can't. And most young men are in a positive *froth* at the thought of her flame dance! Oh!"

That sudden exclamation was the result of her noticing my arrival just as she was about to make a particularly energetic leap towards the ceiling. It took her a moment to regain her balance.

"Hallo, Flottie!" she gushed when she had. "Don't you think it is absolutely *essential* to Rupert's education that he should go and see Lola La Thing-ummy dance? Do *please* tell him it is!"

Hetty Peters was the ward of the Earl of Brabham, and she and Mr. Spencer had known each other since childhood. As it was considered proper that my chemistry lessons should be chaperoned, Miss Peters had been pressed into service as a fellow student, and as a result I had become quite accustomed to a certain unconventionality in her ways. Even so, her behaviour on this occasion seemed unusually bizarre, particularly as I was unable to detect the presence of Mr. Spencer, or indeed anybody else, anywhere in the room.

At that moment, Miss Peters let out a little scream.

"There, Rupert! There!" She began to point wildly at a point somewhere above my head and, as I turned in confusion, I realised that Miss Peters was not alone after all: the Right Honourable Rupert Spencer, his jacket removed and his sleeves rolled up, was hanging from the top of a bookcase in the corner of the room, a good ten feet above the floor, wielding in his spare hand a net very like Miss Peters'.

"Got it!" he cried triumphantly, and cradling the net in one hand he began to clamber back to earth.

"Thank goodness for that," Miss Peters sighed. "Here,

Flottie, help me down. I'm absolutely exhausted. I never thought we'd get them all. I only carried on as long as I did so I could demonstrate to Rupert how fantastically plucky I am. But to be honest, I'm not sure he noticed."

"Butterflies, Miss Flotsam," Mr. Spencer explained, with a friendly grin. He was an athletically built young man, with brown eyes that crinkled at the edges. "I'm making a study of them. A contact of mine was good enough to send me some wonderful specimens, but within moments of them arriving, Hetty here contrived to release the lot of them into one of the highest ceilinged drawing rooms in London."

Miss Peters, still flushed from her exertions, turned a shade redder. "Really, Rupert! That is absolutely untrue! I did just what he told me to, Flottie. Rupert never said anything about shutting the little door. Besides, I thought they looked perfectly happy in their little box, with their leaves and things. They didn't look as though they were all going to fly out just the moment they had a tiny opportunity."

Mr. Spencer had brought over the box in question, a cube of wood and wire-mesh with a little garden of plants in it. "Watch!" he whispered, and he gently pressed his net against the box then pulled back the wooden shutter that acted as a door. Immediately a tiny butterfly of the most brilliant bright blue fluttered into the box and settled on one of the leaves.

"Paris Peacocks," he told me. "From India." Then, in a louder voice: "They've led us something of a dance, I'm afraid. Hetty, will you ring for tea? I think I need refreshment before we can begin our lesson."

While the tea was being poured, Miss Peters returned to her original subject.

"Rupert, darling, don't you think you're being very shortsighted in not taking me to the magic show? I'm sure the Bradshaw twins would both want to take me if you don't, and if they do I shall wear my pink dress, and you know how well I look in that."

"The Bradshaw twins are both colour-blind, Hetty. They told me so themselves. But I'm sure they'll enjoy the show, even if they don't fully appreciate the dress." He turned to me. "Unfortunately, Miss Flotsam, I'm already engaged to address the Marylebone Natural Philosophic Society that evening. It's a group of very eminent men. I can hardly excuse myself by telling them that I wish to witness some conjuring tricks."

"Oh, Rupert! Sometimes you are so *indescribably* dull, I wonder why I want to marry you. I believe you do it deliberately, just to put me off. But it's no good, you know, because I know that *no one* can really be that dull. Besides, I don't believe the Marylebone Natural Philosophic Society actually exists. I think you have made it up just because you'd like it to."

Mr. Spencer looked grave. "I shall put that theory to the society and canvass their views," he replied solemnly.

At that point we were interrupted by the entry of a short, grey gentleman. He was a man of about seventy, impeccably dressed with neatly trimmed hair and moustache, and I recognised him straightaway as the master of the house, none other than the Earl of Brabham himself. Widely known as the Irascible Earl on account of his fiery temper, today he looked more anxious than angry. On his entry, we all rose to our feet.

"Hello, Uncle," Rupert greeted him. "Will you join us for tea?"

The idea seemed to strike him as palpably idiotic. "Tea, Rupert? *Tea?* At this hour? I haven't even had a drop of Scotch yet."

"Hello, Nuncle," Miss Peters responded sweetly. "Do come and join us, even if you only eat the shortbread." She drew him over to the table and guided him down into an empty chair.

"I don't believe you know Miss Flotsam, Uncle?"

"Flotsam? Flotsam? No, I don't believe I do. There were some Motsams in Wiltshire once, I recall. The chap would never stop talking. Ended up running away with a publican's daughter and opening a brothel in Constantinople. Showed a lot more initiative than I ever gave him credit for. No relation, I take it?"

"No, sir."

"Miss Flotsam is very interested in chemistry, Uncle."

"Chemistry?" The Irascible Earl began to growl dangerously. "For *ladies?* Preposterous! One of the few things I can say in your favour, Hetty, is that you've never once shown the slightest interest in education. Now tell me, Rupert, have you seen a newspaper this morning?"

"No, sir, not for a day or two, I'm afraid."

"Then I suppose you won't know anything about it. Never heard of the Malabar Rose, I suppose?"

"Malabar Rose . . ." Mr. Spencer looked thoughtful. "It's a familiar name but I can't quite place it . . ."

"Then you're the only damned fool in London who can't," snapped the earl. "It's a blasted ruby. Everyone's talking about it. It's going on display at the Blenheim Hotel on Boxing Day. Invitation only, and I'm invited. Want you to come with me."

"Me, Uncle?"

"Yes, you! You, dammit! Simple enough request."

"Well, of course, normally I'd be delighted, Uncle, but I'm afraid that evening I'm attending a meeting of the Marylebone Natural Philosophic Society to address them on the subject of . . ."

"The *who?*" The earl snorted dangerously. "Nonsense! Don't believe a word of it. Besides, don't need you all evening. Just want you to come with me to the hotel. About sixish. Viewing doesn't begin till eleven, so you can do what you like in between. Natural philosophers, indeed! Sometimes I think you make it up just to annoy me!" And with a curt bow in my direction, the earl turned on his heel and strode from the room.

"Ahhh!" Miss Peters was the first to speak after the door had slammed shut. "I love it when he's in one of those moods. So much easier than when he's trying to be *nice.*"

Mr. Spencer watched the door still shuddering on its hinges. "Yes, he did seem in good form today. I wonder what that stuff about the ruby is all about? Who do you think can tell us about the Malabar Rose?"

I felt a warm glow of satisfaction. I could. And I did.

THAT afternoon, Mrs. Hudson took me with her to Ealing. I had returned from my chemistry lesson at around lunchtime and found the rooms in Baker Street unusually quiet. Mr. Holmes' study was silent and, from the empty hooks where the gentlemen's hats usually hung, I could tell that both he and Dr. Watson were out. Downstairs, too, there was an air of unwonted calm. The kitchen was immaculate, the only movement the flickering of a flame in the stove. Surprised by this quietness, I made myself busy getting together a little lunch and rereading the lines in the paper about the Malabar Rose. But when Mrs. Hudson finally returned, flapping the dampness out of her coat and blowing hard on her fingertips, it was not the safety of the famous ruby that she had in mind.

"Come, Flotsam. Into your coat! Mr. Holmes and Dr. Watson are out with Inspector Lestrade at the Blenheim Hotel, fretting about the placement of guards and so forth, so you and I have the afternoon off. If we are to help Mrs. Smithers find her son-in-law, there's no time to lose. Men don't just vanish, Flotsam, though I daresay at times they wish to."

We travelled to Ealing by train and then went on by foot to Sefton Avenue, an unremarkable street of sturdy terraced houses with redbrick fronts and small gardens, both front and rear. Mrs. Smithers' house turned out to be at the end of the terrace, on the corner of Sefton Avenue and another quiet street, similar in almost every respect. Before knocking at the door, Mrs. Hudson led me round the corner to examine the house from the rear.

"Note all the details, Flotsam. There is a puzzle here that perhaps we can solve if we understand the shape of the pieces." And, duly encouraged, I noted all I could: the front of the house had a bay window to the front room and a front door set with panes of bright stained glass; the upstairs windows were closed and heavily net-curtained. The rear of the house had smaller windows and a weathered door that opened into the damp, narrow garden. It being the end of the terrace, the house had a third wall, a blind one, solid brick from pavement to chimney with no chink or piercing that might permit escape. In front of this wall, Mrs. Hudson stopped, her toe tapping as if with uncontrollable energy.

"And what have we here, Flotsam?"

"Where, ma'am?"

"Right here." She tapped her toe harder, and I realised she was tapping it to draw my attention to a small metal panel set into the pavement at our feet. It was grey and dull, and didn't draw attention to itself.

"It looks like a coal chute, Flotsam. So they can deliver coal directly to the cellar." She bent down and succeeded in levering it open, then peered into the darkness for a moment. "Here, Flottie, stand next to it for a moment . . ."

She positioned me by the dark gap and looked from my hips to the hole and back again.

"What do you think, Flottie? Could you fit down there?"

"I don't think so, ma'am." The hole was little more than one-and-a-half feet long by a foot wide.

"Hmmm, I think you might be right. Come, let us call on Mrs. Smithers and see what more she can tell us."

At first there was no reply to our knock, but Mrs. Hudson persisted grimly. After a minute or two the door opened, and I recognised the woman who had visited us in Baker Street. Today, however, there was a degree of confusion in her manner that had not been there before, as if something had occurred to unsettle her.

Mrs. Hudson gave her no time for questions.

"Mrs. Smithers, I apologise for this intrusion. Mr. Holmes has one or two further questions he wishes to ask." She lowered her voice. "He would have called in person, but he is detained by this matter of the maharajah's ruby. I'm sure you understand that his presence is required by . . ." With a little gesture of her hand, she signalled towards the sky, as though an altogether higher power was in need of Mr. Holmes' services. Mrs. Smithers followed the gesture with her eyes and gasped.

"Yes, of course. If Mr. Holmes is required personally by . . ." She gave a similar upward gesture. "Well, then I'm sure he must do his duty before he can possibly come and see the likes of me. Please," she continued, remembering her manners, "please come in. My daughter Lavinia is resting upstairs. We have had something of a shock this morning."

With these words she led us into a crowded little front parlour and offered us seats by the fire and cups of tea. Mrs. Hudson accepted the former but was firm in declining the latter.

"A shock, you say, Mrs. Smithers?" she asked, in the most blandly uncurious of tones.

"Well, yes. I suppose I should say *another* shock, for we have not yet come to terms with poor James disappearing. I can only assume that this event is somehow related to the other."

"Perhaps if you would care to explain?"

"Yes, of course. It was something that arrived in this morning's post. A thick brown envelope addressed to Lavinia. At first I thought it must be some little indulgence she had ordered for herself, so you can imagine my shock when she opened it and we saw what was inside!"

"What *was* inside, Mrs. Smithers?"

"Why, it's still so hard to believe! You see, it was bank notes. Piles of them! Two hundred one-pound notes! I've never seen so much money in all my born days!"

Mrs. Hudson looked across at me, and though her face barely changed I could tell by the slight quiver of her eyebrows that this had both surprised and intrigued her.

"And nothing else, Mrs. Smithers? No letter?"

"Nothing! Though I'm sure the money is in some way from Phillimore. He was a quiet man, but he's always done right by my Vinnie."

"And does your daughter agree with you?"

"Poor Lavinia! The child hardly knows what to think. She is quite overcome. But I believe that this strange gift has helped her. 'Dear James,' she said to me, 'Some evil has taken him from me, but this tells me at least that he is safe!' It is a great comfort to her."

"I can quite imagine. But tell me, Mrs. Smithers, can you think of any way that your son-in-law might be able to command such a sum in cash?"

Mrs. Smithers placed her fingers to her cheeks and pondered the question. "It's hard to see how he *could* have done. He's always been a steady worker, of course, but never more than a clerk. And of course, there's been his recent illnesses, too."

The low light of the winter afternoon was beginning to filter into the room, and some of it was falling onto Mrs. Hudson's face.

"He's been unwell?" As she asked the question, her eyes seemed to catch some of that late afternoon brightness.

"Why, yes. It began about three years ago. Phillimore complained of headaches and said that his doctor had recommended a dose of sea air. Vinnie didn't at all like the idea of going off to the seaside with him, so it was agreed he would go alone, to Broadstairs, where he could stay quite cheaply. In the end, he was away for a full ten days, so he must have been quite ill. But he did seem very much better when he came back."

"But the illness returned?"

"It did. He's been prone to ill health ever since, I'm afraid. Every three of four months he'd come over all funny."

"And the cure was always the same?"

"Always Broadstairs, yes. Sometimes he'd stay more than a week, but the last time was only three or four days. Of course, it played havoc with his employment. In the end, Jarvis and Stitch had to let him go, and he's had any number of posts since then. After each illness he'd find himself a new position. For the last five months he's been with Droitwich and Spooner by Marble Arch."

Mrs. Hudson leaned forward. "Do you think you might be able to recall the dates of Mr. Phillimore's various visits to Broadstairs at all?"

Mrs. Smithers looked doubtful. "Well, perhaps if I talked to Vinnie . . . Perhaps between us we might."

"Thank you, Mrs. Smithers. And do you have a picture of your son-in-law to hand?"

"A picture? Of James?"

"A portrait or a photograph, perhaps?"

The idea had clearly never occurred to Mrs. Smithers. "You know, I don't believe we do. We always talked of having one done, of course, but somehow . . ."

"I see." Mrs. Hudson rose to her feet. "Now I suggest you show us around, so that we can see for ourselves any ways in which your son-in-law might have left the house."

Slightly to my surprise, Mrs. Smithers did exactly as she was bid, never questioning whether Mrs. Hudson was truly Mr. Holmes' appointed agent. She proceeded to lead us all over her house, showing us the windows and doors, back and front, on every floor. Mrs. Hudson paused to examine each one closely, and while she did so, our hostess told me more about her son-in-law, as if talking about him was a relief to her. I learned that he was a man of few words. He had met Lavinia at a tea dance, and she had been impressed because he had insisted on paying for her tea. She had found him sober and respectful and endearingly biddable.

That combination, along with a generosity of spirit that he was prepared to demonstrate in suitably material ways, had proved quite enough to win her heart, although whether this had ever been Mr. Phillimore's intention was unclear from his mother-in-law's narrative. She could tell me nothing about his family or his past, only that Mr. Jarvis of Jarvis and Stitch spoke approvingly of the young man. That, and an engagement ring with real stones, had been all the assurance of breeding that Lavinia Smithers required. After that, Mr. Phillimore's history became little more than a footnote to his wife's, and until his series of illnesses there seemed to be very little that Mrs. Smithers could tell us about him. It was as if he had become a shadow in his own home. And if Mrs. Hudson had hoped for more details from the gentleman's wife, she was to be sorely disappointed. We found Lavinia Phillimore dozing on her bed in a laudanum-scented room, a look of beatific happiness on her face, and the contents of the mysterious envelope scattered like rose petals across her pillow.

Two strange things happened before we left the house. The first was Mrs. Hudson's insistence on visiting the cellar, where she spent a considerable number of minutes pacing the floor, and rather longer examining the small cavity in the wall that formed the bottom end of the coal chute.

"Would you be able to climb up there, Flottie, do you think?" she asked me. "If your life depended on it?"

I considered it for a moment, putting my head into the hole itself and peering upwards.

"No, ma'am," I concluded. "Someone my size could fit into the gap, I think, but the chute doesn't go straight up. It's a sort of Z-shape. You couldn't get up there without breaking your neck."

Mrs. Hudson looked dissatisfied with this analysis and continued to peer up the chute for a while longer, frowning deeply. "But if you're right, Flotsam, I just don't see . . ." And with that her speech petered out and a deep furrow of thought seemed to fix itself between her eyebrows.

The second unusual thing happened when Mrs. Hudson asked to be shown where Mrs. Smithers had found the playbill, the one advertising Lola Del Fuego's next performance. Mrs. Smithers directed us to a small drawer by the side of Mr. Phillimore's bed that proved empty but for a pair of brand-new gentleman's gloves. Those gloves seemed to fascinate Mrs. Hudson. They were wrapped in tissue paper as if only recently carried home from the shop, and when unwrapped they appeared to be nothing more exciting than a very ordinary pair of gloves—neither lavishly expensive nor unduly cheap, in fact just the sort of gloves a clerk might be expected to wear. The name of the glove maker stitched inside them was J. Hartington of Kimber Street,

Islington, and they had nothing about them to distinguish them from a thousand other pairs. Yet Mrs. Hudson lingered over them for a full two minutes, turning them over between her fingers as if contemplating something rich and strange.

"These gloves were bought by Mr. Phillimore?" she asked.

"Why, I think so, yes. He mentioned that he needed a new pair the other day. His old pair was quite worn out."

"And he was particular about these things?"

"No, not at all, Mrs. Hudson. James cared little for how he dressed. He would pick up such items from any shop he passed just as he needed them. It is one of Lavinia's constant complaints. She feels he does not take sufficient pride in his appearance."

"I see." Mrs. Hudson seemed to hesitate before going any further, but her next question, when it came, was so unlikely, so patently bizarre, that at first I thought I had misheard.

"Tell me, Mrs. Smithers," she asked, "has your daughter recently received as a gift either a music box, a pet dog, or any variety of clockwork toy?"

WE left the house in Sefton Avenue with Mrs. Smithers' perplexed denials still fresh in our minds. It was clear that nothing on that eclectic list had recently entered the house, and after satisfying herself on this point, Mrs. Hudson seemed ready to depart. While we were indoors, the light had faded and had let in the cold, and some first few flakes of snow were beginning to drift into our faces. Mrs. Hudson seemed unaware of them, and she kept her thoughts to herself as we began to retrace our footsteps towards the station. At the corner of the street, we passed a small boy carrying a holly wreath almost as large as himself, and I realised, with something of a shock, that it was only three days until Christmas.

CHAPTER SIX

The Invisible Worm

Three days to Christmas meant only four days before the Malabar Rose was to be put on display, and that in turn meant a good deal of work for Mr. Holmes and Dr. Watson. The whereabouts of the stone remained a mystery to everyone but Sir John Plaskett, who would arrive every morning with a bounce in his stride and a jaunty whistle on his lips. Even the news that two more of his decoys had almost been seized did nothing to dampen his enthusiasm.

"They'll never find it!" he declared happily. "It's in the last place anyone would think to look. And if I were a thief, even if I knew where to look, I'm not sure I'd dare to make an attempt on it! Too demmed risky!" And he'd guffaw happily with his head thrown back, a laugh that seemed to pain Dr. Watson as he tried to balance marmalade on his morning toast.

"Dash it, Sir John, but what of these latest attempts? Things are getting a little too hot for my liking."

"Oh, don't worry yourself, Dr. Watson. As a result of

these abortive attempts, we now have all the main threats to the Malabar Rose under lock and key. The only one left is this Salmanazar chap, and I'm trusting you and Holmes to deal with *him*."

At that point, just as I was preparing to remove the breakfast tray, there were footsteps on the stairs, and with no warning at all a man dressed as a rat catcher entered the study. He was clad in a soiled jacket and sludge-coloured trousers that ended an inch short of his shoes and revealed a strangely clean and rather jaunty pair of tartan socks. On his head he wore a squashed cap and dangling from one hand was a cage containing three live rats. His face was disgustingly grimy and was distorted by a terrible squint.

"Great God!" exclaimed the major general at the entrance of this unlikely visitor.

"What? . . . Who on earth? . . ." began Dr. Watson, reduced to a stutter of surprise.

In reply the intruder rolled his eyes horribly, and on spying me in the corner set his face into a fiendish leer. I decided enough was enough.

"Will you be having breakfast now, sir?" I asked him. "Or would you be wanting to clean yourself up a little first?"

The man's face fell, giving up both the leer and the squint in the process.

"Damnation!" he muttered. "I had thought my disguise quite foolproof."

"Good lord, Holmes, is that really you?" Dr. Watson rose to his feet and peered at his friend in bewilderment.

"Of course it is, Watson. Who else would be barging in here at this hour? Other than perhaps Sir John, of course."

Sir John's surprise was scarcely less than Dr. Watson's, though he was much better at concealing it. "Mr. Holmes? I can hardly believe it! But what is the meaning of all this?"

Mr. Holmes, restored to equanimity by the gentlemen's

astonishment, gave a low chuckle and began to remove his jacket.

"Do not be embarrassed, gentlemen. Sharper eyes than yours have failed to see beyond these rags these last twenty hours." He looked at me a little doubtfully, as if unable to account for the exception to the rule.

"Yes, sir. Will you be wanting breakfast, sir?"

"In a moment, Flotsam. First, you could pour me a bottle of the excellent brown ale that Mrs. Hudson always supplies. There is one hidden in that large Wellington boot on the mantelpiece."

While I poured the ale, Mr. Holmes explained himself to the two gentlemen. "I have made it my business to find out a little more about the Great Salmanazar and his bag of tricks. Since we took on this case he has scarcely been out of my sight."

"Remarkable, Holmes!" Watson allowed a small pile of pipe tobacco to spill onto the front of his waistcoat. "And he is unaware that he is being watched?"

"Far from it, Watson. Lestrade has detailed a minimum of three officers to follow him at all times. Our friend must think we are a nation of policemen. But I flatter myself that he is not aware of every person who observes him!" He dropped his jacket on the rats' cage and sat down with a satisfied sigh. "It hasn't been easy, of course. The man works through the night on his rehearsals. He spends hours positioning every hook, every rope, every beam."

Sir John, having recovered from Mr. Holmes' unconventional entrance, seemed impressed by this evidence of his energy. "Fine work, Mr. Holmes. Now tell us what you have learned."

Mr. Holmes hesitated for a moment. "What have I learned? Well, I have learned that this Salmanazar is a very deep fellow. He gives nothing away. Although I have dogged his footsteps, he has shown no outward interest in the Malabar Rose. He neither reads the papers nor listens to gossip. He seems entirely intent on his forthcoming performance."

Watson looked a trifle disappointed at this. "So what's the next step, Holmes?" he asked. "I was hoping we'd have the fellow behind bars by now."

"Arrest the Great Salmanazar *before* his performance, Watson? Why, there'd be a riot. Unless they found him with the ruby actually in his pocket, I don't think Lestrade's men would have the nerve. His performance threatens to be the most sensational event to happen in London for years. I hear that tickets are fetching ten guineas apiece."

"Really, Holmes, be serious! Are we to let this chappie lay his plans completely unimpeded?"

"On the contrary, Watson. I feel it is time we confronted him. I would like to see what happens if we can unsettle him a little."

"Ideal, Holmes! When will you do it?"

"Me, Watson?" Mr. Holmes looked over at Sir John and smiled with unconcealed amusement. "Would I go to these lengths to conceal my appearance if I planned to then march into the Regal Theatre and introduce myself to the man? No, my friend, I shall leave that job to you. Later this morning, Sir John and I are to have another look at the arrangements for the ruby at the Blenheim Hotel. I suggest you call on Mr. Salmanazar then and see what you can get out of him."

"Just me, Holmes? By myself? I'm not sure I like the sound of that. After all, this chap sounds dashed tricky."

"Very well." The detective looked across to where I was standing with the breakfast tray, and I felt him fix me with a hawkish gaze. "Flotsam, you have proved an admirable assistant to Dr. Watson in the past. Please get yourself out of that ridiculous apron at the earliest opportunity. You must be ready to leave for the Regal Theatre within the hour."

WITH Mrs. Hudson's help, it took me only a few minutes to transform myself from Sherlock Holmes' maid into the neatly dressed young lady who accompanied Dr. Watson out into the icy rain. Mrs. Hudson had been soothing and unperturbed throughout, pinning my hair for me in front of the mirror and murmuring words of advice as she pinned.

"Keep your eyes open, Flotsam. Don't on any account allow Dr. Watson's questioning to distract you. I doubt if you will learn very much from it anyway. Watch out for the ordinary things, Flottie. Nine times out of ten, that's where you can find the truth."

I digested this advice thoughtfully, but I had something else on my mind.

"Mrs. Hudson, ma'am," I wondered aloud, "how worried are you about the safety of the Malabar Rose?"

"Worried, Flotsam? When the whole might of the nation's police force is available to protect it?"

"Oh, I'm sure it's being wonderfully well guarded, ma'am, it's just that I rather thought you might have wanted to visit the Blenheim Hotel yourself. Just to see what's going on, ma'am."

In front of me, in the mirror, I watched Mrs. Hudson position the last pin so that my hair was held high on my head in the way I'd seen smart young women. She cast a careful look at her work.

"Very good, Flotsam. You wear it well. Now quickly, girl, fetch your hat and let's see you pin it on."

As I carefully positioned the smart little hat that Mrs. Hudson had given me, I couldn't help but return to my original question.

"About the Malabar Rose, ma'am. I'm sure it would be good if you could just keep your eye on things a little bit."

"That's very kind of you, Flottie. But there's plenty to be doing here, what with Christmas coming and the goose still not bought. Besides, I'd like to see this strange business in Ealing settled. Take a look at this, Flotsam."

From a drawer in the dresser she produced a thin, cheaply printed newspaper entitled *Plays and Players*. It was folded open on a column of small advertisements, one of which had been ringed in black ink.

> Reward offered for information regarding the whereabouts of Mr. James Phillimore of Ealing. Apply Rumbelow and Rumbelow, Solicitors, Birch Street.

"I'm not sure what good it will do," the housekeeper mused, "but it can't do any harm, and you never know what might crop up. I've been thinking a lot about James Phillimore's headaches, Flotsam . . ."

"Yes, ma'am?"

"And do you know, I begin to wonder if he really is the rather pale character that his mother-in-law has described."

My journey to Piccadilly with Dr. Watson was a warm and pleasant one. The good doctor went to great lengths to ensure that I was wrapped in blankets against the cold, and endeavoured to entertain me with tales of operations he had performed during the Afghan wars. Despite these, I was still eager to get on with our mission and, after trying the Regal Theatre, we eventually succeeded in tracking the Great Salmanazar to his suite of rooms at Brown's Hotel.

Although *we* were anxious to see *him*, he seemed in no great hurry to see us. In fact, he made us wait in the great crimson-and-gold lobby for fully forty minutes after Dr. Watson's card was sent up, until I began to fear that the good doctor might chew through his moustache or commit some act of violence against one of the marble statues that decorated the hotel's entrance hall.

"Confound the man, Flottie!" the doctor growled. "Where *is* he? Never did like the sound of him, anyway. Don't like a man who does conjuring tricks. It's like playing trick shots at billiards. Not quite gentlemanly. And how can you have a conversation with a man when he's always thinking about how to make your handkerchief disappear?"

"He's supposed to be a very *special* conjurer," I reminded him. "Do you think he might have special powers?"

"Nonsense! The chappie's just a jumped-up fakir, I'll be bound. I daresay a few blunt questions will scare the life out of him."

As Dr. Watson finished speaking, we both became aware that a sallow, Asiatic gentleman in an immaculate dark suit had appeared at his shoulder.

"You are, I believe, the famous Dr. Watson," he stated softly.

"What? Oh, I see. Well, hardly famous, you know," the doctor explained hastily, "though I suppose one or two people have heard of me."

"Indeed, sir. And this young lady?"

"This is Flotsam. Er, *Miss* Flotsam. My assistant."

The man gave a slow, stately bow in my direction, then turned back to Dr. Watson.

"The Great Salmanazar will see you now."

WE found our quarry in the midst of a magnificent room with high ceilings, its walls encrusted with mirrors and heavy gilt panels. Amidst all the grandeur, a slight figure stood facing us, his arm already stretching towards us in welcome.

"Dr. Watson! Such an honour! Do please come in." He ushered us into the centre of the great room with such enthusiasm that we might have been his most particular friends. "Do please take a seat. And of course, your companion, also. Miss Flotsam, I believe. Of course. Please take a seat, Miss Flotsam. It is a great honour."

The Great Salmanazar was far from the imposing figure I had expected. He was little more than four or five inches over five feet, and he had the slight build and lissom grace of a gymnast. He was neatly dressed in the European style, but he had discarded his jacket and stood before us in his waistcoat. He might have been any age between thirty and fifty. His dark hair was heavily lacquered in the Mediterranean fashion, and his moustache was waxed to curl up proudly at the edges. His eyes were as dark as his hair, but from his colouring he might as easily have been a Greek or a Spaniard as an Arab or a Berber. He spoke English almost perfectly with only the faintest trace of an accent.

"Please, at this hour of the day I believe it is considered right to take a drink before one's luncheon. This hotel contains every luxury. Please let me help you to some refreshment."

There was something in the extreme earnestness of his manner that made us feel it would be most hurtful to refuse. I could see Dr. Watson's barrier of formality beginning to crumble a little under the pressure of his host's desire to please.

"Very well, then. I daresay a small Scotch would help to keep out the cold."

"A wise choice. And Miss Flotsam?"

I had no idea what to say, as I had no idea what drink would be appropriate for a young girl to request in such company. For a moment I floundered, until Dr. Watson realised my distress and came to my rescue.

"I always say a glass of champagne at this time of day is the sort of tonic a young lady needs."

"Ah, yes! Champagne!" Our host seemed delighted. "Pol Roger, I think. Allow me . . ."

At that moment, for the first time, I noticed on the table in front of us a small, silver tray, its contents hidden beneath a linen napkin that had been draped carefully over them. The tray must have been there from the moment we entered the room but, distracted by the Great Salmanazar's welcome, I had somehow failed to observe it. Now our host reached down and pulled away the napkin with a flick of his wrist.

The cloth fell away at his touch to reveal a bottle of Scotch whisky, soda water, and a bottle of champagne in an ice bucket. A single champagne flute had already been filled and a stout whisky tumbler already contained a handsome quantity of golden liquor.

"Excellent! Just as you ordered!"

Seeing the expressions of astonishment on our faces, the illusionist laughed softly. "Please forgive me," he chuckled. "Just a small conceit of mine. I must apologise for it. Please, Doctor, the soda water is not yet added. I beg that you help yourself to the required quantity."

"Really, sir!" Dr. Watson had rediscovered his earlier mood, and his moustache bristled. "We didn't come here to see your blasted tricks! I've come about the ruby, sir, and I'm sure you know it."

"Ruby?" Our host hesitated as if the word were new to him. "Ah, of course. A precious stone. And is it a particular ruby that you have come about?"

"Don't pretend you haven't heard of the Malabar Rose!"

"Ah, your English roses! So fragrant, yet so fragile. However, I regret, sir, that I am not a horticulturalist."

I could sense Dr. Watson's choler rising, and to slow it in its ascent, I dared to ask a question of my own.

"Please, sir, have you ever been to the Blenheim Hotel?"

The Great Salmanazar seemed surprised by the question, and he turned to me and eyed me closely.

"The Blenheim Hotel? You forget, Miss Flotsam, this is my first visit to this mighty city of yours, and I stay in this hotel, this Brown's, which has been greatly recommended to me."

"Yes, sir. It's only that there's a piece of writing paper in your jacket pocket. It has the Blenheim Hotel heading on it."

His first instinct was to clap his hand to his chest, as if he still retained his jacket. Realising his mistake, he looked around and saw that item of dress draped casually over the chair beside me. He retrieved it hurriedly and put it on.

"You must accept my apologies if I failed to understand you. I thought you asked if I had *been* to the Blenheim Hotel. I have not. But my fellow performer, Miss Del Fuego, is staying at that hotel. It is from her, this letter that you have observed."

"Well, sir," Dr. Watson cut in, "Miss Del Fuego must know of the Malabar Rose. Anyone staying at the Blenheim could hardly fail to be aware of it."

"I am afraid her letter was entirely confined to matters concerning the performance she is to give." He smoothed down his jacket with the palms of his hands, as if to lay the matter to rest.

"Please, sir," I persisted, "Miss Del Fuego writes in a very strong, masculine hand, doesn't she?"

"Indeed? I am not a graphologist, Miss Flotsam."

"I wasn't meaning to pry, sir, but I couldn't help noticing that the part of the letter I could see seemed to have some sort of floor plan sketched on it."

"Floor plan? Most certainly not." He seemed offended at

the suggestion. "Miss Del Fuego was merely making some suggestions about aspects of the staging. Her diagrams concerned only that."

My questions had clearly put him out, for after that the great illusionist became taciturn and replied to all Dr. Watson's questions by puffing out his cheeks and grunting tense, unhelpful answers. Was he aware of the thefts that had followed him across Europe? He was not a policeman. Had he heard of the Lafayette necklace or the Von Metzen diamonds? He was not a jeweller. Would he agree to remain confined to the Regal Theatre for the whole evening of his performance? Of course. He was not a tourist. The more Dr. Watson battered away, the less forthcoming he became.

Eventually, I could see that Dr. Watson's spirits were beginning to fall. After a few more perfunctory questions along the same lines, he signalled to me his readiness to depart, and we bade the magician a formal and somewhat uncomfortable farewell. As we left, I saw that he had returned to the table where our drinks stood untouched and was thoughtfully covering them with a linen cloth, as if to send them back from whence they'd come.

Outside, Dr. Watson proved rather despondent. "Not much luck there, I'm afraid, Flotsam. Still, your sharp eyes have spotted something, and we must tell Holmes about it at once. We should be able to catch him at the Blenheim. Perhaps he is having a more successful morning than we are."

It was clear from the moment of our arrival there that something had happened to disturb the Blenheim Hotel's usual air of dignified superiority. The first indication of this came as we mounted the steps towards its imposing entrance, only to be confronted by the sight of two uniformed policemen huffing and puffing towards us, an enormous gilded harp carried awkwardly between them.

"Where did he say to put it, Bert?" panted one, as they felt their way gingerly down the steps.

"He said to use our nishiative, you great lummox," his companion replied shortly, possibly annoyed that it had fallen to him to carry the heavy end of the harp.

"And what do you think he meant by that exactly?"

"He meant to get this down to the station on the first wagon we can find and to keep it under lock and key till someone remembers it and wants it back."

"So that's what he meant." The second policeman was less red in the face than his companion but considerably more bemused. "It's amazing what these brainy types will think up, isn't it? I can't see how this is saving the nation. It just looks like a ruddy big harp to me."

At the top of the steps, the doorman was watching this performance and shaking his head.

"I've never seen the like of it," he told us sadly. "Wouldn't hear of using the trade doors at the back, would they? Said they'd been ordered to get everything out by the fastest route, and no questions."

Dr. Watson, still irritated by his unsuccessful interview with the Great Salmanazar, was in no mood to discuss the movements of the hotel furniture. "Tell me, my man, do you know where we can find Mr. Sherlock Holmes?" he asked.

"Mr. Holmes?" The doorman didn't sound overjoyed at the name. "I certainly can, sir. He's in the Satin Rooms. Through the door, then follow the trail of tables and chairs. You can't miss him."

Those directions proved remarkably good ones. Beneath the domed ceiling of the hotel's famous lobby, four perspiring policemen were pausing for breath. Between them, resting at the most disorderly of angles, were two enormous chaises longues. Judging by the faces of the policemen it was likely to be some time before either made it through the great door of the hotel. Then, as we advanced up the great, sweeping staircase, we were passed by further constables carrying, respectively, a small ornamental table, a grandfather clock, a red velvet footstool, a cigar cabinet, an enormous candelabra shaped like an elephant, and a large portrait of the Duke of Wellington of rather doubtful likeness. And when we arrived at the Satin Rooms, the scene was every bit as chaotic as our approach had led us to expect.

The name "Satin Rooms" is perhaps a misleading one, in that it is used both to describe the whole suite of rooms that the maharajah maintained at the Blenheim Hotel, and more specifically to describe the main room itself, which is hung, not with satin, but with finest Indian silk. The rooms had first been taken by the maharajah's grandfather, the sixth maharajah of Majoudh, a man whose life had contained more than its fair share of plotters and would-be assassins. As a result, the maharajah had developed, amongst other things, a morbid fear of corners. He had therefore required his suite at the Blenheim to be remodelled to suit his needs, and the result was an exceptionally large, circular drawing room, domed and elegant, which rather unusually contained four doors and no windows. The doors faced north, south, east, and west, and each of them opened into the same anteroom, in truth nothing more than a large corridor that encircled and contained the main drawing room. The room's only light came from glass panels fitted into the dome above it.

It was in this exceptional room that the current maharajah required the Malabar Rose to be displayed, and it was in this room that we now found Mr. Holmes, Sir John Plaskett, Inspector Lestrade, and a muddled crowd of harassed-looking policemen. Also present, though obscured by the enormous Chinese vase that he was attempting to remove, was the hotel's flustered and protesting manager.

"But Sir John," he was expostulating, "is it really necessary that everything must go? I cannot see how these objects could possibly . . ."

"Everything, Mr. Dupont! The room must be bare but for the plinth where the ruby is to be displayed. Come, man, we're nearly there."

And it was true. By the time Dr. Watson and I had fought our way into the room against the tide of furniture, none of the room's sumptuous furnishings remained in place. The only object of any description left in the room was a slender green column of marble, about four feet high, in the very centre of the room. Mr. Holmes was examining it suspiciously.

"Solid marble, Mr. Holmes. I guarantee it." Sir John tapped it with his cane as if to emphasise the fact. "I selected it myself and brought it here under guard this morning."

"I congratulate you on your thoroughness, Sir John. We cannot be too careful." Mr. Holmes straightened and noticed Dr. Watson for the first time. "Ah, my friend, what do you make of this citadel of ours?"

As he spoke, Inspector Lestrade was ushering out Mr. Dupont and the remaining policemen, leaving just our small group in possession of the room. He then turned to Dr. Watson and gave his own, rather proud, description of the defensive measures that had been put in place.

"With the exception of the four doors, the room is completely sealed, sir. The glass panels in the dome are built into the brickwork and there are no other apertures of any sort. To make sure, I have stationed four officers up on the roof, and I'll keep a guard up there night and day until the ruby is safely removed from this room."

While his audience craned its neck upwards and nodded, Lestrade turned his attention to the rest of the room.

"The walls are made of stone, lined with oak. We have examined each oak panel and can guarantee all are solid. No possibility of hidden doors or secret chambers, or any such nonsense. The floorboards are oak, too, each secured to oak joists. I've had men down there underneath them, and they say it would take a gang of men with heavy equipment to smash a way through."

Sir John nodded approvingly. "Excellent work, Inspector. What about the doors?"

"The south, east, and north doors have already been sealed, sir. Literally boarded up. Each one has an officer on guard outside. All entry now must be by the west door. On the night in question, the ruby will arrive four or five hours beforehand. It will be paced on a velvet display case that Sir John is bringing, and that case will be placed on the plinth in front of a select group of witnesses. The room will then be vacated, and the west door will be chained and padlocked. Two officers will guard each door. I personally shall patrol the antechamber throughout the evening with a group of my most trusted plainclothes men. It won't be possible for an ant to crawl in here without us knowing!"

"Bravo, Lestrade!" Dr. Watson exclaimed. "It would take a miracle to penetrate such defences."

The inspector looked suitably proud. "Thank you, sir. Any questions?"

I knew Inspector Lestrade's final remark wasn't addressed to me, but Mrs. Hudson had always taught me to ask questions, and to my horror I found myself clearing my throat.

"Please, sir," I asked, and suddenly every pair of eyes was upon me. "All those people on guard . . . Why don't they just guard the ruby from *inside* this room? Then they can all see for themselves that the ruby is safe."

A slightly embarrassed silence followed this question as the gentlemen all turned to Sherlock Holmes to explain.

"Ah, Flotsam," he began, with a note of benevolent encouragement in his voice. "It is good to see you thinking for yourself. However, in this instance, I fear you cannot possibly know as much as we do. You are clearly not aware of what happened to the Black Pearl of Castille. When the Great Salmanazar came to town, a committee of Spanish nobles was convened to safeguard it, and they adopted a strategy such as you have described. They locked themselves into a strong room with the pearl, a dozen revolvers, and a rack of duelling sabres."

"What happened then, Holmes?" Dr. Watson asked, clearly as ignorant as I about the annals of foreign crime.

"All went well until the lights were blown out, and the room was plunged into darkness. When light was restored, the pearl was gone."

"No mystery there, Holmes! Clearly one of the fellows had seen his chance and pocketed it."

"Of course, Watson. But which one? The room contained twelve of the proudest men in Spain, each armed with a duelling sabre. To ask any one of them to submit to a search would have been to besmirch his family honour in the eyes of all his peers. Not one of them would agree to it. And besides, it was likely that the pearl was swallowed, so any search would have been futile."

"And the pearl?"

"We'll never know. But I am determined that no such complications should arise here, which is why Flotsam's plan is quite impossible. No, the best way to secure the ruby is to make sure that no one, not even ourselves, has any way of reaching it. Now, Sir John, the guests are to be allowed in to see the ruby at eleven o'clock. I can honestly promise that nothing will have gone awry before then."

"But, Holmes," Dr. Watson exclaimed, "how can you be so sure?"

"I can be so sure, Watson," his friend replied, "because for anyone to overcome all the inspector's precautions and to find a way into this room unnoticed is simply impossible. In fact, I would go further. If anything happens to the ruby while it is in this room, why, gentlemen, then I shall begin to believe this Great Salmanazar really *is* a magician."

CHAPTER SEVEN

The Toy Maker of Kimber Street

It was a slightly bedraggled group that returned to Baker Street that afternoon. A flurry of snow shortly before we left the Blenheim Hotel had made it impossible to find a hansom, and Mr. Holmes, impatient at Dr. Watson's attempts to hail one in the street, had insisted on walking home. As we made our way, the snow turned to sleet, and we trudged back with the sky like a shroud above us and thick, grey slush slopping over our boots.

Each of us was strangely thoughtful, as if fears for the safety of the Malabar Rose were depressing our spirits. For all Sir John's bluff cheerfulness and Mr. Holmes' confident rationality, I was beginning to feel there was some strange power at work that winter month determined to thwart our efforts. And when the sleet turned suddenly to snow again, as if commanded by the wave of a wand, and when that snow grew so dense that the streets were turned quite white by it, and when night fell with a flurry of snowflakes the size of swan feathers, then it wasn't too hard to believe that a strange magic was at work in the dark streets, blinding us to what should have been clear and giving life to strange shadows.

If we needed an antidote to any such thoughts, we found one in Baker Street. The lamps were already lit and the curtains drawn, and from Mrs. Hudson's kitchen crept a smell of rum and nutmeg that whispered to us of Christmas.

"My word, Mrs. H," Dr. Watson declared when she appeared to take the gentlemen's coats, "that's a fine aroma. What treats do you have in store for us?"

"Nothing for tonight, sir, though there's some fine ox tongue and a brace of partridges if you wish to dine at home. But the things you can smell are for Christmas Day, and not a taste for any of you until then. Really, with all this Malabar fuss going on, it's a good job someone has remembered about Christmas."

"I should expect nothing less of you, Mrs. H!" Watson beamed. "I do love a good Christmas dinner! I daresay there'll be goose?"

"There may very well be, sir."

"And plum pudding?"

"It's been ready since September, sir."

"And a good moist fruitcake to go with a glass of spiced port?"

"I made it today, sir."

"Excellent! With icing? I'm very partial to an iced fruitcake, Mrs. H!"

The housekeeper frowned. "An iced fruitcake with spiced port? I hardly think so, sir."

This setback did nothing to dim the good doctor's enthusiasm. "As you think best, Mrs. H, as you think best. That little lot should help to take our minds off this ruby business for a few hours, eh, Holmes?"

But Sherlock Holmes was eyeing his friend with frosty scorn.

"Nonsense, Watson! With the nation's honour trusted to our hands, we cannot for a moment contemplate such frivolities. We shall spend Christmas Day on duty at the Regal Theatre, observing Salmanazar's every move. I have it planned already. You shall be watching the back of the theatre while pretending to unblock the drains."

"But, Holmes! Really! On Christmas Day?"

"Duty, Watson! Duty!"

His companion subsided into a series of muffled grunts. "Perhaps in the evening . . . Get away for a bite of goose . . ." He muttered it more to himself than to his friend.

"After dark, Watson? When the danger is at its greatest? No, by no means. We must prepare ourselves for a long and painful vigil. Now, in the meantime, Mrs. H, I believe you mentioned a partridge . . ."

"I must say, Flotsam," Mrs. Hudson confessed when we were alone by the kitchen fire, "Mr. Holmes' dedication to his cause is a little greater than I had anticipated. To miss Christmas for the sake of that ruby before it has even been stolen! Really! I'm beginning to think that stone is more trouble than it's worth!"

The dark kitchen was at its most appealing just then, warm from a long day's baking and scented with spices. The flames from the fire wrapped us in their warmth and painted the walls with a soothing glow. It was good to be home.

"Ready for a little supper, Flottie?" Mrs. Hudson asked as she began to lay the table.

I nodded contentedly. "That would be lovely, ma'am."

"Good. But we mustn't linger over it, because as soon as we've eaten, it's on with our coats and out again."

For a moment my surprise was less than my dismay.

"Out, ma'am? Out again at this hour?"

"That's right, Flottie. The place we're visiting tonight keeps peculiar hours. It's nearly a week now since Mr. Phillimore disappeared, and I really don't think we can afford to wait."

"Mr. Phillimore?" I asked faintly.

"There's something funny going on there, my girl. And just at the moment, anything that involves something disappearing is surely worth investigating." She paused in her placing of the cutlery and came over to my side. "I ask you because I value your assistance," she said softly. "And because a bright young girl shouldn't be sitting here mending Dr. Watson's socks when she might be out there seeking to explain the impossible."

And so of course I went. And when I stepped out into the cold at Mrs. Hudson's side, into a street muffled by the heavy fall of snow, I felt not the cold of the air on my skin but the warmth of her words in my head. For what challenge could be more alluring than to understand the impossible? If anything was to shape my life, let it be that.

The deepening snow and the bitter cold had emptied the streets that evening so that only a few vehicles and even fewer pedestrians were to be seen on the main thoroughfares, and beyond those, where the maze of London's backstreets disappeared into murky darkness, it seemed that only the rats and their scrawny shadows were abroad.

It soon became apparent that Mrs. Hudson's destination was Islington.

"Do you remember?" Mrs. Hudson prompted me as we nestled together for warmth in a drafty cabriolet. "That's where Mr. Phillimore bought his gloves."

"But, ma'am," I asked, "why are you so interested in where Mr. Phillimore bought his gloves? According to Mrs. Smithers, he would buy his gloves anywhere he happened to be passing."

"Of course, Flottie. That's exactly why I'm so interested."

As I settled down to contemplate that utterance, the cab rolled north and eastwards, through streets of scarcely broken snow. Shortly after we passed the Angel, the cab turned north off Upper Street, and a little farther on it dropped us at the end of a quiet, unremarkable little road.

"This is Kimber Street," Mrs. Hudson explained. "Now, Flotsam, think about it. James Phillimore lived in Ealing, on the west side of London. And he worked in Marble Arch, towards the centre. But this is where he bought his gloves. Now how on earth did he come to be here? What is there here that would bring him so far out his way?"

I peered up Kimber Street. It was a narrow street with a handful of small shops on either side.

"There might have been any number of reasons, ma'am. He might have had business here. Or friends. Perhaps someone he works with. A mistress even."

Mrs. Hudson nodded. "But why would he be on this particular street, Flottie? See how the road narrows towards the end? It ends in a footpath that leads through a churchyard into a crescent of large houses. To go from those houses to the main road, you don't need to go through Kimber Street. No, this road isn't a shortcut to anywhere. The only real reason to turn into Kimber Street is to visit one of these shops."

I looked about me at the drab shop fronts. Only one, towards the end, showed any light. It was hard to imagine someone crossing the city to come here.

Mrs. Hudson held her arm out to me. "Let us imagine the enigmatic Mr. Phillimore walking down this street. Which shop might he have come here to visit?"

The first shop we came to was a faded grocer's shop, its window display dusty and dated. Facing it across the narrow street was a rather mean-looking draper's.

"Neither of those," I decided.

Next came the glove maker's where Mr. Phillimore had made his purchase and, opposite it, a very ordinary tobacconist's.

"Not those, either, I think."

The third shop was tightly closed with wooden shutters, but the legend above the door read "E.A. Husband, Top Pedigree Puppies."

"A pet shop, Flotsam. They sell young dogs to the better-off families around here."

"So that's why you asked if Mrs. Phillimore had recently been given a puppy!"

"Indeed. Yet the answer tells us little. Phillimore might have been purchasing for a lady who is not his wife."

"So you think he came to this street to visit that shop?"

Mrs. Hudson looked unconvinced. "Such shops exist in other parts of town, Flotsam. But it is a possibility. Come, let us move on."

None of the next seven shops offered any suggestion that they might draw their customers from a distance, and I had nearly concluded that the pet shop really was Mr. Phillimore's destination when we came to the shop with the lighted windows. And then I knew instantly, with total certainty, that this was a shop unlike any other anywhere in the world.

All through the shop tiny lamps were burning, shaded with glass of different colours so that they lit the contents of the window with a glow of many different hues. There was gold and green and red in there, and shades of violet and ochre, all mingled together. Between them they lit the window as treasure troves are lit in picture books, and their light crept out onto the snowy street so that the flakes falling on us were gold and turquoise and orange by turns. But it was not the lights that made me gasp, though they filled the window with a magic of their own. No, it was the many devices in front of me that made me stop and stare, each of them turning or spinning or twisting so that the whole shop seemed to be in motion.

"A toy shop!" I gasped, though the words were inadequate, like labelling the finest Swiss chocolatier a sweetshop. Every single one of the items that crowded the window moved by clockwork, the whole ensemble dancing together in the brightly lit cave as if to a wild panpipe tune. There were all the simple toys you might imagine: a jack-in-the-box leapt from a tiny walnut box, then reached behind his back to pull down of his own accord the lid that trapped him, so that he was gone as quickly as he had appeared; behind him a musical box stood open and, as it played, four ballerinas dressed as swans pirouetted to a tune I could not hear. But those were the simple items. Others threatened to overwhelm by their sheer accomplishment. Near the front of the window, a small boy, no more than twelve inches high, was holding a hoop and teaching tricks to an equally tiny poodle. The dog appeared to yap at his ankles with the fluent movement of a real dog, until suddenly it leapt from its base, clean through the outstretched hoop, before returning to his capering.

Farther back, there was a doll's house that appeared to be an ordinary model of a large country house until the figure of a window cleaner on a tiny ladder polishing one of the windows appeared. Attracted by the movement, I was in time to see a window near him fly open and to watch as a maid in bonnet and apron shook her duster clean. Then lights came on in the ballroom, and I watched an elegant couple dance its full length before disappearing through double doors, to be followed by the figure of a footman who gently snuffed out the candles until the room was in darkness.

"What is this place?" I asked, my voice little more than a whisper.

"A place where magic is for sale," she replied softly, her

own eyes still on the spinning toys. "He's been here many years now. His name is Perch. Come, let's go in."

Inside the shop, beyond the window display, the sense of a magic world continued. Strings of brightly coloured beads and sequins hung from the ceiling, shielding the back of the shop from the front like fantastical spiders' webs in a fairy-tale grotto. Strange shapes and structures peopled the shop, but these were still, as if exhausted. I spied a tiny archer and a rocking horse, and a stationary seal with a ball balanced on its motionless nose.

A bell rang as the shop door closed behind us, and as if in response a clockwork nightingale in a wooden tree began to sing. From behind a curtain in the depths of the shop, a man of about sixty-five appeared. He wore a workman's smock and had a pair of thick spectacles pushed onto his forehead, held there by tufts of unruly white hair. The frame of the spectacles was held together with copper wire. I noticed that his head seemed to twitch slightly from time to time, rather as if he had begun to take on some of the motion and man-nerisms of the objects he created. There was little welcome in his voice when he spoke.

"Can I help you? A clockwork doll for the girl perhaps? Something for a shilling that will last until Boxing Day?"

Mrs. Hudson returned his gaze coolly, unruffled by his tone.

"My companion here is rather old for dolls. She is rather more interested in mechanical design. We stood outside your shop and wondered what ratio of gearing you must have employed to create the unusual motion of that Spanish dancer?"

Rather than show surprise at this extraordinary question, he nodded his head rapidly several times, in the manner of someone whose whole life was so dominated by one obsession that there was no surprise when someone, however un-likely, understood and spoke his own language.

"Ah, yes. The Spanish dancer. A fine piece of work." He nodded his head again, a little nervously. "Of course, I can-not tell you how I do it. I never tell." He scanned us again, as if seeing us for the first time. "Most girls just want dolls," he said. "Boys want soldiers. They could buy them any-where, but they come here to plague me. I could make a for-tune selling dolls and soldiers that jerk like fishing lines and break down in a week." He clucked to himself bitterly.

Mrs. Hudson gestured around the room. "But these . . . They are magnificent. You must surely make more from sell-ing one of these than from a thousand cheap dolls."

"Ha! Ha!" The toy maker twitched his head again and grimaced. "There is nothing to be made from these! Noth-ing! Each one costs me a fortune in time and in crafting. If I were to sell any one of them at the cost required to make it, it would be beyond the purse of every man in the kingdom! When I do sell one—and that is rare enough these days—it is less a sale than a gift. And yet the buyer goes away and says to himself, 'Old Perch is expensive. Old Perch cannot charge those prices. I have half a mind to take it back and demand that Old Perch be more reasonable.' Here, look at this."

He stepped across to a shelf where a small tree a couple of feet high stood in an old clay pot. Its branches were bare as if it had long ago succumbed to a lack of attention and to the permanent twilight in which it was kept. It didn't occur to me that it wasn't a real tree until the old man pressed some-thing near the base of its pot and then stood back and waited. At first nothing happened. Then a tinny mechanical tune began to play, something bright and hopeful.

"Watch carefully now," he whispered to me, and I re-alised that as the music played, the tree was beginning to put forth tiny green shoots that grew and opened until, in a minute, the bare branches were hidden by a canopy of leaves.

"You see?" he asked, while the leaves continued to grow. "One of the finest pieces of work I have ever achieved and yet, of what value is it? Who will pay for a tree that grows silk leaves?" He turned away to lead us to another part of his shop, but the tree's music was still playing and when I turned back, I noticed that tiny specks of blossom had appeared and clustered to every branch.

Meanwhile, Mrs. Hudson and the toy maker had their backs to me, and he was beckoning her to a part of the shop where an object the size of a wardrobe stood covered with an old curtain.

"This is something I have just started working on. You may know there is a famous illusionist about to perform in London. His visit has been my inspiration. The mechanism for the figure is still very crude, but I have solved the hard part of the puzzle. Watch . . ."

He tugged away the curtain and for a moment a chill passed through me. Smiling out from the dark corner, life-sized in evening dress, a grinning mannequin leered out at us. His glass eyes seemed to meet mine, and his waxen face combined the features of the living with the pale emptiness of the dead. It was a gruesome rendering of a magician, the sort you might expect to see only in bad dreams. Next to the figure, and of the same height, stood a rough wooden crate with a hinged door. This door Perch pulled open, revealing a low three-legged stool within the crate.

"And now," he declared, "I shall show you something special. You shall be the first to see it. I shall . . ."

At that moment the bell above the door rang and the nightingale sang again, and a middle-aged woman with a fur collar stepped into the shop.

"Excuse me," she began when she saw Perch, who stood with his hand above his head, poised to set into action some hidden mechanism. "Excuse me. I'm looking for a doll for a little girl. Something for about a shilling, I thought."

I watched Perch's features work in wordless rage for a moment, until three rapid shakes of his head brought them under control.

"Please, madam. One moment. I am engaged in a demonstration. Now, young lady," he continued, turning to me, "pass me the top hat on the floor there."

On receiving the hat, he placed it on the three-legged stool and closed the door of the crate.

"Now, remember that the mechanism is still crude," he warned, then clicked his fingers.

As if it had really heard his signal, the mannequin began to move. With a small bow to his audience and a grim, mirthless smile, he reached his hand out to the crate and rapped on it hard three times, then he reached into the pocket of his jacket and pulled out a silk handkerchief with which he proceeded to mop his waxen brow. Finally, eerily, he reached forward and pushed at the door of the crate so that it swung open silently.

"Goodness gracious me!" exclaimed the woman with the fur collar. "The hat's disappeared."

OUR visit to Kimber Street came to an end shortly afterwards. Perch refused to explain or to repeat his trick, despite the insistence of the woman that he should give a second demonstration solely for her. He met her voluble arguments with a sulky silence and finally, as if to escape her, agreed to sell her at a discount a clockwork Rapunzel, whose hair grew longer at the turn of a key. When this transaction was over,

and the woman had left the shop, Mrs. Hudson thanked
Perch for his time and complimented him on his collection,
but only as we were actually leaving the shop did she turn to
him and ask the question that had been on my mind from
the moment we walked in.

"Oh, Mr. Perch," she began, her brow a little furrowed as
she tugged on her gloves. "A friend of mine spoke of calling
here a couple of weeks ago. I wonder, did he purchase anything? His name is Phillimore. You might remember him."

For a moment I thought the old toy maker hadn't heard.
He was engaged in winding a grandfather clock that stood
behind his counter, and when Mrs. Hudson spoke he continued to wind, apparently oblivious. However, it seemed his
head had suddenly bowed a little lower and his face was a little paler, and unless I was very much mistaken, the twitch of
his head became a little more frequent.

"Oh, it's no matter," Mrs. Hudson continued brightly. "I
was just a little bit curious, that's all." And with that, we let
ourselves out into the night.

Outside the toy shop, Kimber Street lay silent under its
thick, white coverlet. By the light of the gas lamps, I could
see the snow still falling, and I could feel the cutting edge of
the winter night keen against my skin. As we followed our
own tracks towards the end of the road, Mrs. Hudson said
nothing, but her brow was furrowed again. I was silent, too,
wondering about the man who had vanished from his own
cellar, and then thinking with a shudder of the wax-faced
mannequin and the empty three-legged stool. Noticing the
shiver that ran through me, my companion paused and adjusted my hat and muffler against the cold.

"You know, Flotsam," she said, "I'm beginning to worry
a very great deal about our Mr. Phillimore."

CHAPTER EIGHT

The Night Before Christmas

Christmas Eve dawned brightly and for a magical hour the sun shone on clean, white snow. For that time, London looked fleetingly like a city in a fairy tale, the sort of scene painted on the backdrops of theatres, where every slate and every sill is neatly layered with snow and every roof dangles icicles like daggers. But even before the night was fully gone, the city had begun to wake, and the smoke of its chimneys was spreading on an east wind. Before long, the early carts were churning the road into slush.

I was out early that morning with errands to run and items to purchase that Mrs. Hudson felt were essential to the proper celebration of Christmas. Because I had other calls to make, I was dressed like a lady in my smart dress and little hat, and the cold soon brought a fine glow to my cheeks. I felt in fine, high spirits, and it wasn't only me. The unusual snowfall had brought the best out of people, and strangers smiled as they struggled past each other on pavements made treacherous by drifted snow. The shopkeepers seemed happy, too. Trade was brisk despite the weather, and in more than one of the places I stopped, an extra package was pressed upon me with the season's greetings. Mr. Herbert at the haberdashery blushed, and gave me a ribbon for my hair, while Mrs. Williamson, the florist's wife, presented me with a sprig of mistletoe "for all those young beaux out there."

"No, don't thank me," she insisted, "it will be them lucky lads that are thanking me. Now get on with you!"

My journey took a detour to include the offices of Mr. Rumbelow, the solicitor. I found him at his desk in a fug of coal smoke and good humour, and when I was shown in by a stammering clerk, he hastened to his feet with a warm smile of welcome.

"Ah, Flotsam! Excellent! Excellent! Come in, come in. You are too warm? Too cold? Just right? Quite so, quite so." He mopped his round and rather extensive forehead with a polka-dot handkerchief and beamed again. "You have perhaps come to see if there has been any response to Mrs. Hudson's advertisement in *Plays and Players*?"

I told him he was right, that Mrs. Hudson was anxious to hear news of the missing Mr. Phillimore. "She seems very taken by the puzzle of his disappearance, sir."

"Indeed, indeed," he nodded sagely. "Mrs. Hudson no doubt has her reasons, Flotsam."

"I wish she was thinking about the Malabar Rose, sir. Mr. Holmes and Sir John are doing everything they can, but if anything was overlooked I'm sure Mrs. Hudson would spot it."

"Ah, yes, indeed. She is a remarkable woman." Having assured himself that I was seated comfortably, he settled back into his own chair. "However, I am sure that Mr. Holmes has matters in hand, Flotsam, and I am now rather looking forward to the performance of this foreign illusionist. I have taken the step of purchasing a ticket for the show myself."

"You have secured a ticket, sir? I thought they had all sold out."

He blushed a little. "Indeed, yes. Quite so. I confess I have paid a price a little higher than that printed on the ticket. As of last night, twelve guineas would appear to be the generally accepted rate." Clearly a little embarrassed by this extravagance, he began to rustle through some papers on his desk.

"Returning to your original inquiry, Flotsam, I regret to say that I have received no response to Mrs. Hudson's advertisement as yet. However, as soon as I do, I shall send word. You may be interested to know that I have received from Mrs. Smithers the sum of thirty pounds to be offered as a reward for information leading to the, er, *rediscovery* of her son-in-law." He tapped the breast of his jacket at the place where his wallet sat, as if to reassure himself that the sum in question was still secure.

I wasn't entirely convinced that Mr. Phillimore's wife, Lavinia, would feel that £30 in return for her husband's reappearance would constitute a suitable exchange, but I didn't like to mention it, so instead I allowed Mr. Rumbelow to accompany me to the door.

"You will no doubt be aware that tomorrow is Christmas Day, Flotsam."

I assured him that I was aware.

"No doubt a busy day for both you and Mrs. Hudson, with Christmas dinner to serve and other such seasonal events to accommodate?"

"Well, sir, Mrs. Hudson will be cooking a goose, but Mr. Holmes and Dr. Watson won't be there to enjoy it because they have to stand guard over the Malabar Rose."

"Indeed? Even so, I feel sure the exertion of preparing a goose must be very great. I happen recently to have taken receipt of a very excellent Napoleon brandy. I wonder, do you think Mrs. Hudson would be, er, *willing* to accept a bottle of it? I'm sure it would be admirable at offsetting any seasonal weariness that she might experience."

I assured him that Mrs. Hudson would be more than happy to accommodate another bottle from his cellar, and at this his face brightened.

"Excellent! I shall send it around at once. And Merry Christmas to you, Flotsam. Merry Christmas indeed!"

From Holborn I made my way towards Bloomsbury, where I had been asked to call upon Miss Peters. As always when calling on Miss Peters, I arrived expecting anything, but in fact the scene that greeted me when Reynolds showed me into the drawing room was one of comparative calm. Rupert Spencer was sitting at the table surrounded by a barricade of weighty tomes, studying something minutely through a magnifying glass. Around him, like rose petals or apple blossoms, fluttered an almost transparent cloud of tiny butterflies in shades of red and pink through to cream and white. In the corner, perched on one of those sets of high steps used in libraries, Miss Peters sat calmly, also reading a book, a large butterfly net dangling from one hand.

"I think the blue ones must been Queens of Patagonia," she was saying, "or perhaps Blue Mormons. Ooh! Hallo, Flottie." Both of them rose to welcome me. "Do you think you might be good with one of these?" She waved the butterfly net at me. Before I could reply, Mr. Spencer intervened.

"Don't answer that question, Miss Flotsam, or she will have you here all day lending her a hand. You see, we have reached something of an *impasse* here."

"Nonsense, Rupert, we haven't reached any sort of pass at all. Not even a pretty one. Any moment now I shall walk out with my head held high and go to the De Courcy's luncheon with my aunt and the Strutheringtons, and everyone will say I did the right thing. So there!"

I looked again at the flight of butterflies. "How *did* they all get out?" I asked. "It can't have been an accident, surely?"

I addressed the question to Miss Peters, and she had the decency to blush a little.

"Well, not entirely, Flottie, no. You see, Rupert spent all yesterday poring over his books and his butterflies and quite refused to come to the ball at Ballestier's because he has to give the collection back today. And even though he's always *so* dull at balls, I was a *little* annoyed with him for not coming because I'd told everyone he'd be there, so when he refused to come, I felt like a deserted wife or something, though, of course, I probably never *will* be a deserted wife because Rupert will probably never marry me in the first place because he much prefers moths and things to people. Even pretty ones."

Rupert Spencer permitted himself a wry smile at this, but Hetty was still in full flow.

"Anyway, when I found him here this morning with his head still in his books as though he hadn't moved all night, I decided I had to do something to *make* him move."

"And so? . . . "

"And so I let them all out," she ended with a flourish.

"And how did Mr. Spencer respond to that?" I asked with a smile, looking across at him.

"He ignored me completely," Miss Peters admitted, and formed her lips into something very close to a pout.

"Which is a much harder thing to do than it sounds." Mr. Spencer looked across at me and smiled. "So now Hetty must either restore them all to their boxes or face the wrath of Lord Clyde, who shall be here to collect them at lunchtime. Lord Clyde is a great enthusiast for butterflies but rather less of an enthusiast for human beings. And he's really rather fierce. He's been known to horsewhip people he feels have treated his butterfly specimens with insufficient respect."

"Oh, all *right*!" Hetty stamped her foot rather prettily and snatched up the butterfly net again. "If you are going to behave like a brute, Rupert, then I have no choice. You two can sit there and pour the tea and never mind if I am breaking my neck chasing stupid Cabbage Admirals all over the place." She proceeded to advance on the nearest butterfly and caught it neatly with a wristy flick.

Ignoring her completely, Mr. Spencer rose and addressed himself to me. "If you please, Miss Flotsam, Reynolds has brought in some tea. Since Hetty is otherwise engaged, perhaps you would be good enough to pour?"

So we sat and drank tea together while Miss Peters stalked the drawing room, berating us for our lack of feeling. Mr. Spencer seemed in very good spirits, telling me of the species he had studied and explaining to me details of butterfly life cycles and anatomy. From there we passed to the subject of Christmas and then to the prospect of the Great Salmanazar's show. As I told him about plans to keep safe the Malabar Rose, Mr. Spencer listened attentively. His shirtsleeves were rolled up, and he looked uncommonly well, his strong brown forearms a contrast to the tiny teacup and saucer that balanced between his fingers. From time to time, Miss Peters would add a word or two to contradict something that he said, and at the mention of the Great Salmanazar she gave a little shriek.

"Ooh, Flottie! I forgot to say. Rupert has found us tickets! We shall see it all for ourselves, though I think they must have been terribly expensive because Rupert positively gulped when Reynolds told him how much they were."

"It's true, Miss Flotsam. They're up to fifteen guineas apiece now. However, Reynolds had rather anticipated my need for them and had gone into the market on my behalf when they still stood at thirteen guineas. At least that's what he claims. If I know Reynolds, I suspect he may have done rather better than that."

I paused with my cup halfway to my lips. "But what about the Marylebone Natural Philosophic Society? Aren't they going to be terribly let down?"

Mr. Spencer blushed slightly.

"Far from it. It turns out that the gentlemen of the Marylebone Natural Philosophic Society have, to a man, decided they would prefer to be at the Regal Theatre. So, in the spirit of scientific investigation, I have decided to follow them."

"That's why Rupert was looking sombre when you came in, Flottie." Miss Peters seemed to be making excellent headway in her retrieval of the butterflies. "He's terrified that the Great Salmanazar will call him on stage and steal his watch, aren't you, Rupert?"

"Nothing of the sort! If I you must know, I'm worried about my uncle."

"The earl?" Miss Peters seemed unsurprised. "Has he been frightening the tradesmen again?"

Mr. Spencer shook his head. "Far from it. And it's at least two days since he wrote anything angry to the *Times*. Worst of all, last night, when you'd gone to the ball, he came in and asked to play cribbage with me."

"Cribbage? The Irascible Earl? No, Rupert, darling, you must be thinking of someone else."

"It's true, I promise. Seemed very anxious to spend some time with me. When I told him that I had a piece of work to finish before I could play, he didn't shout or yell, or any of the things you'd expect. He didn't even fume quietly. He just nodded and said he'd sit and read a book until I was ready."

Miss Peters and I looked at each other. "Read a book?" she asked faintly.

"Yes, truly. *Stirring Tales of Noble Deeds,* I think it was."

Miss Peters and I were prevented from commenting further by a timid knock at the drawing room door, and with immaculate timing the earl himself poked his head into the room.

"Ah, Rupert! Not disturbing you, am I?" he inquired with unusual affability.

"No, Uncle, not at all. Come in and join us. Miss Flotsam is just pouring some tea."

"Tea? *Tea?*" The earl began to growl, in the manner with which Mr. Spencer and Miss Peters were familiar, but before he could launch himself into a full-blooded renunciation of the beverage, something seemed to check him. "Ah, yes. Tea," he conceded. "A refreshing drink, I believe. I would be delighted to join you for a cup."

This was so remarkable a statement, such a total reversal of his lordship's usual preferences, that even Hetty appeared too stunned to reply. She just stood there, gaping at him, waving her butterfly net vaguely in the direction of a Limoges vase. Noting this, the earl seemed to rediscover some of his former energy.

"Oh, for goodness sake, Hetty," he snapped, "put that blasted thing away before you break another heirloom. And I'm damned if I'll have the place turned into a zoo!"

Strangely, this note of resurgent irritability had the effect of putting everyone at their ease, and for a while the conversation became general, with the earl stating in robust terms his views on tariff reform, suffragettes, Welshmen, and the decline of the railways. Even so, although he demonstrated considerable ire on all these subjects, it was clear that some other unspoken issue was on his mind. When Hetty embarked on a long description of the latest fashion in French hats, instead of his normal trenchant views on fashion and the French, he fell silent and pondered.

"Rupert," he began when she had finished. "I was thinking of going to my club tonight."

"Yes, Uncle. You go to your club every night."

"Ah, yes. So I do. But what I meant was, tonight I wondered if you'd like to come with me?"

"Me, Uncle?"

"Yes, you, dammit!" he growled before recovering himself and smiling weakly. "Apologies, my boy. This tea seems to be making me a trifle irritable. Yes, it occurred to me when I was shaving this morning that it would be good for you to come along and meet some of the people there. It must be years since you were last at the club."

Mr. Spencer did a rapid calculation. "Not since I was twelve, I think. If you remember, I was thrown out for setting fire to the Foreign Secretary's whiskers. I seem to recall you were quite cross about it."

"Oh, nothing wrong with some boyish high spirits!"

"No, Uncle. But you had the club alter its constitution so that I wouldn't be eligible for membership for at least eighty-seven years."

"Ha!" gulped the earl unconvincingly. "Ha! Ha! Excellent memory you have! But so long ago! And only a harmless prank. Water under the bridge, and all that. But of course I can see your point. No need to come if you don't wish it. I can stay here with you instead."

"Stay here? With me?" Rupert Spencer was a quick-witted young gentleman under normal circumstances, but this sudden subversion of the established order was clearly causing him to flounder.

"Yes, Rupert, stay here. And you, too, of course, Hetty. We could all sit together and, er, study . . ." Mr. Spencer's jaw began to sag downwards. Hetty simply stared. It took a moment or two before either could respond.

"Uncle, I'm afraid I've promised to take Hetty to the Petershams' Mistletoe Ball tonight. It's a fairly long-standing arrangement, and I know the Petershams are rather expecting us."

To our surprise, the earl brightened considerably. "A ball? Excellent! Lots of people, no doubt. Respectable ones. And the Petershams' is a very solidly built old house. I shall certainly join you! Carrington can take us in the carriage. And Reynolds shall accompany him, in case, er, well, in case we need him for anything."

He rose to his feet.

"If you'll excuse me, I must prepare. Reynolds!"

He put back his head and roared with all his usual force and volume.

"Reynolds! We're going to a ball!" As the door shut behind him, we could still hear his voice on the staircase. "And none of those parvenu new fashions, Reynolds! Lay out some proper clothes! There's nothing wrong with those tails I wore for the Palace the night Ackworth won the Cambridgeshire . . ."

Whatever was affecting the Earl of Brabham, it did not appear to be the spirit of Christmas.

I PASSED the afternoon of that day at Baker Street, a willing accomplice in Mrs. Hudson's plans to prepare for Christmas. In that one hectic afternoon, the goose was stuffed, three brace of grouse were lightly braised, a side of gammon was studded with cloves and baked whole, a large box of vegetables was washed and trimmed, five different sauces were stirred, and a bottle of Chateau Yprieu '62 was carefully decanted.

In addition to the cooking, there was cleaning to be done, beds to be stripped, clothes to be washed, collars to be starched, trousers pressed, silver to be polished, and a great many tradesmen and errand boys to be greeted and dealt with. But if all that work sounds laborious, not for one moment did it feel so; for through it all ran the gathering excitement of the approaching celebration and a burgeoning sense of festivity amongst all our callers, and the knowledge that on Boxing Day the Great Salmanazar would take to the stage and the fate of the Malabar Rose would be decided.

Our day was further enlivened by regular reports from the Regal Theatre and the Blenheim Hotel. At four o'clock, Dr. Watson arrived from the Satin Rooms and reported that all seemed quiet. Mrs. Hudson took one look at the doctor's red eyes and sagging countenance and installed him by the fire with a reviving mince pie and a large glass of brandy and shrub, to such good effect that after half an hour or so he returned to his watch with a spring in his step and a slice of Madeira cake in his pocket.

Twenty minutes later, Sherlock Holmes returned from the Regal Theatre, hungry, unshaven, and with the head of a comedy horse costume slung carelessly over his shoulder.

"Apparently, it is customary at Christmastime for the theatres of London to give themselves over to pantomime," he explained. "You know the sort of thing, Mrs. Hudson: *Jack and the Beanstalk, Cinderella, Aladdin,* lots of lights and costumes and such like."

Mrs. Hudson assured him that she knew what a pantomime was.

"You do? Can't say that I'm an expert myself. Anyway, there's a pantomime troupe booked for the Regal Theatre as soon as the Great Salmanazar departs, and they have been allowed to rehearse there today. I discovered that one crucial scene of the pantomime features two men dressed as a horse." He signalled the bright yellow head, with its red mane and purple polka-dots. "Not a very lifelike horse, apparently. I believe the effect is meant to be comic."

"Yes, sir. The antics of the pantomime horse in these performances are generally considered quite amusing," Mrs. Hudson explained patiently.

"Extraordinary. It merely confirms my view of popular entertainment. However, this horse costume affords an excellent opportunity to observe without being observed. I engaged one of the stagehands to fill the rear half of the costume, and the device served very well for discreet surveillance."

The firm set of Mrs. Hudson's lips never trembled as she grappled with the image conjured up, but I did notice her eyebrow twitch ever so slightly. However, when she spoke, her voice remained serious.

"And has Miss Del Fuego made an appearance at the theatre today, sir?" she asked.

"Miss Del Fuego? No, I gather her rehearsals are complete."

Mrs. Hudson had taken up a pile of laundry, and now she began to fold the top item, a large bath towel.

"It is strange, sir, is it not, that the young man who disappeared from Sefton Avenue in Ealing should have had in his possession a playbill advertising Miss Del Fuego's act?"

Mr. Holmes snorted. "You are still thinking of that domestic tiff, Mrs. Hudson? I can see nothing surprising in it at all. It would appear that the majority of London's male population is agog to witness the famous Flame Dance."

And with that, he allowed Mrs. Hudson to press upon him a parcel of cold pork sausages, a slice of veal pie, and a bottle of brown ale concealed beneath the red mane of the horse's head.

The third report on events followed much later that evening, when Mrs. Hudson and I were sitting at the kitchen table on the brink of retiring. We heard a light tapping at the outside door, and to our surprise Sherlock Holmes entered, leading in his wake Dr. Watson, Sir John Plaskett, and Inspector Lestrade. Mrs. Hudson, who felt her kitchen to be very much her own domain, raised an eyebrow at the sight.

"Mr. Holmes, sir? Can we help you?"

"Of course, Mrs. Hudson, otherwise we should not have bothered you. Dr. Watson has spent the journey here speculating as to what little Christmas treats you might be hoarding away down here, so I volunteered to lead a raid on your larder." He waved impatiently at his colleagues, who appeared every bit as put out by this unconventional approach as Mrs. Hudson. "Come on in, gentlemen, come on in. I'm sure Mrs. Hudson will find you a slice of something and a bottle of ale before you go on your way."

It can't be said that Mrs. Hudson's instinct for hospitality ever failed her, and whatever her feelings about Mr. Holmes entertaining in her kitchen, she kept them to herself; and it was notable that both Sir John and Inspector Lestrade brightened considerably when they found themselves in front of the blazing kitchen fire with glasses of hot whisky in their hands. With snow falling outside and the last hours of Christmas Eve ticking away, it made for a festive scene.

"Now, gentlemen, before we part for the night, let us summarise our position." Mr. Holmes' energy seemed undiminished either by the late hour or by the rigours of his day. "How are things at the Blenheim, gentlemen?"

"All's in order, Mr. Holmes." Lestrade had drained his drink in a couple of gulps and was now looking more cheerful—and a little pinker—than I had ever seen him. "If Sir John can get the ruby to the Satin Rooms safely, then we can be sure it will stay there until the dragoons arrive to take it to the vaults. If anything happens to it while it's under our supervision, why, then it must be that the Devil himself has spirited it away!"

"However, I hardly think that either the public or the

Home Office will be content to lay the blame entirely on that gentleman, Lestrade. They may wish to find a scapegoat a little closer to home."

"You're right, Mr. Holmes." Sir John twirled the end of his moustache into an anxious spiral. "If anything goes wrong, our reputations are ruined. We will be a laughing-stock and a national disgrace." He looked a little anxiously at his colleagues. "However, I'm dashed if I can see *how* any-thing can go wrong. It would take an infantry assault to penetrate the security around the Satin Rooms."

"And you are sure the stone will be delivered safely, Sir John?"

The old soldier chuckled. "Hidden better than a pebble on a beach, gentlemen. And guarded by a veritable Cer-berus. What was that?"

All heads turned for a moment towards the window that faced the area steps. Mrs. Hudson, who had been polishing spoons, apparently with no interest whatsoever in the gen-tlemen's conversation, turned to look, too.

"I thought I heard a noise outside," Sir John explained, still facing the window.

"What about you, Flotsam?" Mrs. Hudson asked. "You were closest to the window. Did you hear anything?"

For a moment all eyes were on me. "Nothing, ma'am," I told her. "Perhaps it was a carriage in the street."

"Or a floorboard creaking," suggested Dr. Watson.

"Or your nerves playing tricks, Sir John," Mr. Holmes concluded. "Come, gentlemen, Salmanazar is being watched by a dozen officers. The ruby is hidden. Our plans are water-tight. I don't think we need to worry about noises in the night. Tomorrow we can meet again to review how things stand, but right now I think we should enjoy another of Mrs. Hudson's excellent drinks."

His companions concurred and more hot whiskies were mixed. Mrs. Hudson then returned to the spoons, only now she polished each of them with a slightly furrowed brow. And none of the gentlemen paid the slightest attention to me, where I stood near the back door with my hands clenched tightly beneath my apron, half-expecting to be found out.

For that night I told a lie. I *had* heard a noise in the darkness outside, I had seen the flutter of a shadow cross the light that fell on the area steps. But I stood still and said nothing. Outside the clock struck midnight. It was Christmas Day.

CHAPTER NINE

The Spanish Dancer

Mr. Sherlock Holmes had declared very clearly his intention to ignore Christmas, but that did not stop him and his colleagues from sitting late into the night by our kitchen fire, raising more than one glass to peace on earth and goodwill to men, particularly those men involved in the guarding of the Malabar Rose. It was not until nearly one o'clock that they had gone their separate ways, by which time Mrs. Hudson had polished all the spoons three times and was beginning to look distinctly impatient. On seeing them go, she had been quick to retire to her bedroom, with a yawned good night to me and a ruffle of my hair by way of Merry Christmas. I yawned, too, and made to head for my own bed, but when I had blown out all the lights except for one candle, instead of retiring I sat down by the fire and waited.

Only when I felt sure that Mrs. Hudson must be asleep did I make my next move, and that was to begin pulling on extra clothes and my heavy coat. Only when I could actually make out her rhythmic breathing did I dare to tiptoe to the front door and let myself out into the bitterly cold night air.

The streets at that hour, on that day, were as empty as they ever were, and there was scarcely a mark in either direction on the freshly fallen snow, nor any sound of horse or harness to ring into the Christmas night. The churches were all darkened now, too, and their doors closed, and even the usual pacing policeman was nowhere to be seen.

The boy called Blue was hidden in the same pool of shadow as before, only this time he was waiting for me. Instead of attempting to run, he stepped forward when he saw me coming.

"I thought it was you," I told him in a whisper. "What have you come for?"

Instead of answering, he looked at me closely, his eyes hesitant.

"I knew you'd come out," he said.

"I thought you might be in trouble. Have you been waiting long? There's snow all over you."

"Them in there." He signalled with his thumb towards the kitchen. "Didn't like the look of them. Looked like policemen. Or preachers."

"That was Sherlock Holmes, Blue. Have you heard of him?"

He shook his head. "Nah. What do I know of that sort? Turkeys that wants pluckin', if you ask me."

"But that's not why you're here tonight, is it?"

He looked at me again, as if still undecided about something.

"Nah. That bloke I told you about. Geezer who said he had work. I went to see him, didn't I?" He turned and looked up the street as he spoke, though I could see nothing there to catch his attention. "Said I could have a job."

I felt a little glow of warmth inside me. "That's wonderful, Blue. What sort of work is it?"

"Sweeping. At a tanner's. Dirty work. 'Spect nobody else wants it."

"But it's a start, and it will keep you out of the hands of the policemen. You *can* make something of yourself, Blue, I'm sure you can."

He looked back at me and began to reply, but something stopped him. Instead he wiped the back of his hands over his forehead as though the snow gathered on his cap had begun to drip into his face. Those hands were tiny—boy's hands—nothing like the hands that his hard, flat voice demanded.

"This gent said I was to stay out of trouble till the job starts."

"And when's that? Do you have long to wait?"

"He wants me on Boxing Day."

"Why, that's only a day away. You can surely keep out of trouble until then."

He looked down at his boots, worn, misshapen items made dark where the snow had dampened them. "There's a man I owe. His name's Monk. We take him stuff, and he pays us. Sometimes he lets us borrow off him."

"He pays you to steal, you mean?"

He nodded, still not looking up. "If we don't pay, he gets his fists out. He's a right hard one. One of the boys, name of Silver, Monk smashed his jaw so hard, Silver can't chew proper anymore. Monk ain't going to let me take no job till I pays him."

I drew in my breath. I began to understand the problem put before me.

"How much do you owe?" I asked. My voice sounded suddenly small. Blue looked up, and for a moment I saw a glimpse of real pain in his eyes.

"Five pounds," he told me.

I think I must have gasped. It was an enormous sum, more than I'd saved in all my life, in all my time with Mrs.

Hudson. I felt my hopes plummeting, all the optimism that had urged me out of the kitchen to this dark rendezvous turned, at a stroke, into a dull sense of dread. And now I had a decision to make. My decision. There was no one there to help me.

The boy seemed to sense my dismay and rattled on hurriedly. "Five pounds is what I owe, but I have some put away. Savings. A wallet I never told him about. It must be nearly two pounds in all."

"So you need another three?"

He nodded, his head hung low again.

"And with that you'd be able to escape from this Monk person?" Another nod. "And start a proper job?"

"A proper job." The words were whispered so low they were almost inaudible.

"I think you'd better tell me about this position you've found. Is it regular work?"

Blue looked up. "He says so. I know someone who works for him. Says it's a good place. Fair pay and regular."

"Who is this employer?"

"Simpson. In Greenwich. Off Tide Lane."

"And this man, Monk, will let you go? You'll really be free of him?"

He nodded again, his eyes back on his boots.

I looked at him, at his bowed head and at the shame and misery in his shoulders. There was a bruise under his ear, the only part of his face visible to me below the pulled-down cap. As I looked, I couldn't help but remember the boy at the orphanage, the way he, too, would bow his head as he pressed close to me, as if by looking down he could escape notice. The thought made something twist inside me, and when I spoke next there were tears in my eyes.

"I have some savings, too. Come on. You have to wait at the kitchen door."

I left him at the bottom of the area steps and crept back into the kitchen. It took me two or three minutes to retrieve my little collection of coins from the hidden place behind the panelling. As I felt for them, I held my breath and listened but there was no sound of anyone stirring anywhere in the house. When I returned to where the boy was waiting, I found him hunched with cold and stamping his feet.

"Here," I said. The money clinked musically as it passed from my palm to his. He looked down at it and then looked me full in the face. For a moment, those pale blue eyes of his seemed cloudy and turbulent, as though struggling with unknown emotions. And then, without any words at all, he was off, clattering up the steps two at a time. At the top, he turned left, stepped smartly past the deep shadows by the front door, and was gone.

I watched him go, partly hurt, partly afraid: hurt at the haste in his going and afraid of what I had done. But worse was the part of me that felt neither thing, the part that watched him go and felt the old emptiness inside me, the emptiness that was worse than pain.

I was about to turn to go inside when a movement in the thick shadows above me caught my eye. I looked up, and as I moved forward to see better, the shadow seemed to move towards me.

"Well, Flotsam," a familiar voice said in the darkness. "You've made your decision. Let's just hope that you've made the right one."

TEN minutes later, wrapped in a blanket in front of a reawakened fire, with Mrs. Hudson's arm securely around me, I cried and I cried and I cried. I don't think I knew why, I only knew that the feelings inside me felt too great to be contained by my narrow frame, and the sobs shook themselves out of me in great convulsions of tears. At first I couldn't even speak, and Mrs. Hudson said nothing, either, just sat solidly with my head on her shoulder and my shoulders nestling under her strong right arm. Two o'clock passed and Mrs. Hudson stirred the fire, and gradually between the tears I began to find words to tell her of my two meetings with Blue and of what I had done. She listened silently, without comment, so that only an occasional tightening of the arm around me gave any sign that she was listening at all.

When I finally ran out of both tears and words, she allowed herself to speak.

"But, Flottie, why did you not tell me any of this before?"

I shook my head and began to sob again. "I knew I was being stupid. But that time at the orphanage . . . Those blue eyes . . . I wanted that boy at the orphanage to be all right."

To my surprise she nodded at this, as if I'd managed to say something that made sense.

"Do you think I've lost my money, ma'am? Was I just being fooled?"

"What do you think, Flotsam?"

"I don't know, ma'am." The tears threatened to recommence.

"Something made you trust him."

That was true, but it seemed hard to remember what. "Perhaps I just wanted to trust him, ma'am."

"Perhaps, Flotsam, perhaps." She stood up then and stoked the fire once more. "I'm going to make you a hot drink now, and then to bed, you understand." I watched her move about the kitchen, unperturbed and unperturbable. She didn't speak again until the drink was warm and steaming in my hands.

"Perhaps your instinct was right, Flotsam," she concluded. "Now we must both trust it for a little and see what happens."

And when I was finally tucked into bed, I slept soundly.

Perhaps Mrs. Hudson knew how much I needed that sleep. Perhaps that is why she didn't tell me at once the things of which she was sure. For Mrs. Hudson's knowledge of the tradesmen and traders of London was unparalleled. And she knew for certain that there was no tanner called Simpson in Greenwich, nor any tannery off Tide Lane.

I woke the next morning feeling rested and strangely calm. At first I could think of nothing but the glorious comfort of my bed, but as my senses began to revive I noticed on the floor the empty purse which once had held my savings. The sight made my stomach tighten with a fleeting sense of loss, but I remembered Mrs. Hudson's observation that something had made me trust in the boy, and after that I felt brighter. Those blue eyes had been so full of feeling. Perhaps it would come right after all.

I knew there was something else I should remember that morning, but at first I couldn't remember what. Then, as if they had been waiting for me to open my eyes, it seemed that every bell in London began to peal at the same time in a great, joyous, tumbling carillon of celebration.

"Christmas!" I gasped and began to pull on my clothes in a hurry. Out in the kitchen, although there was no sign of Mrs. Hudson, glorious order reigned, and the only things not tidied away were a large pan bubbling on the stove and, on the kitchen table, a series of small bundles held together with string. On closer examination, these proved to be the morning's post, and what a post it was! A full five bundles of cards and letters, all addressed to Mrs. Hudson, and, much to my surprise, two neat, crisp envelopes addressed to me. I examined each in turn. The first was white, the second brown. Both were addressed in clear, capital letters that told me nothing about the hands that had written them. I was just about to break the seal on the first when Mrs. Hudson bustled into the room.

"Ah, Flotsam!" she began briskly. "A Merry Christmas to you. The snow's stopped and, as you can see, the postman's already been and gone. However, he did find time to stop for a drop of tea and rum. He tells me there are queues right round the Regal Theatre this morning. There's a rumour that tickets for standing room only will go on sale later today."

She had taken up a large wooden spoon and began to stir the pot on the stove with muscular vigour.

"So much post," I murmured, gesturing at the piles on the table.

"Indeed, and some of it for you, Flotsam."

"I can't imagine who from."

"Well, you can find out shortly. But first there's a bowl of cinnamon porridge to be eaten. Here you are. Plenty of time to read your letters later."

Still a little fuddled by my long sleep, I ate my breakfast in happy silence, contemplating thoughtfully the two envelopes in front of me. Mine had not been the sort of life that had led to old acquaintances, and post of any sort with my name on it was a great and exciting rarity.

As soon as I'd scooped the last spoonful of porridge into my mouth, Mrs. Hudson whisked the bowl from under my nose and began to wash it up.

"Sunday best clothes today, Flotsam. You and I are going out."

"To church, ma'am?"

"No, something rather different. We're going to pay a visit to that dancer you are so interested in."

I felt my eyes opening wide. "Not Lola Del Fuego, ma'am?"

"That's what they call her, I believe."

"But will she see us? Today of all days?"

"Oh, yes, Flotsam. She'll see us. I sent her a little note

yesterday morning, and she was good enough to reply most promptly. We are to go to her rooms at the Blenheim Hotel at eleven o'clock. Which doesn't give us long, so I want you into your smart clothes quicker than a poacher's rabbit."

I needed no second urging, sliding into my smart clothes with what was becoming practised ease. I even made a fair job of pinning my own hair in the way Mrs. Hudson had shown me. When I emerged, the housekeeper was working through her pile of cards, but she looked up when I came in.

"Why, Flotsam, you look more grown up with every day that passes."

I smiled a little shyly at that and joined her at the table. Mrs. Hudson was peering at some chaotic handwriting.

"There's a little note here from Lord Bredonbury, sending his best wishes. At least I think that's what it says. His lordship has never forgotten the time I was able to help him over the little matter of his youngest son and the disappearing pastry cook."

I fingered the first of my two envelopes. "Have I time to open these now, ma'am?"

"Why not, Flotsam? We have a moment or two before we need to set out."

The first envelope was the brown one. Mrs. Hudson had pushed the paper knife towards me, and with something approaching trepidation I sliced it open. In doing so I fumbled it slightly and its contents spilled out onto the table in front of us. There was no letter or note, just a small piece of crisp, white card, printed at the top with the words "Regal Theatre."

The Great Salmanazar
and
Miss Lola Del Fuego

Thursday 26th December

This ticket is for Supplementary Seating
Supplementary Seats are Unnumbered
Doors open from Six O'Clock

"It's a ticket," I said, my voice hushed with awe and hesitant with disbelief. "For the show tomorrow."

"Well, well, well." Mrs. Hudson picked it up and examined it closely. "It's exactly what you say. And in the other envelope? Is there a message in that one to accompany this?"

I shook my head. "I don't think so, ma'am. They're in different handwriting." I opened the second envelope more hurriedly and squinted inside.

"Yes, Flotsam? What is it?"

Without saying anything I reached inside and placed its contents onto the table: another ticket, identical in every way, now rested against the first.

"Well, well," said Mrs. Hudson again. "You have generous admirers, Flotsam."

I didn't know what to say to that, or even what to think about such an incredible occurrence, so instead I rather timidly pushed one of the tickets over to her. "Please, ma'am," I said, my voice a little shaky, "it seems as we shall both see the famous Flame Dance after all."

I WAS whisked away to the Blenheim Hotel in something of a daze. I simply couldn't conceive how either of the tickets had come to be sent to me, and Mrs. Hudson gave me little time to ponder. Before I had a chance to contemplate the great miracle that had befallen me, I was wrapped tightly against the elements and pressed with equal firmness into a rattling hansom cab. There, Mrs. Hudson seized the opportunity, as we sped through the snowy streets, to summarise for me what we knew about the disappearance of James Phillimore.

I listened a little fitfully, still full of a sense of wonder that such a thing—two such things—could happen to me. Who could possibly want to give me such a present? And why? For all that Mrs. Hudson appeared totally incurious about them, these questions both seemed to me as surprising as they were unanswerable.

"So, Flotsam," Mrs. Hudson was concluding, "we know Phillimore disappeared from that house, but we don't know how. But we do know he didn't leave through the doors or the windows."

"Yes, ma'am," I agreed hastily.

"And does that suggest anything to you, Flottie?"

"Er, no, ma'am. It all seems rather baffling."

"It doesn't suggest anything unusual about Mr. Phillimore, for instance?"

"Perhaps he really can make himself invisible, ma'am?"

Mrs. Hudson smiled at this. "I don't think so, Flotsam. Very nearly, but perhaps not quite." She paused for a moment and looked about her. The day was a grey one that threatened more snow, but every house was brightly lit, and there were holly wreaths on every door.

"Cavendish Square," Mrs. Hudson commented. "They always do the decorations well in Cavendish Square. Now, Flottie, two unusual things we know about Mr. Phillimore are his trip to Kimber Street and the playbill with Lola Del Fuego's name on it. I wonder if by any chance the two might be linked."

"But the playbill doesn't mean anything, ma'am. There are so many of them about the place."

"True, Flotsam, but in the case of Mr. Phillimore, I think we can be sure that Miss Del Fuego is not completely unaware of his existence. Nor is she unconcerned about it."

"But how do you know that, ma'am?"

"The note I sent her, Flotsam. A note from someone who

is a complete stranger to her, a note which must have arrived amid many other notes from admirers and well-wishers. And yet a note to which she replied by return."

This made sense. It had surprised me that someone so famous should agree to meet two people such as Mrs. Hudson and myself on Christmas morning. Now I began to see that perhaps it was more than just exceptional courtesy.

"What did the note say, ma'am?"

"Oh, it was very short, Flotsam. Only two sentences. 'The police shall shortly ask you about James Phillimore. I suggest you speak to me first.'"

LOLA Del Fuego proved even more beautiful than I had imagined. She was tall and slim, with strong shoulders and slim hips above what seemed to be the longest legs imaginable. Her skin was pale, but her features were dramatic— full lips, a strong, shapely nose, prominent cheekbones, and dark brown eyes that flashed with fire. Her face was framed by cascades of glorious dark hair.

She welcomed us into her suite with a mixture of courtesy and disdain, dressed in the most remarkable morning dress, a green, silken affair that I viewed with undisguised admiration. It was a suite of considerable grandeur, hung in pale blue silk trimmed with gold. It smelled of roses and exotic perfume.

Having ushered us away from the door, Miss Del Fuego looked us up and down, as if uncertain of who we were and what we represented. Rather pointedly, she neither sat herself nor invited us to sit.

"You are *Señora* Hudson?" she asked at last. Her accent was heavily Spanish, and she hesitated each time she spoke, as if uncertain of her English.

"I am. And this is Flotsam, my colleague."

In reply, our hostess picked up a piece of paper from the table between us.

"I have received this note," she told us, lisping her *s* slightly in the Castilian manner. "I understand it not at all. I think perhaps it is what you call a *threat*. In my country, servants do not send such notes to their betters. So I think I call you here to explain yourselves to me, and if it is threat you make me, I call your English police."

Even though she was looking at us with her head held high and her eyes full of scorn, she still succeeded in looking quite captivating. Her face was attractive in repose; when alive with emotion that attractiveness grew into magnificence.

Mrs. Hudson, however, seemed less impressed. In fact, she seemed more interested in the details of the hotel suite than in Miss Del Fuego's person, and rather than replying immediately, she began to potter around the room, running her hands over pieces of furniture or touching the hangings with her fingers.

Finally she arrived at the picture above the fireplace, an impressive oil painting of ruins in a classical landscape.

"Ah! A copy of a painting by Fabricio, I believe. The original was at Hadley Hall when I was a maid there. Do you know the painting?"

"Phut! It is not paintings that I am asking you about!"

"But such a fine painting. I believe the earl bought it from a countryman of yours, the Duke of Catania. Of course, you will know all about him."

"The Duke of Catania? Yes, I know him, of course. In my own country I have admirers most many."

Mrs. Hudson turned from the painting and looked directly at the dancer. "Did you meet James Phillimore in Paris?" she asked.

Miss Del Fuego lifted her chin, and her eyes glinted dangerously. "Phut! Phillimore! Phillimore! I know no name Phillimore."

Mrs. Hudson shook her head gently. "Ah, but you do. And you want to know why the police are interested in him."

"The police?" She spat the word out with scorn. "What does a person of your position know of the police?"

Mrs. Hudson nodded at the note still gripped in the young woman's hand. "Perhaps you have heard of Mr. Sherlock Holmes? You will see that the address on that note is his address."

The dancer looked again at the piece of paper, and I thought she paled a little. When she spoke her voice was quieter.

"I have heard of this Holmes, yes. And I wish not to be in trouble here with police, that is why I write to you to call."

"I see." Mrs. Hudson seemed to have turned her attention to the plush fabric of the nearest armchair. "And I come to tell you that Mr. Phillimore is suspected of involvement in a very serious crime. If you were found to be assisting him, your stay in London might be longer than you expect."

"No, it is not true!" The young woman's eyes were aflame and her body taut as a spring. "There is no crime. I know this. It is not true."

"And you know nothing of James Phillimore, I think you said."

The dancer took a deep breath to calm herself. "I see what you think. You think, 'If she knows nothing of this man, why does she care?' But your letter with talk of police, and your words of crime, they upset me. I want nothing of trouble. Tomorrow is my last performance. Then I go away. Live happily. Live quiet life."

"Ah, yes. I had heard rumours that you plan to retire." Mrs. Hudson was paying attention again. "The word is that you are to be congratulated."

A genuine flush of pleasure seemed to colour Miss Del Fuego's cheeks. "Ah, the gossip, they know everything. Is true. After tomorrow, I marry. I become wife. I go away."

"You go back to Spain?"

The younger woman shook her head prettily. "Not to Spain. To Canada. My fiancé, he is rich from Canada. He owns much land of Canada. And I, I do not mind the snow to be with him." The smile that had spread across her face lingered for a moment, beautiful in its simplicity, then disappeared abruptly. "That is why these words of police, of crime, they frighten me. My fiancé is very honest man. He not like talk of crime. You tell police, no crime, no James Phillimore, is nothing to do with me."

Mrs. Hudson nodded slowly. "Very well," she agreed after a pause. "If they ask me, I shall tell them exactly that."

And with those words, rather to my surprise, our interview with Europe's most famous dancer was at an end.

THAT afternoon, finding no sign of either Mr. Holmes or Dr. Watson in Baker Street, and receiving no word that either intended to return in time to celebrate Christmas Day, Mrs. Hudson determined to prepare their dinner without them.

"I have never yet served in a house where Christmas has not been properly marked," she declared, "and I certainly don't intend to start now. If there is no one above stairs to do the thing correctly, then we must do their duty for them. Now, Flottie, the goose is in the cold room, and it's ready for the oven. Fetch it out, and let's get started."

We worked as hard as if we had an army of redcoats to feed, and with as much delicacy as if our efforts were to be judged by a banquet of French chefs. Watching Mrs. Hudson's concentration on the minute details of seasoning, I would quite forget that the beneficiaries of her care were no one but ourselves. While we cooked, I had a chance to ask Mrs. Hudson some of the questions I'd been pondering ever since our morning visit.

"Mrs. Hudson, ma'am," I began, "didn't we leave rather early today?"

"You wished to stay longer, Flottie?"

"Well, I'm not sure what we really *learned*. We don't know even if Miss Del Fuego really had heard of Mr. Phillimore before."

"Oh, I don't know, Flottie. I thought we learned some interesting things today."

"What sort of things, ma'am?"

"That Miss Del Fuego is planning to marry. And that she leaps to the defence of a man she has never heard of when he is accused of a crime."

I stirred the soup a little more and pondered for a little longer.

"She's certainly very beautiful, ma'am."

"Yes, Flotsam. A very striking young lady." She leaned over and tasted the soup. "Tell me, Flottie, have you ever heard of the Duke of Catania?"

"No, ma'am."

"Neither have I, Flottie. Neither have I. A touch more salt in there, I think, if you please."

While I was still struggling to understand the implications of all these things, there came a crisis in our culinary campaign when everything seemed to happen at once, when we were so heavily outnumbered by the pots around us that it seemed certain we would be overrun. Like Hector beneath the walls of Troy, Mrs. Hudson commanded as she battled, throwing herself into the thick of the action while directing the forces behind her.

"Quickly, Flotsam! There, on your right. A pinch of sage and then off the heat. And watch on your left. The gravy threatens to boil."

Then, as suddenly as the crisis had arrived, it passed, and an eerie calm seemed to descend upon the kitchen. Each element of our feast stood ready or warming, and the debris of the struggle had all been swept away to soak in the corner by the sink. We stood, weary but triumphant, and surveyed the scene of our victory.

"Do you know, Flottie, I feel that bottle of Chateau Yprieu has been richly deserved. But not yet, of course. I'll begin with a glass of the chilled sherry while you wash your hands and get that apron off. No dawdling now, the food's waiting to be eaten."

When I returned to the kitchen, neat and smelling fresh, the room seemed full of a sense of contentment. By some alchemy, instead of the smell of grease and burning, Mrs. Hudson's cooking had left the room full of rich, tempting smells, and the lamps and the fire filled the room with a soft, flickering light. Mrs. Hudson was sipping her sherry by the fire and behind her the kitchen table stood immaculate as if a duke were dining with us.

"There are three places laid, ma'am," I noticed.

"Indeed?" She looked at her watch and then raised her head to listen. Somewhere at the far end of the street I heard voices singing Christmas carols. "Very good timing," she muttered to herself. As I listened, the voices came nearer, until they were directly outside our door. I heard footsteps on the steps outside, and then the door opened to let in an eddy of snowflakes and the head of Scraggs, grinning merrily.

"How's that, Mrs. H?"

"Very good, Scraggs. Did they take much persuading?"

"Not when I told them they were to come back here for cake at the end of their round."

"I'm pleased to hear it. Now nip up and thank them for me, then get back here sharpish. You've got Dr. Watson's portion of game soup waiting for you."

And so the three of us sat down to eat, and Mrs. Hudson allowed us both a small glass of white wine to accompany the entrées, which was delicious and made me feel like laughing. Just as we were about to move on, there came a respectful tap at the window, and we saw the round and rather balding head of Mr. Rumbelow peeping in.

"Quite wrong of me to intrude, of course," he explained when we had drawn him inside and closed the kitchen doors behind us. "And of course I in no way wish to appear a, er, *scavenger* at the feast. Oh, dear me, no. But Flotsam mentioned that your excellent cooking might be going to waste, and at this time on a Christmas evening my house is somewhat quiet . . ." He caught sight of the dusty bottle that Mrs. Hudson had decanted the day before. "Ah!" he exclaimed in rapture. "The Chateau Yprieu! I have arrived in time!"

To me it seemed that the evening sped by. Mr. Rumbelow told long stories of the Christmases of his youth, spent in Dorset with his eccentric aunt Gertrude. Scraggs performed tricks with dried beans hidden under cups. Mrs. Hudson, after much persuasion, told us how the Irascible Earl narrowly escaped marriage to an Italian countess the year Lecturer won the Cesarewitch. I laughed a great deal, and the fate of my savings and the fate of the Malabar Rose suddenly seemed less important. I was surrounded by friends, and I had tickets for the most amazing show ever to be staged in London.

Then, when it seemed the evening was replete with good things, there was a knock on the front door and there stood Hetty Peters, resplendent in the most alarming mauve ball gown, and the Right Honourable Rupert Spencer, looking strikingly handsome in evening dress.

"We can't stay, of course, Flottie, darling," Hetty explained, pushing past me and heading immediately downstairs. "We've come from the most tedious affair imaginable—at a friend of Rupert's, obviously—and now we're off to something much better and probably quite scandalous where I shall probably drink too much champagne and kiss the butler . . ."

By now she had reached the kitchen and was alarming Mrs. Hudson with an impulsive embrace.

"And, you see, we've bought *presents,*" she went on, "though none for you, Mr. Rumbelow, or you, Scraggs, because we didn't know you'd be here, but I daresay Rupert has some cigars to hand, don't you, Rupert? Anyway, these are from Rupert and me, though of course they aren't really from Rupert because he never thinks to buy presents, do you, Rupert?"

Mr. Spencer smiled enigmatically at this, but had no chance of replying because Miss Peters barely paused for breath.

"That's why no one sensible will ever want to marry him, you see, because generally girls make a fuss about things like that. Mind you, Rupert was very happy to come out for once, weren't you, Rupert?"

"It's true." He addressed himself to Mrs. Hudson. "I don't know what's happened to my uncle, but he's very keen on my company at the moment. Tonight he refused to go to his club and wanted us all to stay in with him. We only got away at all because Hetty bribed Reynolds to play cribbage with him."

At that point in the proceedings, a muffled pop made Miss Peters squeal.

"Oh, Mrs. Hudson! Champagne? Do you think so? Well, since I'm going to drink *far* too much of it anyway, I don't see that it can hurt to start now . . ."

"Champagne, do you say?" A voice behind me made me jump.

"Dr. Watson!" I exclaimed. "And Mr. Holmes!"

"That's right, Flotsam," the doctor beamed. "Duty over for tonight. We've been on the tail of that Salmanazar all day, haven't we, Holmes? But he's safely in bed now, and his door and windows are being watched by a small army of police officers. So I think champagne is in order, eh, Holmes?"

His friend allowed a slightly drawn smile. "Why not, my friend? Let us just hope it does not prove premature. For tomorrow is the day that decides our fate."

"Well, Mr. Holmes," put in Mr. Rumbelow, "I shall be attending the performance tomorrow, so I shall keep my eyes open for any skulduggery."

"Oh, and so shall we, shan't we, Rupert?" Miss Peters added.

"And I've got a place hidden up in the roofing," said Scraggs proudly. "Should be able to keep an eye on things from up there."

And then I heard my own voice, trembling a little with excitement.

"Oh, and do you know? Mrs. Hudson and I are going to be there, too!"

At this someone raised a glass, and all the other glasses followed, all except Mrs. Hudson's. For some reason, a little frown of anxiety had appeared between her eyebrows as though she had remembered something she needed to think about.

"Do you know," she said, looking at the table still laden with food, "since no one has eaten any yet, I think I might ice that fruitcake after all."

CHAPTER TEN

A Disappearing Trick

Every single person there to witness it would always re-member the Great Salmanazar's London performance. From the scamps and urchins who had crept into the wings or hidden themselves under seats, to the sparkling ladies who sat in the boxes; from the girls selling cigars and bonbons, to the moustachioed gentlemen at the back of the stalls who had really come to see the famous Fire Dance; from the light-ing men and the stagehands and the musicians in the pit, to the stout constables in the aisles and the plainclothes detec-tives concealed in the audience, everyone who was there to see it remembered it; and on snowy Boxing Days for many years afterwards they would tell and retell the tales.

Perhaps part of the strangeness of the evening stemmed from the weather, for the whole spectacular show took place at the height of a blizzard. From the first light of dawn that day, the sky threatened snow, and when at nine in the morn-ing the coalman arrived in Baker Street, there was little difference between the shade of his boots and the dark sky above him.

"It will snow, all right," he told Mrs. Hudson as his soot-black horse shifted nervously in its traces; and in reply she looked at the sky and frowned a little and agreed.

"Yes, Mr. Prescott, there'll be snow tonight, and plenty of it. It's a night when sensible, honest folk would stay at home."

But of course they did not. When the first flakes fell that night, there were still ticketless crowds queuing at the doors of the Regal Theatre in hope of a miracle, and the whole of the area around Piccadilly Circus teemed with peddlers and jugglers and loiterers, and people just out to see what would happen.

For rumour was rife. The Malabar Rose was already stolen; the Great Salmanazar was arrested; had fled abroad; had disappeared without trace. The Queen herself was to attend the performance; the Queen had refused to see the show; the Queen had ordered the show to be cancelled to safeguard the Malabar Rose. And through it all, the crowds kept gathering, the price of tickets touched thirty guineas apiece, the taverns and the pickpockets did great business. At the Blenheim Hotel, the great French chef Deslandes served *truite a la Malabar,* and in the Rose and Crown on the corner of Poland Street, the pot boys took bets on whether the foreign magician would magic away the precious stone. The mood of the crowd was patriotic. The British police would stand firm; Sherlock Holmes would foil any plots; Inspector Lestrade was a man to be trusted . . . Six shillings to one said the stone was safe. Eight to one! Ten to one! Hurrah for England and St. George!

The optimism of the crowds no doubt weighed heavily on Mr. Holmes and Dr. Watson as they paced the Satin Rooms, checking and rechecking that nothing was amiss.

At five o'clock that day they were joined by Sir John Plaskett, from his house in Rudolph Place, who brought with him the velvet display box that was to hold the ruby. Ten minutes after that, Inspector Lestrade, who had been with his men on the roof, completed the group. The inspector was brushing snow from his moustache.

"It's beginning to come down thick, gentlemen," he told them. Together they checked their watches and waited for the gem to arrive.

Back in Baker Street, I had found myself chased out of the house just after lunchtime. Mrs. Hudson, busy with household chores and declaring that she had things to do in the afternoon, sent me over to the house in Bloomsbury Square.

"You are to spend the afternoon keeping Miss Peters company, Flottie, and making sure she doesn't get too overexcited. That way, when the snow starts, you can get to the theatre in the earl's carriage. The earl is attending the viewing of the Malabar Rose, but I'm sure he will take the rest of you into town. You can arrive in Piccadilly in style, Flottie."

"But what about you, ma'am?"

"I'll manage fine on foot. There are one or two little tasks to get done first. I want to see Mrs. Phillimore in Sefton Avenue again, for one thing. And I have a call to make on Sir Phillip Westacott, the surgeon, for another."

"Are you unwell, ma'am?"

"Good gracious, no, Flotsam. I'm in the rudest of health. But Sir Phillip is an expert on human anatomy, and just at the moment I find myself quite interested in that sort of thing."

Knowing that Mrs. Hudson's interests could be strangely eclectic, there seemed to be little to say to this. "Shall I see you at the theatre then, ma'am?" I asked.

"You certainly shall, Flottie. Our tickets are for unnumbered seats, but I have had a word with the theatre manager who has agreed to reserve us a pair together. I shall see you there."

At twenty minutes to six that evening, while the first flakes of snow were falling from skies pregnant with wintry intent, I was seated in the Earl of Brabham's brougham, lumbering slowly towards Piccadilly. Next to me, Hetty Peters was bursting with excitement; opposite, Rupert Spencer seemed not at all upset to be foregoing the attentions of the Marylebone Natural Philosophic Society. Only the Irascible Earl seemed out of sorts, checking his watch repeatedly and lowering the window from time to time to berate his coachman.

"Really, the traffic in this town is quite absurd," he growled, gesturing at the street in annoyance. "Must have moved quicker than this in Tudor times! Look at all those damned hansoms! Always think they have the right of way. And that fellow, there, in the victoria! What's he doing bringing his vehicle into the heart of London on a night like this? Must know he's only going to snarl up the roads for everyone else. Fellows like him should have to pay to drive into town!" He lowered the window. "Carrington, if that fellow gets in the way, drive over him!"

Miss Peters wasn't listening. She was gripping my hand and pointing at people in the crowd, uttering little gasps of excitement.

"Look, Flottie! That man there! Doesn't he have a face like a burglar! I bet he's after the Malabar Rose! Oh, goodness, I think I know him. Do I know him, Rupert? The man over there with the red whiskers?"

Mr. Spencer examined the crowd in a leisurely way. "Yes, Hetty. It's the vicar of St. Margaret's. You spilled tea over him at the charity bazaar last month."

"Did I? Are you sure? Oh, *that* vicar. Yes, I remember now. I remember being surprised that you're *allowed* to be a vicar when you look so much like a burglar. It must make his parishioners awfully nervous when he comes calling . . ."

And in that way, in between flurries of snow and volleys of aristocratic ire, we arrived at the Blenheim Hotel, where the earl had been invited to witness the safe arrival of the Malabar Rose.

The contrast between the calm of the Blenheim Hotel and the turbulence outside could not have been greater. The Satin Rooms seemed to float amidst the city's noise like an iceberg of good order in a sea of overexcitement. We approached down the thickly carpeted corridor, past uniformed policemen who, after much deliberation and much checking of lists, eventually allowed us into the antechamber beyond which the ruby was to be displayed. There we found Sir John Plaskett awaiting us, along with Mr. Holmes, Dr. Watson, Inspector Lestrade, and a group of gentlemen in suits whom I didn't recognise. Dr. Watson, on seeing us arrive, gave a happy snort and came over to greet me.

"Ah, Flotsam! Excellent. Dashed pleased to see you. Good to have an extra pair of eyes. Though apparently the ruby isn't here yet. I must say, I wish it would hurry up. All this waiting is beginning to give me the jitters."

Sir John, meanwhile, was introducing the various people present. As well as the Earl of Brabham, the other official witnesses were Sir John, for the Crown; a man with a bowler hat and a moustache called Mr. Bushy who represented the insurers; an Indian gentleman representing the maharajah; and a gaunt, silver-haired gentleman who turned out to be the royal jeweller. When everyone had shaken hands with everyone else, Sir John led us past two more policemen and into the inner chamber itself. The great circular room was just as I'd seen it last, but for one difference: on the slim column of marble at its centre there now stood the elegant velvet case that was to display the ruby. The case, just like the one I had seen in Baker Street, was shaped like a truncated pyramid, with a dimple at its apex where the stone would stand. Without a word the crowd gathered around it. Even Miss Peters fell silent, and I hardly dared breathe lest someone would notice my presence and decide that I had no right to be there.

"Gentlemen," Sir John began. "Three of the doors to this room are already sealed. The fourth we shall lock behind us when we leave. You are all aware of the safeguards in place. Are you satisfied with them?"

There was a general murmur of assent.

"And do you have any questions? If not, all that remains is for me to produce the Malabar Rose itself. I am happy to report that the decoy stones have been completely successful. The Malabar Rose itself has been in a completely unguessable location and has arrived here safely. Now it is time for me to take it back. The Malabar Rose, if you please!"

At first I thought he was looking directly at me, and I began to shrink with embarrassment at such cruel teasing. But then I became aware that behind me the Earl of Brabham was clearing his throat and fidgeting. To my total astonishment, he stepped forward and reached into his jacket pocket.

"Got it here, Sir John," he murmured. "Never let it out of my pocket, you see. Have to admit, I was beginning to get a bit windy, though."

This remarkable revelation caused a stirring of surprise amongst the assembled company.

"My word, sir!" exclaimed Dr. Watson. "Had it all this time, have you? Who'd have guessed it?"

"Who indeed, Watson?" Mr. Holmes coughed modestly. "It took me some time before I realised the stone was likely to be in the possession of a respectable gentleman with no public office, conservative political views, a sturdy coachman, and membership of the same clubs as Sir John."

"But, Uncle," Mr. Spencer was asking, ignoring Mr. Holmes' demonstration of his deductive powers, "you mean it has just been lying around the house all this time?"

"What do you mean, 'lying around the house'?" the earl growled. "It was in my blasted pocket, wasn't it? Why do you think I've been wanting you to accompany me to the blasted club these last few days? Why do you think I wanted to stay in and play cribbage when you wouldn't come? I ask you! Most ghastly few days of my life! Worse than that time I attended the House of Lords. I hardly dared go out, dammit." The earl shook his head, as if in horror. "Cribbage, indeed! Game for old ladies and clergymen! To be honest, I don't know if it's really fit for clergymen, either."

While the earl continued in that vein, the Malabar Rose had been removed from his grasp by the elderly jeweller. I could see his eyes widen as he examined it, and even from where I stood it was easy to see that it was special. The stone he held was not dissimilar in size and shape to the glass replica we had been shown in Baker Street, but there could have been no confusing the two. For the Malabar Rose seemed to burn with a fire at its very heart, and whatever light there was in the room seemed to be captured by it, as if to feed those flames. It was, quite simply, exquisite.

"Magnificent!" exclaimed the jeweller, his eyes still wide. "I have never seen anything like it. Such depth! Such fire!"

The maharajah's representative was studying it closely, too. "Yes, that is the Malabar Rose," he confirmed. "My congratulations to you, sir, on its save delivery."

The ruby was passed to Sir John, who placed it carefully on the velvet case. It fitted perfectly, and suddenly the room didn't feel bare anymore; it seemed to fill with light, as if the

Malabar Rose had furnished it with colour and lustre of its own. At the same time, the assembled group seemed to diminish beside it. We simply stood and watched the fire at its centre twist and flicker and weave patterns of meaning that none of us would ever decode.

The formalities that followed were almost a relief and were quickly over. Receipts were signed and countersigned. The door was sealed behind us with four padlocks, one for each of the signatories, and two constables took up position with their backs to the door. Sir John, Mr. Holmes, Dr. Watson, and Inspector Lestrade stated their intention to stay and patrol the antechamber, while the Earl of Brabham, Mr. Spencer, and those others who were to be there at the official viewing were enjoined to return at eleven o'clock, when the door would be officially reopened. Then our group broke up, and those of us with tickets to the show next door made haste to secure our seats.

THE Regal Theatre was, in those days, one of the smartest in the whole of the country. It seemed to me immense, and even for the most ordinary event it could seat eight hundred people in the most sumptuous comfort. From the rich red carpets of the stalls, to the distant, dizzying heights of the Gods, every box, every balustrade, every dangling chandelier, and every fragment of cornicing was gilded and glorious, and polished till it shone. The different tiers rose above each other in towering splendour so that faces peeping down from the top balcony were little more than pale spots amid the blaze of colour.

Eight hundred seats must have sufficed on most occasions, but that night there were at least a thousand people crammed into the old building. Extra seats had been slotted into the aisles to extend each row, and tickets for standing room had been sold so liberally that it seemed the crowds in the Upper

Circle and the Gods were doomed to spill over into the stalls below. Even at six o'clock, with two hours still to go until the performance began, the theatre seemed full. By the time Mrs. Hudson arrived to take her seat in the stalls, with only ten minutes to spare, the theatre seemed so full it was impossible to believe that those still queuing outside would ever get in.

In the midst of the mounting excitement, only Mrs. Hudson appeared unmoved.

"A very fair crowd," she commented, seating herself calmly and riffling through her bag as if totally unaffected by the atmosphere around her.

"Ah, here we are," she said presently, pulling from her bag a very small notebook. "I jotted down one or two of the things that Lavinia Phillimore told me this afternoon, Flotsam. I thought you might be interested."

I looked at the babbling crowds all around me and wondered how Mrs. Phillimore's recollections of her husband could possibly be interesting at a time like this. Mrs. Hudson, however, was undeterred.

"To begin with, I now have the dates of all Mr. Phillimore's periods of convalescence in Broadstairs. They make fascinating reading. And when I asked Mrs. Phillimore about the large sum of money she received through the post, she told me that she thought perhaps her husband had been dabbling in the stock markets. She remembers seeing a letter that mentioned shares in an iron company and in Canadian railways. Sadly, she's a particularly vapid young woman, and she never seems to have thought to ask him about it."

The influx of people into the auditorium seemed finally to have come to an end. Wherever I looked, it seemed that people were now in their places. Mrs. Hudson nodded towards the stage.

"Look at the front two rows of the stalls, Flottie. It seems that Inspector Lestrade isn't taking any chances."

On looking more closely, I realised that the front two rows appeared to be populated entirely be men in their thirties and forties. Unlike the rest of the audience, none of them were chattering to their neighbours.

"Police constables without their uniforms," Mrs. Hudson whispered. "You can tell. No necks. And look there!" Mrs. Hudson indicated a bent old flower seller in the opposite aisle. "Mr. Holmes has sneaked away from that ruby of his to keep an eye on things after all."

"Mr. Holmes, ma'am? *Her?*"

"Of course, Flottie. Look at the hands. And besides, the flowers are arranged wrong. No flower seller puts the roses next to the tiger lilies."

But before I could reexamine the old woman in the light of these observations, the lights around me began to dim and the audience hushed itself, and the moment London had been waiting for so impatiently had finally arrived.

I could fill many pages in describing the wonders we were shown that night. I had seen magicians before, but I had never seen anything like the Great Salmanazar. At first he appeared rather uncertain, a small man in evening dress who perhaps had wandered out of his depth. But as one extraordinary happening followed another, he seemed to grow in stature until he dominated the stage as surely as he dominated the audience in front of it. We were his entirely, to work as he pleased, and his performance grew into something that defied all sense of reason. At first I was able to think about each trick, to wonder what sleight of hand had accomplished it; but the performance moved so fast, and challenged my reason so rapidly and repeatedly, that eventually I could only watch and wonder. By the time he performed the rope trick, a thousand pairs of eyes were locked on his, and when he disappeared, quite literally, in a puff of smoke, a thousand pairs of eyes blinked in disbelief. A few seconds later, at precisely the same moment, a thousand people became aware that the man they had just watched vanish was, in fact, standing in the aisle of the stalls, twenty yards from the stage, apparently having just witnessed his own evaporation.

Soon we were all so accustomed to the performance of the impossible that when the Great Salmanazar released from his hat in rapid succession a cockatoo, an ocelot, and a fluttering cloud of scarlet butterflies, he might just as easily have produced an elephant and none of us would have thought it in the least surprising.

Finally, when it appeared that the procession of wonders must come to an end, the Great Salmanazar stepped forward and addressed his audience for the first time.

"Mesdames et monsieurs," he began. "Shortly, I shall perform for you a feat that defies all physical laws. You shall see me bound and gagged, secured in every imaginable way, and suspended above you, encaged. But the Great Salmanazar cannot be confined by natural barriers, as you shall witness for yourselves. But first, something a little less taxing. You, sir!"

He pointed with his finger to a portly man seated a few rows behind me. "And you!" He pointed in a different direction. "And you! And finally you, sir! I ask for you gentlemen to stand."

Hesitantly and with obvious embarrassment, four gentlemen rose to their feet. Each was seated at the end of a row, so that they marked very roughly the four corners of the stalls. The Great Salmanazar smiled at each of them in turn.

"Gentlemen, my helpers shall bring each of you a pack of cards. I ask you to select a card from that pack and make a mark on it—a mark known only to yourselves. Your signature, perhaps, or the name of a loved one."

As he spoke, four small boys in red uniforms ran forward

from the front of the stage, and each hurried to one of the gentlemen in question. A short pause ensued as cards were selected and scribbled on, then returned to the boys, who ran back to the stage and delivered them to the magician.

"You see that I do not look at them," he declared, holding them high above his head. "Now I place them safely in my pocket." A thousand people watched the cards disappear into the front of his jacket. "And now, before my incarceration commences, I request a witness to observe that my bonds are genuine."

Almost before he had finished speaking, one of the plainclothes constables from the front row had hastened onto the stage. The Great Salmanazar raised his arms again.

"And so, begin!" he ordered, and at the clap of his hands, the stage was suddenly full of men carrying ropes and tools and all sorts of paraphernalia. A thousand people watched as the illusionist was bound in a straightjacket, gagged, and blindfolded, then tied around with so many ropes that he almost disappeared beneath them. When this binding was complete, he was placed in a sack which was knotted with thick cord, then laid in a coffin that had been carried onto the stage. A pair of carpenters took the coffin's lid and proceeded to nail it down with vengeful thoroughness. Further ropes were then bound tightly around it, and finally two strongmen appeared, puffing and straining, carrying between them a monstrous block of lead the shape of a kitchen weight but two feet square at its base and a further two feet tall. This weight was lifted with some difficulty onto the top of the coffin, and then, while we watched, a crate of plain wood was erected around the whole.

The carpenters worked quickly, and in less than a minute, huge hawsers were being strapped around the crate. Then a mighty iron chain was lowered from the ceiling, and the hawsers were attached to it. A thousand pairs of eyes watched the crate being hoisted into the air until it was fully thirty feet above the stage. We watched it swing for a few seconds and then hang still.

It was at this point that Mrs. Hudson nudged me and showed me her watch.

"Twenty-five minutes to eleven," she whispered. "Twenty-five minutes until the Malabar Rose goes on display."

But I scarcely heard her. Like everyone around me, my eyes were fixed on the hanging box. As we watched it, the auditorium seemed to grow darker and then, as if from nowhere, small fires began to spring up around the stage. Strange, arabesque music filled the theatre, and I thrilled with excitement. The famous Fire Dance was about to begin.

To gasps of wonder, Lola Del Fuego appeared from the wings as if she were floating on the heat from the fires. Her feet seemed scarcely to touch the ground. She was wearing loose layers of white silk that flowed out from her body and were turned red by the light of the fires, until they seemed like flames licking around her. So loose, so insubstantial was the silk that I marvelled at her daring, but the swiftness of the movements and the flickering firelight made it impossible to be sure just how much of that graceful body was displayed. As the music grew faster, the dance became more wild, and as she leapt through the flames, they seemed to clutch at her feet and kiss the tails of silk that trailed behind her.

"Careful, Flotsam." Mrs. Hudson wasn't looking at the dance at all, I realised. "Keep your eyes on the crate if you can."

But I couldn't. It was too much to ask. I noticed that even among the rows of constables, at least three-quarters of the heads had tilted forwards and were following the movements of the dancer.

I had no idea how long the dance lasted. So enchanted was I, so overcome with the wild grace of it, that it might have been an hour, or more. But when the flames died down and the music faded and the applause swept over us like a breaking storm, while the moustachioed hearties were shouting for more and the grey-whiskered gents were waving their programmes, Mrs. Hudson leaned over to me and whispered, "Listen!" And above all the noise, very faintly from the street outside, I could hear a clock striking eleven.

"The Malabar Rose!" I whispered.

"Yes, they'll be opening the doors right now. Mr. Spencer slipped out earlier, along with all the others invited to the event next door."

But before I could start thinking about the Malabar Rose, my attention was caught again by the wooden box that contained the Great Salmanazar. Now, very slowly, to the rhythm of a single drumbeat, it was being lowered back to the stage. The audience, who only a few moments ago had been in such an uproar, began to fall silent again until, as the crate came slowly lower and the drumbeat grew faster, the whole theatre was hushed. When the crate was within six feet of the stage, two strongmen stepped out from the wings and kept it steady as it came lower, until finally it touched the stage and settled there. The drumming was very urgent now, louder and louder with every moment that passed. The two strongmen withdrew. The drumming reached a crescendo and then, dramatically, stopped dead. The silence was almost unbelievable. In my seat by the aisle, I held my breath.

Then came a crash that made me leap in my seat and made the audience gasp with shock. A gloved fist had punched through the board that formed one side of the crate. We watched fascinated as the fist was withdrawn and then with another tremendous crash smashed through the wood once more, widening the hole. Gradually, the Great Salmanazar freed himself from the box. With a final push, he stepped clear of the splintered wood and stood before us, immaculate and unflustered, his arms spread wide as if to embrace our applause.

And applaud we did. It was as if the breaking of the wood had released us from a spell, and now we were properly able to acknowledge all we had seen. The audience rose to its feet in one movement and bellowed its appreciation. Cries of "Bravo!" and "More!" rose above the applause, and the stamping of feet seemed to shake the theatre. A hat was thrown in the air, then another, then hundreds, as if the favourite had just won the Derby. A gentleman in front of me sobbed and waved his handkerchief. A young lady of earnest demeanour was restrained by the constables as she tried to run onto the stage. And amidst it all, the Great Salmanazar was signalling for quiet.

"Please!" he cried, waving his arms. "Ladies and gentlemen, please!" Eventually the noise began to subside. "Please," he cried again, "there is one more thing! Please!" The noise from the Upper Circle took a little longer to die down and when it did the magician spoke again.

"You, sir!" He pointed to one of the gentlemen who earlier had selected a playing card. "I find, sir, that my pocket is empty. I fear I have mislaid your card. Perhaps if you were just to open your pocketbook . . ."

Bemused, the fellow reached into his jacket and took out a leather wallet. "Well, I'll be . . ." he declared, looking up wildly and holding something white in his hand.

"Would that be the knave of clubs, sir?" the illusionist asked.

"It is! It is! The very one. Look!" He held it up to those around him. "My wife's name is signed in the corner!"

By now the other three men were scrambling to pull out their wallets.

"You, sir! The nine of diamonds?"

"Yes, that's right. It's here! The same card!"

"And you! The king of hearts?"

"The same! Here's my name on it!"

"And you, sir!" He pointed to the last of the four. "The ace of spades?"

But instead of smiling back, the gentleman was looking confused, searching through the papers in his pocketbook.

"The ace of spades, I say," the Great Salmanazar repeated.

"The ace of spades is correct, sir," the man agreed, still searching anxiously, "but there is no such card here."

Suddenly the theatre, which had been in an uproar of surprise and admiration, began to fall silent. People looked from the stage to the man in the audience and back again. A certain tension seemed to have entered the magician's body.

"Perhaps then in your pocket, sir."

The man began to go through his pockets with an air of dejection. "I marked it with a cross, so I should definitely know it again. But I can tell you without doubt I don't have it here."

The Great Salmanazar had gone very pale. He seemed to have shrunk in size again, to have become the same uncertain performer who'd first walked onto the stage. I watched him take a deep breath and address the audience.

"*Mesdames et monsieurs,* forgive me. It would appear in this act of physical transportation I have failed. Please forgive me." And with that he stepped back, out of the light and into the darkness, and disappeared from the stage.

To say the audience was taken aback would be an understatement. We sat in silence, confused and a little embarrassed at this unexpected finale. After a few seconds, the curtain descended sharply to the stage and there was a spattering of applause, but for the most part people were too uncertain to clap their hands. A low murmur of surmise and speculation was running through the building, and I turned to Mrs. Hudson. To my total surprise, she was smiling a smile of utter contentment. Sensing that I was looking at her, she turned to me and hastily rearranged her features into more solemn lines.

"Forgive me, Flotsam," she said. "I'm sure this isn't the time to appear too triumphant. But I have just understood the exact whereabouts of our mysterious Mr. Phillimore."

WHEN Mr. Spencer left the theatre that evening, the Fire Dance had just begun. He found it hard to leave, partly because he found Lola Del Fuego's attractions to be in no way exaggerated, partly because neither his uncle nor Miss Peters was at first willing to accompany him, and partly because the sheer pressure of people meant that his progress, when he did move, was slow and wretchedly difficult. He did at least succeed in bringing the earl with him, though Miss Peters utterly refused to budge.

"Don't be silly, Rupert," she hissed. "This is the most thrilling moment of my entire life! Go off to your boring old soiree if you must, but if you try to take me with you I shall scream the theatre down!"

Mr. Spencer, deciding that this was an act of public outrage of which she was fully capable, left her in the care of the elderly archdeacon seated next to her, and accompanied his uncle to the front door of the Regal Theatre. It was there for the first time they fully appreciated the force of the storm that had gripped London while the Great Salmanazar was on stage. As soon as the door opened for them, snow drove itself into their faces with polar fury, and for a moment each man wavered and stepped back.

"My word!" The Earl of Brabham held down his top hat with grim determination. "It's a blasted blizzard. Nothing for it but to struggle through. Mustn't be late!"

At first it seemed there was more snow in the air than on the ground, but when they stepped out into it, their boots sank deep into freshly fallen snow. The storm had emptied the streets. All those bustling crowds and legions of hawkers had been swept away by its force, and the city seemed deserted. By the time the two men had made their way next door, stamping their feet and brushing snow from their coats, it was seven minutes to eleven.

They found a considerable throng of people in the antechamber of the Satin Rooms, waiting for the viewing to begin. Most of them had also torn themselves away from the performance next door, duty dictating that royal invitations must be honoured, even when Lola Del Fuego was on stage. To compensate for this sacrifice, a very fine champagne was being served, and as Mr. Spencer entered the room, the excited chatter was all of events at the Regal Theatre.

"The fellow simply disappeared . . ."

"Splendid trickery . . ."

". . . Seen nothing like it since Sindapour in 'fifty-six . . ."

". . . All mirrors, you know, and then there's the smoke . . ."

". . . Once you know there's a trapdoor, you realise it's really childishly simple . . ."

". . . Wouldn't let any daughter of mine cavort around in public like that, but then of course none of my daughters are really built for that sort of thing . . ."

In the centre of the throng, the Dowager Duchess of Marne was questioning a bishop about his views on black magic, and beyond that a peer from the shires was bribing a waiter to replace his champagne with a whisky and soda. Near the padlocked door, a minor admiral was describing his only-ever naval engagement to a young lady who had mistaken him for someone quite different. They were being watched by Dr. Watson and Inspector Lestrade, who both leaned nonchalantly against the door itself. Next to them, Sir John Plaskett was looking at his watch.

As if this movement was a signal, the other key-holders

disengaged themselves from their conversations and began
to gather around him. Mr. Bushy mopped his brow. The Indian gentleman looked serious. The Irascible Earl looked
slightly irritable. Sherlock Holmes, restored to his usual
costume but smelling faintly of tiger lilies, sauntered casually through the crowds and joined them.

"Come, gentlemen," Sir John urged them, "let us make
no great show of this. Let us remove these padlocks, check
that all is well, then let the party come through to admire
the stone."

One by one the locks were removed. It fell to the Earl of
Brabham to remove the last, but in his impatience he struggled to turn the key and gestured for his nephew to help
him, which is how Mr. Spencer came to be right at the front
of the group when the clocks struck eleven and the doors
swung open.

The lights of the inner room had been left burning, so the
bare interior was brilliantly lit. Perhaps this bright lighting
created a sense of normality and order, for certainly the men
responsible for the Malabar Rose were chatting amongst
themselves as they entered. Mr. Bushy, who was at the back,
even paused to close the door behind him. At first he couldn't
understand why the others stopped talking as he did so. But
Rupert Spencer, from his position at the front of the group,
saw everything with total clarity. He saw the velvet case
empty atop its marble column; he saw the ruby vanished;
the room undisturbed; and he saw, fluttering gently under
the ceiling, translucent against the lights, a single scarlet
butterfly.

CHAPTER ELEVEN

The Ace of Spades

When I arrived at the Blenheim Hotel that evening, shortly after the Great Salmanazar had walked off stage, the scenes that greeted me spoke in equal measures of confusion, consternation, and despair. Mrs. Hudson had sent me to the Blenheim with a message for Sir John Plaskett, and I had jumped at the chance of returning to see for myself a second time the secret fire of the Malabar Rose. But as I approached the hotel, hunched and muffled against the snowstorm, I became aware that ahead of me a group of ladies and gentlemen in furs and frock coats were being herded from the building and out into the blizzard. A single uniformed officer was endeavouring to calm them.

"Inspector's orders, me lady," he shouted over the blast. "A security matter. Nothing to worry about."

"But, Constable, we still haven't seen the ruby!" Her words were almost swept away in the snow.

"Another time, ma'am. There's a little matter we have to sort out tonight. Just routine."

While the constable was fully occupied making himself heard, I seized the opportunity to slip past the melee of top hats and tiaras, into the warmth beyond. But when I got there and stood in the hotel's great foyer, I realised at once that whatever was going on, it was certainly very far from routine. There seemed to be policemen everywhere, running in different directions or forming into groups and looking grave. Mixed amongst them were members of the hotel staff, all of them talking at once: waiters gesticulating, porters shrugging, pageboys pulling faces, and the hotel manager quite literally tearing at his hair while a ring of chamber-maids sought to comfort him with handkerchiefs. Slipping unnoticed through this confusion, I was able to make my way as far as the Satin Rooms before anyone tried to call me back. There, a grim-faced officer found me standing wide-eyed and amazed amid the half-drunk glasses of champagne, the melancholy wreckage of an abandoned evening.

"Sorry, miss," he told me briskly, "no one's allowed in here. All guests are to go to their rooms or else to leave the building. There a sergeant on the door will take your name and address."

"But I have a message for Sir John," I told him, and seeing that this alone might not be sufficient to move him, added quickly, "It's of the utmost importance. It's about . . ." I took a guess. "It's about a sighting of the Malabar Rose."

He raised his eyebrows at that and opened his eyes wide. "Better go straight through, miss. They'll be pleased to see you."

I had expected to discover the inner chamber in the same sort of disorder that had prevailed outside, but instead I found the opposite. There were but five people in the room when I entered and, where I had anticipated chaos and con-fusion, there was only a sombre seriousness and grave, unsmiling faces. The first person I noticed was Sir John, the Hero of Ishtabad, who suddenly seemed very far removed from the scene of his great victories. His face was drawn and pale, and he was pacing to and fro in the centre of the room. Behind him, watching him as he walked, stood Dr. Watson and Inspector Lestrade, both clearly distraught but at a loss for anything to say or do. These three formed a triangle, at the centre of which stood the marble column and the empty velvet case where the Malabar Rose should have been. Compared with the taut, tense figures of these three men, the positions adopted by the remaining pair seemed noticeably bizarre. To the right-hand side of the room, Sherlock Holmes was crouching on his knees and examining the skirting board with a magnifying glass; while to the left, Rupert Spencer was standing with his back to everyone else, his nose in the air, peering up at something on the ceiling. I could think of no reason to account for either activity.

"As I see it," Sir John was saying, "since the stone isn't here, it must now be somewhere else. And dammit! If it's somewhere else, then it must have passed through solid walls!"

All five of them turned when they saw me come in, and Mr. Holmes, who was just getting to his feet, addressed me with a frown.

"Yes, Flotsam? What brings you back here at this unfortunate moment?"

"I have a question, sir, from Mrs. Hudson. She wants to ask—"

"Really! I'm afraid, Flotsam, that we simply have no time to attend to domestic arrangements just now. You must tell Mrs. Hudson to expect us when she sees us. There is no need for her to wait up."

"Yes, sir, but—" I would have explained my errand more

clearly but at that moment Sir John let out a sudden exclamation.

"Of course!" He paused in his pacing and looked up at the ceiling. "Sabotage! It could have been dissolved with acid! An enemy agent on the roof could drip acid through the skylight. Think how much the French or the Russians would love to see our embarrassment!"

Inspector Lestrade, who had allowed a flicker of hope to appear in his face, sank back into his previous gloom.

"You forget, sir. The men on the roof. A dozen of them."

"Ah, yes." Sir John drooped visibly. "A conspiracy between them, perhaps?"

"The men are from different forces, sir, chosen at random. Complete strangers to each other."

"Of course." Sir John looked suitably glum again. "Then there can be no explanation short of sorcery."

At that word, we all looked up. As the meaning of what he had just said dawned on him, Sir John's face suddenly suffused with hope. "By God, I don't know how he's done it, but at least we know who to question. This Salmanazar man, we must arrest him at once, Lestrade!"

Before Inspector Lestrade could reply, Mr. Holmes surprised us all by chuckling dryly.

"Think again, Sir John. In the entire country there can surely be no man safer from arrest than our conjurer friend. There is a whole theatre of witnesses who can testify that he was on stage for the entire evening. And worse than that, at the moment when these rooms were being opened, the Great Salmanazar was nailed in a coffin and suspended from a chain in full view of at least a thousand people."

A long pause followed this observation as its implications sunk in. But Sir John was not to be deterred.

"Even so, Lestrade," he continued, "there is too much coincidence. Perhaps he doesn't perform the crimes himself. Perhaps he has accomplices in his retinue. Anyone in his company is a suspect. You must interrogate them all! And in the meantime, their leader must be arrested."

Inspector Lestrade nodded but looked strangely dubious. However, he was spared the obligation of replying when Rupert Spencer gave a sudden exclamation. We all turned to him and found him looking down and smiling with tremendous satisfaction. Slowly and steadily he held out his hand towards us, and I saw that resting softly on the palm was a single red butterfly.

"Of course!" Dr. Watson exclaimed. "I'd forgotten all about that butterfly. Now how the devil did that get in here?"

It seemed that no one had an answer to that, but the smile persisted on Mr. Spencer's face.

"I can't tell you how this comes to be here, gentlemen, but I can tell you what sort of butterfly it is. I *thought* the name was familiar. This butterfly is *Atrophaneura pandiyana*. They're found in the southeast of India. In English this species of butterfly is called a *Malabar Rose*."

Sir John groaned and rubbed his eyes with the ball of his hand. "Like a blasted fairy tale! A precious stone turned into a butterfly."

"Precisely," agreed Mr. Spencer. "As if at the wave of a wand."

A long silence followed, and during it Dr. Watson noticed for the first time that I hadn't left the room.

"Still here, Flotsam? I think perhaps you should be getting back. Mrs. Hudson will be getting worried about you."

"But, sir, I have a message from Mrs. Hudson for you." I produced a folded scrap of paper and passed it to him. He flipped the paper open and read it aloud.

"'Sir, I have an urgent question for you and I would be

grateful if you could return Flotsam with the answer. I should be greatly obliged if you could ask Sir John exactly how the entrance hall of his house in Randolph Place is currently furnished?'"

Sir John's face flushed with anger as he heard this, although I noticed that Mr. Holmes, Dr. Watson, and Rupert Spencer all seemed to have pricked up their ears.

"Randolph Place, eh?" mumbled Dr. Watson.

"The entrance hall furniture . . ." Mr. Holmes pondered.

"I wonder what she means?" muttered Mr. Spencer, thoughtfully.

"It means the woman's mad!" declared Sir John, seizing the note and tearing it into pieces. "Bothering me with such nonsense at a time like this!" He turned to me. "That is all, girl. Now run along."

"But, sir, there's one other thing. Something I noticed just before I came in."

"Yes, what is it?"

"This had been pushed under one of the champagne glasses, sir. Perhaps I should show you exactly where I found it—"

"But what *is* it?"

"It's a playing card, sir. Just an ordinary playing card, I think, except that it's an ace of spades, and the ace has got a great big cross through it."

THE Great Salmanazar was placed under a sort of house arrest later that night. His arrest was not an official one because of the number of witnesses to his whereabouts at the time when the stone was stolen. Nevertheless, he was made to understand by Inspector Lestrade that any attempt to leave his suite of rooms at Brown's Hotel would be regarded as an attempt to flee the country. Inquiries by Lestrade's men had proved that the playing card I found in the Satin Rooms was the one selected during the Great Salmanazar's show. The gentleman who selected it turned out to be a retired dentist from Cheam who had told his wife that he was attending a dinner of Dentists For Temperance. Although anxious that his name would not appear in the *Dental Times* or the *Cheam Parish Gazette,* he was sufficiently clear minded to be sure that the mark on the card was his.

This was enough for Lestrade, who took the decision to confine the magician to his quarters. As a precaution, similar steps were taken against Lola Del Fuego, and the rest of the Great Salmanazar's entourage was rounded up and confined to the Regal Theatre under police guard. The pantomime that was due to be staged there was cancelled "due to unforeseen circumstances." Meanwhile, a statement by Sir John to the newspapers explained that the viewing of the Malabar Rose had been postponed while Scotland Yard investigated "certain foreign elements" believed to pose a threat to its safety. The statement was reassuring in its tone, but it remained to be seen if the British public would be easily reassured.

Inspector Lestrade, who had appeared at first quite crushed by the blow that had befallen him, became transformed at the thought of decisive action and was soon directing investigations with the energy of a desert dervish: warnings were sent to all ports; policemen were recalled from their holidays; all known receivers of stolen jewellery were to be hauled in for questioning so as to take them out of circulation; honest jewellers across the Home Counties were roused in the early hours and warned to be alert to anything unusual; a man from the Natural History Museum was dragged from his bed to supply a list of any lepidopterists who might keep live specimens of the Malabar Rose butterfly; and finally, two constables were placed at the door of the chamber from which the ruby had vanished, to ensure that nothing would be touched prior to a further examination the following day.

If the events of the night had one happy outcome for me, it was that they appeared finally to have persuaded Mrs. Hudson to take an interest in the Malabar Rose. For when Dr. Watson, Mr. Holmes, and myself returned to Baker Street at half past four in the morning, I found her wide awake and eager to hear every detail I could recall. She had kept the fires burning throughout the house in anticipation of our return, and there was something to lift the spirits of all three of us in the sight of our windows glowing orange over the snow-lined street. I felt Mr. Holmes' shoulders straighten a little at the sight, and Dr. Watson mumbled something about joy in the morning.

"Indeed, my friend. An apt observation. This engagement may be lost, but the battle is far from over. Up to now this has been all about setting guards, but now it becomes a matter of pure reason, Watson! Pure reason! And I think it can safely be said that no greater practitioner of that activity can be found than here in Baker Street. Now come, let us see what restoratives the excellent Mrs. Hudson has prepared for us."

In that murky December dawn, the two gentlemen went to their beds comforted by hot buttered rum and by sheets that had been warmed for an hour or more in front of a blazing fire. For me, there was the comfort of the warm, dark kitchen, so safe and orderly that you felt no magic, however extraordinary, could ever disturb its placid calm. Guided by Mrs. Hudson's promptings, I recounted everything I could remember about events that night, until my eyes became heavy, and the housekeeper, tutting at herself for her thoughtlessness, wrapped me in a blanket and half-carried me to my bed.

There, however, sleep seemed to abandon me. From where I lay, I could see the shadows from the street falling across the kitchen floor. Just the ordinary shadows, but they made me restless. I found myself remembering the empty velvet case where the ruby should have been, and then my own empty purse, now bereft of the savings that had once been special to me. Eventually, I rose and slipped quietly to the kitchen window. Outside, the street lay motionless under the snow. No one signalled. No one called. No figure lurked there, waiting for me.

After that, I slept.

AT eleven o'clock the following morning, Mrs. Hudson and I were surprised by a knock on the kitchen door and the appearance of Mr. Holmes in a rather splendid silk dressing gown, paisley-patterned pyjamas, and a pair of stout, woollen rugby socks.

"Mrs. Hudson," he commenced, "I wonder if I might join you for a few moments. I imagine you are not unaware of events last night. I'm sure young Flotsam has informed you of the salient points."

"She has, sir." Mrs. Hudson, without apparently pausing in her polishing of Dr. Watson's boots, succeeded in ushering Mr. Holmes into the chair by the fire and in indicating with a nod that I was to bring him a bottle of his favourite brown ale.

"Mrs. Hudson, I have not forgotten that in the past your powers of observation have proven unusually acute for one of your sex, and I wondered if you would be prepared to give me your own observations on last night's performance at the Regal Theatre. I witnessed some of it for myself, and for the rest I have read the police reports. But perhaps you might have noticed something they did not."

Mrs. Hudson's response to this was surprisingly even-tempered. She simply put down the boot she was polishing, wiped her hands on her apron, and seated herself opposite Mr. Holmes.

"Very well, sir. I hope I can be of some help. And if Flotsam here will join us, she can correct me if I leave anything out."

With that simple introduction, the housekeeper proceeded to describe the performance of the Great Salmanazar in remarkable detail. From time to time, Mr. Holmes would ask a question but mostly he listened in silence, sipping his beer and running the tip of his tongue over his lips as if in great thought. When Mrs. Hudson came to the part of the evening when the Great Salmanazar was being nailed into the coffin, the great detective leaned forward eagerly, and remained in that pose until the narrative was concluded.

"So tell me, Mrs. Hudson," he began, after at least a minute of silent musing, "you feel this Salmanazar was definitely *inside* the case when it was hoisted into the air?"

"Yes, sir."

The kitchen was bright that morning, much brighter than usual because of the snow that lay outside. Nevertheless, a shadow appeared to have fallen over Mr. Holmes' face. He looked gaunt and troubled.

"That is the opinion of everyone who witnessed it, Mrs. Hudson. And I have no doubt you are right. But it would be convenient to believe otherwise, to believe that by some magic power he really had taken wings and transplanted himself into the Blenheim Hotel."

"Then you do not believe that, sir?"

He snorted with a mixture of derision and disdain. "Most definitely not! The facts of this case are clear. The Great Salmanazar never left the theatre. Neither he nor anyone else entered the room where the Malabar Rose was on display after the door was secured. The Malabar Rose did not evaporate into thin air, nor did it turn into a butterfly. No one but an idiot would believe such nonsense!"

"I say, Holmes, *there* you are!" Dr. Watson had appeared at the kitchen door, tousled and a little bleary-eyed, his army greatcoat pulled on over his nightclothes. "Thought you might have gone out."

"Not at all, Watson. I am hearing Mrs. Hudson's account of last night's flummery."

The doctor, yawning prodigiously, made his way to the fire and sank down into the seat vacated by Mrs. Hudson, who had risen and was beginning to make tea.

"I say, Holmes," he began a little plaintively, "I couldn't help but overhear. If you really think this chappie was in the theatre all the time, then how did he magic away the ruby from under our noses?"

"Ah, Watson! So sure of the culprit! So unwilling to think ill of those around you!"

"Eh? Sorry, Holmes, not sure I understand. Think ill of whom?"

"Well, Watson, my ideas are not yet formed, but let me ask you this. Did anyone break into the Satin Rooms by force last night?"

"Definitely not, Holmes."

"And did anyone achieve such an entry by guile?"

"You mean, sneak past us? Don't think so, Holmes. Can't see how they could have done it."

"In fact, everything we know, and all the evidence available to us, says that nobody entered the room after the last door was sealed?"

"I suppose that's right, Holmes, yes."

"In that case, Watson, are we not forced to conclude that the Malabar Rose left the room *before* the door was locked behind us?"

"Eh? Before? Can't have happened, Holmes. We were all there. Saw the wretched thing being put on display."

"But there came a point when you turned your back and left the room, did there not?"

"There did."

"And did you look back after that?"

"Can't say I did, Holmes."

"There were people who left the room after you?"

Dr. Watson scratched his head. "Yes, there must have been. Yourself. Mr. Spencer. Miss Peters. Flottie. And Inspector Lestrade."

The great detective turned to me. "Do you agree with that, Flotsam?"

I coughed politely. "I think perhaps Inspector Lestrade and I were in front of you, sir."

Dr. Watson looked perplexed. "Really, Flottie? Well, if you say so . . ."

"So exactly how do *you* remember it, Flotsam?" Mr. Holmes inquired.

"Miss Peters was before me, sir. But Sir John and Mr. Bushy and Mr. Choudrey, they were all behind me."

"No, no, Flotsam," the doctor exclaimed. "I'm sure that's wrong. I'm pretty sure the last ones to step away from the ruby were Lestrade, Miss Peters, and the Earl of Brabham."

"You see, Watson?" Mr. Holmes was smiling broadly. "Every person who was there will remember it slightly differently. But did you actually look back and see that the ruby was in place at the moment just before the door was locked?"

"No, Holmes, I can't say that I did."

"So as far as you know, it's possible that the last person to leave the Malabar Rose's column could have slipped it into their pocket."

"Certainly not, Holmes! I don't believe that for one moment!"

"But you cannot swear they did not."

"Well, not swear it, exactly, but . . ."

"My point precisely. What about you, Flotsam?"

"No, sir."

"You mean you also cannot be sure it was not stolen before that moment?"

"No, sir. I mean that I'm certain the Malabar Rose was there as the door was locked. I remember looking back and admiring it."

"Ah." The detective looked a trifle nonplussed for a moment, but rallied gamely. "Of course, that theory was merely a piece of idle speculation, but no doubt some similar simple explanation will exist. It is merely a matter of finding it."

Mrs. Hudson interrupted this demonstration of analytical thought by placing in front of her employer a large tea tray and two plates of generously buttered toast. "I'm sure that's true, sir. Now, I fear Flotsam and I have an urgent errand to run this morning, so I'll serve breakfast in the study in half an hour, if that's convenient."

"As you please, Mrs. Hudson," replied Mr. Holmes carelessly, polishing off a thick slice of toast with great relish, "though I have little need for physical sustenance at a time such as this. However, before you rush off on whatever domestic matters require your attention, I have one further question to ask you."

"Yes, sir?"

"It's about the performance of the Great Salmanazar. You say you are certain that he was physically present inside the suspended crate for the duration of the Spanish woman's dance."

"Yes, sir."

"Then how do you explain the playing cards reappearing in the gentlemen's wallets? And how did the ace of spades come to be found just outside the room from which the Malabar Rose was stolen?"

Mrs. Hudson had been busy preparing to go out, but the

question made her pause. To my surprise, it was me she was looking at, not Sherlock Holmes.

"Well, you see, sir," she began a little hesitantly, turning slowly to face her questioner, "the secret of that trick is very simple indeed. The cards the gentlemen signed never reached the illusionist's pocket. Each of those four gentlemen was offered a pack containing only *one* denomination of card, so the Great Salmanazar knew exactly which card each of them had selected. Then, when the gentlemen had marked their cards, the page boys who carried the packs were responsible for slipping the marked cards back into their wallets *before* they returned to the stage."

"But how could they do that, Mrs. H?" Dr. Watson puzzled. "Surely the audience would have noticed even if the gentlemen themselves did not."

"No, sir. We were all being distracted by events on stage. And what if those boys in their smart uniforms had been recruited from the ranks of our finest pickpockets? It would be as easy for them to remove and return a wallet as it would for you to light that pipe."

"I see . . ." Mr. Holmes was nodding thoughtfully. "So the cards returned to the illusionist were not the signed ones?"

"Of course not, sir."

Dr. Watson appeared less than convinced. "But what about the ace of spades, Mrs. Hudson? How did that come to miss its mark? It was a signal blunder for it to be dropped so near the scene of the crime!"

"On the contrary, sir. That is the most elegant part of it. By charging one of his boys to slip the card unnoticed into the Blenheim Hotel, the Great Salmanazar has rather cleverly drawn attention to himself, and has no doubt diverted the police from the real solution of the puzzle."

Mr. Holmes stroked his chin and thought for a moment. "Your theory appears to fit the facts, Mrs. Hudson, but sadly it is pure speculation. You cannot be certain that any part of it is true."

"Only one part of it, sir," and here the housekeeper gave me another swift glance, a glance of such solicitude that I understood before she said another word what it was that I was about to hear.

"You see," she went on, and I knew her words were directed at me, "I had a very good look at the page boy who came closest to us. I was right by the aisle, so I could see him a good deal better than most people. There can be no doubt, sir. The boy in question is a known thief."

She turned to me then, her face full of feeling.

"Your description was an excellent one, Flottie. In the whole of my life, I have never seen such remarkable blue eyes."

CHAPTER TWELVE

The Unexpected Arsonist

When I thought of Blue, it wasn't the loss of my money that hurt, although that small sum was all I had ever saved, and the knowledge of its existence had often comforted me on nights when memories of my former destitution slipped into my dreams. No, far worse than the pecuniary loss was the hurt at being so deceived, and the shame and anger at my own stupidity. I had trusted him, that boy with blue eyes, and he had cheated me. I had trusted him for no proper reason, only because once a small child had pressed close to me; because once I had known a boy who was blameless. Perhaps I had trusted him because I could still remember that picture of a mother who wasn't my own. How he must have mocked me for all that sentimental kindness! How he must scorn those people so careless with their money and so foolish in their feelings! That day I followed Mrs. Hudson down the snow-mantled streets in silence, these thoughts twisting inside me and turning a bright morning dark with unhappiness.

So occupied was I with my own inner musings that I little cared where Mrs. Hudson led me, and barely gave a thought to the purpose of our journey. My companion sought neither to comfort nor distract me, content instead to let my thoughts wander where they would. It was not until she came to a halt on a busy street corner that I thought to look around at where our path had led. I found to my surprise that we had already come as far as Piccadilly, and that Mrs. Hudson had stopped opposite the stately entrance hall of the Blenheim Hotel.

The two policemen on duty at its entrance were the only visible indication of the previous night's disturbances, and the crowds that thronged the streets were too concerned with safe navigation of the treacherous pavements to show any curiosity at their presence. Mrs. Hudson drew me close to her and placed her hand on my shoulder.

"You're a brave young woman, Flotsam. I know this morning's news has been a blow. But I fear we need to keep our wits about us if the Malabar Rose is to be returned swiftly to safekeeping. Now, I'm quite curious to see for myself the room where the ruby was put on display. Do you think you can show me?"

"Yes, ma'am. But I'm afraid the rooms are guarded now, and there are orders to let no one go in until Inspector Lestrade has examined them again."

Mrs. Hudson nodded at this, but I noticed that her eyebrows twitched as if with a flicker of amusement.

"Well, let's see what can be done, shall we, Flottie? I daresay we'll find a way."

The calm façade of the Blenheim Hotel proved wildly deceptive, for inside its grand lobby, a considerable proportion of the previous night's chaos remained. Puzzled guests were gathered in small groups around leather armchairs, answering questions put to them by perspiring police officers. At the reception desk, a selection of the more irate were pressing for answers to a variety of questions, all posed simultaneously and at escalating levels of loudness. Daunted by the ferocity of these questions, a young man with red hair and whiskers was endeavouring to redirect their ire by flapping his arms plaintively in the direction of any policeman who happened to pass.

Aided by this general disorder, it was a simple thing to steer Mrs. Hudson through the crowd and to lead her up the grand staircase without anyone paying us the slightest attention. From the top of the staircase, a wide corridor led to the Satin Rooms, and at its end we paused, aware of the sentries placed ahead of us.

"Flotsam, am I right in thinking that the door guarded by those two constables leads to the room in question?"

"Yes, ma'am. That's the door to the inner chamber. There are three other doors, but those have all been boarded up."

"And those two policemen are the only ones on duty?"

"There are two more patrolling, ma'am. And then there's the pair on the stairs we've just passed. And all the ones down in the lobby, too."

"I see." Mrs. Hudson was regarding the two constables thoughtfully. "Tell me, Flottie, have you ever noticed what men do when a fire breaks out?"

"A fire, ma'am?" It seemed a peculiarly random question.

"Yes, Flotsam. A big fire. One that seems likely to get out of hand."

"I suppose they do the sensible thing, ma'am."

"And what would that be?"

"Move anything valuable that may otherwise get caught in the blaze, and then get some proper help in fighting the fire."

"Yes, you might think so, Flotsam. That would be eminently sensible. The truth, however, is rather different."

"Ma'am?"

Mrs. Hudson was carrying with her a particularly large bag, and now she reached into its depths and produced a box of matches. "I think a demonstration is in order. You see those curtains at the top of the staircase?"

"Yes, ma'am."

"Well, Flotsam, when I give the nod, I want you to set them alight."

"Ma'am!" I gasped. "Not really! I can't!"

"I don't think anyone is looking, Flottie. They're all far too busy. Now, when you're sure the fabric is truly ablaze, you need to scurry away into the crowd downstairs and watch what happens."

I looked at her and waited for her to smile at her own joke. I even began to smile for her. But her face was serious, and she seemed to be calculating the distance between the curtains and the nearest policeman.

It says a great deal for the force of Mrs. Hudson's personality, and even more for the trust I placed in her, that I was prepared in the end to do as she asked. Nevertheless, it was with a fluttering heart and slightly shaking hands that I took up my position by the heavy drapes that were my target. At first it seemed impossible that my presence there would not excite suspicion, that I would not immediately become the focus of every eye in the hotel. But the moments passed and no notice was taken of me, so, at a sign from Mrs. Hudson, I bent to my task.

The fire caught slowly at first, but the flames were silent, and I found I had ample time to slip discreetly down the stairs before the blaze was noticed. In fact, even when I had reached the crowd below and could see the flames licking dramatically up the curtains, no one seemed to be aware of the danger. In the end, it was a throaty cry of "Fire!" from a familiar voice upstairs that gave the alarm.

The effect of the cry on those around me was dramatic.

While the women grasped for their bags, every man in the room rose to his feet and, as if with one mind, rushed towards the fire. Although some moved quicker than others, in a few seconds every man in the place was heading for the stairs, some crying out, some knocking over tables, some removing their jackets to beat at the flames, others with no firmer plan than to shout their advice as loudly as possible to the greatest number of people. However, despite the urgency of the men downstairs, all were beaten to it by the four policemen stationed near the Satin Rooms. All four came rushing down the corridor and appeared at the top of the stairs together, where they proceeded to leap around the burning curtains in a paroxysm of excitement. They were quickly joined by their colleagues from the stairs and, in only a few seconds more, the volunteers from the hotel lobby began to swell their numbers. The press of excited people rapidly became so thick that it was hard to make out the fire at all, and the air seemed a good deal thicker with their shouts than it was with smoke.

Despite the total lack of any coherent plan, the frantic flapping of jackets eventually began to have some effect, although at least three garments ended up adding to the general conflagration. In the end someone thought to haul the curtains from the wall, and a great many feet set about stamping on the smouldering remains with energetic satisfaction. As they did so, I saw Mrs. Hudson edge past the assembled company and come placidly down the stairs, so very unremarkable and so utterly ordinary that I was probably the only person present to notice she was there.

"So, Flotsam," she chuckled on joining me by the main door, "do you feel that demonstration has helped to answer my question?"

"You mean men always do that when there's a fire, ma'am? Just rush around and get in the way?"

"Well, perhaps not *all* men. But a great many of them,

and on most occasions. Never underestimate the masculine urge to be seen to be *doing,* Flotsam. Even the ones who are really better suited to thinking will suddenly insist on showing off. Usually not very well. Now, some fresh air, I think."

We pushed our way out into the street. The sun was still bright on the snow, but our breath was white in front of us.

"So did you manage to see the Satin Rooms, ma'am?"

"Oh, yes, Flotsam. There was nothing to stop me once the constables had rushed off."

"And what did you find?"

Her eyebrows trembled a little at the question, but her voice was as steady as always when she replied.

"The inner chamber was exactly as you described it, Flotsam, and exactly as I expected. And yet I think I've found something there that the gentlemen should know about. If Mr. Holmes and his colleagues had cleaned as many rooms as I have, they would perhaps look at the contents of a room in a rather different way." She changed her bag from one hand to another and adjusted her muffler. "But before I do, I am only too aware that Sir John never gave you an answer to my question about the furniture in his hallway. So our next stop, Flotsam, is Randolph Place, to see for ourselves just how his hallway is furnished."

In the event, when we arrived in Randolph Square, Mrs. Hudson left me holding her bag at the foot of the steps while she approached Sir John's bright red front door and knocked smartly. From where I stood I could see the door opened by a grey-haired butler who, after a few words from Mrs. Hudson, seemed to brighten markedly and beckon her inside. When she emerged a few minutes later, it was with a satisfied smile on her face and with the suspicion of a wink in my direction.

"Come, Flotsam. Things are taking shape very nicely. Sir

John Plaskett's butler turns out to be the uncle of a young girl I was once in service with. He's a nice old man, and very eager to help, but he's afraid his memory isn't what it was. Apparently, there was a night before Christmas when he left a downstairs window unlatched, and the incident is clearly playing on his mind."

"And the furniture, ma'am?"

"Just as I had anticipated, Flottie. Very sparse. No large items, only a small table and a couple of small chests."

"But, ma'am, I really don't understand why that matters. I don't know what it means. In fact, I don't know what *any* of this means. Why *are* you interested in Sir John's furniture?"

At that, Mrs. Hudson pulled up sharply and looked at me, understanding dawning in her face.

"My apologies, Flotsam," she said softly. "You make me realise how remiss I have been these last few days. I have been keeping things to myself and leaving you to draw your own conclusions."

"I'm sure you mustn't blame yourself, ma'am. I know how busy you've been lately, especially with Christmas and everything." I paused there, a little embarrassed. "It's just that I'm not sure I've drawn *any* conclusions about anything just yet. I've no idea why we're interested in Sir John's house. I don't know how the Malabar Rose disappeared. And I've no idea why you're so interested in that man Mr. Phillimore who disappeared in Ealing."

"Ah, yes! Mr. Phillimore." The housekeeper nodded approvingly. "We have been very lucky there, Flottie. Who would ever have connected his disappearance with the ruby, eh? If Mrs. Smithers hadn't brought her problem to us, we'd never even have heard of him. And if that was the case, then we'd probably have no idea where the ruby is at all."

"But *do* we have any idea where the ruby is, ma'am?"

She squeezed my hand then, and her voice was full of reassurance. "I promise you, Flotsam, the Malabar Rose is in very safe hands. But there still remains out there a man who's determined to steal it. A man driven forward by the greatest force of all."

I pondered that for a moment. What force did she mean? Hunger for power? For wealth? For influence?

Mrs. Hudson seemed to read my thoughts. "No, Flottie. None of those. Something much greater." She squeezed my hand again. "Love, Flotsam. That is the greatest force, the most powerful of them all. And that is the force we face now. The gentleman we seek is in love."

FOR the rest of the journey home, Mrs. Hudson entertained me with various observations that she hoped might prompt me to form some conclusions of my own. As she talked, the bright sunshine of the morning faded around us and gave way to the grey drudgery of a winter afternoon. Above us, dark clouds were building from the east, trapping beneath them the city's exhalations of soot and smoke. This dark breath flecked the air with black, and the cheeks of every passerby were quickly smeared, as if by the city's dark fingerprints. Soon the white cape of the night before had become the grey overcoat of a malevolent day. And in the east the wind was rising. It would be another hard night. Mrs. Hudson, however, refused to be intimidated by the weather.

"So, Flotsam, what's the most significant thing we know about Mr. Phillimore?"

"He disappeared, ma'am."

"He certainly did. There's been quite a lot of disappearing going on these last few days. But Mr. Phillimore has been disappearing from time to time for a while now, hasn't he?"

"You mean his trips to Broadstairs, ma'am?"

"That's right. Those mysterious trips to Broadstairs. For

three years there has been a fascinating regularity to those little trips of his. And other things have been happening at regular intervals, too."

"Jewel thefts, ma'am. And magic shows."

"And nothing in the great scheme of things to connect Mr. Phillimore with either. But suddenly something has changed. Mr. Phillimore has disappeared. Now what has changed recently, Flottie?"

I thought hard. "You mean before he disappeared, ma'am?"

"Before or shortly after. For instance, what has changed about the Great Salmanazar's shows?"

"I don't know, ma'am. They say his tricks get better and better. And of course now he has Lola Del Fuego performing with him, and that means even bigger crowds."

"Ah, yes. In Paris and Berlin, his last two shows, he performs with the famous Lola. And a little later a humble clerk in Ealing disappears."

"But, ma'am, there's *nothing* to connect those two things. There's nothing to connect him to the Great Salmanazar's show at all."

"The card for Lola's show found in his room, Flottie?"

"Lots of men must have taken those home, ma'am."

"The fact that Miss Lola agreed to see us when we mentioned Phillimore's name?"

"Perhaps she really *was* just scared because you'd mentioned the police."

"The fact that both Mr. Phillimore and the Great Salmanazar appear able to vanish into thin air?"

"I'm sure there's an explanation for both those things, ma'am."

A gust of cold wind tugged at Mrs. Hudson's collar, and she pulled her coat closer together at the neck.

"Very well, Flotsam, if none of those arguments persuade

you, I shall have to draw your attention to Mr. Phillimore's socks."

"His socks, ma'am?"

"If you remember, he kept them in a drawer close to his bed. I took a very close look at them."

I dimly remembered Mr. Phillimore's sock drawer and its collection of little round bundles crammed closely together.

"What about his socks, ma'am?"

"Their colour, Flotsam. They were all very muted shades, very like a clerk's socks should be. But for one pair. A pair of pale lilac socks that leapt out at me straightaway. Not just because they were lilac, you understand, but also because they were made of very fine silk. They were quite a cut above anything else in that drawer. Have you seen many men in lilac socks, Flottie?"

I screwed up my eyes and tried to recall. "Not that I remember, ma'am."

"No, they haven't really been worn over here. But in Paris last summer they were considered the very height of fashion. Every gentleman was wearing them." She shook her head sadly. "Though what a room full of men in lilac socks must have looked like is anyone's guess. Now, what do we know about Mr. Phillimore's shopping habits?"

"He didn't care much about his clothes, ma'am. He just bought what he needed where he happened to be."

"Precisely. So where would he be when he bought those socks?"

I hesitated. "Well, I suppose he *might* have been in Paris."

"And not just in Paris. In a very grand part of Paris. Those were very fine socks. Now, are we to suppose he had merely run short of socks? Well, that's possible. But then we have to consider the necktie . . ."

"The *necktie,* ma'am?"

"At the back of his wardrobe, almost as though he'd pushed it out of sight deliberately. It was quite different from all his others. And he'd left the label on it. 'Philippe Sagars, Paris.' A very expensive piece of neckwear, Flottie. Now, I can't believe he had forgotten to pack both socks *and* ties. No, I think something happened to him in Paris to make him go out and buy expensive new clothes."

My mind raced. "A disguise, ma'am? Perhaps he was on the run! Perhaps he dressed up to make his escape?"

The housekeeper tutted while we paused to cross the road. "Really, Flottie, a moment ago you maintained he was innocently in Broadstairs. Now you have him pursued through Paris by who knows what manner of ruffians. No, I think the explanation is a little more commonplace than that. I've always found there is one thing more than any other that drives unfashionable men suddenly to buy new clothes, Flottie."

This time I understood without prompting. "I see, ma'am. You mean love again."

"That's right, Flottie, that's exactly what I was thinking. Mr. Phillimore was in Paris and in love."

"But, ma'am, that's all just *speculation.* Mr. Holmes would laugh at us if he heard all that."

"Of course he would, Flotsam. And he'd be right. But for one more thing."

"And what's that, ma'am?"

"It was just an idea I had one day when I happened to be passing down here."

She stopped and pointed. We were halfway down a small alleyway that provided a shortcut through towards Baker Street. The walls of the alley had been covered with layer upon layer of posters and advertisements, each new bill pasted on top of its predecessors, most of them now weathered and peeling. The poster Mrs. Hudson was pointing at was some months old and torn in places, and stained dark by the rain and the black London fog. But for all that, it was still clearly legible.

Mr. John Grovsner Johnson
presents
A Spectacular Show
A Variety of Famous Acts
including
The spectacular, the amazing,
THE BRINDISI BROTHERS!
Gravity-defying Acrobats

THE REMARKABLE CYCLING BUTLER!

GRIMALDI'S HUMAN AUTOMATONS!

The famous voice of
SALLY SHYE, THE SHOREDITCH NIGHTINGALE!

Conrad Phelps, Conortionist
The Rubber Man of Bow Bells!

A freak of nature!
Spectacled Jack the Memory Man!

Fido the Fiddling Hound!

And much, much more!

THE WINDMILL ON THE GREEN
June 4th–29th

I read it all three times but to my disappointment was seized by no sudden revelation.

"As I say," Mrs. Hudson went on, "that poster gave me an idea of why James Phillimore was in Paris." I noticed that as she spoke her eyes seemed to be locked on something a long way away, and her face was full of thought. "Yes, indeed. It all fits. Think about it, Flotsam, and if you need a clue, ask yourself this: Just how did the Great Salmanazar escape from that coffin when we know beyond all doubt that it had been properly nailed down and then chained up tightly *from the outside*?"

CHAPTER THIRTEEN

Surprises at the Mermaid

We returned to Baker Street to find the familiar rooms plunged into an unwonted gloom. Dr. Watson had retired to his room with a headache and the stated intent of cataloguing his collection of unusual Oriental artworks. Mr. Holmes had taken up his violin and was filling the house with music of the most exquisite melancholy, music that made me think of silent pools in dark and distant forests. In our absence, neither gentleman had thought to light the lamps or throw any coals on the fire, even though the afternoon was a cold one and the rooms were full of shadow. On realising this, Mrs. Hudson tutted loudly and pulled on her apron.

"Follow me, Flotsam," she growled beneath gritted teeth, and I followed in her wake as she bustled into the study.

"Now, sir," she exclaimed as the startled detective broke off from his playing. "You two gentlemen have eaten none of the luncheon I laid out for you—the shutters, Flotsam—and

you've let the fire go quite out. I can't see that being cold
and hungry and surrounded by darkness—the lamps, Flottie, if you will—is going to help either of you solve any mysteries. Rather than catching chills here, I'm sure you'd be
better off out and about, interrogating villains or something."

As I saw to the lamps, she dropped nimbly to her knees and
began to breathe some life into the dying fire. Mrs. Hudson
had the sort of lungs that rendered bellows redundant.

"Really, Mrs. Hudson!" Mr. Holmes countered weakly, "I
cannot permit such a disturbance! For those who are
strangers to the ways of pure reason it may be hard to understand, but I assure you that the solution to our problem
lies in cerebral agility, not in the mundane bullying of witnesses that Inspector Lestrade considers so vital."

"I daresay pure reason will not be hampered by a cold
mutton chop, sir. Nor will it be fatigued by a bit of lamp-
light or a touch of warmth. Now, if you don't mind, sir . . ."

And with magnificent disregard for the detective's objec-
tions, she continued to blow life into the fire.

The cessation of the violin very quickly alerted Dr. Watson to a change in the prevailing mood, and in only a few
moments he appeared from his bedroom. The sight that
greeted him evidently cheered him greatly.

"Did you mention a mutton chop, Mrs. H?" he asked
hopefully.

"I did, sir. On the table by the window." She straightened
up and wiped her hands on her apron. "And you'll find a
portion of curried goose there, too, should you fancy it."

"Splendid, Mrs. H!" Dr. Watson advanced to where
lunch had been laid and began to load his plate while Mrs.
Hudson and I continued to make the place as comfortable
and welcoming as possible. Mr. Holmes watched his friend
with some dismay.

"Tell me, Watson, can you really eat so heartily when faced with such a crisis in our affairs?"

There was a note of suffering in his tone that clearly touched Mrs. Hudson, for she paused in her tidying.

"Don't despair, sir," she said, and although her tone was bright and encouraging, I recognised a certain earnestness in it, too. "I'm sure that the Malabar Rose will come to no harm. Indeed, were it not for the fact that there are still some dangerous characters out there, I might even tell you . . ."

"Mrs. Hudson!" Mr. Holmes interrupted crossly. "I'm grateful for your encouragement, and I realise that I sought your opinion earlier, but I hardly think that you are best placed to understand the situation as a whole. I suggest you leave that to Dr. Watson and myself."

"As you say, sir." It seemed that Mrs. Hudson would accept this rebuff and simply return to her chores, but there remained a gauntness in Mr. Holmes' face that made her try again. "This may be a strange time to raise the subject, sir, but I wonder if I might say a few words about Mr. Phillimore, the gentleman who disappeared from Ealing. His mother-in-law called here, if you remember, sir."

"The domestic dispute in Ealing, Mrs. Hudson? I fear that if you wish to discuss that, you have sadly misjudged your moment. This is very clearly not the time. I would ask you not raise the subject again. Now, if you would leave us, perhaps Dr. Watson and I might be able to concentrate on the matter in hand."

So Mrs. Hudson and I withdrew; but while I seethed with indignation, Mrs. Hudson seemed no more perturbed than if some proud old lady had refused her offer of a seat on a crowded omnibus. Indeed, on returning to the kitchen, I found the housekeeper in a magnanimous mood.

"You can see that the two gentlemen are very anxious

about things, Flotsam, and anxiety can do terrible things to people. I'm trusting you to look after them this evening. See that they eat properly, and if Mr. Holmes touches that violin, go in and ask him to tell you about his treatise on strangulation. That will cheer him up."

"Why, ma'am, are you going out this evening?"

"I am, Flotsam. I have been invited to call on old Lord Boothroyd at his house in Berkeley Square. I was able to do his lordship a small service in a matter involving a Swedish opera singer and a two-way mirror, and his lordship has been good enough to remember me ever since. While I'm away, Flottie, make sure you keep the fires going and see if you can get on top of all the darning that needs to be done. And whatever you do, don't let anyone touch the fruitcake in the pantry. I have plans for it."

"Yes, ma'am," I replied obediently, wondering absently how, at a time when so many things seemed urgent, Mrs. Hudson had time to worry about fruitcakes or to call on elderly peers of the realm.

"And remember, Flottie," she continued, almost as if she had divined my thoughts, "at this moment in time we must try anything to prove a link between James Phillimore and our theatrical friends. At the moment, our only evidence is a rather flimsy silk tie. And we're going to need a considerably more substantial bond than that!"

ALTHOUGH I scarcely marked them at the time, it was those words that returned to me later in the day, when I decided to seek out Dr. Watson in the study. Mrs. Hudson had left at four o'clock, and after her departure the place fell quiet. Mr. Holmes retired to his room with four bottles of brown ale; Dr. Watson rested fitfully in the study behind a copy of the *Times*; I darned socks quietly in the orange warmth of the kitchen. Despite the silence, it was easy to believe that all three of us were, in our own way, grappling with the problem of the Malabar Rose.

At half past four, Dr. Watson could contain himself no longer and sought some refuge in action: in this case, a brisk constitutional through the winter streets. He returned a quarter of an hour later, damp of foot and red of face but looking better for the exercise.

"Ah, Flottie," he smiled when I appeared to help him out of his coat. "Just the person. I bumped into Mr. Rumbelow at the corner of the street. He was on his way here with a message for Mrs. Hudson, which I insisted I could deliver for him. He kept telling me how urgent it was, as if he thought I might not remember. Now where did I put it? . . ."

"I'm afraid Mrs. Hudson has gone out, sir. It's her afternoon off. She may not be back till much later."

Dr. Watson pulled a face. "Out, eh? I must say, that's a blow. Mr. Rumbelow was most insistent. Ah! Here it is." He held up a crumpled envelope, and we both regarded it with some concern. "I tell you what, Flotsam, why don't you open it on her behalf? Just in case it's something that can't afford to wait. I wouldn't like Mr. Rumbelow to feel I hadn't taken proper steps. Of course, you are welcome to come and find me in the study if you think it is a matter in which I can be of assistance."

I hadn't really imagined myself taking up this offer until a glance at the contents of the note changed my mind. Ten minutes later I found Dr. Watson looking much better in a pair of dry trousers, with a restorative glass of brandy and soda water clutched firmly in his hand.

"Ah, Flotsam!" he greeted me brightly. "All is well, I hope?"

"Yes, sir. It's just that I think Mr. Rumbelow's note might be quite important after all. You see, after Mrs.

Smithers' visit here, Mrs. Hudson placed an advertisement in a newspaper called *Plays and Players*."

"Quite right, too. Just what Holmes recommended. About a Mr. Phillips, was it not?"

"Phillimore, sir. Well, there's been a reply. Mr. Rumbelow has received a note from an actress called Fidelma Fontaine saying that she has information about Mr. Phillimore. She said she could be found at the Mermaid Theatre in Stepney after eight o'clock in the evenings. But her note to Mr. Rumbelow was delayed and only reached him this morning. And tonight is her last performance there."

Dr. Watson nodded wisely. "I see. So after tonight she might be anywhere. Very awkward. The Mermaid Theatre, you say? That must mean Shakespeare, I suppose. I've always been fond of the Bard. There's that one about the chap in the hat . . ."

"Will it really be Shakespeare, sir?" I wondered. "I thought the Mermaid in Stepney might be a little more . . ." I struggled for the right word but couldn't quite find it. "Well, rather more *popular* than that."

"Ah, yes. I see. One of these modern melodramas, you think? Well, it's all the same to me, so long as it's nothing by that Oscar what's-his-name. I never seem to get the jokes." He pulled out his watch. "I think I can see my way to a satisfactory solution here, Flotsam. Mr. Holmes has no need of me this evening, and although Stepney's the other side of town, we can give it a go and try to get there for eight. Very likely we'll be able to grab a word with this Fontaine woman before the curtain goes up. What do you say?"

What I said was yes, and ten minutes later Dr. Watson and I were rolling through town in a hansom cab. So excited was I at the thought of taking action on Mrs. Hudson's behalf that I had only half an ear for my companion's stories of strange customs among the Afghan tribes. For, I reasoned,

Fidelma Fontaine was on the stage, and so was Lola Del Fuego, and that was a connection of a sort. Perhaps this might be the real evidence Mrs. Hudson was seeking! Inside my shoes, my toes curled with excitement, and I thrilled at the prospect of imminent discoveries.

The cabdriver had been instructed to drop us at the stage door of the Mermaid Theatre in Stepney and, although the request appeared to surprise him, he clearly knew his way and had no trouble finding it. It is fortunate that was the case, for the stage door was situated down such a dark and dingy alleyway, a damp passageway so strewn with rubbish, that it seemed impossible the doctor and I would ever have found it for ourselves. I could see my own opinion of our destination reflected in Dr. Watson's face as he handed me down from the hansom, but I was pleased to see that he was determined to proceed. As the cab rattled away from us, he advanced to the low door and rapped firmly on its frame.

In response to his knock, a small panel set into the top of the door was pulled back and a pair of eyes, already narrowed with suspicion, peered out at us.

"What jer want?" an old man's voice asked gruffly.

"We're here to see Miss Fontaine," Dr. Watson replied. "At her own invitation," he added hastily, as the narrow eyes narrowed further. Dr. Watson took out his card. "Tell her I am calling on behalf of Mr. Rumbelow, the solicitor."

After a moment of hesitation, a thin hand was extended and the card vanished. The panel shut hastily behind it.

"Dashed impudence!" Dr. Watson exclaimed. "I can hardly be taken for one of those stage-door chappies who hang around and importune young ladies of the cast, can I, Flotsam?"

Before I could respond, the panel in the door snapped open again. "She can't see yer now. She's gettin' dressed. She says to go round the front. Tell the boy on tickets that Maud says you're all right. I'll come and find yer when she's done an' bring yer backstage."

We had little choice but to follow these instructions, for the panel was slammed shut almost before the last syllable was spoken. Thankfully, when we did as we were told and made our way to the front of the theatre, we found a very different face to the Mermaid. For we found she stood on a wide and bustling street, no doubt the heart of Stepney, and despite a clear sky and the bitter cold that accompanied it, the crowds abroad that night were both loud and boisterous. In contrast to her rear, the front of the Mermaid was vibrant with activity, and Dr. Watson and I were forced to join a short queue at the ticket office.

"After you, guv'nor," offered a short man in a squashed hat whose arrival coincided with our own. "All the fun of the fair, eh? In for a treat tonight, ain't we?"

"Indeed," muttered Dr. Watson rather coldly, and he tightened his grip on my arm.

At the ticket window we discovered that the mention of Maud did indeed secure a pair of tickets for which all payment was refused. Dr. Watson's attempt to ask what time the performance began was met with a knowing grin.

"Started half an hour ago," the ticket man told us. "But don't worry, guv'nor, you're in time for the good bit."

By this point in the evening I think Dr. Watson was beginning to have misgivings. Indeed it was clear from his increasing pallor as we mounted the stairs towards the circle that he was really quite alarmed, but with complimentary tickets and an appointment to keep, it was clearly nigh on impossible for him to turn back.

"I trust, Flotsam, that we shall meet nobody we know here tonight," he mused as we ascended. "And if there is anything in tonight's performance that is in any way, er, *distasteful* to you, then we shall leave at once."

"Yes, sir," I assured him, now more curious than ever to witness the spectacle that lay ahead.

Once we had reached our seats, however, the first acts on stage did a great deal to put Dr. Watson at his ease. The first was a fire-eater with an enormous droopy moustache who, once he had tired of fire, turned his attention to swords, daggers, forks, and any number of items of hardware. He left the stage to polite applause that the doctor joined in readily, more I believe out of relief than out of genuine pleasure. Next, a small girl appeared and sang a song about meeting the Queen and then dying, which met with rather less applause generally, but for which Dr. Watson clapped very loudly indeed.

"Very good! Very good!" he repeated warmly. "A truly heartrending performance!"

After that a man appeared with a dog and a tandem and, after many humorous false starts, man and dog together cycled the tandem twice around the stage. Then came a man who made shadows with his hands, and who followed the usual array of animals and birds with some rather rude shadows that I pretended not to understand.

When the shadow-man came off, a curtain near the back of the stage was raised to reveal a hanging trapeze suspended between two high platforms. There seemed to be a short pause in proceedings then, for one or two latecomers were admitted right at the front of the stalls. Watching them scurry to their seats, I found that one of them stood out in particular, for she was a young lady of rather graceful and lissom appearance who appeared genuinely surprised and intrigued by the sight of the trapeze on the stage above her. Indeed, such was her curiosity that she ventured to take one or two steps up the narrow stair that led to the stage itself.

"Wrong way, love!" a voice shouted from somewhere in the stalls, and a good deal of laughter followed it, but although she gave a vague smile over her shoulder, the young woman seemed neither to understand the import of the cry, nor to realise that by now the attention of the theatre was beginning to focus on her. So unaware was she, indeed, that she tiptoed delicately up the remaining steps until she stood on the very edge of the stage. The sight of the hanging trapeze seemed to fascinate her, and her eyes never left it as, almost in a trance, she moved into the centre of the stage.

By now the audience had fallen silent but for one or two nervous giggles. "Really," Dr. Watson rumbled nervously, "isn't there a stage manager here to rescue that unfortunate woman from this ridicule?"

Apparently there wasn't, for just then the young lady noticed for the first time the ladder that led up to one of the platforms. It seemed to prompt her to some sort of decision, for she moved towards it with sudden decisiveness, to the accompaniment of one or two ironic cheers from the crowd. At the foot of the ladder, however, her progress was checked, for both her wrap and her skirts stood as clear impediments to her climbing it. Apparently aware of the difficulty posed by the wrap, she reached to her neck without hesitation and unfastened its tie, letting the garment fall to the floor behind her.

If the audience had been silent before, now it was also tense and motionless. Dr. Watson's jaw appeared to have dropped several inches.

Freed from the confines of her wrap, the young lady now made haste to place her hands on the rungs of the ladder, but at the last moment a thought held her back, and she began to peel off her long, elegant gloves. A sound almost like a sigh seemed to escape from the audience, as if everyone had breathed at once. Next to me, Dr. Watson's jaw closed and fell open again but words failed to emerge. Only by repeating the exercise could he make himself heard.

"My word!" he gasped, limply.

Now with her arms bare to the elbow, the young lady seemed happy to return to the ladder, and tried her first steps upwards. However, it was instantly clear that something was wrong, for she wobbled dangerously and stepped back to the ground with a slight squeal of alarm. It wasn't difficult to see that the cause of her difficulty lay in her elegant evening shoes, and these she hastened to kick off. But now another difficulty presented itself, for she was looking down with great concern at the pair of fine stockings that were now threatened by the forthcoming climb.

"My word!" exclaimed Dr. Watson a second time, apparently immobilised by shock. But by now the rest of the crowd had found its voice.

"Don't spoil 'em!" it cried.

"I'll hold 'em for yer!"

"Too good to go climbin' in!"

Dr. Watson's jaw dropped even lower. Next to him I bit my finger and watched with wide-open eyes, too surprised and shocked and fascinated to do anything but stare. I knew I should be scandalised, and I was, but I was achingly anxious to keep watching, to see what could possibly happen next.

The lady's stockings were removed in a trice, very deftly and as discreetly as could possibly be done, but not without offering to the crowd a glimpse of creamy white calves that caused a ripple of almost anguished appreciation to run around the theatre.

"Come, Flotsam, we must go." Dr. Watson found words at last, but his eyes were still wide with shock and so fixed upon the stage that they defied all his attempts at moving them. As for me, I don't think I could have moved if I'd tried, so paralysed was I with a mixture of horror and of glee.

By now the lady was halfway up the ladder, but it was clear to all who observed her that her skirts were a considerable impediment to her. The audience was now not backward with its advice.

"Watch out! You'll trip!"

"They're in yer way!"

"May as well hang for a sheep as a lamb!"

With a grateful glance at her advisers, she began to fumble with the hooks and eyes at her waist, and for a moment I thought that Dr. Watson would finally cry enough. But the effect of such outrageous indecency on the good doctor was to fix him to the spot as surely as if pinned there by an Afghan lance.

"My word," he said again as the skirts fluttered to the stage.

Needless to say, the remainder of the young lady's ascent followed a similar pattern, so that by the time she launched herself, with magnificent athleticism and to whoops of applause, onto the waiting trapeze, her remaining garments were so few and so scanty that they could only be said to protect the very last vestiges of her modesty.

It was clear to me that the young lady's skill as a trapeze artist was very considerable, but I fear that by this stage of proceedings the crowd was paying scant attention to it. Nevertheless they cheered and yelled encouragement at every move she made, and when she finally came to take a bow on one of the elevated platforms, they rose to their feet and cried for more as if no other act could ever satisfy them. Dr. Watson rose, too, and blinked like one awaking from a dream.

"My dear Flotsam, I'm appalled . . . That you should witness such common lewdness is unforgivable . . ." He paused to mop his brow. "Come, we shall leave at once and complain to the manager. I shall raise a public outcry against what we have witnessed here tonight!"

However, before we could move away from our seats, a tiny, hunched old man materialised at the end of our row.

"Oi, Mr. Watson," he called out, gesticulating at us with strange, crablike movements of his arms. "You're the lucky one all right. Come on! Come on! She'll see yer now."

CHAPTER FOURTEEN

A Theatrical Family

The prospect of seeing Miss Fidelma Fontaine at even closer quarters clearly inspired in Dr. Watson something very close to panic. When the old man repeated his gesture, causing those seated around us to begin to take an interest, Dr. Watson turned to me in desperation.

"Really, Flottie, we can scarcely call upon her now. After seeing her . . . After seeing her so . . . I mean, it's not to be thought of! We must leave at once."

"But Dr. Watson, sir, Mrs. Hudson is relying on us."

As I knew it would, the idea had a powerful effect on him.

"Of course, yes. We mustn't forget that. I wouldn't wish Mrs. Hudson to think we had let her down . . . Even so, such a woman! No more than a common hussy. I have met girls like that in India, Flottie. Simply not to be trusted. Ignorant, coarse . . . *Must* we, Flotsam?"

"Just one or two questions, sir."

"Very well, there can be no harm in that, I suppose. But then we must certainly leave."

So saying, he allowed me to lead him to the end of our row, where our guide awaited us rather impatiently. As soon as we had disentangled ourselves from the rest of the audience, he ushered us with a strange, sideways gait out of the auditorium and down labyrinthine combinations of stairs and corridors, until we came to a room crowded with performers. It smelled of hot bodies and greasepaint.

"Here yer go," our guide muttered. "She'll see yer now." And with that, he disappeared into the crowd, leaving us awkward and embarrassed in the middle of the room. For amid that gathering of show people neither Dr. Watson nor I could be described as inconspicuous, but the poor doctor stood out particularly: tall and respectable and hurriedly removing his gaze from a naked thigh here or a plump corsage there.

"Can I help you, ducky?" A woman in a dancer's costume came to our rescue, her body trim as a teenager's, but her face beneath the paint nearer forty than fourteen. Dr. Watson, who had been looking down, found himself staring into the depths of a plunging cleavage and had to readjust rapidly the direction of his gaze.

"Why, yes, madam. We have an appointment to see Miss Fidelma Fontaine."

The dancer signalled with her thumb towards a door marked "Filly." "Maud!" she shouted at the top of her voice. "Admirer come to see you. Old enough to know better."

"Why, really, madam!" Dr. Watson began, blushing with indignation, but before he could say more, I dragged him away towards the door we'd been shown.

"Come on, sir." I urged him. "Just one or two questions and then we can go."

I knocked at the door, and a woman's voice called "come in" in a surprisingly pleasant, well-modulated voice. And if our hostess' voice was not the one I had expected, then neither was the scene that presented itself to me on entering. I had expected a room characterised by decadence, with a central figure sprawling in luxury amid admirers while calmly sipping gin or painting her nails. Instead the room was small and ugly, lined with bare brick, stained in places by damp, and it contained no decoration of any kind, being as spartan as a monk's cell. The sole person in it was the young lady from the trapeze, and it was clear from her bare feet, and from the bare legs that showed beneath a thick, camel-coloured woollen dressing gown, that she wore no more now than when we had seen her last. Instead of preening herself in front of a mirror, she was engaged in packing large piles of books into a box.

She turned to us as we entered and gave us the same, lovely smile that we had seen before, albeit in rather different circumstances.

"Dr. Watson, I believe? Oh, and you must be . . ."

Her voice, as I had already noted, had no obvious accent; she might just as easily have been welcoming us to a tea party at a rural vicarage.

"My name's Flotsam, ma'am. Dr. Watson was good enough to bring me to see the show."

"Was he?" She raised an eyebrow and turned it on him, then turned back to me. "I'm surprised he considered it suitable. I hope you didn't find it too terribly shocking."

"Oh no, ma'am. Well, that's to say, yes, a little. I mean, perhaps more surprising than shocking, I think. And, ma'am, the way you did it all was so very *wonderful!* I mean, you were just *brilliant* on that high wire."

She smiled at that, a smile full of warmth and pleasure. "Why, thank you, Flotsam." Then she turned to my companion. "And you, Dr. Watson, are you scandalised?"

Dr. Watson, finding himself in a very small room with a very attractive young woman in a state of near undress, was clearly very far from comfortable; but I could see that what unnerved him even more than her bare ankles or the loose-ness of her dressing gown across her bosom, was the direct-ness of her question and her total composure in our presence. He had clearly anticipated all sorts of feminine coyness or trickery, perhaps even blushing shame, but nothing like this.

"I . . . Well, I confess, madam, that it is not, er, not quite the sort of entertainment to which I am accustomed."

"I'm very pleased to hear it, Doctor," she replied with all seriousness. "You will perhaps credit me with an awareness that what I do is not considered very respectable, not even by the men who come here every night to witness it."

"Pah!" exclaimed Dr. Watson. "They should be ashamed of themselves! What does that crowd know of respectability?"

"Oh, I think you wrong them, Doctor," she replied lightly. "Only yesterday one of them caught me by the stage door and insisted that I must repent and seek the Lord, or else face eternal damnation. And he must have been very genuinely concerned for my soul, as I know for a fact that he had witnessed my sinful display at least half a dozen times."

"The blackguard!" It seemed that in his great distaste for his fellow-theatregoers, Dr. Watson had temporarily forgotten his own moral outrage. "You should have poked him in the eye!"

"On the contrary, I quoted him something from Thessa-lonians. I think that startled him rather more."

It clearly startled Dr. Watson, too. "Thessalonians? I see . . ."

She laughed at that. "Why, Dr. Watson, I don't believe you've ever read a word of Thessalonians in your life! Now, please don't stand there all awkward by the door. I have three chairs, so please make use of one. And you, Flotsam. Here, sit by me . . ."

Dr. Watson, still clearly ill at ease, took the seat that was farthest from our hostess and nearest the half-packed box of books. Almost instinctively as he sat down, he peered at its contents.

"Why, Sir Walter Scott!" he exclaimed. "One of my favourites! Are you an enthusiast?"

Sitting down, with her dressing gown rising up her calf and her body half-twisted towards us, she was perhaps more beautiful than she had been on stage. I found myself thinking of Lola Del Fuego. I had thought her beautiful, too, but hers was a kind of rare, unworldly beauty that seemed to set her apart. The woman before me now was beautiful in a much more believable way; she was someone you might actually meet in real life. And where Lola's dark, flashing eyes had seemed part of her defences, the eyes that were now turned in amusement on Dr. Watson were open and engaging.

But Dr. Watson was clearly unaware of them, looking instead—and with undisguised enthusiasm—at a tartan-bound copy of *Waverley*. His absorption made her smile.

"I've read a lot of Scott, yes, Doctor. *Old Mortality* is a very interesting work."

"The one with all the religion in it? Not really my thing, I'm afraid. But I've always thought *Ivanhoe* is rather splendid. A tremendous yarn!" He grinned at his fellow reader with honest pleasure, then remembered who she was and looked down in confusion. "So, er, all these books are really yours, Miss Fontaine? Keats, Longfellow, Shelley . . . and yet you . . ." His sentence was swallowed by his own embarrassment.

She faced him with unruffled calm. Even if she had been fully dressed, she could not have been more composed.

"Yes, Dr. Watson. You have seen how I make my living. It seems to surprise you that I can also read a book."

"Well, I, er . . . Really, Miss Fontaine . . ." It clearly *did* surprise him, even as he tried to deny the fact.

"It's not what I would have chosen, but I am not ashamed

of what I do, Doctor. And, please, none of this *Miss Fontaine.*
That's all nonsense. You can call me Maud. Or, if you prefer,
Miss Phillimore."

At that, I couldn't prevent myself from letting out a
squeal.

"*Miss Phillimore?*"

"Yes, Flotsam. That's my real name."

"Related to Mr. James Phillimore?"

"My brother. That is why I responded to your advertisement."

"Do you know where he is, miss?"

Her face fell a little. "No, I'm afraid not. That's why I
wrote to Mr. Rumbelow when I saw his advertisement. I
thought perhaps someone might have come forward . . . You
see, my brother seems to have disappeared."

"Oh." The disappointment in my voice was clearly evident. "I'd hoped you could tell us where to look. We need to
find him, you see. His wife . . ."

"His *wife*?" For the first time that evening, Miss Fontaine—Miss Phillimore—looked disconcerted. "My brother
is *married*?"

"Why, yes. To a lady in Ealing. It was her mother who reported him missing."

For a moment a silence fell as both she and I digested
what we had learned. In the end it was Dr. Watson who
spoke first, his voice surprisingly gentle.

"Perhaps, Miss Phillimore, if you were to tell us a bit
more about your brother . . ."

She straightened. "Yes, of course. I'm afraid I don't really
know him very well, so perhaps I should start at the beginning."

"WHEN my father met my mother," Miss Phillimore began,
"it was one of the great surprises of his life. My father was a

highly respectable corn merchant in Sussex, a man of very comfortable means and of considerable reputation. My mother, in contrast, was a dancer, one of a chorus of dancers performing at the Alhambra. The two met—it's not clear how—during one of my father's infrequent visits to London, and he returned again a fortnight later. It was during that visit that their decision was made, and after the shortest possible engagement, my mother was plucked from the troupe at the Alhambra Palace and transplanted into a prosperous Georgian farmhouse in the countryside near Pyecombe.

"There can be no doubt that the advantage of the match was all on her side, for as well as a comfortable income and a house surrounded by orchards, she also gained a husband who was devoted to her and, in the course of time, two healthy and affectionate young children. My brother James was born but a year after their marriage, and I arrived barely twelve months later. We were fortunate children in every way, for both our parents doted on us, and we had as our playground a fine old house, and beyond it the great sweep of the South Downs."

"Ah, the Downs!" sighed Dr. Watson. "You know them well?"

"As I know myself."

"They're a grand part of the country. Out in Afghanistan, I used to dream of them."

Miss Phillimore smiled at him.

"I am pleased they have a place in your heart, Doctor. If my life had followed the path intended for it, I should never have left them. Yet that life was not to be, for there was something in my mother's heart that none of her good fortune could ever quite vanquish. It seems she always entertained a secret yearning for her former existence that prevented her from settling into her new world. It was she who taught me as a child of four the rudiments of the trapeze, and I realise now that those afternoons in the orchard, with a swing slung over a branch, were not filling her with peace, as they did me, but stirring memories of her own past."

Miss Phillimore paused for a moment. Her dressing gown had fallen open a little, and she absently drew it closer to her.

"My father was unaware of his wife's discontent or, if aware, too puzzled by it to know how to respond. It is my belief that for all his great love for her, she always remained a mystery to him. And whether that is true or not, there came a day which altered our lives forever. I was five at the time, and my father had taken me with him to market, leaving my mother and brother at home. When we returned, we found her gone, and my brother gone with her. It was the last time we ever saw her."

When Miss Phillimore paused this time, it was because I had reached out and laid my hand on hers.

"My father made inquiries, of course," she went on, "and soon learned that she had returned to her life on the London stage. I don't think he ever tried to see her, though. The loss and the betrayal had so affected him that he was a broken man. His spirits never recovered from that blow, and, although he lived long enough to celebrate my seventeenth birthday, his career and circumstances went into decline from the day my mother left. They never recovered. His business failed, and his debts mounted. Our house was sold when I was ten, and a succession of houses followed, each smaller and less reputable than the last. When he died, I was left with nothing."

Dr. Watson was listening most attentively to this narrative, and at this point he puffed out his cheeks in sympathy. "So that is how the fates led you to London?" he asked.

"That's right, Doctor." She met his gaze and smiled a sweet, sad smile. "You must think I have fallen very far."

"Why, no!" he mumbled awkwardly. "That is to say, I

quite understand . . . Innocent young girl . . . Left alone . . . Devilishly difficult . . . Tragic circumstances . . . Dashed awkward . . . Same thing myself, no doubt."

This last comment made her smile again, but with a sparkle in her eye.

"I fear your talents may not be suited to it, Doctor. But I, unfortunately, had few options. The day after my father's funeral I came to London in search of my mother. It took me two months to discover that she, too, was dead and that I was left an orphan. By then, what little money I had was all spent. But in my searches I had met many who remembered my mother and had offered to find me work if I should need it. As I retained some acrobatic skills from my youth, I found myself eventually employed on the trapeze. Oh, do not look so concerned, Doctor! I assure you that for many years, as I made my way, my performances really were confined to the trapeze. But the competition is fierce, and there are many who can hang prettily from a swing. If I was to continue to find work, I knew I had to make my performance different.

"I hit upon the idea for my current performance only a few months ago, and already it has changed everything. I don't deny that the first time I performed it I was indescribably nervous, but it has been such a success that I have had no time to feel ashamed or cheapened. And next week, for the first time in my career, I am to be top of the bill at a theatre in town."

She pointed to the box of books. "You see, the punishment for my fearful indecency is to escape the Stepney Mermaid."

Dr. Watson swallowed awkwardly. "Very pleased to hear it, Miss Phillimore. No place for a young lady . . . Rough crowd . . . Scoundrels out there . . . Upsets me to think . . . Bare brickwork . . . Damp, no doubt, too . . . Much better off in town."

He swallowed again.

"And you, er, never married? Dashed strange . . . Attractive young girl . . . Reads Keats . . . Likes the Downs . . . Admirers, surely . . . Surprised no nice young man . . . Take you away from all this . . . Can't imagine why . . . Society too prudish . . ."

He tailed off with a gulp and studied the cobwebs above the door with great interest. Miss Phillimore watched him for a moment, a quiver of amusement on her lips.

"In my profession, Doctor, I meet very few young men of the sort I might wish to marry, and of course, those I do meet have no desire to marry me. Not many are willing to take the risk my father took."

"And your brother, Miss Phillimore," I put in, afraid we were drifting a little off the point. "What about him?"

She nodded and gave a sad little shrug.

"Nearly fifteen years passed from the day my mother took him away to the day I met him again. Even that meeting was by chance. I had asked after him, of course, but I had never been able to track him down. Growing up at my mother's side, he had very soon been encouraged to fill the role of child entertainer, so he had gone under many strange names. Then one day we found ourselves in the same theatre, and by some miracle we succeeded in recognising each other. Our reunion was a joyous one.

"As a child performer, my brother had been a tremendous success. He had indeed earned more at the age of eight than my mother ever earned. The stage was the only life he knew, and he basked in his success. However, by the time I was reunited with him, his stage career was over, and he had become a disappointed man. It appears that his particular act had not survived the transition into manhood. He had found himself slipping down the bill until one day he slipped off it altogether. And to make it worse, he was in love with his childhood sweetheart, a very pretty young girl called Polly Perkins. As James' success evaporated, hers was growing, and it was soon clear she was destined to top the bill in playhouses well beyond Stepney. It became harder and harder for the two to keep in touch, and her successes only served to emphasise his failure. Eventually, James refused to see her anymore, saying he didn't want to be a blight on her career. He declared that he was to abandon theatre work altogether and would take a job as a clerk."

"But you kept in touch, miss?"

She shrugged again. "He sort of disappeared. I had no idea where he worked or even what name he went by. But at the beginning of every month he always came to watch my act. Mostly he wouldn't even stay to talk—I think coming to the shows made him sad. He would just watch from the stalls and wait until he'd caught my eye, then leave. But this month he didn't come. I have been watching for him every day, but nothing. So when I saw the advertisement in *Plays and Players,* I determined to write in the hope that there might be some news."

Dr. Watson was nodding understandingly at this, as though there was nothing else about James Phillimore that his sister could possibly add. But, in contrast, I was almost beside myself, tapping my feet and burning with excitement as the full import of Maud Phillimore's words began to dawn on me.

"One thing, miss. It's really important. What was your brother's particular talent? What act was it that he found himself unable to continue as an adult?"

"Why, it is a common story for performers in his line. As children, there are many who can be flexible, but only very few retain that ability undiminished into adulthood."

Dr. Watson was looking puzzled. "I'm sorry, I didn't quite catch that . . ."

Miss Phillimore gave a wry smile. "As a child my brother was mostly known as Folding Freddie, the Boy in the Box. He could fold himself up to the size of a football. His speciality was appearing out of especially large top hats. Yes, Flotsam, that's right—my brother was a child contortionist."

Just as I had experienced problems in getting him there, so it was with some difficulty that I eventually dragged Dr. Watson away from Miss Phillimore's dressing room. He had clearly been most affected by the story she had told us, and in addition, having found a safe haven, he seemed most reluctant to brave again the storm of greasepaint that prevailed outside. Nevertheless, eventually my repeated urgings succeeded in raising him to his feet, and the good-byes we said to Miss Phillimore were both grateful and sincere.

"Mrs. Hudson will find your brother, miss," I reassured her. "I'm sure she'll have news soon."

"Indeed!" confirmed Dr. Watson. "I'm sure she will. Er, if she were to find anything of interest to you, where might we be able to contact you?"

"I shall be at the Oriental for the next twelve weeks, Doctor. A message will reach me there."

"Ah, the Oriental! Near Victoria. Pleased to hear it. Very handy for Hyde Park. Thoroughly recommend that as a place to take exercise. Even in this weather. Not quite the Downs, of course, but can't be beaten for a good constitutional."

"I shall be sure to take your advice, Doctor," she told him solemnly, and the pair shook hands before Dr. Watson allowed himself to be hurried outside. Once we were out in the cold air, I allowed my urgency to show.

"A cab, sir! We must hail a cab!" I insisted. "We must get back to Mrs. Hudson as quickly as we can."

"Really, Flotsam? Anything you say, of course. Not sure I fully understand the rush, though."

"Miss Phillimore's brother, sir. What we have learnt tonight explains how he disappeared. You see, there was a coal chute from the street to the cellar, sir, but we didn't think of it as a way of escape because someone would have to bend double to use it. But that's exactly what James Phillimore can do! He may not be able to tie himself in knots like the professionals anymore, but I'm sure he's still able to squeeze himself into a very small space!"

"I see," Dr. Watson replied, with no great conviction. "Folding Freddie, indeed! Very droll! But can't see why it's urgent, Flottie. Nothing to be done about it tonight."

"Yes, that's true, sir. I just want Mrs. Hudson to know as soon as possible. *Please,* sir, let's keep moving!"

"You don't feel we should have offered to help Miss Phillimore pack her books, Flottie?"

"No, sir. She'll manage very well without us. And besides, sir, she *was* rather scantily dressed."

"Eh?" Dr. Watson looked momentarily nonplussed. "Ah! Yes. See what you mean. A bit indelicate to linger, perhaps. Still, we mustn't blame the young lady for her unfortunate circumstances. Great strength of character . . . Admirable fortitude . . . Very thick dressing gown . . . Nothing improper . . . Tragic tale . . . Fine woman . . . Ah! There's a cab!"

So saying, he darted into the street, his arm raised enthusiastically, and a minute later we were on our way back to Baker Street.

For all my haste, it was late by the time we reached home. The heavy snowfall of the day before had been broken by the ravages of the day's traffic into a ghastly, syrupy slush, which the night air was now freezing into black and unforgiving ice. Our horse was properly shod for such weather, but many were not and progress through the busy streets was slow. It was about midnight when I bade good night to Dr. Watson and slipped downstairs to the glowing sanctuary of the kitchen.

To my surprise, not only was Mrs. Hudson still awake, she was busily at work icing the fruitcake that had gone uneaten on Christmas Day. By the time I arrived, the rich darkness of the cake was already enclosed in a thick crust of royal icing sugar, and Mrs. Hudson was at work decorating the surface with swirls and patterns that were as elegant and detailed as marble friezes.

She welcomed me with a nod of the head and a raised eyebrow.

"Now, young Flotsam, if you are going to start attending music halls in Stepney with older gentlemen, I shall have to start worrying about you."

"But, ma'am," I stammered, "how could you *know*? . . ."

She nodded again, this time at Mr. Rumbelow's note, which I had left lying open on the kitchen table.

"Oh, I see! I know that note was really for you, ma'am, but I thought you'd want to talk to Miss Fontaine before she moved on to another theatre and we lost her address. And you weren't here, you see, so when Dr. Watson offered to take me . . ."

Mrs. Hudson dusted her hands against each other briskly.

"You did quite right, Flotsam. Though I'm a little surprised at Dr. Watson for taking you to such a show. I imagine he expected something rather different."

"Oh, he *did,* ma'am. You should have seen his face when Miss Fontaine started taking off her clothes! And although I'm calling her that, it isn't her real name at all. Guess who she *really* is, ma'am?"

Mrs. Hudson was unknotting her apron. "Go on, Flottie."

"She's Maud Phillimore, ma'am. She's James Phillimore's sister!"

Rather than throw up her hands or whistle or make some other gesture of surprise at this revelation, as I had secretly hoped she might, Mrs. Hudson merely nodded serenely.

"Is she indeed? That's very good work, Flotsam. Very good work indeed. And she will no doubt have told you about her brother's peculiar talents?"

"So you know that already . . ." I couldn't help but feel a little disappointed that my discovery had been anticipated, but in no more than a moment my excitement returned. "You see, ma'am, that's how he was able to vanish from the cellar! And I know all about his past, too. His mother ran away to go on the stage. Do you think that's what he's done?"

"I do, Flotsam, at least in a manner of speaking." She checked her icing with a damp finger, then straightened and smiled at me properly. "You've done very well tonight, Flottie, you really have. You have clearly learned a lot about our Mr. Phillimore's past that I know nothing about. I suggest we make ourselves a hot drink and swap tales. But first, what do you think of my icing?"

I studied the fruitcake carefully. "It's beautiful, ma'am. But I thought you didn't approve of iced fruitcake?"

"Oh, well, Flottie, there's a time and a place for everything. Now, you change into your night things while I boil the kettle, and then we'll settle ourselves down in front of the fire and see what's what."

After following her instructions, I was soon nursing a steaming cup of lemon and honey, and telling Mrs. Hudson all about my outing to Stepney. For the most part she listened in silence, though when I described Dr. Watson's response to the antics of Fidelma Fontaine, our eyes met, and she allowed herself a little chuckle. When I told her how I'd discovered that James Phillimore had once been a child contortionist, I got excited all over again, only to remember that Mrs. Hudson had already arrived at the same conclusion.

"But how could you *know* that, ma'am?" I asked. "After all, it's hardly a very likely thing."

"No indeed, Flottie. Though I had begun to suspect some days ago, when I saw the mention of a contortionist on that poster. That is why I sought advice from Sir Phillip Westacott, the notable anatomist. You see, once you've discarded Mr. Holmes' rather fanciful suggestion about how James Phillimore disappeared, the coal chute really *was* the only way out of that house without being seen. And once you know that, then it must follow that Phillimore is able to fold himself into very small spaces. And, of course, after that all sorts of things made sense."

"Like what, ma'am?"

"Oh, like how the Great Salmanazar was able to pull off his little act of escapology," she said carelessly, with a little wave of her hand. "And how the Malabar Rose disappeared."

With that, she rose quite calmly from her seat and began to look for something in the drawer of the kitchen table.

"How the ruby disappeared, ma'am? I don't understand. There was nowhere to hide in that room, ma'am. The only thing in there was the marble column where the stone was displayed, and that was solid. He couldn't have hidden in there, ma'am."

She found the piece of paper she was looking for and returned to the fire.

"Far from it, Flottie. He most definitely wasn't anywhere near the Malabar Rose when it disappeared. In fact, he was suspended above a packed audience at the theatre next door at the time."

"Ma'am?" I was completely confused by then. But Mrs. Hudson was unrolling a large, scrolled piece of paper.

"Here, look at this, Flottie. I borrowed this from old Lord

Boothroyd when I visited him this evening. He is one of the last of the Gallivanting Grandees who made such a splash in the sixties. They never missed a show, no matter what or where, and Lord Boothroyd never missed a pretty face, especially when it came to filling his country house at weekends. Nobody knows more about the different acts that have appeared in London over the last thirty years than he does. I've spent a fascinating evening listening to him—acrobats, dancers, Chinese tumblers, he's seen them all." Mrs. Hudson paused to sip at her drink. "The only problem was that I was looking for someone called Phillimore, and that name didn't seem to ring any bells with his lordship. He knew all about Boneless Boris, the Birmingham Bender and Articulated Anders, the Artful Austrian, but nobody he mentioned had a name like Phillimore. It was only when we went through the old playbills that we had a piece of luck."

I looked at the paper she had spread in front of me. It was a little yellowed and brittle with age, but otherwise it was like other playbills, the headlines full of names I didn't recognise, all in very large print.

"His lordship had mentioned the name 'Folding Freddie' a couple of times before we found this particular playbill. He remembers him well—a small boy who used to hide in tiny boxes so he could burst out at comical moments and shout 'Are you goin' to kiss 'er?' Very popular, he was. But it wasn't until we came to this bill that we made the link. It's the very first billing of his career."

Mrs. Hudson's finger guided my eye to the tiny print right at the bottom of the paper. At first I wasn't sure which line she meant, and I peered at "Abe Hammond's Performing Seals" and "Kitty Keats, Child Poet" before I found the line I was looking for: "Folding Freddie Phillimore, the Infant Surprise."

"So that's how you knew! And it means we know exactly

how he came to disappear in Ealing!" I paused, suddenly struck by a thought. "But we don't know *why*, ma'am. That still doesn't make sense."

"Doesn't it, Flotsam?" The housekeeper chuckled to herself. "Here, have a look at this."

She tapped her finger on the playbill, about half way up the list. "Polly Perkins, the Clapham Canary," I read.

"Polly Perkins, ma'am? That's the girl he was in love with later on."

Mrs. Hudson nodded. "Lord Bothroyd remembered Miss Perkins very well, Flottie. She began as a tot, singing popular songs, but according to his lordship she grew into a very attractive young woman. He doesn't know what happened to her, though. One day she was on her way to the top, the next she dropped out of sight. He supposed she must have married someone respectable and settled down."

"And did she, ma'am?"

Mrs. Hudson chuckled. "Lord Bothroyd has a remarkable collection of old papers about the stage, Flottie. Eventually, we dug out this."

She showed me a picture of a young girl in an old-fashioned white dress. She must have been about eleven or twelve, but her dark hair was trimmed into tight little ringlets of the sort that had been fashionable then. Underneath was printed the legend "Polly Perkins, Popular Songbird." Mrs. Hudson was eyeing the picture with evident satisfaction.

"Does she remind you of anyone, Flottie?"

I looked again, thinking of the young girls I'd known, trying to match them to the picture before me. Then, quite abruptly, those childish features seemed to rearrange themselves in front of me: an adult nose, full lips, cheekbones where there had been girlish fat. And a pair of passionate dark eyes, flashing from under locks of dark hair.

I looked up, my face full of wonder.

"Why, Mrs. Hudson, not . . ."

"Of course, Flotsam," she confirmed with a small smile of satisfaction. "And I think there can be no doubt now that James Phillimore is a man who needs watching."

That night was the first for some time that I did not think of the boy with blue eyes. For now the hurt I felt was crowded out by a sense that pieces of a puzzle were beginning to fit together. The thought filled me with a restless excitement, so that when I lay in bed that night it was with images in my mind of stage tricks and exotic dancers, and of love amongst the stage lights.

Perhaps this mental turmoil is why I didn't notice anything strange about the shadows cast onto the kitchen floor by the streetlamp outside. Had I been studying the patterns of light visible from where I lay in bed, I must surely have seen a long, slim shadow that fell into the room from the road outside as it passed to and fro across our window. Backwards and forwards it paced, like a restless shade undecided in its hauntings. But that night my eyes were heavy, and I didn't see the dark figure creep down the area steps and very silently try the latch on the kitchen door. No sense of foreboding disturbed my slumber, no shiver stirred my sleep. Not even a vague sense of relief that, for once in my life, I had remembered to bolt down the latch of the kitchen door, to keep the night at bay.

CHAPTER FIFTEEN

Perch Revisited

The next morning was unusual in that both Dr. Watson and Mr. Holmes were up very early. After the lethargy of the previous day, Mr. Holmes now appeared seized with exceptional energy. He was dressed long before his breakfast was served and passed the time before its arrival conducting experiments that involved pulling pieces of cotton across the floor at complicated angles. When I placed his tray before him, he immediately pounced on the boiled egg he spied there, proceeding to balance it on a large pile of books that he had constructed in the centre of the room. Then, for the next hour, while his breakfast cooled and his toast hardened, he occupied himself with a variety of elaborate manoeuvres, all of which involved a lasso of cotton looped around the egg, which was then hoisted, pulled, or dragged from its base by a network of carefully connected threads. Mrs. Hudson, when she observed these activities for herself, smiled encouragingly and left him to it.

Dr. Watson, on finding that his friend's fierce concentration

precluded all conversation, declared his intention to take a
stroll in Hyde Park and paused only to change his necktie
for a rather colourful cravat. Mrs. Hudson, too, seemed anxious to leave the house, for she rushed through the routine
jobs of the morning with the most unusual haste. While I
was still laying the fire in the gentlemen's study, she popped
up to tell me that she had business to conduct with Mr.
Rumbelow and that she would be gone all morning.

She must have seen some disappointment in my face at
this news, for her expression softened, and she offered me the
prospect of something far more interesting than a visit to
the solicitor's offices.

"If the gentlemen do not require us this afternoon, Flotsam, I rather think it is time we had another word with
Perch, the toy maker. Perhaps we could arrange to meet at
his shop at five this afternoon?"

It was an invitation I accepted gladly, and one which
piqued my curiosity. Peering out of the window as Mrs.
Hudson emerged into the street below me, I wondered where
the old toy maker fitted into our story. Would he be able to
tell us the answer to the whole mystery? As I watched, Mrs.
Hudson made her way along the pavement below me, looking around her as she went as if enjoying the fragmentary
sunshine. A hansom cab slowed beside her, but she dismissed
it with a shake of her head and continued on foot with all the
vigour of a woman intent on a good walk. It was just as I was
turning away from the window that I noticed her check suddenly. Across the road from her, another cab had slowed almost to a halt in order to manoeuvre around an unloading
dray, and I watched astounded as Mrs. Hudson darted across
the road and swung herself with remarkable agility into the
moving cab just as it was pulling away. In a few seconds
more, it had turned a corner and disappeared from sight.

Before I could ponder the meaning of this remarkable behaviour, my eye was caught by another familiar figure. Miss
Peters, looking as fresh as a Michaelmas daisy, had entered
Baker Street from the other direction and was making her
way to our door. Her progress along the crowded pavements
was easy to follow, for her advance was marked by the erratic
behaviour of the many gentlemen who insisted in sweeping
off their hats in a manner designed to capture her attention,
but which mostly succeeded in hampering their fellow pedestrians. Totally oblivious of this, Miss Peters smiled sweetly
and rather vaguely at the crowd in general and, on noticing
me in the window, gave an exquisitely lovely smile and a
wave of her hand. Without waiting to witness the impact of
this on the young men in her path, I hastened downstairs to
the front door and waited for her knock.

However, when after a longer interval than I had expected, her knock finally came, I found that a little of the
serenity had gone from her face. She was holding a note in
her hand, and she looked puzzled.

"Hello, Flottie," she began. "Do you know, the *strangest*
thing just happened?" She looked again at the note. "A
small boy just gave me this. Just now, when I was about to
ring the bell. 'For the lady wot lives inside,' he said." Her
voice fell naturally into a very fair impersonation of a Cock-
ney urchin. "Then he just darted off. Oh, it *is* exciting here!
Every time I come, something mysterious happens. Mrs.
Hudson's always up to something, isn't she? Living here
must just be the most *wonderful* thing, Flottie. So much
more interesting than tea parties with Lady Londonderry
and waltzing with the Walters boy."

She sighed deeply, as if the hardship of her life was almost
beyond bearing.

"Still," she continued, brightening again, "it's not every

girl that gets to deliver mysterious messages, is it? Come on, let's see what it says!"

I hesitated. "But if it's for Mrs. Hudson, don't you think . . ."

"Oh, nonsense, Flottie! He didn't *say* it was for her, did he? It might just as easily be for you! Oh!"

The exclamation coincided with her tearing open the note, and as it dangled open in her hand, I saw at once why she had gasped. The message was not handwritten at all. Instead it consisted of one sentence, made up of different letters clipped from newspapers. The effect was dramatic, and it shocked us both into silence. I had never seen anything like it.

sTop yoUr SnOopiNg oR face tHe consEqueNcEs

"Oh, Flottie, whatever does it mean?" Miss Peters asked breathlessly.

"It's a warning," I replied, my eyes narrowing. "For Mrs. Hudson. Someone doesn't like what she's doing."

Miss Peters took a deep breath and began to shake her head. "Goodness, Flotsam! What on earth is Mrs. H up to now?"

IN the end, Miss Peters insisted on spending most of the day with me. Having digested the meaning of the strange note, her spirits rebounded to their earlier heights with remarkable alacrity, and her plan for ensuring that my own spirits followed hers was simplicity itself.

"We are going back to Bloomsbury to have luncheon with Rupert. Then we are going to Verity's to look at their new hats. If there's a safer place in the world than Verity's, I can't imagine what it must be like! And wait until you see the hats just in from Paris, Flottie. They are so unutterably beautiful; I almost want to weep just at the thought of them. And after Verity's, we'll take tea at the Ritz and eat absolutely as much as we can, and then, if we can fit it in, we'll go to Bertorelli's for chocolate. That ought to be enough to calm us down, I think. Except, of course, that the waiters at Bertorelli's are all so fantastically handsome that I find it quite hard to be calm when I get there."

I explained to her that I was engaged to meet Mrs. Hudson at five o'clock. Miss Peters tried to insist on accompanying me, but the image of Mrs. Hudson questioning Mr. Perch with Miss Peters in tow seemed so utterly far-fetched that I quietly determined to slip away alone. Nevertheless, Miss Peters proved such excellent company that as we walked back towards Bloomsbury, I already felt my good humour returning.

It also turned out that Miss Peters had news about the theft of the Malabar Rose. Rupert Spencer, it seemed, had been made responsible for talking to London's community of butterfly experts with a view to finding out more about the specimen found in the Satin Rooms.

"And he's been so *boring* about it, Flottie. Really! Butterflies, butterflies, butterflies, all day long. How *can* a man as handsome as Rupert be interested in something so dull? We might think they're very pretty and all that, but to him they're just creepy crawlies with wings, you know. But that's the trouble—he *loves* creepy crawlies. He really *must* marry me, you know, just so I can save him from himself. Otherwise, he'll just become one of those tedious, dusty old men with butterfly collections. And I know exactly what they are like because I've been forced to take tea with them all week. He calls them lepidopterists, which as far as I can see must be the Latin for dusty old men. There was one of them who was being so crushingly dull that in the end I said to him in my grandest manner, 'Really, sir, do you not think you should have some interest in your life *other* than insects?' But instead of him shrivelling up in shame, he just laughed as if I'd deliberately told a very funny joke. And then it turned out that he was the Chancellor of the Exchequer. Well, really! I'm not sure I'm happy that the nation's finances are in the hands of a man who spends his money on moths. If I ever *did* get a vote, Flottie, which would probably be a terribly bad thing for the country, I'd be sure not to cast it in favour of any party that includes lepidopterists."

I felt a smile of my own beginning to form, but I suppressed it hurriedly. "Tell me," I asked instead, "what has Mr. Spencer found out from all these men?"

"Well, Flottie, it turns out that the butterfly they found in the Satin Rooms really was the kind called Malabar Rose, which is just too peculiar, isn't it? I keep telling Rupert that the Great Salmanazar must have waved his wand and done it by *magic,* but he doesn't seem to find that in the least bit funny. Anyway, it seems that what really happened is that, a few weeks before, someone bought a dozen specimens of Malabar Rose butterflies from a man in Newbury. Or was it Newmarket? Or Newark? *Somewhere,* anyway. The man doing the selling, wherever he was, had a lot that were just chrysal-thingies, and he sent them by post before they hatched."

"And where did he send them?" I asked, hoping that Miss Peters' sense of geography might not have collapsed altogether.

"Oh, to an address in London somewhere. Can you imagine getting a pack of creepy, wriggling things pushed through your door like that? Yuck!"

"And can you remember whereabouts in London?" I persisted as patiently as I could, wondering if it would be bad manners to shake her until she answered.

"Oh, I don't think so. You know how bad I am at remembering things. Now, let's see . . ."

"Not to the Great Salmanazar, I suppose?"

"Don't be silly, Flottie. I'd have remembered *that.*"

"Might it have been an address in Ealing?"

"Ealing? I don't think so. I keep thinking 'Billingsgate,' but it can't have been that. Why would someone send butterflies to Billingsgate? And besides, I think there was some connection to toys . . ."

"Toys? It wasn't sent to someone called Perch in Kimber Street, was it?

"That's it, Flottie! Perch! I knew it was something to do with fish." Miss Peters glowed prettily at her own cleverness and smiled randomly at a young man passing on a bicycle, who reacted by wobbling with surprise and almost colliding with an omnibus.

On arriving at the house in Bloomsbury Square, I found Rupert Spencer at home and able to confirm for himself the story that Miss Peters had sketched out. Although nobody could be sure how the butterfly had been introduced into the Satin Rooms, it seemed certain that it must have passed through the hands of the toy maker, Perch. Mr. Spencer had called on Perch that morning but had found no one at home. But, he declared firmly, he had given the name to Lestrade, and he was pretty sure that Mr. Perch was going to have a few questions to answer.

When, in turn, I told him about how the toy maker had already crossed Mrs. Hudson's path, Mr. Spencer nodded thoughtfully, his brown eyes pensive and resting on my own.

"So she's onto something, is she? I thought she must be. We should have known that Mrs. Hudson would have an idea or two of her own." He smiled again then, his eyes crinkling at the edges, and faced with the honest warmth of that look I almost told him of Mrs. Hudson's plan to call on

Perch that very evening. But fearing that she might not welcome a crowd of companions, I kept silent, and watched Mr. Spencer help Miss Peters to another slice of ham, and thought how nice he was.

And at a quarter to five that evening, as I made my way on foot through the dimly lit streets that led to Perch's shop, I rather wished I had made a different decision. I had forgotten how quiet those streets were, how inimical to strangers. The winter night comes on very quickly in London when you are a little nervous or a little lonely, and that night, to my surprise, I found I was both. I hadn't set out like that. I'd said my farewells to Miss Peters full of excitement at the thought of joining Mrs. Hudson. But with every step I took away from the lights of Islington's Upper Street, I found my confidence diminishing. The streets were very quiet just there, devoid of any of the commercial bustle I knew from central London, and by half past four they were empty but for occasional pedestrians, straggling their way homeward through a freshly fallen layer of snow. The houses turned blind eyes to the street, their faces set in fixed and haughty frowns. And yet, as I passed them, there grew in me a sense of being watched, and I found myself shrinking deeper into my collar and keeping to the shadows. I would have given a great deal then to have had Rupert Spencer striding along beside me.

At the corner of Kimber Street, I paused and let myself sink for a moment into the snow-wrapped silence. I'd hoped to meet Mrs. Hudson before this, as she made her way here, but when I turned to look behind me, I could make out nothing but the shadows and the pale pools of gaslight on the snow. I gathered my collar close to my neck and continued rather hastily along the row of shuttered shops to where the toy shop stood.

As I approached, I noticed that this time there was no glow of lights from the old man's shop as there had been before. And then, peering into the gloom, I realised that two figures were standing in the shadows near its door. Before I had time to worry about who they were or what they wanted there, one of them moved a little into the light, and I recognised Mrs. Hudson's formidable figure. Her companion, however, I didn't recognise: an elderly woman, hunched and rather scrawny. She seemed to be engrossed by her own conversation.

"Gone, I tell you. Into thin air. He was there last night when I passed by back from the Angel and Trumpet. Working on something at the back of the shop, he was. But this morning his door was open to the street, and when I went in looking for him, he was gone. Gone! With all his tools still on his bench, like he'd been carried off by angels straight to heaven." This thought made her cackle, a thin, reedy attempt at laughter that ended in a cough. "Or the *other place!*" she concluded. "Most likely to the other place! Heh! Heh!"

By now I had joined them, and Mrs. Hudson welcomed me with a nod.

"Thank you, Mrs. Griffiths," she said firmly, drawing the conversation to a close. "Since the place is unlocked, I think we'll just have a little look around before we go."

And quicker than the old woman could reply, Mrs. Hudson seized my arm and thrust me through the door of Perch's shop.

The sight that welcomed us was very different from the one that had greeted our first visit. Then, the whole shop had glowed with light, and there had been more movement than the eye could easily take in. Now there was darkness and shadow, but much worse than that was the stillness. It seemed intense, unnatural, as if an enchanter's spell had been cast over the figures that surrounded us. The poodle in the window had slumped into immobility, the hoop above its head forgotten; the Spanish dancer had stopped dancing, as if in the grip of a grim paralysis; and even the jack-in-the-box had failed to return to its box and hung, distended and limp, where it had fallen.

"So old Perch has gone, has he?" Mrs. Hudson murmured. "I wonder what's become of him?"

But instead of replying, I told her as rapidly as I could what I had learned about Perch and the butterflies, and about the warning note thrust into Miss Peters' hand.

"I see," she mused as I brought my tale to an end. "I rather expected something of the sort. I have been taking care in my wanderings. But now, I think, we need to work out, if we can, what has happened to Perch. You take the front of the shop, Flottie, and I'll take a look around the back."

"And what are we looking for, ma'am?"

She looked sombre for a moment. "Anything we can find, Flotsam. And let's hope it's nothing grisly."

Perhaps it was those words that put the thought into my mind, but as I began my investigation of the darkened shop, the unease that I had felt earlier began to grow. However hard I tried to be practical, I was unable to rid myself of a slight wariness and the feeling I was being watched. As I moved amongst them, the lifeless eyes of Perch's mannequins seemed to follow me, and I began to fancy that each of them was somehow *waiting* for something to happen: waiting for me to discover something, or else to leave them to their silence. At one point I brushed against the half-sized figure of a soldier, only to cry out when his hand jerked instantly upwards into a crisp salute, as if caught sleeping on guard duty. However, his salute was never completed, for his energy waned with the action only half-complete, and his hand sank slowly to his side, as though sleep had once again overcome him.

Startled by my cry, Mrs. Hudson thrust her head out from behind the curtain that separated Perch's workroom from the front of the shop.

"Back here, Flottie," she beckoned. "There's something you should see."

In the back of the shop, safe from the eyes of the street, Mrs. Hudson had felt able to light a candle, and by its light I could make out the outline of a crooked, cramped work-shop, the benches covered with objects in a state of semi-construction. The item that had excited Mrs. Hudson's interest turned out to be a wooden crate which she had found pushed under one of Perch's workbenches. As she unpacked it, I saw that it contained a number of much smaller boxes in various stages of completion, some empty, some with complicated mechanisms fitted neatly into them. Folded amongst them, almost black in the dim light, were a number of lengths of thick, luxurious velvet.

Mrs. Hudson placed one of the more complete boxes on the bench in front of her. As well as four square sides, this one had been fitted with a hinged top in the shape of a trun-cated pyramid. Mrs. Hudson wrapped a part of the dark fab-ric around it.

"Does this remind you of anything, Flottie?"

My heart gave a leap. "Of course, ma'am!" It was as if the pieces fell into place with a huge and satisfying rush. "I un-derstand it now, ma'am! I'm sure I do."

Mrs. Hudson chuckled to herself, a low, happy chuckle. "Evidence at last, Flotsam. Real, solid, tangible evidence. How careless of Perch to leave these things behind. I think our visit must have panicked him, for it seems he left in an almighty hurry. Now we just need to find where he's gone."

I returned to my search of the front of the shop, peering into dark corners and under furniture, not entirely sure what I was looking for. Although it had filled me with an uncommon sense of enlightenment, Mrs. Hudson's discovery had also added to my feelings of apprehension. The workbenches abandoned in mid-task; the objects left behind that should have been destroyed; the stock of the shop unsold and untended: these things preyed on my mind. And while they did, each set of unseeing eyes followed me as I passed.

Determined to keep my imagination in check, I tried as hard as I could to thrust these thoughts from my head. After all, there was no reason why anything should have happened to the old shopkeeper. There were a hundred and one reasons why he might have gone away, none of them in the least bit sinister. Why should I be thinking the worst? People didn't just disappear. At least not usually. Why should I think he did?

It was at this point in my investigations that I came to the clockwork magician.

For a moment, I thought of calling out to Mrs. Hudson. His face was hideous, frozen in a mocking, inhuman grin. His eyes seemed to follow me in a deathly leer. But I wouldn't run away. I took a deep breath and waited patiently until I had regained my composure. One should investigate calmly, I told myself, or not at all.

The large crate that stood next to the mannequin was the size of a man, its door firmly closed. It was in this crate that Perch had placed his hat before it vanished. It was also, I realised, the most capacious, most practical, most obvious place to hide something in the entire shop. Especially if it was something large. Something the size of a man . . .

Once again I hesitated. The arm of the mechanical magician had come to rest reaching out towards the door, in such a way that I would have to touch the arm to reveal the contents of the crate. And confronted with this obstacle I found

I had no great enthusiasm for touching that pale, waxen hand. In my head I heard Miss Peters' voice, all wistful, saying, "It must be *wonderful* to have so much excitement, Flottie!" And I sincerely wished that she were with me then, for I felt sure that she would have flung open the door without a second thought. Emboldened by this reflection, I reached out, shut my eyes, and tugged the door open . . .

"So now we know what happened to Perch." Mrs. Hudson's voice sounded at my shoulder, uncommonly grave and sombre. I realised I still hadn't opened my eyes. "He's on his way to a better place, Flotsam," she continued, "and there's little we can do about it now."

"You mean . . ." I could hardly bear the promptings of my own imagination, and yet they still seemed better than opening my eyes.

"Yes, Flotsam. Cape Town. I've heard the climate there is wonderful. And as good a place as any to hide a guilty conscience. I don't suppose he'll be needing those anymore."

Blinking my eyes open, I saw that she was pointing into the crate, where, instead of the crumpled, bloodied corpse that I had fully convinced myself must be lying there, there was nothing but a pair of broken spectacles. Apart from those, the crate stood empty.

"But . . ." I stammered, "I thought . . ."

"Yes, Flottie, I admit I was a little worried, too. But look, I found this in the next room. It's a typed note confirming a first-class passage to South Africa on the *Queen Sophia*. She must have left Southampton at noon today. Whatever Perch's role in all this, it would appear his employers are not ungenerous."

"But what's to be done, Mrs. Hudson? Is there nothing to be done to stop him?"

Mrs. Hudson's answer to that question was never clear, for as she began to speak, the silence of the shop was fractured by a terrible crash of glass, and the toy shop's front window crumpled into fallen shards. Amid the fragments, a half-brick pitched onto the floor and rolled to a rest at our feet. Before either of us had time even to flinch, the brick was followed by a burning oil lantern, thrown so that it shattered against the wall beside us. From it, in a moment of liquid beauty, flowed a great, golden arc of flame.

CHAPTER SIXTEEN

The Clockwork Thief

That evening, Mr. Holmes' study in Baker Street played host to a select gathering of those most concerned with the fate of the Malabar Rose. Mr. Holmes had been the first to return and had been surprised to find his rooms unlit and the grates uniformly cold. Ever the practical man, he had attempted to light the fire in the study by means of a flask of spirit of naphtha, which he happened to notice at the front of his own chemical cabinet. While he was engaged in this rather perilous activity, Dr. Watson entered the room, whistling brightly and sporting a cravat of alarming yellow and blue swirls. It was an adornment wasted on his friend, who at that point was close to losing his eyebrows to the conflagration he had engendered.

"Where the devil have you been all this time, Watson?" he snapped impatiently. "We have a major case on our hands, our reputations hang by a thread, and in the middle of it all, I find you have taken yourself off somewhere. To make matters worse, we don't have a fire, and the place is as dark as a morgue."

"Sorry, old man," his friend replied, his equanimity undented. "Went for a stroll in the park. Hyde Park, you know. Thought it would be good for my constitution. Most refreshing. It's amazing what a walk can do for you. I feel a new man." He paused and sniffed the fire suspiciously. "Mrs. Hudson not in then?"

"Evidently not," Mr. Holmes observed dryly. "I should hardly undertake this task for recreation, should I?" He pulled out his watch. "Watson, it's nearly seven o'clock on one of the shortest days of the year. You cannot have been in the park until this hour."

The doctor flushed slightly. "May have stopped off for a pot of tea, too. Just to refresh myself, don't you know? Get the old grey cells working . . ."

"Really, Watson," Mr. Holmes returned rather testily, "this is most unlike you. We are expecting Sir John Plaskett and Inspector Lestrade at any moment and, as you have no doubt divined, neither Mrs. Hudson nor Flotsam is anywhere to be found."

Dr. Watson took a step away from the fire, which was threatening to ignite the objects on the mantelpiece above it.

"A bit rum, that," he decided. "Never known Mrs. H to let us down before."

"There may be more grounds for concern than you imagine, my friend. Look what I discovered on Mrs. Hudson's kitchen table."

He produced from his pocket the strange note that I had received earlier that day and placed it in front of his companion.

sTop yoUr SnOo*p*iNg oR face tHe *c*onsEqueNcEs

Dr. Watson studied it with such incomprehension that it might have been a species of exotic fish.

"But surely this note is intended for you, Holmes? Mrs. Hudson must have forgotten to bring it up."

"You think so, Watson? I fear you are overlooking an important detail."

"And what is that, Holmes?"

"If you cast you mind back over recent events, you may notice that we haven't actually *done* any snooping yet. It is not a word I would choose to describe our activities at any time, Watson, but I'm afraid, however we describe them, we haven't done anything even remotely resembling it since the Malabar Rose disappeared. We have pondered a great deal, but we have done rather less. This note was composed by someone who feels threatened. And it is hard to conceive that anything we have done recently would threaten even the most timid of criminals."

Dr. Watson considered this hypothesis. "Hmmm, I take your point, Holmes. But really, why would anyone wish to threaten Mrs. Hudson?"

Mr. Holmes paused, and for a moment seemed unsure how to express himself.

"It has gradually come to my attention, Watson, that Mrs. Hudson may not be quite like other housekeepers. Though her mental capacity is inevitably limited by her gender, I have noticed that on occasion she shows uncommon speed of thought for one of her sex. And I fear that in the last few days she has rather taken to heart that drab little case in Ealing . . ."

"You mean there might be something in that disappearance tale after all? Dashed inconvenient of her to let it get in the way of *your* investigations though, Holmes."

"Indeed, Watson. Nevertheless, I confess to some slight

feelings of anxiety on her behalf. For now, however, there is little we can do. I have created a very fine fire. If you were to light the lamps, I feel we can go ahead with our appointment this evening as if nothing were amiss."

That something was amiss, however, was apparent from Mr. Holmes' demeanour that evening. His discussions with Sir John and Inspector Lestrade centred on their attempts to break the alibi of the Great Salmanazar, and on their questioning of the rest of his troupe. The illusionist however had shown them the straightest of straight bats, simply insisting that, as he was on stage in front of a thousand people at the time of the theft, their questioning was both pointless and impertinent. And indeed, on coming up against that immoveable defence, their further investigations inevitably foundered. This failure left both men vexed and short tempered, and when, for the fourth time, Mr. Holmes crossed the room to peer through the window, Sir John's patience finally gave way.

"Really, Mr. Holmes!" he snorted. "We are involved in an issue of unparalleled importance, one which the Palace itself has placed in our hands, and frankly we have made an appalling mess of it. I hardly think it unreasonable to expect your undivided attention for an hour or two."

Mr. Holmes turned from the window. "You must forgive me, Sir John. I am concerned about my housekeeper. She was expected home rather earlier than this . . ."

"Your *housekeeper*, Mr. Holmes?" the soldier exploded. "Really, sir! I hardly see how your housekeeper can be of the slightest interest to us when we are facing both national disaster and personal disgrace of the most public kind."

"Which shows how little you know Mrs. Hudson, Sir John," Mr. Holmes smiled. "However, I agree that for now we must apply ourselves to the problem in hand. You say you have rounded up a large number of London's known criminals?"

According to Dr. Watson, it was at that point in proceedings—and with the most impeccable timing—that Mrs. Hudson's feet were heard in the corridor outside, and her firm knock rapped on the study door.

If I were to attempt a comparison, I should say that she swept into the study that evening the way a battleship sweeps into harbour: purposeful yet somehow majestic. In contrast, I trailed in her wake like a slightly damaged tender, painfully aware of the dark smuts on my cheeks and the slightly singed skirts around my ankles.

Our appearance was clearly dramatic, for all four gentlemen leapt to their feet upon our entrance.

"My word, Mrs. Hudson! What has happened?" Dr. Watson gasped, and I realised that all four were eyeing with astonishment the great dark trails of soot and ash that covered us.

"We have been most concerned, Mrs. Hudson," Holmes added. "And I see we were right to have been."

The housekeeper looked down at her blackened hands and her scorched dress and dismissed them with an imperious wave of her arm.

"It's nothing, Mr. Holmes. Flotsam and I have had a little difficulty with an oil lamp, but both of us are unscathed. Some excellent work by Flotsam with a blanket, and the assistance of some passing navvies, has seen us through the crisis. We are far more concerned that we were not present to light the fire here, sir. What must you think of us?"

Without waiting for reply, she busied herself in dabbing at the fireplace with the hearth brush.

"Think nothing of it, Mrs. Hudson," Mr. Holmes reassured her. "I'm sure it must have been an extraordinary circumstance to keep you from your duties."

"Oh, I fear not, sir. Just a little trick we discovered about making jewellery disappear. I'm afraid we were much amused by it and rather lost track of the time."

At her words, Sherlock Holmes looked up sharply and even Dr. Watson blinked a little.

"Eh? What's that, Mrs. Hudson? Something about making jewels disappear?"

Mrs. Hudson continued with her tidying. "Oh, it's nothing, sir, I'm sure. Nothing that you and Mr. Holmes will not already have thought of, sir."

The two gentlemen exchanged glances and Mr. Holmes cleared his throat a little hastily.

"Of course, Mrs. Hudson. I daresay you're right. Dr. Watson and I have indeed formed one or two theories of our own. But perhaps in the course of your domestic duties you have hit upon something that would be of interest to our guests here. What do you say, Sir John? Shall we hear more?"

The old soldier tutted in exasperation. "Really, Mr. Holmes, at a time like this . . ."

But before he could finish his sentence, Mrs. Hudson had risen to her feet and curtseyed politely.

"If you please, sir, Flotsam and I could do with five minutes to tidy ourselves up. If we could return then, I have something downstairs that I shall bring with me. Perhaps it will be of interest . . ."

And almost before Mr. Holmes had time to acquiesce, she had bustled out, dragging me behind her as a comet drags its tail. When the doors had closed behind us, she turned to me and winked, then led me chuckling back to the kitchen.

OF course, the truth behind our escape from Perch's toy shop was very much more complicated than Mrs. Hudson's summary of the situation had made it sound. However, it might have been a very great deal simpler had it not been for Mrs. Hudson's insistence on returning to the back of the shop to retrieve the half-built boxes that we had examined earlier. For after the first shock of flames had spread across the floor, it was clear that a path remained open that led to the front door. Quicker almost than the flames, Mrs. Hudson had thrust me bodily through the gap and into the night air. But instead of remaining with me, she then turned back into the shop, darting past the flames with easy grace and a surprising fleetness of foot.

My instinct was to follow her, but no sooner had I seen her figure disappear into the smoke than I heard shouts behind me, and I was taken up by a gang of Irish navvies who were looking for a shortcut to a nearby public house. Like the male guests at the Blenheim Hotel, their response to the flames was to rush as close to the fire as physically possible while shouting contradictory instructions to their friends. But unlike the guests at the Blenheim, this group of men was used to working together and were of a practical bent, and so, to my relief, were able to sort themselves out rather more quickly. One of them quite quickly marked the fact that the shop next door displayed in its window a pile of rough blankets. Reasoning that if the fire were allowed to burn unchecked then not only the blankets but the shop's entire stock would be in peril, the decision was taken to smash through its window and to arm themselves with whatever would be most helpful in fighting the flames. And so, equipped with heavy blankets, my new allies proceeded to beat at the fire with sterling vigour and some highly descriptive vocabulary, whooping and cheering when they realised that I had joined their ranks and was flapping away with a blanket of my own.

Mrs. Hudson, having heaved the precious box of evidence to safety through a back window, had returned to the blaze armed with a broom, and the energy with which this two-fronted attack was prosecuted meant that within a few minutes the last vestiges of fire were being extinguished. The timely arrival of the navvies had caught the blaze before it had fully taken, and although we had all breathed in rather too much black smoke, the only lasting damage done was to Mr. Perch's collection of toys. I couldn't help but feel a terrible sadness when I saw what magnificent pieces of work had been lost. The boy and the poodle were completely destroyed, and the magnificent clockwork dolls' house had been gutted by the flames so that it resembled a real country house in the aftermath of a genuine fire. The saluting soldier who had startled me earlier was slumped on his side, apparently fatally wounded. And next to the crate where Perch had made the hat disappear, nothing remained but a heap of scorched clockwork. The waxy magician who had so terrified me had melted completely away, and gone with him, forever, was the secret of his remarkable trick.

It had taken Mrs. Hudson and me some time to extricate ourselves from the hubbub that followed the blaze. Indeed, Mrs. Hudson refused to leave until we had seen our Irish friends happily installed in the snug bar of the Angel and Trumpet at the expense of Mr. Perch's grateful neighbours. That the attack on Mr. Perch's premises was an act of arson seemed widely believed, but neither the navvies nor the neighbours had spied the perpetrator, and his identity and motives were the subject of much discussion when Mrs. Hudson finally signalled that it was time for us to depart. Then, with her salvaged box wedged firmly between us, we had returned to Baker Street in a speeding hansom, and had hastened directly to Mr. Holmes' study.

There, after some hasty ablutions and a change into respectable clothing, Mrs. Hudson and I felt able to rejoin the gentlemen. We found them ready to receive us: Sir John, with some embarrassment; Lestrade, a little impatiently; Mr. Holmes with sly amusement at the confusion of his guests; and Dr. Watson, still wearing his bright cravat, with a very full glass of whisky. Mr. Holmes' fire appeared to have recovered from its strange method of ignition and was burning brightly, and Dr. Watson, with typical enthusiasm, had lit every lamp in the room. It made for a warm and welcoming scene.

There was something welcoming, too, in Mr. Holmes' face as he greeted Mrs. Hudson on her return.

"Now, Mrs. Hudson," he began, "I believe you said something about jewels . . ."

"Yes, sir," she agreed, "though what I know, I've found entirely by accident while giving a helping hand to Mrs. Smithers in Ealing, sir."

How much of the original tale Mr. Holmes remembered was unclear, but Mrs. Hudson started at the very beginning, reminding him of Mrs. Smithers' visit to Baker Street and then moving on to our own visit to the house in Ealing, our examination of its windows and doors, our inspection of its cellar and our observations concerning Mr. Phillimore's wardrobe. She spoke at some length about the cheap gloves that had recently been purchased in Islington and explained patiently about the Parisian fashion for lilac socks.

Outside in the quiet streets, more snow was falling. Inside, in contrast, the study had grown very warm, and from some hidden corner a tiny moth had appeared and was flickering helplessly around one of the lamps, as if released by the heat from its winter slumber. When Mrs. Hudson began to describe our first visit to the street in Islington where the gloves had been bought, I could sense that her audience was growing a little restless. She had not gone a great deal further before Mr. Holmes felt called upon to intervene.

"All this domestic detail is no doubt fascinating to one of

your profession, Mrs. Hudson, but I fail to see of what interest it can possibly be to us. We have rather more significant matters with which to grapple than the colour of a clerk's socks. And I fear you will never persuade Inspector Lestrade that his detectives would be more effective if better acquainted with Parisian fashions!"

His remark was met with a small ripple of mirth, and I sensed in Sir John and Inspector Lestrade a growing embarrassment at the situation in which they found themselves. Mrs. Hudson, it was clear, was failing to hold their interest.

However, rather than be cowed by their attitude, Mrs. Hudson appeared as serene and confident as if she were explaining the best way to bake scones on the range downstairs.

"Forgive me, sir. Domestic commonplaces are a housekeeper's business. Now, tell me, sir." Her tone seemed suddenly firmer and more determined. "What exactly were you looking for when you searched the Satin Rooms after the ruby's disappearance?"

Mr. Holmes arched an eyebrow and exchanged bemused looks with his colleagues.

"Why, Mrs. Hudson, we were looking for any possible way an object the size of the Malabar Rose could have been removed from that room."

Mrs. Hudson nodded knowingly.

"Yes, sir. I rather thought so. I worked for a lady once, sir—I shan't mention her name—who was sent an unsigned letter telling her that one of her maids had stolen a large silver candelabra from her drawing room. Now, this lady had long held suspicions of that particular maid, and she was delighted to have these suspicions confirmed. She went straight down to the drawing room to see for herself the truth of the matter, and when she saw the candelabra wasn't there, she called the police at once."

"Very unpleasant," Dr. Watson sympathised. "Had a man in Afghanistan once who used to help himself to my snuff. Damned if I could ever catch him at it, though. Did they ever track down the stolen candelabra, Mrs. H?"

"Oh, it was still in the drawing room, sir. Someone had moved it to a table on the other side of the room. But the lady of the house couldn't see it there, and neither could the police."

"But why on earth not?"

"You see, they weren't expecting to find it, sir. The lady hoped that it had gone, and the police, well, they'd been told it was missing so it never occurred to them it might still be in the room. It was only when the girl who did the dusting went to work that the situation was resolved."

At the denouement of this little tale, Sir John let out an impatient exclamation, and even Sherlock Holmes looked exasperated.

"A very amusing little story, Mrs. Hudson, but surely you aren't suggesting that the ruby was still in the room, and yet somehow we failed to find it?"

"Yes, sir," Mrs. Hudson replied, her face impassive.

"You mean you *are* suggesting that?"

"Yes, sir."

At this, Sir John could restrain himself no longer. "Do you take us for fools?" he spluttered furiously.

Mrs. Hudson looked at him calmly. There was a slight pause.

"Going back to Mr. Phillimore, sir," she went on, "I mentioned there was a toy maker's shop on the street where he bought his gloves . . ." Inspector Lestrade rolled his eyes at the mention of Mr. Phillimore's name, but it was going to take more than that to deflect Mrs. Hudson. "Flotsam and I visited that shop today, sir, in the hope of finding a good doll for a shilling. But instead we found some interesting bits and pieces, sir. I have with me something I'd like to show you."

She moved purposefully to the door but paused by the lamp where the moth still fluttered. Very carefully she reached out and caught it between her cupped hands, and then left the room in silence.

When she returned a minute later, it was with a small parcel loosely wrapped in brown paper. This she placed solemnly on a small chest marked "Cords, Garrottes and General Strangulation" that stood beside Mr. Holmes' chair. Then, without any drama or fanfare, she pulled away the brown paper to reveal a velvet jewel case, lying open to reveal a velvet pyramid on which a large stone might be displayed.

"Good lord!" exclaimed Dr. Watson, recognising it at once. "It's the replica case. You remember, Holmes. Sir John left one here on his first visit."

"Very nearly, sir," Mrs. Hudson corrected him. "It's certainly *quite like* the replica case, but it is not the same one. Let me show you something."

She rummaged for a moment in the deep pocket of her apron, and it was noticeable as she did so that now, with the appearance of the jewel case, her audience was suddenly paying much closer attention. Even Sir John had leaned forward in his chair in order to observe the case more closely. I don't know what magic or drama I was expecting from Mrs. Hudson at this point, but I remember being most surprised at the object she produced from her apron—a neat, blue duck egg of unremarkable appearance. I was clearly not the only one to be a little taken aback, either, for four sets of eyebrows shot up in surprise.

"An egg, gentlemen," she explained, in case there was any doubt. "You'll agree, I hope, that it is about the size of the Malabar Rose. Now, watch . . ."

She reached down to the jewel case and balanced the egg on the apex of the velvet pyramid, so that it perfectly filled the hollow intended for the ruby. There was another quickening of interest in the room now, and I could see all four gentlemen edging closer in their seats, intrigued to discover the meaning of the demonstration.

"So what now, Mrs. Hudson?" Dr. Watson asked, slightly puzzled.

Mrs. Hudson looked up at the clock. "We wait, sir. Timing is very important to all this. The timing needed to be perfect, you see. Probably Perch is the only man in the kingdom capable of getting it exactly right."

"Eh? I'm not sure that I follow, Mrs. H," Dr. Watson grunted. "What exactly are we waiting for? It's not about to hatch, is it?"

"Ssssh! One moment, sir."

She was watching the clock intently now. The hands stood one minute short of the hour, and I realised she was waiting for the clock to strike. Even Dr. Watson seemed to sense the importance of the moment, and he, like the rest of us, fell silent and watched the minute hand as it edged slowly towards the perpendicular.

That minute seemed to take an age to pass. Mrs. Hudson, for all her apparent serenity, appeared as absorbed as the rest of us. As we watched, the silence thickened around us, stirred only by the ticking of the clock. So when, with a click, the minute hand finally edged home, that noise was enough to make me jump, and the chimes that rang out seemed to boom like church bells. But the egg, which we were all now studying with unashamed intensity, did nothing. It continued to sit where the ruby should have been, looking faintly ridiculous. When the last stroke of nine faded away and still nothing had happened, there was a general shifting in seats and, from Sir John, another exclamation of impatience.

"What now?" he demanded.

But his question went unanswered, for at the very moment he spoke, *the egg began to move.* A faint whirr of clockwork started up from somewhere inside the case and, as we watched in astonishment, the velvet pyramid on which the egg rested seemed to shrink into itself, so that very gradually, very gently, the egg was being lowered into the dark base on which it stood. Fascinated by its progress, we watched until the pyramid had become a hollow and the egg had reached the floor of the case. When it could sink no lower, the velvet slopes that supported it began to open, creating a hole through which the egg fell softly. For a moment it rested upright, its balance almost perfect, but then, inevitably, it toppled to its side and rolled away, out of sight into the concealed depths of the box. The opening of the velvet panels had another effect, too, for as the egg disappeared, something small came fluttering upwards into the light.

"That moth!" I gasped, and Mrs. Hudson nodded, as the tiny creature flapped up into the shadows in search of a dark crevice in which to hide. Now, with the egg hidden and the moth released, the velvet sides of the pyramid were moving upwards again, and by the time the minute hand of the clock showed two minutes past the hour, the jewel case was exactly as it had been before—but for one significant difference: the egg, instead of resting on top of the case, was now securely hidden inside it.

The impact of this demonstration on the four gentlemen was no less than extraordinary. Suddenly all four of them were on their feet, all talking at once.

"Remarkable," Holmes declared, his eyes bright with excitement.

"Astounding!" Watson boomed, while Inspector Lestrade seemed too stunned by what he had seen to offer any sort of comment beyond the word, "Blimey!" repeated over and over.

Sir John, however, was reacting very differently.

"But it can't be true!" he gasped, an observation he repeated, apparently in the hope that someone would support it. He alone appeared to be greeting Mrs. Hudson's demonstration with horror rather than relief. "The case the ruby stood on came from the royal jewellers," he told us. "I received it from them myself and brought it to the Satin Rooms in person."

"Hmmm, Sir John has a point, Mrs. Hudson," conceded Dr. Watson. "I can't see the royal jewellers pulling a trick like that, what?"

"The boxes were switched, sir." With the demonstration safely complete, Mrs. Hudson's air of complete serenity had returned. "A visitor called at Sir John's house a few days ago. The butler allowed him into the entrance hall, but found him gone almost as soon as he had turned his back. Of course, he hadn't really left the house. He had hidden himself in one of the chests that decorates Sir John's hall, along with the clockwork jewellery case that he intended to substitute for the real one. That night, when the household was asleep, he emerged, found the original case in Sir John's study, switched the two, and left by a downstairs window. The timer was already set, of course, and the chrysalis of the butterfly was on the inside and on the point of hatching."

"It seems a dashed complicated way of doing it, Mrs. H,"

"Oh, no, sir. It had to be done like that. If there had been any sign of breaking and entering, Sir John would have been immediately on his guard. But this way there was no sign the switch had taken place. The butler found an unlatched window the next morning, but being a man of advancing years he assumed he had simply failed to close it properly on his nightly rounds."

"But how did they know what the jewellery case looked like, Mrs. H?" Dr. Watson asked. "And how could they possibly have made a copy beforehand?"

"Really, sir," Mrs. Hudson replied sternly. "All the jewellery cases made by the royal jewellers are made to the same design. It is their special feature."

"I don't believe a word!" Sir John's colour had deepened to a rich burgundy, and the veins were standing out in his temples. "That bit about the chest is ridiculous. The chests in my hallway are tiny. Honestly, Mr. Holmes," he continued, almost imploringly, "no man could fit himself into one."

"Mr. James Phillimore could, sir. A man with what they call double joints. He was also able to squeeze himself up the coal chute in Sefton Avenue. And incidentally, that's how he could assist the Great Salmanazar in his escape trick."

"Eh? Sorry, Mrs. Hudson, don't quite follow."

"It's very simple, sir. Mr. Phillimore is concealed in a box that is made to look like a huge lead weight. That weight is balanced on the coffin, apparently to make it impossible for the illusionist to lift the lid. When the whole works is concealed in the crate, Phillimore releases himself from his own box and uses the tools he has with him to release his employer."

"So they were in it together! Er, in the crate, I mean." Inspector Lestrade appeared to be catching up. "That must mean they planned to retrieve the ruby later."

"Precisely, sir."

Mr. Holmes was beaming with delight. "But this is excellent news! Inspector, what happened to the jewel case after the ruby disappeared? We must fetch it at once and recover the ruby."

Lestrade pointed towards Sir John, who by now had sunk low in his chair and was holding his face in his hands. "I believe, Mr. Holmes, that Sir John took the case home with him. That's the last I saw of it."

"Sir John?" Holmes asked, his spirits still buoyant. "You have it safe?"

The old soldier was shaking now, his hands still pressed to his face. "That's just the problem, Mr. Holmes. You see, there was an *event* last night. At my home. I didn't mention it. It didn't seem important."

"An *event,* Sir John?"

"A burglary, Mr. Holmes. My house was broken into. A back window was smashed. Mr. Holmes, the jewel case is stolen."

CHAPTER SEVENTEEN

Miss Del Fuego's Last Dance

That night the snow fell deep on London, choking the gutters and sealing off alleyways, muffling the hooves of horses and the grinding of factories, blotting out the view of Big Ben as if a curtain had fallen on it. But no amount of snow was enough to cool the temperatures in Baker Street as the four gentlemen responsible for the Malabar Rose considered what was to be done next. Sir John's announcement had stunned us all, but Mr. Holmes and Inspector Lestrade were the first to recover. Mr. Holmes was quickly on his feet, pacing his regular beat in front of the fireplace. His eyes gleamed with energy, and it was clear he was not downcast.

"A second chance, gentlemen," he mused. "And this time we have a real crime to investigate, with broken windows and physical evidence. Lestrade, who have you got on the case?"

"I'm not sure, Mr. Holmes. This would probably have gone to McAdam." Lestrade's brain was clearly racing. "I can get down there straightaway to take over. You're right, Mr.

Holmes, this gives us a chance. We know where we are with a common burglary. And at least we know the Malabar Rose cannot yet have gone far."

"This man, Phillimore. You must get a description from his wife, Lestrade. Then alert the ports. Close the doors on him!"

"Of course, Mr. Holmes. We can make life damned hot for him now. But what should we do about the Great Salmanazar?"

"Keep him under house arrest for now. He was clearly involved. You may soon have sufficient grounds for a formal arrest."

"Let's hope so, sir. Sir John, will you accompany me? I will need to rouse your household and question them about events last night."

The two men left immediately, the one grim-faced but determined, the other still sadly downcast. After their departure, Mr. Holmes continued his pacing.

"A daring crime. They were unlucky that I came to hear about the disappearance in Ealing. Had I not been aware of that, they might have made good their escape."

I looked across to see how this would be greeted by Mrs. Hudson, but the housekeeper appeared serene rather than outraged.

"Let's see, Watson," Mr. Holmes continued. "What would you do now if you were in this fellow's shoes?"

"Make for the coast, Holmes. Show a clean pair of heels. I'd want to get out before the alarm was sounded."

"Precisely. Let's see . . . There was a night train for France from Victoria last night but, given the time of the burglary, it is impossible that he could have caught that. What about the early trains to the channel ports?"

"If you please, sir," Mrs. Hudson cut in quietly, "I didn't

like to mention it earlier because I thought the other two gentlemen would make a lot of fuss, but I don't think Mr. Phillimore will be heading for the coast."

"You don't? You think he might lie low, wait for the outcry to die down?" He paused to consider. "I think not, Mrs. Hudson. No, I fear you do not understand the intricacies of the criminal mind. I am convinced he will head for the Continent."

"No doubt he would, sir, but, you see, he doesn't have the ruby."

"*What?*" I have never seen Sherlock Holmes look more totally astounded. He paused in his pacing and glowered at his housekeeper. "Explain yourself, Mrs. Hudson," he demanded.

"It's as I say, sir. He doesn't have the ruby. He has the case, but the ruby wasn't in it."

"It wasn't?" Mr. Holmes was scowling now. "Then who in God's name *does* have it?"

"I do, sir."

"*You do?*" I have never known such a gaunt man appear so close to apoplexy. "Is this a joke?"

Mrs. Hudson allowed herself a smile. "Well, I daresay there is quite a funny side to it, yes, sir." She nodded to herself, as though the conversation was about nothing more important than the next day's dinner menu. "You see, as soon as I visited Perch for the first time, I found myself wondering how the old toy maker might be able to help with the execution of a jewel robbery. Once you had ruled out the impossibly elaborate, there weren't many options left."

Mr. Holmes and Dr. Watson exchanged glances. "That's all very well, Mrs. Hudson," the detective growled, his teeth clenched. "But I understood you to say you actually *have* the ruby in your possession."

"I do, sir. When Flotsam and I went to the Satin Rooms

the day after all the excitement, I took with me the replica jewel case that Sir John had left us. And when I was able to sneak into the room itself, it was a moment's work to swap the replica for the case I found there. That's the one I brought away with me, sir." She pointed to the jewel case that still stood beside his chair.

"But *where is the ruby,* Mrs. Hudson? We must tell Sir John at once."

Mrs. Hudson might have appeared impassive as she considered this question, but from where I stood I could detect a slight stiffening of her jaw.

"If you don't mind, sir, I'd rather not say."

"You'd rather *what*?" Again I feared for Mr. Holmes' heart.

"I say, Mrs. H, we can't have that, you know," Dr. Watson put in. "It's not quite on. Can't just keep it, you know. And, besides, we need to know where it is so that we can look after it properly."

Mrs. Hudson looked him squarely in the eye. "I don't wish to be rude, sir, but it seems to me that the fewer people who know where to find it, the safer it is."

"But we could put it in safe hands! Get it into the vaults at the Bank of England."

"That's true, sir. But if you do that, you'll never see Mr. Phillimore again. He'll just slip away. Now if you were to use the Malabar Rose as bait . . ."

"My word, Mrs. Hudson!" Mr. Holmes spoke with the air of a man seeing light after many dark months. "That's just the thing! I see that you are truly benefiting from your proximity to genius."

"Yes, sir. Thank you, sir."

"But how would it work, Holmes?" Dr. Watson wondered.

"Simple, my dear Watson. Phillimore is out there somewhere, wondering where the gem is. If we could persuade him that it was being held in a certain place . . ."

"Sir John Plaskett's house, for instance, sir."

"Indeed yes, Mrs. Hudson. If we could get word to him that the Malabar Rose is hidden in Sir John's bedroom, he would surely make another attempt on it."

"And we could be waiting, Holmes! Splendid!" But then a cloud of doubt passed over Dr. Watson's face. "Er, how would we get word to him, though? We don't know where he is."

Mrs. Hudson waited patiently for Mr. Holmes to respond, but when he hesitated she coughed politely.

"If it were mentioned in passing to the Great Salmanazar, sir, might he not get word to his accomplice?"

"But the Great Salmanazar is being held incommunicado in his hotel, Mrs. Hudson. He won't be able to contact his friend from there."

"Yes, sir. That's why I think we should help him escape."

IT was nearly midnight and the city was already deep in snow when the council of war at Baker Street finally drew to a close. The idea was simple. Dr. Watson would visit the Great Salmanazar the next day and, in his own inimitable manner, would mention that the Malabar Rose was safe in Sir John's hands. Then, when our plans were laid, the police guards at Brown's Hotel would be lured away, allowing the illusionist to abscond.

"He will be too wary to lead us to Phillimore directly," Mrs. Hudson explained. "You see, he'll be half-expecting to be followed. But he'll find some discreet way of getting in touch with his partner in crime, you can be sure of that."

"And then, when Mr. Phillimore comes calling on Sir John, we shall be ready to strike!" declared Sherlock Holmes.

"In the meantime, Mrs. Hudson," muttered Dr. Watson rather anxiously, "I do hope you've got that ruby hidden somewhere damnably safe!"

. . .

By the time the clocks struck twelve that night, the household in Baker Street was on its way to bed. I was the first to get there—on Mrs. Hudson's orders—and as I lay with the blankets pulled up to my nose, I could tell from the peace upstairs that Dr. Watson and Mr. Holmes had also brought their day to a close. Last to bed was Mrs. Hudson. Instead of retiring straightaway, she took up another pile of laundry and began to fold it into neat piles. For half an hour by the kitchen fire, her face lined with thought, she lined up the edges of sheets, measured folds, divided, and then subdivided, all with Pythagorean exactitude. At the end of that time, she took up a copy of the *Gazette* and turned to the pages that listed sailings, then found the columns concerning departures to Canada from the south-coast ports. Only after she had studied it for many minutes did she nod to herself and take up the lamp and retreat to her room. By one o'clock, the house was silent.

Silent, but not still. For on the kitchen floor, unnoticed by me as I slumbered, a shadow twitched. As if aware that, in the whole street, it alone was blessed with motion, it paused for a little time before moving again. This time the movement was very clear and determined: and the shadow grew and threatened to fill the room. At the same time, a very faint creak frayed the edge of the silence, as if weight was being lowered onto rusty metal. Slowly and softly, someone crept down the area stairs.

Had I woken then I would have seen the shadow transformed into a dark figure, its form still indistinct as it came close to the kitchen door—so close that it might have been listening, as if to see what stirred. Then, almost inaudibly, something began to scrape at the kitchen lock. A thin wire was slipped between the door and the jamb, a connection was made, and with breathless care the inner bolt was worked slowly inwards until it slipped from its hold, and the door swung open.

The figure didn't hesitate, slipping into the kitchen shadows, then turning and pressing the door closed behind. Then silence, a pause to listen. No sound, only the hush of a sleeping house. Then more listening—intense, concentrated listening, as if there was a need to press beyond the silence, to go behind it, to the steady breathing of the hidden sleepers. At last, as if navigating on the extremes of its senses, the figure began to move. Skirting across the pool of streetlight that filtered onto the kitchen floor, it crept with clear purpose to a small door in the corner of the room. A small, familiar door. My door.

When I awoke that night, there was a dark hand over my mouth. Weight pressed down on me, hot breath was on my cheek, an urgent whisper in my ear.

"Flotsam! Flotsam!" A small voice, a child's voice. A voice on the edge of panic. "Sssh, Flotsam. It's me. Blue. It's me."

"Blue!" I thought the word rather than spoke it, for his hand was still pressed on my mouth. I pushed it away angrily and, recovering my equilibrium, gave him a furious push with all my strength so that he stumbled backwards and hit the wall.

"What are *you* doing here? How dare you?" My fury was fuelled by the shock. "If you think you can get more out of me, well, you're wrong. You took it all already. A job, you said! And to think I believed you! I know what you were doing at the Regal Theatre that night!"

I made no attempt to lower my voice. I was too angry for that. Anger shot through me with all the pain that comes from trusting and being deceived.

"Sssh, Flotsam," he begged again. "*Please.* If they catch

me, it'll be the Scrubs for me." In the darkness I could see him reach inside his thin, tatty coat and bring out a small canvas bag. "Look, I've brought it back. What you lent me. Every penny of it. Here, count."

He threw the bag onto the bed as if not daring to come any closer. It landed on the nest of blankets with a metallic clink.

For a moment I just looked at it, too shocked and surprised to think clearly. But then, as it had landed so close to my hand, it seemed obvious to reach out for it. In silence I emptied its contents onto the blanket.

There was enough light from the kitchen for me to know beyond doubt that he was as good as his word. Three gold sovereigns, clean and pure and perfect. My lost savings restored. Restored by a thief. A cheat. A liar. I looked up uncomprehendingly. He must have seen by the sagging of my shoulders that my anger had gone, for now he dared to come forward and perch himself on the foot of my bed.

"I've been trying to get it back to yer. Honest. But there's always coppers an' 'tectives an' all sorts roun' here. So it's took me some time. But it's all there, it is."

"Yes, Blue, it's all there." I looked down, overwhelmed, suddenly full of guilt for all the anger I'd been carrying with me. "But I don't understand. I gave you this to settle your debts, so you could make a clean start. But that was lies. There was no job where you said. And Mrs. Hudson saw you picking pockets at the theatre."

"She did *not!*" Suddenly his small face was full of fire. "I wasn't picking pockets. I *wasn't*. I was putting stuff *into* pockets, I was. Playin' cards, that's what they were gettin'. Nothin' wrong with that, is there? No law 'gainst *givin'* folks stuff, is there?"

In the dim light I could sense rather than see that he was flushed with indignation.

"No, that's true," I agreed. "But . . ." I paused. "Perhaps you should just tell me everything."

And this time he did, I was sure of that. If only because there seemed no reason to lie now.

"What I said, 'bout a clean start, it was the honest truth, it was. I knew that I needed to buy myself out. But I never had the money. I used to just sort of dream that someone 'ud give me money out of the blue—just give it, honest-like, so I could get away. An' I knew just what I'd do if I had it."

"What would you do?"

"You heard of a place called New Zealand? Everyone says it's the place to go. There's chances out there for someone like me."

At first I thought he was lying again. This tiny, Thames-eel of a boy who knew nothing but London, to be dreaming of a land so strange and so far away—it seemed impossible to believe. But then the faint light from the street fell for a moment on his face, and I saw those amazing blue eyes lit up with something pure and wonderful. They were the eyes of a visionary, a dreamer grasping for his dream.

"What sort of chances, Blue? I've heard it's hard over there."

"I don't mind hard. And I'm quick, and I learn fast. Faster 'n anyone. Oh, not book stuff. Ain't never been learnt none o' that. But how to do things. Mend things. An' I can sell. Can sell anyone anythin'. I just ain't got nothin' to sell." His eyes drifted back to me. "So I've been savin'. For the boat. But it takes so long to save, 'cos all I steal I have to give most of it back to the gang. So I just lies awake at night an' dream."

When he paused, I didn't speak. I felt too moved by the feeling in his voice.

"When I saw you, Flottie, that night when you grabbed

my hand, I sort o' felt like you weren't the same as the others. Dunno why. Just knew you was different. And then yer goes and gives me that money. No one's ever done that. Not ever. Made me feel all funny, it did. So I took it to old Monk, the gang-master, and I told him I was quits, that he'd never see me again. An' he never will."

"And the theatre, Blue? What was that all about?"

"That was the job I told you about. Didn't like to tell you what it was, 'cos I thought you'd not like it much, so I made something up. But this thin guy come up to a mate o' mine in the street, told him there was three guineas for him and his mates if we does some work for him and never tells no one. *Three guineas,* Flottie. Think of it! An' easy work too. So I took the money an' did the work, then come straight here to give you back what's yours."

Perhaps it was because it was late and I was tired, but there was something in his tale that brought a lump to my throat. I suddenly felt small and humbled.

We talked for a long time that night. I learned that he was only a little short of the total he needed for his boat fare. He had no idea how he'd raise the remainder, but somehow he left me believing that he'd find a way. In return for his confidences, I told him why there were always so many policemen around the house and ended up telling him the whole story of James Phillimore: how his wife was looking for him and how Mr. Rumbelow was holding a reward of £30 for anyone who found him, how Mr. Holmes was setting a trap for him, how Mrs. Hudson had somehow managed to snatch the Malabar Rose from his grasp.

But that was not the end of that night's talk, for when Blue came to leave I noticed a reluctance in him to step out into the night. At first I thought it might be the cold that deterred him, and I tried to persuade him to take my winter coat. But it was soon clear there was something quite different on his mind. Eventually, he reached into his pocket again and drew something out in his closed palm.

"That first time you spoke to me, Flottie. You asked me if my name was John."

"You reminded me of someone, that's all."

"And you said about a picture."

"That boy I knew had a picture," I explained.

"Pictures have writing, don't they? To tell yer who they are."

"Some pictures do."

"I reckon you can read, Flottie." He was looking at me appraisingly.

"Yes, Blue."

"Can you read this?"

He opened his palm and showed me, resting in it, a slim oval locket. It was too dark to see the detail, but when I took it from him he struck a match, and by that dancing light I could see it plainly.

"You open it there," Blue whispered. "See? You pushes that . . ."

The locket sprang open, revealing the portrait inside. A young woman smiling, indescribably lovely. The softness of that face, the smiling eyes with their mixture of love and laughter . . . I remembered her so clearly. And, had any doubts remained, the words on the back, engraved in sloping letters, would have dispelled each one.

> *To John, my loving husband*
> *For always and forever my life, my love*
> *Your wife for always,*
> *Sarah*

Before I could read it aloud, the match flickered out.

"What's it say, Flot?" Blue was trying not to let his eagerness show. "I've never had anyone to ask before, you see. Does it say her name?"

"Her name's Sarah. I think she's your mother," I told him. "The locket was her gift to your father. He was called John. It says she really loved him." I couldn't hide the catch in my voice. "And, Blue, you and I, we've met before."

THE day that followed the heavy snowfall dawned grey and uninviting. The snow clouds hung low over the city, and the smoke from London's chimneys, trapped by the dark canopy above them, filled the air with a grey drizzle of soot. The streets that day were a bad place to be. Traffic struggled and tempers flared. The drifted snow was quickly churned by scrabbling hooves, and the pristine whiteness of midnight was churned into the filthy slush of dawn.

Dr. Watson, attempting an early morning walk in a mauve-and-green necktie, was quickly beaten back by the dirt and the confusion.

"How is it, Mrs. Hudson, that we can run an empire that spans the globe, but we can't manage to keep a path open between Baker Street and Hyde Park on a snowy morning?"

"No doubt the situation will improve, sir. Indeed, I trust it does, for Flottie and I have a call to make this morning. And indeed, you yourself will be calling on the Great Salmanazar this morning, will you not?"

Dr. Watson appeared gloomy at the prospect. "That's right, Mrs. Hudson. Must play my part. And I don't mind. It's just that I was very keen to fit in a walk in the park this morning."

"In this weather, sir?"

Dr. Watson looked suddenly nonchalant. "Oh, what's a bit of snow? Can't let it get in the way of a good walk, can we? Tell me, Mrs. Hudson, what do you think of this necktie?"

"A very colourful garment, sir."

"You think so?" Dr. Watson sounded doubtful. "I'm not sure myself. I might go and change it for something with a bit more *character* . . ."

And with that, Dr. Watson pottered back to his room, humming in rather a carefree manner.

"Now, Flotsam," Mrs. Hudson continued when he'd gone, "as I said, we have a call to make. An urgent one. The future happiness of any number of people is at stake. Who knows, it might even affect the colour of Dr. Watson's neckwear. So less of your yawning and on with your coat. I've known cats in creameries yawn less than that."

I felt this remark could not be allowed to pass, so as we readied ourselves for the rigours of the streets outside, I explained to Mrs. Hudson about my nocturnal visitor. She listened with great attention, and when I told her about the return of my savings she vowed to improve the locks on the kitchen door. When I described how Blue's locket had proved that he really was the helpless child who had once clung so close to me, for some reason the telling of the story made me cry. Mrs. Hudson said very little but allowed the tears to flow, diverting me deftly into a tearoom off Paul Street so that when at last the sobs ran out of strength, I was faced with a steaming bowl of hot milk and a hearty plate of cinnamon toast.

While the toast was being demolished with an appetite surprising in one so watery-eyed, Mrs. Hudson explained by way of a diversion that we were on our way to see Lola Del Fuego.

"And a very different sort of interview it will be this time," she declared menacingly and, as it proved, entirely correctly. For the Lola that we found at the Blenheim Hotel had none of the sheen or the freshness that I remembered from our first interview. She was still an imperious beauty, though now there were dark circles under her eyes and a hollowness in her cheeks, as if anxiety had pinched them tight. At first she refused to see us but relented even before her message of refusal had reached us. When we were shown into her rooms, she flew at us in a grand Iberian passion.

"Ah, so it is you!" she raged. "You, who since your visit to me all things go wrong! I am here like a bird in a cage. Your police say, no, I cannot leave. Cannot walk in the streets. Cannot send letter to man I will marry. I know nothing what goes on, only you lose your silly ruby and you think, 'Ah! Lola is foreigner, she has not friends here as she does in Spain. We say she steals stone. Then all is happy.'"

Her eyes flashed venomously. "But is not true. I dance while ruby is lost. I dance. Many, many people see. So soon I go from here, and then you will see what happens, all you who treat me like so."

Mrs. Hudson showed no sign of flinching in the face of this storm. She simply waited until the tirade had run its course, returning the dancer's gaze with unruffled composure. Then, when the accusations had run out, she began slowly to unbutton her coat, as if readying herself for a long interview.

"Now then, Polly Perkins," she began sternly, "I think we might all get on a little better in plain English, don't you?"

On hearing these words, the dancer paled as if all the passion and defiance had drained from her. Even so, she mustered her strength for one last, brave stand.

"Poll-ee? Who is this Poll-ee? Is not my name. I am Lola Conchita Santa-Maria De La Cruz, and I speak the Spanish of Castille."

"No, you are Polly Perkins, and you speak the English of Clapham Junction. Judging by your accent, you have never been to Castille, or indeed any other part of Spain, in your entire life. Now, my girl, I've no time for charades. If you don't give up this ridiculous pretence at once, I'm afraid you're going to find yourself in a great deal of trouble."

For a moment the younger woman hesitated, and I watched a succession of emotions play across her features—surprise, anger, fear . . . At the end of them all came a sudden and unexpected surrender, and I watched a tense, watery smile appear on her lips. When she spoke, it was with the undisguised accent of south London.

"So, you've found out about me. I can't say I mind. I need someone to talk to more than I've ever needed anything in my life, and that's the truth." Her lips trembled a little. "It's driving me mad, being kept here with no idea what's going on! If I don't find out, I shall go insane, I know I shall."

She turned and beckoned us deeper into her suite of rooms, still struggling to control her emotions. "I'm sorry. I must stay calm. And you're both cold. Come here, by the fire."

As we divested ourselves of our outside coats and began to warm our hands, Lola—Miss Perkins—was watching us with a curious expression.

"I've heard of you," she said after a pause. "My cousin was in service. She said you helped her when she dropped some sort of old pot."

"The Hardwick Ming vase? But her name was Thompson."

"Yes, she was from the other side of the family."

"I remember her well. I hear she is doing very nicely as a seamstress in Barnstaple now. And I believe Lord Hardwick is no longer trying to have her thrown into chains. Now . . ." She fixed the dancer with her most reproving stare. "Now, your beau, James Phillimore, is making a great deal of trouble. The way he's going, he's likely to end up behind bars for a very, very long time."

"*No!*" The hair comb Miss Perkins was playing with snapped abruptly between her fingers. "That can't be true!" she pleaded. "He's not a bad man! It's that Salmanazar! It's him who should be in the dock, not my Jimmy!" She broke down in a fit of weeping and covered her face with her hands. "Oh, Mrs. Hudson! I love him so! I've always loved him! I can't bear for anything to happen to him. I can't bear for him to go to prison. I'd rather give him up altogether than have that happen!"

Mrs. Hudson guided her gently into an armchair, but her voice was still stern. "It might yet come to that. Mr. Phillimore has a wife, you know."

Miss Perkins' shoulders began to shake with even greater wretchedness. "I know," she whimpered. "But only because he was trying to forget me! She doesn't love him as I do! She cannot! I know she cannot!"

Mrs. Hudson eased herself into the chair opposite the stricken woman and signalled with an eyebrow for me to settle myself beside her.

"Now then, Polly Perkins," she said softly, " I think the best thing you can do is to tell us everything right from the beginning . . ."

AND that is how I heard for the second time how James Phillimore's mother ran away from her home in the South Downs to return to the London stage, taking with her the young son who had been left in her charge on that fateful afternoon. With that desperate act began Mr. Phillimore's long journey from privileged country childhood to becoming, briefly and almost accidentally, the most wanted man in Britain.

The experience of his early years, after his mother's return to the grubby stages of the East End, was not, however, entirely without parallels. Like him, Polly Perkins had been brought up in London's seedier halls of entertainment, and the two had been thrown together from an early age. Each had been there to watch the other's first, infant steps into the limelight, and each had been there to support the other as they had grown into seasoned child performers. The boy contortionist and the girl singer were soon seen by those around them to be particular friends, and that friendship grew and became something fonder as they began to leave their childhood behind them.

But adulthood brought change, and Folding Freddie's rather straightforward act did not translate to the adult stage, while his sweetheart's voice grew clearer and more beautiful every day. Yet that same voice cracked with emotion as Miss Perkins told us how Phillimore's career had begun to crumble.

"It never mattered to me that he wasn't successful," she wailed. "I would have loved him if he'd been a dustman or a chimney sweep. I just wanted him to be with me! But his pride wouldn't allow it. He hated that I had money and he didn't. He took to avoiding all his old friends, and he told his casual acquaintances that he was going to start a new life somewhere else. Then one day he just disappeared. He left me a note to say he loved me too much to hold me back, that one day I would forget him and would thank him for what he had done. But I couldn't forget him! Not for a day. I went abroad and turned myself into Lola Del Fuego, but I never forgot him. All that time when there were counts and dukes and who knows what begging for my company, I could only think of how we used to laugh together, how he'd put his arms around me and make me feel I was the most special person in the world. By the time I went to Paris to perform with the Great Salmanazar, I'd almost forgotten what Jimmy looked like, but I still missed him. I missed him every day."

She looked up at us then, and smiled bravely through the tears. Polly Perkins had given up some of Lola Del Fuego's exotic veneer, but she seemed to me to have gained a beauty of a different sort: the sort of simple sweetness you glimpse sometimes amid crowds on busy streets, and which makes you for a moment forget the greyness of the day around you.

"I'll always remember that day in Paris when he walked in," she told us with a faint glow rising to her cheeks. "I felt my heart miss a beat, and I thought I was going to fall to the ground. After all that time, to have him suddenly walk into the room so completely unexpected! And I could see he felt the same. It was like we'd never stopped thinking of each other. From that moment, we knew we had to be together. Oh, we knew it was wrong! Don't think that we didn't. But the touch of his fingers made me feel like I was melting, and there was nothing I wouldn't give up just to be with him."

At that first meeting she learned that Phillimore was Salmanazar's secret collaborator. He had been recruited by the illusionist because since his retirement he was no longer known in theatrical circles, and because he had not lost his simple talent for folding himself into tiny spaces. He was Salmanazar's most jealously guarded secret, appearing only on the eve of performances and then disappearing again immediately afterwards, so that even the stagehands didn't know how the magician was escaping from those tightly chained crates and those nailed-down coffins.

"But Jimmy soon came to know about Salmanazar's other business," Miss Perkins confided. "He knew about all those famous thefts, but he never had nothing to do with them!" Miss Perkins became defiant at the thought. "He knew how Salmanazar used his act to slip away, knew about all the big robberies, but he was paid to keep quiet. He never got involved in any of them, at least not until . . ." She hesitated, looking anxiously up at Mrs. Hudson. "At least not until this time."

"And what was different about this one, Polly?" Mrs.

Hudson inquired, though I think both she and I already knew the answer.

"Oh, Mrs. Hudson! It was because of me!" Her shoulders began to shake again, and her rather lovely lips trembled. "We planned to escape together, to get away from his marriage and from Salmanazar and everything. Jimmy said his wife wouldn't miss him if he left her enough money instead. He said if we were rich we could give her money to make it all right, and then we could go and live together somewhere abroad, where nobody would find us. We only wanted enough to get away, honestly we did!"

The thought of that shared dream brought more tears rolling down her cheeks, and we waited quietly until she was able to go on.

"Jimmy knew that Salmanazar needed help to steal the Malabar Rose. The police were watching him now, you see, but none of them knew a thing about Jimmy. He could come and go as he pleased. So they struck a deal and planned it together. Salmanazar liked Jimmy. He offered to share the whole value of the ruby, but Jimmy said he only needed enough to live a quiet life in Canada. He said too much money would make people notice him."

She stifled another sob.

"So you see, it's *my* fault that Jimmy's in trouble. But he never stole anything before this, Mrs. Hudson! He never did!"

"And he hasn't stolen very much yet." It seemed to me that Mrs. Hudson was speaking more to herself than to the woman before her. "There's breaking and entering, of course. And an empty jewellery case stolen from Sir John Plaskett. And there's the small matter of attempted arson with the aim of destroying criminal evidence. But at least he hasn't got the Malabar Rose. I'm afraid if he succeeds in getting that, there's little hope left for him at all . . ."

Miss Perkins' pallor had become even more marked during this summary of her loved one's position. "Oh, Mrs. Hudson! What's to be done?"

In reply, the housekeeper looked her firmly in the eye and spoke with unexpected urgency.

"Listen carefully to this. Your future depends on it. You are in a very difficult position. There are some who might consider you an accessory to the Great Salmanazar's crimes. You may need to make a very hasty escape if you are to avoid a spell in prison."

"Escape without Jimmy?" She shook her head desperately. "No, I won't! I would rather let them take me!"

"And spend the rest of your youth stitching sacks in Holloway? What would your Jimmy say to that? No, here's what you will do, my girl. When you receive word from me, you will slip out of here any way you can. The fire escape may be your best bet. Then you'll take the first train to Portsmouth. Take only the bare essentials with you, and on your arrival find somewhere cheap to spend the night. At four the following afternoon, go to the offices of the Meyer and Stallard Steam Company and wait at the rear door. The *rear* door, mind. Is that clear?"

"The rear door, yes."

"Wait there until seven o'clock. If no one comes to find you before seven, go in and tell them your name. Your real name. There'll be a ticket waiting for you. Use it to go to Canada, and don't look back."

"Just go as I am? Leave everything behind? But, Mrs. Hudson, I've worked so hard to make a little fortune for myself. Back in Paris I have a house and savings . . . If I run away as you suggest, I lose everything!"

"If you do not, any chance you have of seeing James Phillimore again will be lost forever." Mrs. Hudson spoke with such a note of authority in her voice that to contradict her would have taken the courage of a lion.

"And Jimmy?" Miss Perkins asked meekly.

"Jimmy must take what comes. By the time you reach Canada you will know exactly what the future holds for him."

Miss Perkins nodded meekly at that, and then asked the question that I was asking myself.

"But, Mrs. Hudson, why would you help me like this? You don't even know me."

However, it was clear from the look in Mrs. Hudson's eye that she had no inclination to elucidate.

"Oh, I have my reasons, young lady," she stated shortly. "You don't need to know what they are. We may not meet again after today, so in parting I'll leave you with some advice."

"Yes, Mrs. Hudson?"

"Simply this. If in the future your path leads you to domestic happiness, I recommend that you always pay very careful attention to your loved one's socks. Now good day to you, Miss Perkins."

CHAPTER EIGHTEEN

Midnight in Trafalgar Square

The case of the Malabar Rose reached both its climax and its conclusion on the night in which one year ended and the next began. It had taken Dr. Watson until the morning of the thirtieth to obtain an interview with the Great Salmanazar that was not closely observed by one or the other of Inspector Lestrade's officers. When the chance finally arose, Dr. Watson, by his own account, gave an excellent performance in the role of bluff old fool, and was able not only to inform the illusionist that the Malabar Rose was being held at Sir John's house, but also to intimate to him that the evening of New Year's Eve might be a time when the attention of that gentleman's police guards was most likely to waver.

Those seeds having been planted, the study in Baker Street became a place where plans were laid and relaid, where decisions were taken boldly and then quietly reconsidered. Sherlock Holmes and Dr. Watson were pressing in their desire to include at least Sir John and possibly also Inspector Lestrade in the Baker Street confederacy.

"After all," argued Dr. Watson, "deliberately setting free this Salmanazar chappie so that he can bait the trap for Phillimore is all very well, but what if we lose him? There'd be the devil to pay! We'd become a national laughingstock, Holmes!"

"We won't lose him, Watson," Mr. Holmes returned reassuringly. "You and I will dog his footsteps every inch of the way. When it's clear that he's found a way of communicating to Phillimore the whereabouts of the ruby, we shall perform a citizen's arrest and take him back into custody." He broke off and frowned at his pipe. "Even so, Mrs. Hudson, if we are expecting this man Phillimore to break cover at Sir John's house, I admit I'd be happier if there were a dozen sturdy constables to back us up."

But Mrs. Hudson was adamant that the police should not be told anything until we had Mr. Phillimore in our hands. And since Mrs. Hudson was the only person who knew the *real* whereabouts of the Malabar Rose, her preferences carried rather more weight than the two gentlemen's combined.

In the meantime, we began to decide exactly what role each of us would play. It was agreed that Dr. Watson and Sherlock Holmes, both heavily disguised, would be responsible for following the Great Salmanazar and making sure he didn't escape. Then, to our great surprise, Mrs. Hudson refused to play any role at all, insisting that it was her night off and that she had half a mind to visit a relative of hers in Sydenham, a suggestion that provoked alarm and despondency in equal proportion amongst her coconspirators.

"But who will distract all the policemen on duty at Brown's Hotel, Mrs. H?" Dr. Watson asked. "That's the key to this whole thing."

"I'm sure we can leave that to Flottie, sir," Mrs. Hudson assured him.

Sherlock Holmes peered at me over his violin, which he had raised to his chin but had not yet begun to play.

"And do you feel you have it in you to be sufficiently distracting, Flotsam?" he inquired.

"I'm not sure that I do, sir," I replied honestly, "but I certainly know someone who does."

IT's fair to say that Miss Peters showed no reluctance whatsoever when I explained to her that she was required, single-handedly, to lure a dozen different policemen away from their posts. If I had expected a display of maidenly modesty, I was to be severely disappointed.

"Really?" she gasped, when I explained to her the task ahead. "Oh, Flottie, you *are* an angel! You know how much I always want to help with Mrs. Hudson's plots and plans. No, I don't think I need you to explain it all in detail, really I don't. I'm sure it's all very clever, but you know how I never really understand Mrs. Hudson's adventures until she explains them very carefully right at the end. I think for now I'll just stick to the policemen, shall I? You know, I've *always* liked policemen, ever since I was six, and one of them arrested me for tying fireworks to the door of the post office. Or was it the vicarage? Well, *somewhere* with a door, anyway."

When I wondered aloud if Rupert Spencer would altogether approve of her flirting with uniformed policemen, she simply laughed the question away with a little shake of her head.

"Oh, *of course* I shan't tell Rupert. I shall tell him I'm going to the Winter Ball and that I intend to dance all night with the Walters boy. He never seems to mind when I do that. He just smiles and shrugs. It's *most* unflattering. Anyway, I'm sure he won't be jealous however many policemen I flirt with. And if he *was* jealous, well, that would just be simply *too* divine . . ."

"But how will you do it?" I asked, marvelling at her confidence. "After all, there are twelve of them."

She giggled rather charmingly at the thought. "Don't you worry about it, Flottie. I have a plan. I'm very good at plans, you know, it's just that nobody ever notices. I forget it myself sometimes. But don't worry, it's all going to be *too* easy. I shall pick you up tomorrow night at seven. Make sure you are dressed in your very smartest clothes. I shall be wearing that pale blue evening dress, and I shall be looking really rather heavenly."

At which thought she smiled and began to talk about hats.

FOR all the unusual severity of the winter weather, it seemed that the citizens of London were determined to celebrate the dawning of the new year with considerable enthusiasm. Right from the moment when the shops began to close on the evening of the thirty-first, it seemed that everyone from the humble clerk to the rather tipsy costermonger was making his way into town with a mission to drink a toast or two to the new year, to the old year, to Her Majesty, to Olde England, to his fellow topers, perhaps even to the Malabar Rose, which surely, it was generally agreed, should be put on show without further delay.

As a result of this great influx of revellers, the streets were congested, the theatres sold out, and the public houses were heaving with crowds and good humour. At the Tudor Rose, off The Haymarket, a woman dressed as Britannia was singing ribald sea shanties to generous and raucous accompaniment. Down by the river, a crowd had gathered, and bets were being taken on which of two monkeys would be quickest up the mast of the schooner *Percival.* In at least a hundred different streets small boys were setting off firecrackers, and a hundred different grandmothers were recalling that, when the Duke of Wellington was prime minister, young lads used to know some manners. In Trafalgar Square, the pantomime troupe that had been barred from the Regal Theatre in the wake of Salmanazar's show had decided to put on its own, impromptu performance at the foot of Nelson's Column; and soon after they had raised their makeshift curtain, a crowd of cheering hearties was roaring on Baron Bounder as he pursued Widow Wellbeloved around the fountains, and was weeping as the principal boy vowed to win the heart of the beautiful princess, even though he had no fortune to his name but a handful of beans and a rather shapely pair of legs.

Before leaving Baker Street and placing ourselves at the mercy of these boisterous elements, Mrs. Hudson and I found a little time to talk quietly as we completed our daily chores. Mr. Holmes and Dr. Watson had already left to take up their chosen positions near Brown's Hotel, positions where they felt they could observe the Great Salmanazar's movements without themselves being seen. Without them, a restful hush fell on the house.

"So, Flotsam," Mrs. Hudson began when the last pan had been scoured and the last glass polished. "If things happen as we plan, by dawn James Phillimore could be in the hands of Inspector Lestrade. What do you think of that, eh?"

The question took me by surprise a little. "I suppose that's a good thing, ma'am," I told her. "After all, he's a desperate man. Who knows what he might do?"

"Yes, desperate to get away from London, Flotsam. And desperate to escape Lavinia Phillimore. Desperate to be with Polly Perkins somewhere where there are no theatres. I wonder, Flotsam, is that really so bad?"

"But, ma'am, people can't go stealing things just because they want them!"

"Can't they, Flottie?"

I blushed, remembering that Mrs. Hudson and I had only met when I, in desperation, had attempted to steal a cabbage from Scraggs' barrow.

"Besides, James Phillimore hasn't really done much wrong yet, has he? Oh, I know he's *trying* to, but that's rather different."

"But he tried to burn us alive in Mr. Perch's toy shop, ma'am!"

"Oh, I think we just happened to be in the way when he was trying to destroy the evidence that connected the toy shop—and him—to the Malabar Rose."

"And then there's his wife, ma'am. He seems to have forgotten about her completely."

"Well, Flottie, he sent her that pile of notes, enough to keep her in dresses for quite a long time. But you're right, my girl. It would not do for us to forget Mrs. Phillimore, would it?" She picked up a stray dishcloth and folded it into a neat square, then folded it into triangles, reconsidered, made it once again a square, and placed it carefully on top of a pile of plates. "Good luck tonight, Flottie. And remember, if Salmanazar succeeds in getting word to Mr. Phillimore about where the ruby is, we can expect the attempt on Sir John's house to follow very rapidly. You'll need to be on your toes, girl."

She had advanced as far as the pantry and was peering into it, her face pensive.

"Mrs. Hudson, ma'am, you aren't really going to Sydenham tonight, are you?"

She favoured me with an approving smile. "Of course not, Flotsam. But I've got a little idea of my own for tonight that I didn't want to tell Mr. Holmes about. There's someone I want a quiet word with and this would seem to be my only chance. Which means I may not be back here to guard the ruby tonight if anything goes awry."

"You mean the ruby's *here,* ma'am?"

"Wherever else would I keep it, Flottie? Yes, it's here, though you're better off not knowing exactly where. Now, if there's any time tonight when you think things are going wrong, I want you to come back here and keep watch. Lock all the doors and shout for a policeman if anyone tries to get in. And Flotsam? If anything were to happen to me tonight, I'd hate to think of that iced fruitcake going to waste. Do you think you can promise me to get the whole thing eaten in the next few days, while it's still nice and fresh?"

And with that great weight off her mind, she smiled happily and set about a detailed inventory of all our tinned goods and preserves.

Miss Peters arrived to collect me on the stroke of seven o'clock, and arrived in some style, comfortably ensconced in the Earl of Brabham's carriage with Carrington, the earl's coachman, impassive on the box.

"Well, my uncle wasn't using it," she explained gaily, "and Carrington always likes to keep an eye on me, don't you, Carrington?"

It was hard to tell from Carrington's delicately raised eyebrow if that was the case or not, but he certainly steered us out of Baker Street with great care, the carriage picking its way through the evening traffic with the quiet dignity of a dowager duchess at a village harvest fair. To my great surprise, our path led not to Brown's Hotel where Salmanazar was being confined to his rooms, but to the very headquarters of those guarding him, to Scotland Yard itself. There

Miss Peters instructed Carrington to set us down, and to wait close at hand for our return.

"But Hetty," I asked as we climbed the steps to the door, "who will be here at a quarter to eight on New Year's Eve?"

"Well, Flottie, I think quite a lot of people." She pulled a small card from her bag and studied it. "Yes, honestly. Tonight is the night of the annual Scotland Yard sherry party, which may sound pretty ghastly to you and me, but I'm hoping it's when all those detectives go absolutely wild on too much amontillado and start throwing canapés at the Lord Mayor of London. I know it's happening because my uncle was invited, but he said he'd rather spend the night on a bare mountainside with a sabre-toothed tiger eating his entrails, so I rather think he wasn't planning on coming. So, Flottie darling, we shall jolly well go in and see for ourselves . . ."

The appearance of Miss Peters in a shimmering blue evening gown seemed to dazzle the sergeant on duty to such an extent that he could barely manage a polite "good evening" as we swept through the door. And when the vision in front of him demanded to see someone very important *at once,* he had to shake himself a little before he could respond.

"Er, may I know what it's about, miss?"

"Oh, yes, officer, you *must* hear all about it. You see, it's the most appalling tragedy, and it's taking place *right now.* If something isn't done soon, I hate to think how it will end. I told the Earl of Brabham that if I came here someone was *bound* to help."

"The Earl of Brabham, miss? Er, yes. Of course. In that case . . ." He signalled to a rather pimply youth who was lurking somewhere behind him. "Mills, go and fetch down the chief inspector. Tell him it's urgent."

"A chief inspector?" Miss Peters whispered in awe. "A chief inspector sounds *terribly* important."

"Oh yes, miss. Of course, if you'd been here earlier, you could have spoken to Sir Marcus Stewart himself, but he's had to go on somewhere else."

"Oh, I'm sure a chief inspector will be quite good enough, officer. I'm sure he'll be able to sort out *everything.*"

This touching belief was one she repeated at great length to the gentleman himself when he finally appeared—a tall, rather portly man, grown a little rosy through too much oloroso and an overindulgence in Scotland Yard mince pies. He listened in something approaching bewilderment as Miss Peters gave him the details of the disaster that only he could avert. The Below-Stairs Ball at the Mecklenburg Hotel was disastrously short of eligible men, she explained; any number of footmen, gardeners, butlers, and the like, had failed to arrive; the housemaids and under-cooks of London were on the brink of collective hysteria for want of sufficient dancing partners; Miss Peters knew that in an emergency you could always trust a policeman, and she had noticed a dozen dashing representatives of the force on duty at Brown's Hotel, just a short distance from the Mecklenburg . . .

"I'm sorry, miss," the rosy gentleman replied a little uncomfortably. "Those men are on special assignment. Very important work. I'm afraid you'll have to look elsewhere for reinforcements."

"Oh, but surely you could spare *some* of them, Chief Inspector? You see, I have six tickets here, and I'd just love to think they were going to proper, manly young men. Policemen have numbers, don't they, as well as names?"

"That's right, miss."

"Well, couldn't you just send, say, the even-numbered men along to the ball? I'm sure five or six of your men would be enough to guard *anything.*" Her eyes began to go a little misty. "And it's such an important night for all those young girls. They so rarely get to go out. For them, events like the annual Scotland Yard New Year's Eve sherry party are just an impossible dream . . ."

It didn't take long for the chief inspector's resistance to crumble. Miss Peters was looking particularly fetching that night, and long before she had finished describing the happy lives that the young women of London would live if only they were fortunate enough to marry policemen, I could see that the gentleman before her was utterly captivated. When she finally finished speaking, I swear it took him a full five seconds to notice.

"Eh?" he started. "Oh, yes. Of course, Miss Peters, of course. I must say, I can't see why it needs a dozen of them at Brown's. Six should be plenty. After all, they've only got to keep an eye on one chap." He turned to the pimply boy. "Mills, take these invitations from Miss Peters to the lads on duty at Brown's and tell the six with the highest service numbers to attend the event at the Mecklenburg Hotel with immediate effect. That's an order from me personally. Now, ladies," he continued holding out his arms to us, "perhaps you'll allow me to help you to a glass of the Lord Mayor's excellent sherry . . ."

It took half an hour and two glasses of sherry before Miss Peters and I were able to return to the earl's carriage.

"Well, Flottie," my companion sighed happily as she flopped down beside me and squeezed my hand, "I think that went rather well, don't you? That nice man seemed so pleased when I told him the earl would be inviting him to dinner. He's clearly never met the earl, has he? And that's six of the twelve out of the way already. What fun!"

"But Hetty, what was all that you told him about the Below-Stairs Ball?"

"Oh, it's all true, Flottie. It's a terrible event, and it happens every year. It's organised by a woman called Mrs. Mayhew who's the sister of Lord Tolpuddle. She thinks it raises the spirits of what she calls the domestic classes. Well, of course, the domestic classes can all think of much better things to do with an evening off than to spend the evening with Mrs. Mayhew, so every year all her friends are forced to buy bucketloads of tickets and then bribe their servants to attend. This year the going rate at our house was five shillings a head, an extra day off over Christmas, and either a tray of chocolates or a bottle of port. And even then Reynolds says he had trouble finding any takers." Miss Peters rolled her eyes at the thought of it, and looked out of the window. "Oh, we're not moving! Carrington, why aren't we moving?"

"You haven't told me where to go yet, miss."

"Haven't I? How perfectly ridiculous of me. To the Savoy, if you please, Carrington. The Savoy!"

As Carrington jerked the carriage into motion, I found myself worrying that perhaps Miss Peters had forgotten that there were six more policemen who needed to be removed.

"But why the Savoy?" I asked. "Shouldn't we be going to Brown's?"

"Oh, no, Flottie! The Savoy is the place! That's where Sir Marcus Stewart is. You know, the really, really important policeman. The Duchess of Dorset is holding a soiree. And don't worry, Flottie. I've made sure we're actually invited to this one."

If you had asked me that morning about the likelihood that I should ever in my entire life attend the soiree of a duchess, I should have laughed at the question. Had I known that such an event was precisely where my day was leading, I should have been seized by so great a fit of anxiety that I should probably never have been able to rise from my bed.

However, Miss Peters seemed to have no concerns whatsoever on my behalf, merely laughing musically when I pointed out that it was surely not the duchess's intention to invite anyone such as myself, that she would be highly unlikely to invite even Sherlock Holmes, and certainly not his housemaid.

"And then there's my clothes! I can hardly turn up dressed like this!"

"Nonsense, Flottie! Stay close to me and everyone will think it's just me being peculiar. They're used to that. And to be perfectly honest, by the time we arrive they'll all be rather merry and probably won't notice us much at all."

Although it rather saddened me to agree, I had to concede that there was perhaps some truth in this last statement, for our arrival at the Savoy seemed to go largely unmarked by the glittering crowd gathered at the duchess's behest. Miss Peters guided me rather deftly around a ruddy-faced butler who was there to announce the guests, and then we found ourselves enveloped in the swirl of elegant men and women who eddied around the salon in seemingly inexhaustible waves. It is hard to say exactly how Miss Peters came to be introduced to Sir Marcus Stewart; harder still to say how he came to be clutching six tickets for the Below-Stairs Ball while simultaneously calling for the constable on duty. To this day, I am convinced that Sir Marcus was only vaguely aware of the instructions he gave the constable, so intent was he on assuring Miss Peters that her concern for the hapless housemaids of London did her great credit and was a cause that he would dearly like to discuss with her at greater length.

"Here, Andrews, I have some orders for the men at Brown's Hotel," he told the uniformed officer. "The six with the lowest service numbers are to proceed at once to the ballroom of the Mecklenburg Hotel. They are to dance till dawn, you understand. No shirking. I want a full report from each of them tomorrow morning, with full details. And woe betide any of them who try to sneak off to the punchbowl when they should be waltzing! Now, Miss Peters, I was just mentioning the tiger hunting I did in Bengal last spring . . ."

Miss Peters apparently found the tigers extraordinarily fascinating, for she refused to hear of anything else for a good half hour. Only when at least half a dozen of the creatures had been stalked and dispatched and transformed into rugs did she begin to look around her.

"Ooh!" she gasped suddenly. "There's the Bishop of Lichfield! How wonderful! Flottie and I simply adore the Bishop of Lichfield, don't we, Flottie? Those sermons of his! So uplifting! And so very *long!* I particularly love that one about kindness to animals. You won't join us, Sir Marcus? No? Are you quite sure? Oh, well, if you really don't want to . . ."

She guided me with the lightest of touches towards an elderly gentleman in a clerical collar and then, quite suddenly and with something very like a footballer's shoulder charge, diverted me unceremoniously through the door of the salon and out into the hall beyond.

"Quickly, Flottie," she whispered. "Back to the carriage!"

"But why? We've done our bit now. And I want to know if he really *is* the Bishop of Lichfield, or whether you've just made that up."

"Of course I've made it up, Flottie! I don't even know where Lichfield *is.* But any minute now that funny little magician is going to be on the run in London, and I simply *have* to know what happens next. Come on, through those doors there. Ho! Carrington! Excellent! Now straight to Brown's Hotel. And, Carrington . . . Drive like the clappers!"

· · ·

SHERLOCK Holmes and Dr. Watson, in order to be able to follow the Great Salmanazar both closely and discreetly, had taken the decision to disguise themselves as ordinary labourers, and had taken up positions where they could easily observe all the comings and goings from Brown's Hotel. It was with considerable astonishment that they witnessed the departure of all twelve policemen, noting, but not understanding, the reason for the high spirits with which they made their way to their next assignment; and on seeing them go, the two gentlemen had redoubled their concentration, anticipating at any moment the appearance of their quarry. Mr. Holmes, his face blackened and strangely anonymous in the guise of a working man, lurked in an archway opposite the main entrance. Dr. Watson, predictably ill at ease in the rough garments he had been allotted, was a hundred yards to the left, on a corner from which he could view both Holmes' position and the narrow street leading to the hotel's rear entrance. Helped by the crowds and the darkness, they blended easily into the scene, even Dr. Watson appearing in some way camouflaged amongst the array of other flushed and rosy faces that spilled from the public houses around him.

Miss Peters and I, however, had none of those gentlemen's advantages. Rather than blending into the crowd, Miss Peters was dressed with the express purpose of standing out from it, and our arrival in the earl's grand and ornate carriage could in no way be considered surreptitious. It was hard to see how the Great Salmanazar, or indeed any passerby, could fail to notice us. Dr. Watson certainly did, for he waved at me merrily before remembering his disguise, and turning his wave into an elaborate and bizarre scratching of the head.

"Keep walking," I whispered urgently to Miss Peters. "We'll have to pretend we're on our way somewhere else. Mr. Holmes will be awfully cross if he thinks we're getting in the way of his plans."

"I know!" Miss Peters decided brightly. "In here!" And before I could do or say anything to dissuade her, she had darted with great swiftness and no little enthusiasm into a public house of the very roughest appearance.

Although I was sure that Miss Peters had never before seen the inside of a London tavern, it soon became equally apparent that this London tavern had never before seen anything quite like Miss Peters. On a less rowdy night, her arrival would certainly have turned every head in the place and would almost equally certainly have reduced the regular drinkers to silence. That night, however, the crowd was squeezed so tightly together that only those in the immediate vicinity of the door were aware of our arrival, and those that were—nearly all of them men—looked at Miss Peters and blinked in astonishment. In reply, Miss Peters smiled back her most winning smile.

"Oh, Flottie, it's really rather jolly in here. *Much* nicer than I imagined. I love men in flat caps, don't you? They always look so *sensible.* Now, where's the waiter, do you think? We shall need a table for two, in the window, so we can watch what's going on outside."

Over the din of the assembled company, I tried to explain that there were no waiters in establishments of this sort and that you had to purchase your drinks from the public bar, but from the serene smile on her face it seemed that she could make out very little of what I said.

"Yes, we probably *should* have some champagne," she shouted back. "What a pity we didn't think to reserve a table." She examined the crowds around her again. "Really, Flottie, a lot of people seem to be staring at us. It must be my dress. I *told* you it was simply too beautiful for words. Look, that man in the window looks like a gentleman. I think we should ask to join him at his table, don't you? It's just the perfect place to keep watch, and I must say that he looks rather dashing from behind. I do *so* like a man with broad shoulders."

I looked to where her finger was pointing and saw a well-dressed young man with brown hair staring intently out of the window. His back was turned to us but even from a distance there was something about him that looked extremely familiar.

"But, Miss Peters," I exclaimed, "isn't that Mr. Spencer?"

"*Rupert?* No, of course not, Flottie. It can't be. Rupert distinctly told me that he was going to the New Year gathering of the Kensington and Chelsea Society of Chemists. I remember it because it sounded a more than usually dull way for him to see in the new year. When I told him I was going to dance all night with the Walters boy, he looked rather pleased and said something about it keeping me out of trouble. So it can't possibly be Rupert, can it?"

At just that moment the gentleman turned round. It was Rupert.

Miss Peters gave a shriek that was audible to at least two dozen drinkers, and she began to push forward forcefully.

"*Really*, Rupert! What *are* you doing here? Oh, I see it all! It's some sordid affair, isn't it? And in a place like this! How dreadful for you! I must rescue you from her clutches at once . . ."

"'Ere, what's this?" asked a man with a pint of stout who found himself thrust to one side by Miss Peters' determined progress through the crowd.

"Gent's been caught by his missus, Fred," his friend told him. "Tasty bit o' goods, too. You'd think he'd have the sense to stay at home."

If Rupert Spencer heard any of that, his only response was to wave cheerily in our direction and then to clear a path for us to his table, where he settled us on low stools and began to chuckle to himself.

"I should have known it, Hetty! And you, too, Flotsam! As if you two would let all this Salmanazar business go by without taking a hand yourselves. It serves me right for not thinking of it before! If I'd thought about it sensibly, Hetty, I'd have locked you in the cellar before I came out."

"Well, I like that! Really! Flottie and I have every right to be here, haven't we, Flottie? We like it here. And besides, I shouldn't be talking to you at all. You told me you were going to be in Kensington."

Mr. Spencer's eyes crinkled at the edges. "A change of plan, Hetty. I found the Society of Chemists every bit as dull as you had imagined them. And, besides, I thought Mr. Holmes might need some help. But tell me, are you not concerned that the Walters boy is without a dancing partner tonight?"

"Oh, Rupert! As if I care!" She took his hand fondly. "Now tell us, did you see all those policemen going off duty? That was all because of me, you know."

As she spoke, I was watching Mr. Spencer, whose profile was framed by the windows behind him, and my eye was caught by a movement in the street beyond. A slight figure moving deftly through the crowds slipped furtively passed the window.

"Mr. Spencer!" I cried urgently. "Who was that over there?"

He turned towards the street, suddenly tense. "Where, Flotsam? . . . No, I don't see." Suddenly his knuckles tightened on the back of his chair. "By jove! There's Sherlock Holmes on the move! Come on! The game's afoot!"

The three of us were on our feet in an instant, pushing through the packed mass of revellers towards the door, but out in the cool of the street we had to pause to look around.

"The Great Salmanazar must have slipped out while we were talking. Now where . . ."

"There! There's Dr. Watson, sir! If we cut down Mermaid Alley I think we can head him off!"

"Excellent! Well done, Flottie. Look, the three of us will move quicker if we spread out, and that way we'll have less chance of missing them. I'll take the other pavement. Wave like mad if you need to attract my attention."

"Isn't he wonderful, Flottie?" Miss Peters sighed as we watched him go. "He's so good at pretending to be masterful. And he really is incredibly handsome, isn't he? Even though he's so totally hopeless at polite society, I'm sure there must be hundreds of girls wanting to marry him, you know . . ."

But I didn't reply. The chase was gathering speed, and we had given the leaders a considerable head start. I had no breath for chatter and found myself at times forced into a half-run in order to keep up. Miss Peters, sensing my urgency, fell in behind me and did her best to follow.

The Great Salmanazar set a fierce pace, leading us first north towards Oxford Circus, then south again, always keeping to the busiest streets where his cover was greater, and where it was harder for any pursuer to follow. From time to time I glimpsed him, his collar pulled up and one gloved hand grasping an envelope close to his chest; but more often I was able to keep on his trail by the sights I caught of Sherlock Holmes or Dr. Watson, who despite the surging crowds were clinging to their quarry with grim tenacity.

"That letter in his hand," I gasped to Miss Peters, "it must be a note to Mr. Phillimore telling him where the ruby is supposed to be. We've got to let him post it, and then we can pounce. As soon as it's out of his hand, we're free to grab him."

Miss Peters nodded. She was a little flushed by now, and it was clear from a number of despairing glances downwards that the damage done to her evening gown during the chase was preying on her mind every bit as much as the fate of the Great Salmanazar. However, before she had time to put her anguish into words, we were off again, and even quicker than before.

Now the illusionist seemed to be moving with a definite plan. He picked his way neatly through the warren of streets that led to Covent Garden, and there I nearly lost him, for on turning the corner I found the market square one seething mass of humanity. Amidst the groups of people walking, laughing, dancing, even wrestling with each other, it was impossible to make out the direction taken by the Great Salmanazar. But just as I began to despair of the chase, Rupert Spencer popped up at my shoulder.

"Over there! See? It's Sherlock Holmes. Follow him!" And he was off in pursuit without waiting to see if I'd understood. Miss Peters and I darted after him, and a moment later I saw Dr. Watson ahead of me. Following determinedly in his tracks, we soon found ourselves once more in touch with our prey.

Twice we saw the Great Salmanazar approaching post-boxes and each time he hesitated with the envelope in his fingertips; each time we waited breathlessly for his message to be dispatched. But on both occasions he looked about him, changed his mind, and continued his flight through the crowds.

From Covent Garden we were led onto Long Acre and then down Bow Street and onto the Strand. There, an over-turned fruit barrow caused a blockage and allowed us to creep much closer to the head of the chase, which was just as well, for when the magician reached Charing Cross, something peculiar happened. He had paused for a moment on the kerb, facing towards the church of St. Martin, when a small boy ran up to him, apparently to beg. The Great Salmanazar seemed to be reaching into his pocket to find a coin when something the child said caught his attention, and he bent down to listen. The boy signalled with his arm up Duncannon Street, and the magician followed the gesture with his eyes and nodded. I held my breath and waited for the note to change hands, but the boy scuttled away, and the Great Salmanazar, gripping the envelope a little more tightly, strode purposefully up Duncannon Street and towards Trafalgar Square.

If any place had become the centre of that night's bacchanals, it was the great square around Nelson's Column. That huge space was teeming with merrymakers so that the foot of the column was entirely obscured, and the lions that guard it seemed to float on the shoulders of a dancing crowd. Even as we approached, the press grew greater, and I found myself carried forward and thrown against Dr. Watson.

"Flotsam?" he shouted above the hubbub. "Are you here? Excellent! Don't let him out of your sight. It should be any minute now that we need to grab the fellow!"

Then the eddying tide of people drew me away from Dr. Watson and threw me into the arms of Rupert Spencer, who grinned warmly and pushed me forward in the direction of Nelson himself.

In the very centre of the square, the scene was one of utter bedlam. As well as the throng of people drinking from flasks or bottles of beer, and shaking hands with everyone, there seemed also to be taking place a pageant of strange and wonderful figures that looked as if they had arrived directly from a medieval carnival. A beautiful princess in a pointy hat and silver robes danced with a boy in a jerkin who, I realised when I was thrown closer to him, wasn't a boy at all but a fine-looking girl with close-cropped hair. Around them, three men dressed as autumn leaves capered in circles, a man in a full suit of armour blundered in circles and attempted to pour brown ale through his visor, and, above them all, on the lip of the fountain, a pantomime horse kicked and whinnied like a thoroughbred.

"It's the pantomime troupe!" Dr. Watson yelled when we were thrown together again. "They've been performing here tonight. Watch out! There he goes!"

I peered through the tumult and saw the dark figure of the magician moving away from the centre of the square, towards a lamppost where another small boy was leaning, apparently waiting.

"My word! Here we go!" Watson roared, and pressed forward keenly. "As soon as that note is out of his hand, let's get him!"

As we pushed and shoved to get clear of the crowd, I saw the Great Salmanazar close in on the boy. No word was spoken but the envelope was passed from one to another, and the boy took off like an arrow from a bow. For half a second the illusionist watched him go, but then a great cry went up not ten yards behind him, and I saw the wiry figure of Mr. Holmes bursting from the shadows and hurling himself forward. While the smaller man was still looking up, Holmes dove forward and launched himself horizontally at his prey.

Had Mr. Holmes been a yard closer when he leapt, the force of his tackle must surely have crashed the magician to the cobbles, and our work that evening would have been done. But that single yard gave the Great Salmanazar a chance to react, and although his movement was instinctive rather than planned, it was enough for the main force of Mr. Holmes' dive to glance off his hip. The force of the collision staggered him, but he rode the challenge with a stoutness and sureness of footing astounding in a man so slight, and, while Mr. Holmes' momentum carried him five yards past, the magician clutched at a passerby, regained his balance, and took flight.

Now it was a chase in earnest. Disguise was abandoned and all stealth was gone. The Great Salmanazar had a ten-yard start over Dr. Watson and was running for all he was worth. I followed behind as rapidly as I could, but was quickly passed by a recovered Sherlock Holmes, gaunt and tense and sprinting like an athlete. In open country our prey would have been quickly gathered in and, sensing this the illusionist tried to turn back to the centre of the square, where the thronging crowds promised shelter. This change of direction saved him, for Rupert Spencer had made ground to head him off, and five yards more would have taken the magician straight into his arms. But the sudden swerve changed everything, wrong-footing the younger man and allowing the older to double back and narrowly escape Dr. Watson's clutching fingers.

Seeing this, Mr. Holmes was quick to adjust, and he and Dr. Watson were able once again to close on the fleeing figure. The Great Salmanazar must surely have been grasped there and then had it not been for the unfortunate intervention of Baron Bounder, the pantomime villain, who chose that moment to lunge drunkenly after a pretty young girl dressed as a daffodil. This lunge took him straight into the path of the detective and his companion, and brought all three crashing down into a heap. Mr. Spencer, in swerving to avoid the melee, found himself pitched straight into the arms of the daffodil, who took advantage of this astonishing good fortune by holding onto him tightly and kissing him as many times as she could before he was able to escape.

While this catastrophe untangled itself, the Great Salmanazar had broken clear of the pursuing pack, and I saw him pause and look around. But at this point it seemed that his luck had changed, for his momentum had carried him almost exactly to the spot where Miss Peters had halted to remove her beautiful and totally impractical shoes, one of which appeared to have shed its heel. On looking up and finding herself face to face with the object of our pursuit, she squealed excitedly and, with great presence of mind, threw her fur stole over his head and kicked him in the shins.

This unexpected assault clearly disconcerted the little magician, and it took him a few moments to extricate himself, first from the fur, then from Miss Peters. Finally shaking himself free, and realising that his pursuers had begun to pick themselves up and regroup, he looked around and seemed to make a decision. His haphazard progress had now taken him to the part of Trafalgar Square that faced the Admiralty Arch. Perhaps the sight of the Mall beyond appeared to offer him respite from the chaos of the square, or perhaps his eye was caught by the pink-and-yellow costume of the pantomime horse, which had abandoned its place by the fountains and was now dancing for a small group of admirers under the arch itself. Whatever his reasons, the Great Salmanazar set off in that direction, still with a lead of twenty yards over the pursing pack, which now, rather to my surprise, had me at its head.

Had the fugitive kept to his course and taken the chase onto the Mall, he must surely have escaped, for the various mishaps behind him had taken their toll, and none of the men giving chase were moving as freely as they had before. However, at that precise moment, the pantomime horse finished its dance and for no obvious reason jogged off placidly into a little alley that ran away to the left. The Great Salmanazar, perhaps hoping for narrow streets to hide in, paused and looked behind him, hesitated, and then darted after the horse and into the alley.

"Yes!" Mr. Holmes cried. "We have him! I know that street. It's a dead end!" He and I came to a halt at the alley's entrance and waited for the rest of our allies to catch up. "In there!" Mr. Holmes signalled. "See where the alley turns to the right? He's gone round that corner. But the road runs only another fifteen yards before it comes to an end. We have him trapped!"

As if to support Mr. Holmes' grasp of London's topography, the pantomime horse chose that moment to reappear, shooting rapidly out from around the corner as if startled to find that the Great Salmanazar had followed it there. Finding itself in front of a reception committee, the horse gave a nervous tap dance and then, sighting the reassuring figure of Widow Wellbeloved drinking gin straight from the bottle, gave a little bow and scurried off.

"Now," said Mr. Holmes, "let us form a line and advance together. I think between us we will be more than a match for the fellow."

And so we edged forward together and turned the corner five abreast. It was clear from the very first glance that Mr. Holmes' description of the little backstreet was an accurate one. The blank walls of high buildings enclosed all three sides of it. No one could possibly escape from it without coming past us.

But the first glance told us something else, too. Something had gone wrong. Some trick of magic had been performed. For where we expected to see the great magician, hunted and cowering and ready to surrender, there was no one but a young lad perched jauntily on a dustbin and smoking a cigarette.

"Scraggs?" I gasped in bewilderment as the five of us stopped short.

"Oh, hello, Flot," he chirped. "And Mr. Holmes, and Dr. Watson, too. How jolly!" He clambered off the bin, putting out his cigarette as he did so. "It's a funny place, this. I was sitting here having a quiet smoke when two blokes in a comedy horse costume came round the corner. As soon as they saw me, they ran off again, then you arrived. A bit strange, eh?"

"But Scraggs, what about the man who came in here just after the horse?"

Scraggs stared back at us blankly.

"A man, Flot? Just now?" He shook his head. "Sorry, there's been no one. Just those two blokes in the horse outfit. I've been here ten minutes, and I can tell you there's been no one."

At that moment, with slow, portentous certainty, the chimes of Big Ben began to fill the night around us, and we listened in silence as the great bell sounded twelve times.

"Midnight," observed Scraggs. "And since we're all gathered together so handy, like, perhaps I can be the first to wish you all a very happy new year."

CHAPTER NINETEEN

An Unexpected Boy

It was quite some time before Sherlock Holmes and Dr. Watson could bring themselves to accept that the Great Salmanazar had truly disappeared. Every dustbin had to be searched, every drainpipe tested to see if it might have offered a means of escape. A single metal door was discovered sunk into one of the blind brick walls, presumably a rear entrance to one of the grand buildings around us. But the door was rusted fast and had clearly not been opened for years. Finally, we searched the cobbled floor of the alley for drain covers that might lead to the sewers. To Mr. Holmes' delight, one was found near the corner around which the Great Salmanazar had disappeared. However it took the combined efforts of Mr. Spencer and Dr. Watson to lift it, and when the latter was prevailed upon to peer inside, he reported that there was nothing to be seen but darkness and nothing to be heard but dripping water and perhaps the scurrying footsteps of a rat.

"Damned smart piece of work if he made it down there,"

Watson grunted. "And ruby or no ruby, I'm dashed if I'm going down there after him."

"Very well, my friend." Mr. Holmes' face was a ghastly white in the gaslight. "I daresay that the solution of the conundrum will present itself to me presently. But first there is a great deal to be done. We must alert Lestrade to this fellow's escape. We'll soon have every policeman in the city looking for him. I'm sure he can't get far. And we must get to Sir John's house as quickly as we can, for the magician managed to send his message, and we can expect his accomplice to make an attempt on the ruby at any time. We must be there to welcome him."

"Of course, Holmes." Dr. Watson brightened. "We can still save our skins, can't we? After all, if we can lay hold of this chap Phillimore, and if we can persuade Mrs. Hudson to hand over the Malabar Rose, then I daresay the Home Secretary will be pleased enough, eh? Do you fancy coming with us, Mr. Spencer? We could do with a strong chap like you."

Mr. Spencer looked at Miss Peters and raised an eyebrow.

"I'd be delighted to join you, Dr. Watson, but first I think I should take Miss Peters home." Miss Peters spluttered at this, but Mr. Spencer carried on regardless. "I'm sure Hetty would agree that a young lady whose dress is torn *quite* so much as hers is would be likely to attract the wrong sort of attention during a secret vigil."

With these words he looked rather pointedly at her ankles. Miss Peters looked down, gasped, and stepped smartly behind me so that my skirts shielded her from his gaze.

With Hetty apparently rendered speechless, Mr. Spencer grinned at me and Scraggs. "What about you two? Are you joining the vigil at Sir John's?"

"Not me," said Scraggs hastily. "I've got a job to do for Mrs. Hudson. In fact, I should be off now. Don't know what I'm doing lazing around here. Come with me, Flot?"

It was tempting to say yes, but I was remembering Mrs. Hudson's last words to me. I had promised that if things went awry, I would return to Baker Street and lock myself in. And now, with the Great Salmanazar having vanished into the night, it seemed prudent to live up to my promise.

FOR all the crowds that spilled onto the streets, for all the revelry and ribaldry in the air that night, my journey home felt a long and lonely one. The more desperate I became to reach my destination, the slower my progress seemed to become. As I left the crowded streets near the Haymarket and Piccadilly Circus, I began to quicken my pace, and in the emptier streets around Savile Row, I was on the brink of breaking into a run. The ruby was unguarded, I reasoned, the Great Salmanazar had escaped, and Mrs. Hudson's plans were in disarray. It was up to me to guard the rooms in Baker Street, up to me to see that the Malabar Rose, whatever its hiding place, remained safe until morning. As my heart raced at the thought, the first snow of the new year began to drift gently to my feet.

The farther I travelled from Trafalgar Square, the sparser the crowds became, until, as I entered Baker Street, the only traffic passing me was the occasional hansom cab, and the pavements ahead of me were empty but for one or two well-wrapped revellers hurrying to their beds. The snow must have started earlier here, for already a layer as thin and crisp as white crepe paper had settled over the cobbles. With no one around to observe me, I ran the last hundred yards as fast as I could, still struggling to contain the anxiety that was welling up inside me.

My first sight of home calmed me, however, and leaning against the rails I took a moment to regain my composure and recover my breath. I could see from the unbroken snow

that nobody had set foot on either the stone steps up to the
front door or the iron steps down to the basement area since
the snow had started to fall. How long ago was that? Twenty
minutes? Half an hour? The knowledge reassured me, and
when I took out my latchkey and descended the area stairs, I
had even begun to laugh at myself for worrying so much and
with so little provocation.

But it was laughter that soon died on my lips, for on de-
scending the iron staircase I found the kitchen door not
quite shut, the latch not flush in place. Surely Mrs. Hudson
would not have left it ajar in that way? She had been anxious
that the place should be properly guarded . . . I wished then
that I'd made less noise on the stairs, that I'd jangled my key
chain less carelessly, for if any intruder had been waiting in
the shadowy kitchen, they must surely now be aware of my
arrival.

For a tiny part of a moment I was tempted to step away,
to turn back into town to seek out Scraggs or Rupert
Spencer and ask them to accompany me. But I had promised
Mrs. Hudson I would stand guard, and that was what I intended to do. So I steadied myself against the iron stairs,
then with my key between my fingers and my heart in my
mouth, I swung open the kitchen door and peered into the
darkness.

Apart from the streetlight behind me, the only light in
the room came from the dying embers of the kitchen fire.
Shadows lurked in each corner, but they were familiar shadows, friendly companions in a place I knew so well. I listened for any sound of movement but there was
nothing—nothing strange or unusual, nothing to make me
nervous or on edge. And when I stepped forward and lit the
oil lamps, everything seemed as it should be: as neat and as
pristine as Mrs. Hudson always left it. Even so, I had already
learned that appearances could be deceptive, and armed with

a lamp I proceeded to search every corner of the room. When that failed to show me any sign of intrusion, I moved onto the pantry, the cold room, then Mrs. Hudson's bedroom, and finally my own. Emboldened by the unsullied sense of order that prevailed around me, I moved on to the rooms upstairs. My nervousness was now replaced with ruthless efficiency, and I determined to make sure that I was alone in the house and that our defences remained unbreached.

Only when every room had been scoured for signs of disturbance did I allow myself to relax. I made sure to check that all the doors were firmly bolted, and then I built up the fire and made myself a cup of hot milk, the drinking of which was accompanied by a warm sense of satisfaction. I was properly on duty, and everything was in order. The bolts were drawn, and I was impregnable. Let anyone try to carry off the ruby now! Then, putting all thoughts of the Great Salmanazar out of my head, I settled down to wait for Mrs. Hudson.

But I waited and waited. In truth I think I had expected her return to follow shortly after mine, so I wasn't really prepared for so long a vigil. The clock outside struck two, but still she had not appeared. Nor was there any sign of Dr. Watson or Mr. Holmes, and I realised that any noise from the street outside had long ceased. With the celebrating crowds long dispersed, the roads around Baker Street seemed quieter than usual. I began to realise how tired I was, and when the clock struck the next quarter it roused me from the edge of sleep and made me blink. From then on I struggled grimly to stay awake, while my body betrayed me by slumping comfortably in front of the fire, and my thoughts began to drift into slumber. I let my head fall back onto a cushion, and I noticed dully that the oil lamp on the kitchen table was burning low. I knew I must refill it, but the lamp was a long way away, and in a moment I would move and see to it, but for now the fire threw a softer light than the lamp, and I would rest a moment and watch the shapes in the embers for a few minutes more . . .

When I next stirred, the kitchen lay in darkness. The oil lamp was out, and the fire had burned so low that the only light was a smudge of orange in front of me. It would be wrong to say that I awoke, for my body remained asleep, so heavy in its slumber that to move anything but one sleepy eye would have been impossible. But something in my consciousness had flickered into waking, and one small part of my brain told me that the shadows had changed. Something had moved.

It is hard now to explain my reaction to what I saw that night, hard to convey the utter weariness that seemed to weigh on every limb or the paralysis that gripped my thoughts almost as tightly as my body. In one corner of the kitchen, not far from where I dozed, there was a small, low wooden chest that we used for kitchen linen. It was no more than two feet across and less than that in height, and in my search of the kitchen it had never occurred to me look inside something so small. But now, as I looked, another movement in the shadow caught my eye, and the lid of the box began to lift as if raised by an invisible hand.

I should have screamed or jumped to my feet, but I simply could not—it was as if fear, like an opiate, had numbed my senses, giving me no choice but to watch. From inside the box a dark arm appeared. It was followed by another, easing the lid upwards until it fell open, revealing narrow shoulders and a head too dark in the half-light to be blessed with features. Slowly, like a shade emerging from the underworld, the dark figure emerged from its box.

At no point had it made the slightest sound, and only when it turned and stepped out into the kitchen did I hear its footfall on the stone flags. That sound, tiny as it was, broke the spell that bound me and suddenly I found my feet, rushing as fast as I could for the kitchen door, for the street that lay beyond. I had surprise in my favour, for as soon as I moved I heard a gasp of astonishment behind me. But my own precautions proved my downfall, for when I reached the door I found the bolts pushed firmly home, and as I struggled to release them, the dark figure was upon me. His arms went around me, and he lifted me bodily back into the kitchen. As he did so, the light from outside fell on his features, and I saw for the first time the face of James Phillimore.

To my utter surprise, it was a kind face. I had imagined villainy, cunning, relentless determination. But pale as it was, and lined as if by years of disappointment, I sensed in it no malice, no pleasure in the task it contemplated. Before that night I had never imagined what he looked like, thinking of him only as the faceless clerk of Ealing, the man of whom his own wife had never bothered to own a portrait. Even in his crimes, he was strangely faceless. We knew about his socks and his ties, but nothing about the looks of the man who wore them; and in his appearances for the Great Salmanazar his role had always been to lurk unnoticed, his presence unguessed at by the stagehands around him. He had somehow stolen into the story of the Malabar Rose by stealth, leaving no trace behind him but his name.

But now, suddenly and shockingly, he was real, with strong arms forcing me back into my chair.

"Not a word!" he whispered urgently. "Any sound at all and I will gag you, I swear I will." Then he reached behind him for one of Mrs. Hudson's immaculately folded sheets and began to knot my hands together behind the back of the chair.

"I know who you are!" I told him fiercely, suddenly angry at his bullying. "You're James Phillimore. We know all about you."

He smiled, and even though his lips were pinched with anxiety, it was not an unpleasant smile. "I've come to fame too late then. Look, I don't want to hurt you but, by God, I swear I will if I have to. I haven't come this far to fail now. Now tell me, *where is the Malabar Rose?*"

I met his eye without flinching. "It's at Sir John's house. Sir John Plaskett. He's got it."

"Liar!" he cried, and I glimpsed then something of the passion that gripped him. His breathing was unsteady, and there was a desperation in his voice that he fought to control. "I've been watching Sir John. Him and that policeman, they haven't a clue where it is." He fixed me with eyes that flared with anger. "No, it's that housekeeper who has it. She took it from the Blenheim Hotel. Oh, I'd be away and clear with the stone in my pocket by now if it wasn't for her! Now *where is it?*"

He shook me then, but there something in the way he did it that made me suddenly sorry for him. He was angry, yes. I could see that. But not angry at me, not even angry at Mrs. Hudson, angry at the fates that had thwarted him, and angry at his own helplessness. It was the choking, flailing desperation of a man who has reached for his dream but cannot quite catch hold of it.

I waited until he took his hands from my shoulders, then looked him in the eye and replied quite calmly.

"I don't know where it is. Mrs. Hudson wouldn't tell me."

Something in my voice clearly convinced him, for he stepped away and began to look around him.

"Very well," he replied. "I'll start upstairs. You're coming with me, though. I want to keep an eye on you."

The ransacking of our rooms that followed was on an unimaginable scale. Working at a ferocious pace, he moved through Mr. Holmes' and Dr. Watson's rooms, turning out every drawer, emptying every chest. The neatly catalogued filing cabinets were toppled to the ground, and every tray ripped from them and overturned. Nothing was spared. Soon the neat and tidy rooms were lost beneath a carpet of debris. When he failed to find anything resembling a ruby in any of the cabinets, he produced a knife and began to cut out the upholstery of chairs and to disembowel cushions, cutting the throats of pillows so that they bled white feathers into the air.

While he did all this, his forehead was beaded with sweat, but, strangest of all, he *talked*. At first, he gave a muttered commentary on his searching, but soon it was clear his words were not intended for me but were a fiery, fractured monologue aimed at the fates with which he duelled.

"Please," he muttered over and over. "Please, please let me find it. I swear it will be the last thing. I'll go away. Away. Never ask anything more." He overturned a small cabinet full of letters written in invisible ink. "It isn't for *me*. I was prepared to let her go, to let my life drain away in Ealing if it meant I didn't pull her down. I asked nothing then. Nothing! And not once did I complain. Not once! But then you sent her back to me. I never asked for that! And she loved me. She loved me!" He sliced through the leather arms of an armchair. "It's for her. All this is for her. So she can have the things she deserves. Not for me. None of it for me."

Suddenly he dropped to his knees amid the wreckage of the room and put both hands to his face.

"Oh, God! Please show me where it is! I love her. I love her so."

He remained in that position for some moments, weeping soundlessly, apparently oblivious to my presence. When he finally rose to his feet, there was a grim determination in his face.

"It's as I thought," he said. "She's hidden it downstairs."

If I found the destruction of Mr. Holmes' study difficult

to witness, the chaos now unleashed on Mrs. Hudson's kitchen filled me with despair. That place was my sanctuary, and to see it so defiled was to feel my whole life overturned. Worse even than that was the certainty in my own heart that this was where the Malabar Rose was hidden. At any moment he might discover it! Even now he was in the pantry, swiping food off the shelves to see what might be concealed behind. And while the crashing and the banging continued, I listened for the striking of the clock. It was after three now. Surely Mrs. Hudson would come home soon?

Finally, when every inch of the kitchen and the adjoining bedrooms had been devastated by his search, Phillimore came to stand before me.

"That trapdoor there, where does it lead?"

"There's a little cellar."

He looked at me for a moment. I was still tied to my chair. He had carried it with him as he moved me around the house so that in every room I had been tied down and there had been no chance of escape.

"I can't take you down there with me. So I'm afraid I must make you a little more secure."

He had already tied me by my wrists, but now he took another sheet and secured me by the ankles, too. Then he placed a handkerchief in my mouth and tied a pillowcase tightly around it.

"That should hold you," he said, and stooped to pull open the bolt that kept the trapdoor in place.

I had allowed myself to be gagged with no great struggle because I was sure the cellar was too obvious a place for Mrs. Hudson to have hidden the Malabar Rose. Every moment he spent there was time when the true hiding place was safe. It was therefore with some satisfaction, bound and gagged as I was, that I watched James Phillimore take up the oil lamp and descend the ladder, leaving me alone and in near darkness.

My instinct as soon as he had gone was to see if there was anything to do to loosen my bonds. My first attempts were aimed at working free my hands and feet, but in both cases I quickly found that the knots binding me were tight and would not easily give. However, before I could test them to any significant degree, I heard something. Not James Phillimore's triumphant progress of destruction. Something quite different: an indistinct sound of scraping from one corner of the room. It was too dark to make out what had caused it, but just as I was beginning to believe that it had been something moving in the street outside, I heard it again—the creak of iron grinding slowly over iron.

Downstairs, I could hear boxes crashing to the floor and being kicking open. But now my attention was entirely focussed on one corner of the room. Despite the darkness, I could make out a movement there now, and my heart raced at the sight. *Someone was unbolting the kitchen door.* Not from the inside, but from the outside, with a wire, working it through the crack of the door. My rescuers, whoever they were, had arrived!

But their progress was clearly very slow. And there was very little time left: very soon James Phillimore would return to the kitchen. Already the bangs and thumps from below were diminishing in frequency, as if his search was drawing to a close. I waited motionless, hardly daring to breathe lest it should attract his attention, while the thin scraping noise continued.

Down in the cellar, I heard James Phillimore curse softly and then fall still. I imagined him looking around, surveying the chaos he had caused, uncertain what to try next. Meanwhile, above his head, the drawing of the bolts seemed to have hit some sort of difficulty, for although the top bolt was now undone, all movement of the lower bolt seemed to have ceased. I strained to detect any further movement, but all I could hear was a creak from below as Phillimore took hold of the ladder and began to place his weight on it. Then, just as he began to ascend, the bolt began to move again. But surely it was too late? I could hear Phillimore climbing the ladder. Any moment now his head would reappear . . .

Then, abruptly, with a loud metallic screech, the final bolt shot free, and the kitchen door burst open and crashed back against the wall. Caught off balance, a small boy tumbled through it and caught hold of the kitchen table to steady himself.

"Blue!" I cried uselessly, for the word was completely smothered by my gag. Luckily, Blue ignored me. Three strides were enough to take him round the table to the mouth of the trapdoor, and he reached it just as James Phillimore's head poked into the room.

"Wha . . .?" the older man began, taken aback by the sight of this unexpected boy looming over him. But Blue had clearly understood the fleeting nature of his advantage, and with a great firmness he slammed the trapdoor hard upon James Phillimore's head.

His victim had only time to mutter a gasp of surprise before the door struck him and slammed shut. The sound of its slamming was followed a moment later by the soft thump of Phillimore's body hitting the floor below.

"Coo," my rescuer remarked, quickly placing himself on top of the trapdoor. Then he looked up at me, his blue eyes wild with surmise. "Blimey, Flottie," he exclaimed. "Who the bloomin' 'eck was he?"

CHAPTER TWENTY

The Icing on the Cake

It was some time before I could answer Blue's question, as first he had to untie my hands and feet, and then remove the gag from my mouth. Then, when I could speak, I insisted that we lift the trapdoor and investigate whether Mr. Phillimore was still alive. A cursory examination carried out from six feet above his fallen body showed our victim to be unconscious but breathing regularly.

"Just knocked 'im out," Blue commented with some satisfaction. And I agreed, though to be on the safe side I still insisted on relocking the trapdoor before we moved on.

"His name's James Phillimore," I explained. "He's the one who went missing from his wife."

"The one there's a reward for?"

"Yes, that's the man. I'd forgotten about the reward. Why, Blue, you might get some money! We can ask Mr. Rumbelow all about it. He has the money in cash so perhaps he can give you something today!"

"Mr. Rumbelow . . ." He lingered on the name. "That'd

be good, Flottie. You can ask him for us. Just think of that. A reward . . ."

"But what are you *doing* here, Blue? You couldn't have known that I needed rescuing."

He shook his head. "Came to say good-bye, Flottie. There's a boat leaving for New Zealand late tomorrer. A mate can get me a place, cheap like. I've got just about enough to get me there, and I'll trust to luck after that. So I came to tell yer. Gave me a right shock when I saw you all tied up, an' that geezer heading down for the cellars. What was 'e after?"

"The Malabar Rose. He didn't find it though."

"You mean it's here?"

"Somewhere."

Blue let his eye wonder over the chaos that surrounded us. The floor was littered with broken plates and shattered glass and all manner of displaced objects.

"Think o' that, eh! A ruby big as a bloomin' egg somewhere at me fingertips!" He dwelled on the thought for a moment, then turned back to me and shrugged. "But what would I do with a ruddy great ruby? You can't flog somethin' like that in a back alley, can yer?" He signalled to the trapdoor. "What about him?"

"Prison, I suppose. It's sad really. I don't think he wants money for himself. He just thinks he needs it because of a girl."

"Pah! Serves 'im right then." Blue smiled cheerfully, then stiffened in his seat. "Listen. Voices!"

He was right, although they were still very distant. Somewhere along Baker Street two people were approaching.

"I'm off, Flot. Don't want to meet no one. And they're sure as shovels to be comin' here. There's always folks comin' and goin' here in the middle o' the night."

"But you don't need to rush off, Blue. You've done nothing wrong."

"Nah, don't fancy stayin'. An' besides, I got somethin' else to do tonight. Got to see a man about somethin' . . ."

He reached out then and put his arms around me. I remembered the tiny child in the orphanage, too frightened to touch anyone for fear of a scolding, and a lump rose in my throat.

"Good luck, Blue," I whispered.

"And to yerself, Flot."

He winked at me then, with the finest blue eyes I'd ever seen, then turned and walked away, out of the kitchen, up the area steps and out into the snow-lined night. When Mrs. Hudson and Scraggs entered the kitchen a minute later, I was still sitting quietly, letting him go.

IF I had expected Mrs. Hudson to register any consternation or dismay at the destruction of her lovingly ordered kitchen, I was most definitely disappointed. If she felt any surprise at all at the devastation that greeted her, it was expressed in the raising of a single eyebrow as she surveyed the scene.

"So he's been here, has he?" she asked, as much to herself as to me, and then bustled over to where I was sitting and placed a hand on my shoulder while she surveyed the damage.

"Yes, ma'am," I replied. "Mr. Phillimore, I mean. He tied me up."

"And has he been gone long?"

"Gone? Oh, no, ma'am. He's still here. I've locked him in the cellar."

It was only then that I had the satisfaction of seeing Mrs. Hudson surprised, for on hearing this news both her eyebrows twitched upwards, and she rewarded me with a look of unabashed approval.

"Scraggs," she declared, "I think Flotsam has something

of a story to tell us. See if you can revive the fire while I light some lamps. And let's try not to tread on any of the best china, shall we?"

It is hard to imagine that a room so thoroughly ransacked could ever be considered welcoming, but such was Mrs. Hudson's power to bring order to chaos that her simple instructions proved enough to transform the place. Soon the lamps were lit and the night shut out, the fire revived, and the fallen chairs righted amidst the wreckage and arranged around the table. While all that was being accomplished, I told them how Mr. Phillimore had appeared from the linen chest and had wreaked havoc throughout the house, only to be laid low by my friend with the blue eyes.

Mrs. Hudson listened attentively, and when I had finished my tale she tiptoed gingerly over to the pantry and peered inside. After studying the debris for a brief moment, she returned to the kitchen table, her face content.

"He didn't find it, did he, ma'am?"

She gave a little snort in reply. "Certainly not, Flotsam. He only looked in the places he himself would have hidden it." She looked across at Scraggs and chuckled. "The male brain is like that. If he'd found the stone tonight, I'd have eaten my . . ." She paused, the shadow of a smile on her lips. "Well, never you mind *what* I'd have eaten. Now, enough of all this chatter. I think it's time we had a word with the famous James Phillimore. From the noises down below, it seems he's come to."

Scraggs paused in his tidying and looked up with considerable enthusiasm.

"Shall we tie him up, Mrs. H?"

"Oh, I don't think so, Scraggs. I don't think we'll find much fight left in him. But perhaps you should keep yourself between him and the door, just in case. Now, let me see . . ." She bent down, and from the debris at her feet retrieved a dusty brown bottle. "Ah, just as I thought. The Wellington port. And not too badly shaken by the look of it, which is a great blessing. Flotsam, while we fetch up Mr. Phillimore, would you be so kind as to decant this very, very carefully? I think tonight we deserve a little celebration."

Mr. Phillimore, when supported from the cellar and placed in a chair, cut an extremely sorry figure. The blow to his head clearly pained him, but more dispiriting to him than the physical discomfort appeared to be the stern face of Mrs. Hudson and the determined figure of Scraggs barring the doorway. Our captive was bruised, outnumbered, and defeated, and on all counts he knew it. He seemed to shrink into his chair, a thin, tired man with despair etched across his features. He eyed Mrs. Hudson with dull foreboding.

"Why have you haunted me this way?" he asked. "I've seen you. Always on my scent. Visiting my wife, harassing Polly, advertising for information about me. And taking away the ruby. I saw you in the hotel that day, you know. If it wasn't for you, I'd be on the way to Canada with the ruby in my pocket by now."

"Mr. Phillimore," Mrs. Hudson's voice had a steely edge to it and she fixed him with her sternest gaze. "Mr. Phillimore, I care very little for rubies. But some good men were tasked to guard that stone, and they were faced with ruin by your little plot. And Mrs. Smithers, your mother-in-law, has been genuinely concerned for your safety. More concerned than you deserve."

Mr. Phillimore bowed his head at that, apparently not so hardened as to be completely beyond shame.

"Now I've something important to say," Mrs. Hudson went on. "Shortly, Inspector Lestrade of Scotland Yard will be here. You will be charged with breaking and entering, theft, arson, illegal imprisonment, and attempted murder.

You will be taken from here to a prison cell, and you will remain in one for a very long time."

"No!" he cried. "It's not like that! All those things you've said. They're not true! I've done so little. Just some errands for that man, Salmanazar."

Mrs. Hudson continued to eye him coldly.

"Tonight I delivered to Mr. Rumbelow, the solicitor, a statement by the Great Salmanazar explaining precisely how the two of you plotted to steal the Malabar Rose. It tells precisely how he came to recruit you to help with his act, how he was looking for a contortionist of sorts, someone who was no longer known in theatrical circles. He's put it all down. How you first helped him in Budapest, how you bound up his cut hand the night he stole the Romanoff tiara. He says it was you who planned the theft of the Malabar Rose from the start."

"That's not true," he groaned. "Not the last bit. It was all his plan. It was *he* who knew all about Perch. It was *he* who thought of changing the real jewel case for a mechanical one. He even insisted on finding the right sort of butterfly to put in the case. That was the sort of showman he was. He wanted the whole world talking about him."

"That may be true, Mr. Phillimore." Mrs. Hudson rose from the table and gathered up a pile of laundry that had earlier been tipped to the floor. She selected a single sheet and began to fold it while Mr. Phillimore looked on, wondering, his attention seized by something in her tone. "But the Great Salmanazar has escaped to Spain leaving only his statement behind him. Your great friend Polly Perkins has escaped, too, you know. That leaves only you, and the police will be keen to have a scapegoat."

"What? Polly has gone? But why?"

"Because by telling her your plans, you had made her an accessory." Mrs. Hudson looked up from her laundry and impaled him with a stern glare. "Now, you still have a wife here, and a good, honest mother-in-law. If you were to stand trial the full story would come out—all about you sneaking off and them not guessing, and all about you and Miss Perkins. It would cause them terrible embarrassment and distress. Much more distress than you have caused them so far. To spare them that, I am prepared to offer you an alternative."

Such was the power of her presence that Mr. Phillimore said nothing, but for the first time since we'd hauled him from the cellar, I saw a tiny gleam of hope in his eye.

"In two hours' time," Mrs. Hudson continued, "a train leaves Waterloo for Portsmouth. You will take that train. It's the slow train, stopping at every station, so it will be breakfast time when you arrive at Portsmouth Harbour. As soon as you get there, you will go to the front door of the offices of the Meyer and Stallard Steam Company. The *front* door, mind. You will stay there until five o'clock, waiting for someone to come and find you. When they do, you have a choice. They will have a pair of tickets for a boat departing for Canada. You can either accompany them on that boat, or remain in this country and wait for the police."

Mr. Phillimore was looking mystified. "The choice seems an easy one. Who will it be, this guardian angel sent to take me away?"

In reply, Mrs. Hudson shook her head. "You will find out tomorrow. However, it is possible no one will come to find you. If they haven't come by five o'clock—and the timing is vital here, you understand—then you will find your way to the *back* door of the offices. Wait there. The instruction remains the same. Someone will be looking for you, and when they find you, go with them."

"And if no one comes to that door? What then?"

"Oh, they will, Mr. Phillimore, they will. In that respect you are a lucky man."

"But why all this mystery? Why can you not tell me who I am looking for?"

Mrs. Hudson sighed. "I can't help thinking, Mr. Phillimore, your time is better spent making yourself scarce than asking unnecessary questions."

At this, Mr. Phillimore began to rise, only to sink once more back into his chair.

"But what's the point?" he sighed. "Without Polly, what's the point? Oh, I know how generous your offer is. I don't fully understand why you should do so much to help me. But without Polly, there's no future for me anywhere. I might as well stay here and rot in gaol."

Mrs. Hudson nodded and finished the folding of a second sheet before reaching into her apron and passing him a slim, cream envelope.

"As it happens, I spoke to Miss Perkins earlier this evening, before she fled. She asked me to give you this."

Mr. Phillimore took the letter with a look of awe on his face and with fingers that trembled as he opened it. The note was clearly short, for by following his eyes I could see that he reread it a dozen times before folding it reverently into his pocket.

"She begs me to go," he said quietly. "She says it would break her heart for me to be locked away. She says that if I love her I must escape, even if it means we can never be together."

For a long time after that, he sat with his head bowed. A stillness settled on the room around him, a stillness so intense it seemed I could *hear* it, a stillness only broken when Scraggs, very softly, stepped away from the kitchen door. When Mr. Phillimore finally looked up, his eyes were moist with tears.

"Very well," he whispered hoarsely, rising to his feet. "I don't understand why, but Polly says I am to trust you. The Meyer and Stallard Steam Company, you say?"

"That's right, Mr. Phillimore. The *front* door."

"Then I shall go." He took one step towards the door and paused, almost as if he expected us to stop him. When nothing happened, he continued to the door and there, with the night beckoning him, he paused once more.

"I have a sister . . ."

"Yes, we know. We will get word to her of what has happened to you."

He nodded briefly, then turned away, and in a moment he, too, had vanished into the night.

I CAN'T pretend that I wasn't bursting with questions about Mrs. Hudson's decision to release the man we had spent so long plotting to catch. However, after witnessing Mr. Phillimore's departure, neither Scraggs nor I had opportunity to ask a single question before Mrs. Hudson cleared her throat and began to direct the clearing up of the disordered kitchen. If it occurred to either of us that such an operation might reasonably have waited until the following day, it was a thought that Mrs. Hudson's stern demeanour was sufficient to put out of our heads; and we found ourselves stacking china, repopulating shelves, rescuing provisions, and filling the dustbins with broken glasses. We had already returned the pantry to a semblance of order and had largely cleared the floor of debris when we were disturbed by a timid knock at the kitchen door.

"Mr. Rumbelow!" I cried on opening it, the blinking, slightly bewildered-looking lawyer being the very last person I expected to find on our doorstep in the early hours of the first morning of the year.

"Er, yes," he mumbled. "It is indeed me. Quite so. And if I may be so bold, a happy new year to you, Flotsam. And to you, Mrs. Hudson. Scraggs, you're here, too? Extraordinary hours you all keep . . ."

We shepherded him into the kitchen and seated him by the fire.

"I must say, sir," Mrs. Hudson observed, "your own hours are a little unusual this morning. And you appear a little put out. Is there anything we can do for you?"

"*Do* for me? Do for *me*?" Mr. Rumbelow seemed to find the question astonishing. "But *you* sent for *me*, Mrs. Hudson. Just now. And I came as soon as I could. Unfortunately, I have suffered a slight mishap on the way."

Mrs. Hudson and I exchanged puzzled glances.

"A mishap, sir?" she asked gently.

"Well, in truth, something a little worse than that. A failing in my professional duty. I cannot imagine what my client will say."

Mrs. Hudson decided help was needed. "Flotsam, the moment for that port has finally arrived. If you would be so good as to fetch Mr. Rumbelow a small glass of it . . . Now, sir, please go on."

"That boy you sent, Mrs. Hudson. I fear he is not entirely honest."

"Sir, I've sent no boy for you this evening."

"You have not?" The stout solicitor half-rose in his seat and then sank back down with a groan as a terrible understanding dawned. "Then I've been tricked, Mrs. Hudson! Most blatantly, cunningly tricked!" He passed his hand weakly over his forehead. "A quarter of an hour ago I was roused by a young boy. He said that you required my presence here most urgently to attend to the case of James Phillimore. He said you asked most particularly that I should bring with me the reward money that his wife had placed with me. A sum of thirty pounds, if you remember."

"I see, sir." Mrs. Hudson nodded soothingly. "Here, try a little of this."

Mr. Rumbelow sipped at the port and closed his eyes for a moment in quiet contemplation.

"Ah, yes! The Wellington port. Quite sensational. And so few bottles left . . ." He opened his eyes again. "But I scarcely deserve it. You see, when I had pulled on my clothes and returned to the street, the boy was waiting for me. Helped me on with my overcoat, he did. Well, naturally I expected him to accompany me here, but no sooner did we step off the pavement than he simply ran off. And do you know, the little scamp took my wallet with him!"

While Mr. Rumbelow paused to mop his brow, Mrs. Hudson gave me a questioning glance.

"Tell me, sir," I asked timidly. "This boy, did you notice if he had blue eyes?"

Mr. Rumbelow sat up as if startled. "Why, Flotsam! How remarkable! Do you know, that's the only thing I noticed about him. The boy had the most striking blue eyes imaginable."

I couldn't help but smile at the news, and Mrs. Hudson let out a long, low chuckle.

"So justice has been done. I think you can enjoy your port after all, sir. It seems that James Phillimore's captor has found his own way to claim the reward."

"Reward, Mrs. Hudson?" A new voice from the edge of the kitchen interrupted us, and I saw that the door into the basement area had opened a little to admit the head and shoulders of Sherlock Holmes. "I fear our vigil tonight has had no reward. We have waited all night for that man, Phillimore, to walk into our trap and we'd be there still if we had not seen the error of our ways. I'm afraid your plan has failed, Mrs. Hudson."

"Ah, Mr. Holmes," Mrs. Hudson beamed. "I'm very pleased to see you. Now you two gentlemen come in here and get yourself warm. There are a few things you need to know."

"Not just the two of us," the detective replied. "We had two assistants in our watching. And I fear they are as cold and dispirited as we are."

He pushed the door open to reveal, alongside Dr. Watson, the shivering forms of Rupert Spencer and Hetty Peters.

"But, Hetty!" I exclaimed. "I thought Rupert was taking you home?"

"Well, you know, Flottie," she began brightly as they were ushered in, "I rather think Rupert thought the same. But, *obviously*, I wasn't going to miss the fun. So when we got home, I went upstairs and climbed out of the window."

"Oh, Hetty, you didn't!"

Rupert Spencer manoeuvred her a little closer to the fire with a wry grin.

"I'm afraid she did. Apparently, the next door's footman witnessed the whole episode. They needed to revive him with brandy, I believe."

"What nonsense, Rupert! I'm inclined to think he rather enjoyed it. He certainly didn't seem in any hurry to stop looking."

"Rooted to the spot in horror, no doubt," Mr. Spencer concluded and then turned to listen to Mr. Holmes, who was interrogating Mrs. Hudson.

"You say there's something we need to know, Mrs. Hudson? Is it about the whereabouts of James Phillimore?"

"No, sir," she responded calmly. "I'm afraid Mr. Phillimore has fled the country."

"He has? About the man, Salmanazar, then?"

"No, sir. I'm afraid he has fled the country, too."

"You know this for certain?"

"I do, sir."

He looked around and nodded wisely.

"I see from the state of this kitchen that there are things you no doubt wish to share with us. But if you can't tell us the whereabouts of those two gentlemen, Mrs. Hudson, then I'm afraid that little you say can be of any comfort to us."

"Oh, come, sir. You were asked to safeguard the Malabar Rose and that stone is now safely in front of you."

"I do not see it, Mrs. H."

"No, sir. But you see a large iced fruitcake. Now Flotsam here knows that I abhor an iced fruitcake. This will be the only one of its kind you are ever offered in this house, sir. However, there is no denying that a thick layer of royal icing sugar can hide any number of flaws beneath its surface. It is a trick that any cook learns at her mother's knee. Perhaps we shall have a slice presently. It is hardly the ideal accompaniment to the Wellington port but, after all, it *is* New Year."

"Great Scott!" Dr. Watson exclaimed. "You mean the world's most famous ruby is inside that fruitcake?"

"Of course, sir. If Mr. Phillimore had ever worked in a busy kitchen, he would have thought of that immediately. But, of course, if he ever had, I wouldn't have hidden it there."

Sherlock Holmes eased himself out of his coat and reached for his pipe.

"You know, Watson, Mrs. Hudson is right. We may have made no arrest, but the plot to steal the Malabar Rose has been thwarted, the plotters are fled, and the stone itself is safe. The gentlemen of the press will be able to announce that a dangerous plot has been foiled, which will reflect well on both the government and ourselves, so all in all the Home Secretary has every reason to feel pleased. He could scarcely ask for much more, could he, Mrs. Hudson?"

"Oh, but he could, sir. That is what I wished to tell you. You see, I thought it would be helpful if you could tell him where to find a few other things, too."

Mr. Holmes raised a quizzical eyebrow. "Such as?"

"Such as the Godolphin sapphire, sir. Or the Von Metzen diamonds or the Star of the Danube. Or the Rheims altarpiece or the Lafayatte necklace. Or the Plevski emeralds. Or even that dreadful jewel-encrusted camel that was stolen in Naples."

"But those things have all vanished," put in Dr. Watson, clearly confused. "Each was stolen in the most mysterious of circumstances."

"Yes, sir. By the Great Salmanazar. But they are all very difficult to sell, so he kept them all in a strongbox in Paris while he decided what to do with them. The key to the strongbox is over there, sir, next to the fish kettle."

Dr. Watson sat down heavily.

"Do you know, Mrs. Hudson," he muttered faintly, "I rather think you're going to have to start right at the beginning."

The fire was built up so high that our faces were brightly lit as we sat around it and listened to Mrs. Hudson's explanations. Fresh coals hissed satisfyingly in front of us, and Scraggs had been tasked with roasting chestnuts over the flames, so that every now and then a nut would leap in the pan or sigh sweetly at us as the heat began to work its changes. The Wellington port had been shared around, although Mrs. Hudson had taken great care to steer some of the company in other directions. Mr. Holmes had been furnished with a bottle of brown ale, Dr. Watson with a substantial glass of brandy and shrub, and Miss Peters with a glass of champagne and a slice of lemon, a combination which she insisted was all the rage that season at London's most fashionable establishments.

From time to time in the telling of her tale, Mrs. Hudson

would break off to savour the port, providing an opportunity for one of the rest of us to leap in with a question.

"So we know now how they made the ruby vanish, Mrs. H," Dr. Watson commented at one such moment, "but I don't understand all the rest. I mean, how did that magician chappie make himself disappear this evening. We all saw him go into that alley. And then the wretched fellow simply vanished under our noses!"

Mrs. Hudson nodded calmly at the row of faces turned to her.

"Well, you see, sir, their plan was going fine until I got hold of the ruby. They had thought that once the ruby had vanished, they had all the time in the world to obtain the mechanical jewel case. After all, there was no reason for anyone to guard it particularly closely. But after I had spoiled that plan, they were lurching from one crisis to another. James Phillimore attempted to burn the evidence of how Perch's box could make the stone disappear. You see, once we could prove that, the authorities would be willing to track down Perch, and Perch was the weak link in their chain. So they packed him off to South Africa as quickly as they could."

"Yes, Mrs. H, but you haven't answered Dr. Watson's question about events this evening." Mr. Holmes' tone made it clear that he knew the answer himself but wished his friend to have it explained in very simple terms.

"No, sir. I'm coming to that. Our plan to trap James Phillimore was a good one, but I confess that there was one detail I was uncomfortable with."

"What was that, Mrs. H?"

"It was the fate of Mr. Phillimore and the Great Salmanazar if we handed them over to the police. They may have been charged with conspiracy to steal, but the evidence against them was scanty. Perch could link Phillimore to the crime, as it was Phillimore who commissioned the boxes. But there was nothing much against Salmanazar. I could imagine a botched arrest followed by a hasty acquittal. So instead, I thought it would be helpful if I arranged to have a little word with our great magician."

"But how did you manage that, Mrs. Hudson?"

"Oh, quite simply, sir. I just helped him to escape this evening."

"*You?* But *how?*"

"That boy who bumped into him by Charing Cross station told him what to do. The Great Salmanazar knew he was being followed, you see, and he was lost in a strange city. So I simply gave him the message to follow the pantomime horse. Of course, only the British really know what a pantomime horse *is,* but he soon grasped the idea, and he was able to follow the horse into the alley by Admiralty Arch."

"That's right, Mrs. Hudson," Dr. Watson agreed. "*We* saw all that happen. But how do *you* know so much about it?"

Mrs. Hudson looked at him in great surprise.

"Why, sir, who do you think was inside the pantomime horse?"

"Eh? What? You mean? . . . *You?*"

Mr. Holmes chuckled at his friend's confusion. "Of course, Watson. Surely it is obvious? I'm surprised that even you haven't grasped it by now."

Mrs. Hudson nodded gravely at the great detective. "Of course, sir, as you will no doubt have realized, Scraggs and I were in the horse costume at the start of the evening. When safely out of sight in the alley, Scraggs and the magician swapped places. Like a true showman, the Great Salmanazar proved rather adept at playing the rear end of the horse. After that, it was all easy. I escorted him to his hotel room and we had a little talk. I pointed out the serious view taken by British justice of attempts to steal the Queen's jewels. I talked a little about the determination of the police to make an arrest and a little about the state of our prisons. After a little, he was very eager, in return for a boat ticket and a promise of a safe journey, to tell me the whereabouts of all his past prizes."

"But, Mrs. Hudson," Rupert Spencer put in, "you've just said that the evidence against him was scanty. Why should he cooperate like that?"

"He cooperated, sir, because I was able to show him a statement I'd obtained earlier in the day from Miss Lola Del Fuego. In the hands of any police force in Europe, it would put him behind bars for the rest of his life. You see, through working with him so closely, she and James Phillimore had learned a good many of his secrets."

Dr. Watson snorted. "But if you had that sort of evidence, Mrs. H, why let the fellow go at all? Why, we could have him safely under lock and key already."

Mrs. Hudson took another sip of port before replying.

"Well, sir, this way we get all the other jewels back. But I confess that wasn't my main reason. You see, sir, he's simply far too good a magician to waste away his life in gaol. What good would that do for anyone? The Great Salmanazar really is from Spain, it turns out. He learnt his skills very humbly, as an itinerant magician in the villages of Andalusia. Once I had his agreement that he would return directly to that region and never again attempt to leave it, then I was quite happy to let him go."

"But how can you be sure he will stick to any such an agreement?"

"Because he knows I have Miss Del Fuego's letter, and that I will not hesitate to use it." She rolled her wine glass between her fingers, so that the port seemed to glow with the light from the fire. "And you know, when all was settled, when he saw that his adventure was finished, I rather think the prospect ahead of him did not wholly dishearten him. He talked at length of his days on the lanes of Andalusia, the winter snows and the dust in summer, and the welcome in every house he came to. Very moving it was. He told me of all the small children in tiny, unvisited villages, who would run out a mile or more to greet him. I like to think they will have a performer amongst them who once held the whole of Europe under his spell. Yes, gentlemen, I'm inclined to think that more good will come of the Great Salamanzar returning to the mountains of Spain than in keeping him rotting in a crowded British cell."

"And James Phillimore?" Dr. Watson asked. "What has become of him?"

She looked at me, and for a moment one eyelid flickered meaningfully before she turned back.

"The full story of James Phillimore will remain a mystery, I fear, sir. However, it appears his wife in Ealing has received word that he has fled the country never to return. So I think we have no alternative but to assume we have heard the last of him. He was never really a proper criminal, sir, just as he was never really a proper contortionist."

"And Lola Del Fuego?" Miss Peters asked. "What happened to her?"

"Also gone abroad. Her love for James Phillimore, and his for her, is one of the more moving aspects of this story. It seems that all along she was willing to give up her fame and her wealth just to be with him. I think it was his idea that she could only be happy living in luxury, and it was that mistake that drove him to steal the Malabar Rose."

"So, Mrs. Hudson," Mr. Holmes concluded, "the protagonists are all fled. Their plot is broken, and their careers over. Tonight we shall cut your excellent cake, and tomorrow the Malabar Rose shall be placed on public display in all its glory. Tell me, would you find it in any way embarrassing if I was to raise a glass and drink your health?"

If I had questions still to ask, I decided then that they could wait a little. For by then the chestnuts were ready to eat and the level of the port was falling steadily. By the time both were finished, Miss Peters was asleep on Mr. Spencer's shoulder and the first sounds of traffic were to be heard in the streets outside.

"Time for me to go," mumbled Mr. Rumbelow, looking at his pocket watch.

"Indeed, sir," concurred Mr. Holmes, prodding Dr. Watson when he realized that his friend was beginning to nod off in front of the fire.

"What about this, sir?" Mrs. Hudson asked, indicating the iced cake that sat in front of us. "Would you like to cut it now?"

She held a knife out to him, and he reached to take it, then seemed to change his mind.

"Do you know, Mrs. Hudson, until we get it safely to the Home Office, I think the Malabar Rose may as well stay where it is. Though, I fear that way you lose an excellent fruitcake."

"They're never so good once they've been iced, sir." She shook her head and rose to see the gentlemen to the door. "I'm afraid it's a bit of a mess up there, sir. You must do what you can tonight, and Flottie and I will sort it all out tomorrow. And as for the rest of you," she continued, turning back to the kitchen, "it's high time you all got some sleep. So back to your homes and into your beds, before I get you to do the washing up. Oh, and a very happy new year to you all, as well."

We stood in the kitchen doorway and watched them go, Scraggs yawning hugely, and Miss Peters barely awake as Mr. Spencer supported her up the iron steps. The last, weary snowflakes of the night drifted to the ground in front of us. Soon it would be day.

"Tell me, ma'am," I asked as we turned back into the kitchen, "was it *you* who told Mr. Phillimore's wife that he was going abroad?"

"It was, Flottie. I went to see her yesterday, when I was confident we'd trap him one way or another. I told her that her husband had been foolish, that he was destitute and on the run, and that the only chance for him was to escape to Canada to start a new life. I told her that he would be waiting for her in Portsmouth, and I explained very clearly that if she valued him and wished to be with him, that she was to go to the offices of Meyer and Stallard. To the *front* door, Flotsam. I told her to take the money he had sent her, as it would be all they had. And I made it as clear as I could to her that if she did *not* travel to Portsmouth, if she did *not* reach him by five o'clock this evening, that he would depart without her, and she would never hear from him again."

"You told him to go with whoever comes to the front door, ma'am."

"That's right, Flotsam."

"And if no one comes by five, he's to go to the back door."

"Indeed, Flottie."

"Where Miss Perkins will be waiting?"

"No doubt."

"But if Mrs. Phillimore travels to Portsmouth, too? . . ."

"Then he has a wife who loves him."

"But what would happen to Miss Perkins?"

"She will travel on a different boat, to a different part of Canada."

I considered this arrangement thoughtfully.

"I don't imagine Mrs. Phillimore will much like the thought of Canada, will she, ma'am?"

"You may be right, Flotsam."

"She's very fond of hats, and she has plenty of money now."

"She does indeed."

"So what will happen, ma'am? Who will end up where?"

Mrs. Hudson had picked up a sheet from a pile of crumpled laundry that had been pushed hastily into the laundry chest. She waited until she had folded it into a perfect, crisp white square before she turned to answer my question.

"That's really not for us to say, Flotsam. Events will take their course. We don't need to know what happens next."

I nodded as if I understood, but made a mental note to visit Ealing in a fortnight's time, to see if Mrs. Phillimore still lived in the house in Sefton Avenue.

"You went to a lot of trouble to help Mr. Phillimore, ma'am. All that planning and those boat tickets. I don't really know why. Was it really because you wanted to save Mrs. Smithers and her daughter from scandal, or was it because Lola Del Fuego loved him so much?"

"Oh, a bit of many things, Flotsam. I didn't need to worry about the cost of the tickets. I think Mr. Holmes will be happy to cover our expenses. So perhaps the thing that really decided me was Dr. Watson's neckwear."

I blinked at her in astonishment.

"Those lurid cravats, Flottie. Surely you've noticed them?"

"Why, yes, ma'am . . ."

"And his walks in Hyde Park? It is a strange time of year to develop such a habit."

"Hyde Park, ma'am?"

She appeared to be concentrating her full attention on the folding of a large double sheet, but I saw her eyebrows twitch very slightly.

"I saw a playbill in town yesterday, Flottie. It appears that a trapeze dancer called Miss Fidelma Fontaine is performing at the Oriental Theatre. And it occurred to me that the Oriental Theatre is not very far from Hyde Park."

"Why, ma'am!" I exclaimed. "You mean . . ."

"I mean no more than I say, Flottie. But I confess it has occurred to me that Maud Phillimore has disadvantages enough already. The additional scandal of a brother in gaol would hardly encourage the attentions of an honest man."

I spent a moment considering this and decided that perhaps I should observe Dr. Watson's behaviour a little more closely in the months ahead.

"Do you think he will want to write the story of the Malabar Rose, ma'am?"

"Oh, perhaps he will, Flotsam. But as always I shall insist he doesn't mention us. I don't think we were cut out for the limelight."

I sat and gazed into the fire for a moment longer, trying to work out what it was about the case of the Malabar Rose that still worried me.

"Just one more thing, ma'am," I asked at length. "Mr. Phillimore really *did* try to steal the ruby, ma'am. Are you sure it's all right to just let him go?"

"Your friend Blue, Flotsam. I believe he tried to steal your purse . . ."

"Oh, yes, ma'am but I . . ."

Mrs. Hudson raised her eyebrows and began to fold the next sheet. Instead of continuing with my reply, I looked into the fire and considered the case of Blue and the case of James Phillimore, and all the things they'd taught me about appearances and disappearances, about despair and love. I suppose those thoughts led me onto other things, and while Mrs. Hudson worked her way peacefully through the rest of the sheets, I remembered something that in all the excitement I had almost forgotten: I had a mystery of my own to solve. So when Mrs. Hudson had finished folding the last pillowcase, I was still thinking of the unexpected tickets I had received on Christmas Day. And when she spoke to me, I didn't even hear her, for I was utterly lost in contemplation of a future that seemed to teem with secret admirers.

Read more from Rhys Bowen's Constable Evans series that has "well-drawn, engaging characters and vivid sense of place. A definite winner."
(Peter Robinson)

Evan's Gate   0-425-20198-8
A five-year-old vanishes from a seaside caravan park—and Welsh constable Evan Evans must consider all the suspects. But he can't help wondering if the abduction is related to the disappearance of another girl twenty-five years ago. Now, he must build a difficult case against a possible double murderer.

Evan Only Knows   0-425-19607-0
Welsh constable Evan Evans knows that village life is not as peaceful as it seems—and now his job takes a turn toward the tragic when the man accused of killing his father is suspected of murder once again.

Evans Above   0-425-16642-2
Constable Evan Evans expected idyllic Llanfair to be a calm oasis far away from the violent crime of the big city. That is, until a string of murders erupts in the town, putting every "charming eccentric" under suspicion...

"Satisfying as a Guinness pint...the perfect book to curl up with on a rainy day." —*Booklist*

Available wherever books are sold or at penguin.com

Penguin Group (USA) Online

What will you be reading tomorrow?

Tom Clancy, Patricia Cornwell, W.E.B. Griffin,
Nora Roberts, William Gibson, Robin Cook,
Brian Jacques, Catherine Coulter, Stephen King,
Dean Koontz, Ken Follett, Clive Cussler,
Eric Jerome Dickey, John Sandford,
Terry McMillan, Sue Monk Kidd, Amy Tan,
John Berendt…

You'll find them all at
penguin.com

*Read excerpts and newsletters,
find tour schedules and reading group guides,
and enter contests.*

Subscribe to Penguin Group (USA) newsletters
and get an exclusive inside look
at exciting new titles and the authors you love
long before everyone else does.

PENGUIN GROUP (USA)
us.penguingroup.com